The Stone
Rainbow

Also by Helene Wiggin

Dancing at the Victory Café
Days of Bread and Roses
Trouble on the Wind
In the Heart of the Garden

The
Stone Rainbow

Helene Wiggin

PIATKUS

For more information on
other books published by
Piatkus, visit our website at
www.piatkus.co.uk

Copyright © 1999 by Helene Wiggin

First published in Great Britain in 1999 by
Judy Piatkus (Publishers) Ltd of
5 Windmill Street, London W1
email: info@piatkus.co.uk

The moral right of the author has been asserted

A catalogue record for this book is available from the British Library

ISBN 0 7499 0517 4

Set in Times by Palimpsest Book Production Limited,
Polmont, Stirlingshire

Printed and bound in Great Britain by
Biddles Ltd, Guildford and King's Lynn

In memory of my sister, Audrey
1935–1977

Acknowledgements

Many thanks to 'Cos' and Dorothy Cosgrove of 'Cosgrove's House of Colour', Rimington, Lancashire, for all their help in sparking off this story and Lisa Kennedy, bridal designer of 'Sugared Almonds', Earby, who helped with the dress-making details.

I am indebted also to Morag Williams, the curator of the Crighton Royal Hospital Museum,
Dumfries, and Margaret Boyle who both gave freely of their time to further my research.

Thank you to all the people of Kirkcudbright who shared wartime memories, especially Peter MacAdam, the Stewartry Museum, Galloway News and Margaret Crosby of the Tourist Information Board for such a cheery welcome. I acknowledge Adam Gray's excellent wartime anecdotes in his 'Borgue Academy' for giving me some local insight.

*'Life is a rainbow which also includes
black'* – Yevgeny Yevtushenko,

*'My heart leaps up when I behold
A rainbow in the sky:
So it was when my life began
So it is now I am a man:
So be it when I shall grow old,
Or let me die!
The child is father of the man'* –
William Wordsworth, *'My Heart Leaps Up'*

1

FREYA'S NECKLACE

'A golden yoke
Forged with pride
Worn with sorrow.
Circlet of chains
And stones polished
Like glass tears.'

A Wednesday Afternoon In May 1949

It was like cycling straight into an oil painting: into a canvas of sea and mountains, islands and shore, into a rainbow of colours as far as the eye could see. A brassy sun hung in an enamel blue sky; the turquoise sea shimmered underneath, lapping on to dark rocky outcrops and islands overlooking Fleet Bay, two sides of this canvas framed by brown-mauve hills to the north. The foreground glinted with dots of shorebirds fishing on the edge of the tide: gulls, wagtails, waders, and black and white flashes of oyster catchers kleep-kleeping in alarm at the sight of a small boy careering towards the sand, shouting, 'Come on, Auntie Netta! Race you to the beach!'

The young woman skidded to a halt, her fingers pumping the brakes of her sit up and beg bicycle, the wind whipping strands of red-gold hair across her eyes, blinding them from the seascape for a second. She paused to drink deep the precious scene for it had been carried with her into exile so many times, tucked safe at the back of her mind in reserve for dreich Yorkshire evenings.

The picnic to Castlehaven and Carrick Sands was always the high point of her holiday back home in Stratharvar; a precious ritual. Who would be first to catch sight of the shoreline and the barrack-like towers of the huge 'cow palace' at Corseyard, or run around the walls of the Viking fortress? It

3

was always Gus who was first to scatter the brown Ayrshires from their grazing as he tore across the green machars.

Netta wheeled her pushbike slowly over the humps, scouring the coastline to see what had changed since their last picnic a year ago. Thankfully there were no jagged stumps of wartime coastal defences to spoil the beach, no barbed wire and fences with KEEP OUT signs thrown up on other coasts when fear of invasion was real.

'Come on, Auntie Netta, you're such a slowcoach!' yelled Gus as he turned impatiently. His aunt was not in her usual hurrying mode but plonked herself down on a grey boulder while he skimmed pebbles over the surface as she had taught him on her last visit. There's no rush, she thought to herself, we have this day all to ourselves to explore together. This is our time.

Usually her visits followed a familiar route march. First she would arrive in Kirkcudbright by train, but, this time thanks to the loan of some petrol coupons she arrived in style in an old Ford van, parking by the harbour square. Then she usually stopped to steady her nerves with tea and scones upstairs in the Paul Jones Tearoom before catching the bus, looking out over the harbour as if from the prow of a boat, admiring the fishing fleet anchored in the estuary. This time she watched from the window for a glimpse of her stepmother, Peg Nichol, puffing along the street in her faded cotton frock and handknitted cardigan, weighed down with the weekly shopping; her wicker basket stuffed with extras from the High Class grocers in Cuthbert Street. With her was young Gus in shorts and Aertex shirt, itching to go crabbing somewhere on the edge of the harbour.

Netta liked to tiptoe up behind the boy to surprise him with an ice cream cone from Angelini's Café. She'd watched him gulp it down while Peg sniffed about spoiling his dinner and warned him not to put sticky fingers on the car bonnet. Then they all piled into the van to wend their

4

way westwards around the twisting lanes towards the coast and Brigg Farm.

Gus was already sunburned, having shot up inches since Netta's last visit. The journey gave them all time to pass pleasantries, to warm to each other again for the sake of the child who bounced up and down in the back with the messages. Gus was dying to know what goodies Auntie Netta had brought from England in her leather case and hatbox.

She watched for the first sights of home: the bumpy track up the hill towards the grey Galloway farmhouse which stood four-square, lintels edged with red sandstone, attic windows jutting out of the roof, glinting in the afternoon sunshine.

Her father, Angus Nichol, would be hovering somewhere in the courtyard of the old whitewashed farm buildings ready with his usual gruff greeting, ruddy face weatherbeaten by fifty summers, sandy hair frizzled by salt and sun. Gus raced up the stairs ahead of her, hovering by the door of her old childhood bedroom with its iron bedstead, pegged rug and wash stand. The summer curtains were thin and barely closed, faded by sunshine from the southern aspect. He hovered excitedly while she unpacked, eyes scanning her luggage just in case . . .

'Thank you for my birthday present. I've got a farm and tractor and loads of cars now. Jamie Paterson's got a wee sister called Maisie and I've got a new calf. Do you want to see my pageant costume? We made helmets out of silver paper with real horns. The Sunday school teacher said mine was the best, so she did . . . and I got my photo in the paper, do you want to see it?'

Gus raced off down the passage to bring back a crumpled account of the carnival procession from the *Galloway News* and his battered Viking helmet. She looked down at his dark pixie face with its shock of black hair and those piercing blue eyes; such a strange mixture, more Irish than Scots.

'How long did this take you?' asked Netta, amazed by

5

his achievement. 'It's very good. Did Father find you the horns?' Gus nodded, eyes still fixed on her luggage. One of their rituals on her arrival was for the suitcase to be opened and Gus to finger through the piles of clothing for any lumpy packages. 'What's this in your shoe? Is it a shoehorn?'

'No.'

'Is it toothpaste?' Netta shook her head with a smile. 'Look and see.' It was a rolled up copy of the *Beano*. Gus ferreted about until he also found the packet of Liquorice Allsorts and the picture book and crayons. 'Thanks, Auntie Netta! Come and see my toy farm. Father made it for me.'

His whitewashed bedroom at the back of the farmhouse was changing from an infant's bedroom to a *Boys' Own* den, with battered pre-war toys and half-made models cluttering the floor. He had a homemade wooden garage crammed with Dinky toys; a high bed covered with a candlewick bedspread in airforce blue. A moth-eaten stuffed animal of uncertain breed was tucked by the pillow. Yumpy had gone everywhere with Gus when he was small, on picnics and car rides, now he was relegated to the bed. 'I spy Yumpy!' Netta laughed and Gus looked crestfallen. 'Mammy says I'm too big for a suckie.'

'I expect Yumpy's too old to play now so he stays in bed all day to keep it warm for you,' Netta reaassured him. Trust Peg to give the orders. All the Nichols were secret suckie sniffers. Netta's old rag doll still sat on a wicker basket chair in her Griseley home. It was sad day when a little boy must give up his comforter but she supposed it was for the best.

'Tea, folks!' Peg shouted from the banister rail. 'Wash yer hands afore ye sit down, Gus!' He dunked his hands in the bathroom wash bowl and they trooped down together into the kitchen. There was a fine spread of ham and eggs, and a custard trifle with hundreds and thousands melting rainbows of colour on to the cream.

This was the moment when Netta always knew that she

was a visitor and no longer a daughter of the house ready to take her family as she found them. Hands were washed, napkins unfolded and the holiday began.

On the first evening she would usually walk around the fields to view the stock with Father, admiring his fine herd of Ayshires and his field full of Belties, the black Galloway cattle with a white band round their middle, famous for providing succulent beef.

There had been Nichols around Stratharvar for two hundred years: Nichols who had supped with Rabbie Burns at the Murray Arms in Gatehouse of Fleet; Nichols who had built up a dairy herd second to none in the district, supplying produce to the huge creameries; Nichols who carved their names on the black oak desks of Stratharvar school and lined the pathways of the parish kirk.

The farm lay nestled in the hollow between two hummocks, sheltered by trees, a good mile from the coastal gusts. Above it were some ancient cairn stones set on a hilltop.

On her second day back Netta would always walk up to the top of the hill for the panoramic view over Wigtown Bay. On the third day she took herself off shopping to Castle Douglas. The fourth, if it was fine, would be a ride to Gatehouse of Fleet and Mossyard beach so Gus could collect the beautiful shells blown off course by the Gulf Stream. Then on the fifth day came their picnic ride to Castlehaven, to the small galleried broch heavily restored but still a magical haunt.

To Gus it was a real fort where pirates were driven off the rocks by warriors and old sea dogs were repulsed from Carrick Shore, but its origins were as old as the ports and townships of the Stewartry itself, part of an ancient Gallovidian defence system. He was too young yet to understand the technicalities but already he had a feel for its history.

Now Gus had abandoned his own tricycle in favour of the slippery rock pools. Netta watched his progress as she sniffed the briars and honeysuckle gorse, the hedgerows full of blossom, the sculpted shapes of thorn bushes carved by the sea winds, that tangle of sea and meadow flowers and salt wind – the smell of home. The cows grazing on the shoreline ignored their intrusion after a while so she unloaded her knapsack, unpacking Peg's contribution of thick Spam sandwiches, a bottle of still lemonade, ginger buns and slices of fruit loaf. This was the mid-week ritual of Netta's stay which was always observed, rain or shine; the solemn waving off, the race to be first to see the sea, the picnic and the story.

For as long as she could remember, Netta had loved this special place where the pink marsh orchids glistened in late spring, the wild flowers lined the inner walls of the fort now encrusted with lichen and rocky alpines in the crevices, the squills the grassy promontories. Here they could pretend to be guards on sentry duty, imagining life in Viking times. Gus had caught her excitement about times past and Netta fed him stories of the Norse Gods in Valhalla and Asgard. For each visit she prepared another tale from the lives of Odin, Thor, Baldur and Loki, who had fought terrible battles against evil monsters and goblins.

Once she had found a battered copy of the *Lives of the Gods* in the Griseley Bookshop. Censoring all its more bloodthirsty details, Netta had prepared her story for this visit. The storytelling usually came after Gus had stuffed down his picnic in order to let his meal settle before they pedalled off on the rest of their day.

'What's it today? he asked, munching his apple. He knew their routine by now.

'Another story of the old Gods and the rainbow bridge, I think. I thought we might look at one of their Goddesses for change . . . Freya, wife of Odur, who lived with their daughter Hrossa in Asgard. This is the story of Freya and the necklace Brisingamen.' She told him the story of the young Goddess who, against her husband's wishes, went off in search of the mountain of the Giant Women, the Goldsmiths of

Middlearth, leaving her child with her husband in the palace. Freya was lured by dwarves who kissed and entrapped her. Then, when she found the Goldsmiths and they showed her that golden necklace, Freya clasped it and it seemed to make her more beautiful than ever. On her return to Asgard her husband had gone away in search of her and she was sorely distressed. She searched all over the earth for him but he never returned and she was left heartbroken.

'What did she do next?' asked Gus, puzzled.

'She kept on searching and stood on the Bifrost bridge, the rainbow bridge between heaven and earth. Remember we've been there before? Some say she stood there weeping like a fountain until Goddess Frigga came out to comfort her and remind her that she still had a beautiful daughter, Hrossa, to look after. From then on Freya wore that cursed necklace, not out of pride but out of shame. When she weeps, her tears fall as rain on the earth and sometimes we see her rainbow bridge with all the colours of the world in it.'

Gus fidgeted, disappointed with this girlie story. There were no monsters in it ... He munched the rest of his apple in silence before racing off again on his trike to lead the way to Carrick Sands, past the big house at Knockbrex which stood back from the rocky inlet like a toy fort. He wanted to see if the tide had washed up any messages in ships' bottles on the beach opposite Ardwall Island among the seawood and flotsam, driftwood and metal strewn over the grey pebbles and sand. This time he was in luck.

'Look! Come and see, Auntie Netta! I've found a helmet.' Gus was waving an object excitedly. He watched his young aunt in her pleated shorts and plimsolls, picking her way through the boulders and shingle to the line of seaweed where he lifted up a leather helmet like a dead animal, slimy and with barnacles clinging underneath. He'd noticed that when he walked with her in town she always got wolf whistles from the seamen on the harbour. She pretended not to notice but he saw her freckles go pink.

Now she shuddered as he offered the mask for her to inspect. The face that must once have donned this pilot's mask was probably sunk fifty fathoms deep in some lonely grave at the bottom of the Irish Sea like Long John Silver.

'Put it down, it might have fleas!' His aunt shook her head, not wanting to touch the slimy object.

'Mammy'd say that.' Why did grown-ups hate getting dirty and muddy and greased up? 'Do you think it was a Spitfire pilot's or a Jerry's?' Gus and his friend Jamie would play war all day long if allowed to.

'I don't know, dear.'

'Did you know any soldiers who were killed in the war?' Gus asked in his matter-of-fact voice, hoping she would tell him another adventure story like the ones in his comic. She nodded but said nothing. Why did everyone always clam up when he asked about the thing called war? He knew it was a great big adventure he had missed out on. The big boys played Japs and Jerries in the playground, knocking the littler ones over, but Mammy said nice boys didn't fight. Gus was secretly a pirate so he always fought back. Netta was family and she didn't usually mind. Now his auntie was staring out to sea and looked sad, like the woman in her soppy story.

He looked down, poking among the seaweed. 'Have you got a golden necklace?'

'No, but my mother had a lovely one made from polished pebbles all the colours of the rainbow: amethyst, amber, quartz, turquoise, all linked together with a golden chain. Father bought it for her on their wedding day.'

'Do you wear it?'

'No, Peg has it.'

'Why? I've never seen it but I'll ask her to show it to us,' said Gus, burying the helmet in the sand.

'No, Gus, I'd rather you didn't.' He could tell by her pursed lips that he was not going to be told why but it was worth another question.

'Jamie Paterson telt me that you're no my real auntie. Are you ma big sister then?'

Netta shrugged her shoulders. 'Something like that but I like being called Auntie . . .'

Sometimes it was hard to understand who anyone was. This auntie kept coming back to Galloway, taking him on trips, telling him all about people in the brown photographs until he fell asleep with her chunnering. Mam sniffed a lot when she arrived and plumped up the cushions just as she did when the Minister called after church and she had to hide the *Sunday Post* out of sight quickly. But Carrick Shore was their special picnic spot and Gus liked his auntie's company sometimes. No one else would play French cricket with a piece of driftwood or spot oyster catchers, rock pipits, seagulls and bobbing sand birds for his I Spy Club.

As the afternoon wore on the sky darkened and an anvil of heavy cloud over the bay threatened an outburst. It was time to turn back eastwards again to Brigg Farm, home for evening milking. He wished he had a proper bicycle not a trike. Trikes were for babies and the wheels kept sticking in the gritty tracks, making his legs tired.

This picnic outing marked the turning point of each visit. The days would run quickly downhill after that. Netta watched Gus bending over his collection of shells and thought of herself at that age on the same shoreline, watching her mother painting, her wispy red hair fading outwards at the sides, hunched over her sketching or looking up to capture the brightness of the beautiful scene.

Griseley seemed so far away, with its dark stone dykes and tall chimneys, sooty mills amongst grey fells where time dragged. While in Yorkshire she yearned for this place.

11

Now, her time here was ebbing fast, this rationed time. Netta remembered that she was here for a purpose.

It was time to make demands again. She must not go back to Yorkshire empty-handed this time. Don't forget your New Year's resolution. You can do it! was the vow she had made to herself a week ago. Now there were only a few days left to execute the mission but courage was failing her as it always did.

The next day it poured down, heavy driving rain blown in from the sea lashing the grey walls of the farmhouse. Netta made herself useful mending Gus's torn trews and fixing buttons to his shirts. She could relax if there was a thimble on her finger and a needle in her hand. Peg was baking in the kitchen, listening to the wireless, not in a talking mood. Counting the days, no doubt, until this visit ended. Gus had gone to play at his friend's farm, out of their hair.

Netta took the mending basket into the cool parlour with its dark treacle-coloured paintwork, black oak furniture and heavy moss green velvet drapes at the window. The china cabinet gleamed with china cups and saucers, souvenirs from Musselburgh and Largo Bay. On the walls were sepia portraits of the Nichols family in suits and black bombazine dresses with white mutches – stern, forbidding ancestors who had frightened her as a child. There was the smell of old soot and damp and disapproval in this room. She spotted two of Grandpa John Kirkpatrick's watercolours of Kircudbright harbour and the Toll Booth. The two fishing boat sketches that had always hung close by were gone but she could see faint marks on the distemper where they'd left their mark. His paintings were becoming sought after. He'd been a colleague of Hornel and Jessie King and the other famous Kirkcudbright painters.

Stepping back into the parlour was like stepping back a hundred years. Nothing much had changed but the drawers of the cupboard were neatly tidied out, lined with fresh copies of the *Galloway News*. As she rooted round to find the old photograph albums she fished out sepia postcard scenes, rosette prizes from cattle shows, Sunday school attendance tokens. Nothing of interest to her here. Her world had turned and left this Stratharvar way of life far behind many years ago.

The first album was in the bottom cupboard: a heavy leather-bound book with a stiff gold clasp, full of yet more ancient Nichols posed in their finery, sturdy Galloway farmers with handsome faces. A smaller album was full of Peg's old family photos: Peg MacBain, her stepmother, as a young girl in uniform, stiff and starchy even then. She was after all one of Mother's distant cousins who'd come to nurse the invalid and stayed on to wed the widower. There was one unframed photograph of Peg and Angus on their wedding day outside the parish kirk porch, looking awkward in the sunlight. The photo was pristine, still in its cream folder with tissue paper lining. There was a blue leather album of Gus in his toddler days and Netta closed that quickly. Where was her picture taken with Mother at Ayr? Where were her own baby days kept? There was only one picture of her, grinning in pigtails; a line-up on the bench outside Stratharvar School when she was nine before Peg came and her world changed forever.

All that sixth day indignation rankled in Netta's mind. Eventually she sought out Angus with a mug of tea as he was tidying up in the byre.

'I was looking for a snapshot of myself when I was a bairn to show Gus and yon one of Mother to take back to Griseley with me. Where would I be finding them?' Angus paused, looking at her square on with his blue eyes.

'Don't be asking me then, it's Mother's stuff. What's brought this on, Netta?' he replied.

'Nothing, only it's about time I took some more snaps back

with me to put on my own mantelpiece. Tell me where to look?'

'That's Peg's department, she had a clear out a while back. She did say the drawers needed sifting through. She's awful sensitive on that score. Best not to fash her with it. I'm sure they're put away safe somewhere.' Angus slurped his tea quickly and returned to his job, not looking at his daughter.

Why did she always have to tiptoe around her own home on eggshells in case she cracked the fragile veneer of welcome? Why did she have to behave like a visitor or a prisoner on parole? All she was asking for was some blessed snapshots, but Netta could feel her heart thudding at the thought of facing Peg with the real demands of her mission. It felt like asking for the Crown Jewels. Why did her courage always fail her at the last? Was it because all her past was shut away in some press, out of sight in a neat box labelled: DO NOT OPEN?

Early On Friday Morning

Netta woke with a start from a dream. Mother was still drifting away from her, far out to sea on a boat, bobbing on the waves while she was left alone on the shore, trying to keep the misty figure in sight. Netta stumbled out of bed half asleep, fumbling for the light, crying out as she stubbed her toe. Why were there always these same dreams, yearnings for the sound of beloved voices and shapes? This dawn half-light promised only shadows and echoes, silhouettes on the wall made by lamplight. She felt as small as in that school snapshot, a child again in a Fair Isle jumper and tartan kilt.

One morning Netta had gone to school in sunshine, rushed out of the door to catch the school charabanc which stopped for her at the end of the track and returned home to only tears, silence and darkness. Mother was asleep on the bed, cold and different. 'Say goodbye to your mammy, hen,' urged Peg MacBain gently, but Netta turned away in disgust. 'That's no my mammy!' she cried, rushing down the stairs and into the darkness. The sky was flushed with autumn constellations and she had searched in vain for a shooting star to wish her mother back home again.

The world was painted in such different colours then, when Mother was alive, Netta thought as she sat on the bed. Mother was the smell of treacle scones and honeycomb, warm butter and currant spices; the smell of all the colours of the rainbow in her artist's palette. Yet how quickly all those familiar colours and smells had faded when she'd passed away. Mother had been one of the only good and certain things in Netta's life. It was she who'd first said that the rainbow in the Galloway sky was really the handle of God's basket, carrying the whole world safely through storms and tempests. Mother had said it was made of silken threads. Father had roared in disbelief: 'Come, Jeanie, don't fill the bairn's head with the jewels of untruth. It's stuffed with enough nonsense as it is.' Mother just looked up from her sewing and smiled so sweetly.

'What's the world without colour, Angus Nichol? Why, the very ark of the rainbow is in the child – the sunset in her hair, the sea-shifts blue and green in her eyes, the sand and pebbles dust her cheeks. Is she not a very rainbow of God's mercy?' Her loving words made Netta's red hair and freckles just about bearable.

'She pleases the eye, as well you ken, but it's the colour of her heart which will be the making of her. Rainbows are nothing but tricks o' light on water and there's no ark without tears, Jeanie.'

So the heavens darkened and the light went out of her world when Mother was taken away in that wooden casket and put in the cold earth. It was hard even now to think of that sad time, all dressed in black and grey.

There was so little left to remind her once Peg got her thick ankles under the table at Brigg Farm. Father looked sad and his moustache drooped above a clown's downcurved mouth. He worked all day in the fields with his men and came home silent. Netta knew that he never looked at his daughter again without wincing for she was the image of his loss.

How quickly Mother's things were cleared away from Netta's loving touch: her tortoiseshell hairbrushes and combs, the silver-topped bottles, the bangles and beadwork purse and that special necklace. Her clothes were packed away and the cupboard rattled with empty hangers on the rod. Each time Netta came home from school there were further changes. Peg MacBain did not go back to Kilmarnock but stood at the range dishing out meals and clean laundry, feeding the hens and polishing the dark oak. Soon the smells of home became Peg's own peculiar sour smells, of meat pie and scouring powder. Her smalls hung over the pulley to dry. Netta wished she would disappear. Peg loomed over her childhood like a dark shadow, black hair peppered with oatmeal, pinafore floury and greasy over her heavy bust and rounded belly. Netta always thought of her as a plain clothes and porridge sort of woman.

Angus Nichol changed with her staying. Netta saw that he could look at Peg now without wincing and they shared little jokes. Netta was too young then to recognise the signals but she sensed a strange dark smell of a different spice in the air.

All these thoughts raced through her head again as she dressed quickly and made for the narrow staircase up to the loft with her lamp. She must not leave empty-handed again, without her photographs and everything else that belonged to her.

'Who is that up in the loft?' Peg stirred from her sleep. Angus chuntered and snuffled but did not move. Until that buzzer in his head woke him for the milking he was dead to the world. Peg could hear footsteps above. Surely Gus was not awake at this hour? It must be Netta rooting through the cases. Angus had said she was on about photographs. Let her search, there was nothing up there of interest. The sooner that young woman was on her way back south to England the better. Her visits had to be tholed, but her coming brought Peg out in itchy bumps. Like the proverbial bad penny she rolled up each summer with her fancy presents and now swanking a

17

borrowed motor car. They were not fooled for one minute by all her dainty clothes and eagerness to please. Netta was only a jumped up seamstress for all her big ideas, making fancy gowns for women with more money than sense. It was about time the girl faced the truth and settled down to her life in England.

Netta was far too like Jeanie Kirkpatrick for Peg's comfort: the same red-gold hair and tall graceful figure. 'A race horse out of a stable of nags,' Angus had laughed, describing Peg's second cousin. He was gey proud of his beautiful wife and pretty daughter which made Peg all too aware of her own dumpy figure, the dark brows which almost met over the bridge of her nose and double chin. Peg had learned early that plainness was her lot but that didn't make her useless and fragile like poor Jeanie who, for all her beauty, was weak in her chest. Peg had proved to be the sturdier of the two, a reliable workhorse. She had been glad enough to escape the drudgery of life in Kilmarnock even if it was only exchanging one kitchen sink for another, and that isolated down a track two miles from Stratharvar, the nearest village.

No one could ever fault Peg's housekeeping. You could see your face in her polished surfaces and her thrift in the darned heels of Angus's stockings. She kept hens and ducks, helped with the cheese making, scoured the dairy and kept bees. Each Sunday she warmed the pew in the parish kirk and was a stalwart of the Ladies' Guild. Had she not answered the call of war duty by taking in evacuees from Glasgow? What she had been called to do in the name of mercy was above the call of Christian duty. And was it not she who kept all those toerags up to scratch with moral lectures, meals and motions? Peg firmly believed in regular bowel movements as the key to health and happiness: Beecham's Pills, Syrup of Figs, Sennacot tablets . . . she was a martyr to them all.

What was that stampeding above her head, enough to wake the dead? She would have to rise and give that girl a piece of

18

her mind, disturbing them at this hour! There was no making any sense of Netta. What a disappointment to her father she had proved; a thorn in their flesh right from the start. After all they had done for her, still she kept wanting more.

Peg spied her photograph in its silver frame on the windowsill. The child had spoiled that portrait with her scowl. Resentment still festered like a pluck on the chin. Netta had even spoiled their wedding day, the minx, with all that business with they beads! How would Peg ever forget the scene?

September 1937

Peg ordered the party dress from Wee Alec Kerr, the travelling out-fitter, from their 'Children: From Cradle to Young Miss Galloway' catalogue. It was to be Peg's own special surprise for Netta to soften the blow when she told her the news. Peg had even collected the outfit from the store herself, packaged it in brown paper and left it on the table for the girl to find after school.

'What's this? It's no my birthday . . .'

'It's for you, a braw new frock for the wedding.' Peg straightened herself, waiting for the blast.

'What wedding is this then?' Netta fixed her piercing blue-green eyes on Peg in disbelief. 'You're no marrying my pa, are you?' She rummaged through the packaging and took out the turquoise taffeta frock with its puff sleeves and stiffened underskirt, flinging it across the floor. 'I'm not wearing that!'

'You'll do as you're told, you ungrateful lassie! I declare tae God I'm no having you turn up at ma wedding in black mourning. Pick it up at once! It's been ordered especially. Think yourself lucky. Many a wee lassie would think herself Princess Elizabeth in yon bonny goon. Try it on, I chose the shade to go with yer hair.'

'You're no my mammy and you cannae make me!' Netta picked the frock off the floor as if it was a duster and flung it on the kitchen table. 'I'm no going to yer rotten wedding! Who said you could marry my pa? He's married already.'

20

'Aye, but your mammy's away to live with Jesus, God rest her soul, in a far better place out of all her earthly suffering. Yer faither needs a woman about the house and since I've been doing this job for months, we decided it was aboot time we settled things properly afore the tongues of all the Stewartry start to wag.'

'You're never going to be my mammy, I don't like you,' answered Netta, mouth pursed tightly in defiance.

'And I don't like you much so that's the truth telt and the devil shamed! We'll both have to make the best of it.' Peg stood firm with her arms folded over her bosom.

'Nobody asked you to come here,' snapped Netta, trying to fix her gaze out of the window and in the yard.

'As a matter of record, young lady, as I recall my second cousin Jeanie Nichol herself begged me to help yous all out when she took to her bed . . .'

'We'd've managed!' came the fierce reply.

'Och, aye! I didna see you soiling yer fingers in the byre or at the sink.'

'I do the hens.'

'And the hen money has brought you this fine dress to be my flower girl. You ought to be grateful I'm asking you. Look, this has real smocking on the bodice. I'll treat you to some sandals with straps and long white socks . . .' Peg could see the child wavering. Wee Alec had chosen well for her but Netta didn't want to give Peg the satisfaction of acknowledging it. 'It'll have to do,' she said grudgingly.

'It'll have to do! I ought to give you some laldie for yer cheek! A good skelping is what you need, not a new dress.' This argument was going nowhere.

'My pa loves my mammy, not you.'

'Well, she's no here to get his meals on the table or warm his bed. I may be no good with the painting or much to make a portrait of, but he knows this plain woman's grateful. I'm strong, built to last . . . more than yer poor ma was, being sae delicate. Besotted though he was by her fair looks and artistic

21

fingers, she was a town incomer not an in-born country bred like me.'

'Are you going to give him a bull calf then?' Country girls knew all about birthing and offspring and Netta was no exception.

'Wash your mouth out!' Peg's arm swung out to clip the cheek out of the child. Netta ducked and darted to the door.

'Just you wait till I tell Faither about yer lip.'

'I don't care, I hate you! I shall tell my mammy what you've done. It's no fair!' The girl raced across the yard up the track towards the top of the hill.

Peg turned back to her chores. Taking on Netta Nichol was the price she must pay for a warm fireside. 'Dear God, send me enough cloth to warm her coldness,' she prayed and straightened out the dress. Once there were other weans at the hearth the girl would soon fall in line.

On the morning of the wedding Netta took her time fixing up her liberty bodice and the garters round her white stockings. Peg had starched her petticoat and bound the child's wiry hair into tight ringlets. The dress was hung up ready for the trip to church. Angus was looking stiff and shiny in his best suit. His hair plastered down, his cheeks flushed from the drinking spree at the Stratharvar Hotel. Peg had squeezed into the dark pink two-piece suit that just about skimmed over her bulk, thanks to her new Spirella corset. She had let Mary MacCrindle shampoo and set her hair into a crimped wave flat against her ears and she wore her new floppy straw hat to one side. The finishing touch was the necklace of polished stones that Angus had pushed towards her in its blue box.

'Here's something to go with your outfit. It's yours now. Shame to waste a good bauble.'

He did not touch her or offer to put it on her neck. When he looked at her there was only resignation and gratitude in his eyes, never a spark of desire or admiration. Peg could live with that. When she gave him a son, then she might shine brighter in his eyes. She was sitting by the dressing table when Netta appeared in the doorway.

22

'You can't wear that!' She pointed to the necklace in horror. 'It's my mammy's, not yours!'

Angus turned sharply to his daughter. 'Of course she can. I bought it for Jeanie. It's for me to gie it to whom I please.'

'But it's mine! Mammy said it was for me to have the rainbow necklace. She can't have it!' The child stood defiantly, expecting him to back down.

'Haud yer wheest! She did no such thing. Jeanie wore it on her wedding day. Peg is yer mother now.' Angus made towards the child.

'That pink blancmange is no my mother. If I can't wear my beads, I'm no going to yer wedding . . .'

He dragged the girl, taffeta skirts rustling, out into the passageway and took his razor strap to her backside. 'This is for cheeking Peg on her wedding day! Never talk to my wife like that again or you're no a daughter of mine. This is her home now. You can stay in your room all day for all I care but Peg can choose what she wants to wear without your permission, missie. Do you hear me?'

Steely-eyed, red with tears and with a stinging backside and crumpled dress, Netta stood stony-faced with the rest of the small congregation gathered for the service. Later they went to the Stratharvar Hotel for high tea and she drank lemonade while the grown-ups drank whisky. Then Netta was sent to stay next door with the Patersons for a long weekend while Peg and Angus took the train to Edinburgh for their honeymoon.

Peg had no stomach to wear Angus's gift after all the carry on. A dead woman's promise had spoiled the pleasure of it all so she made do with the corsage of roses and white heather. The necklace was put carefully back in its box and she never touched it again.

23

May 1949, Friday

Peg lay wide awake now. Only two days of the visit left. It was no use stirring up old wounds. Netta could turn the attic over all morning if it kept her out of the kitchen. What she's really after is no up there, Peg thought to herself, and it's no hers for the taking either.

Netta opened the trap door and sniffed the dusty air. A moth fluttered towards her lamp, casting flickering shadows. The floor was cluttered with the flotsam and jetsam of departed Nichols packed in boxes and cabin trunks; a musty graveyard, overgrown and neglected in the usual out-of-sight, out-of-mind way of most attic dumping grounds. All the history of the ancient family must be at her feet but she was in no mood to explore the distant past.

What she was looking for would be tucked away in cardboard boxes and leather attaché cases; stuff flung up here in the last ten years or so. It would take some sifting through so she would start at her feet and work backwards. The dust was gritty in her throat and her back was aching already but Netta was not deterred. Even if it took all day she would find the bits and pieces of her past among this lot. She would not give Peg the satisfaction of ignoring her requests. There were so many important details of her own journey that were hazy; her memories were often distorted and all mixed up in her brain.

Netta edged herself down on to the floorboards and cleared a space for the lamp. She dusted the nearest square box and opened it. It was a gas mask of all things! How she had hated fire drill and air raid warnings, the smell of the rubber up her nose choking her like a dentist's mask sending her to sleep. She was made to carry this wretched box across her chest for a whole year until they grew lax at the School and she transferred to the Academy. Inside the box was tucked a handwritten programme for some concert but it was not in her own fancy script but a misspelt list of items. The wartime concerts, of course, with the evacuees from Glasgow. Glory to heaven! There was one bright spark in her schooldays which had brought fireworks to Stratharvar: Wilma Dixey and her brother Malky, the Lang Gang; Miss Lennox and Miss Murchison, their teachers. What a shot in the arm to such a dozy village they were! How Netta wished she had a snapshot of them all lined up on the stage for that first Christmas shindig but film was scarce and saved for only the most important occasions. The coming of the evacuees had been a shock to Stratharvar School and they had certainly changed the direction of her life forever. 'Oh, Dixie!' Netta sighed. 'We were always trouble, you and me. We didn't have a very good start, did we?'

September 1939

A few weeks after war was declared the Dixeys exploded into Brigg Farm like Catherine wheels: a girl of ten with a shock of straw-coloured hair which stood up like Strewwelpeter's, and a small boy of about six with knees like doorknobs who looked as if he'd not seen a square meal in years. They seemed to be labelled up and parcelled in brown paper, carrying gas masks and paper bags, following behind Peg's ample rump like stray pups. Netta, being in her Anne of Green Gables *dreamy phase at the time, was not looking forward to sharing all her things with strangers. It was enough trying to be nice to Peg as part of her war effort.*

The Nichols were late getting to the Hall where the fifty-two evacuees from Glasgow foisted on Stratharvar were gathered for selection and distribution. The hall was in chaos with kids tearing round more like squealing piglets running amok in an auction market than at a sorting office. The best ones had long been chosen: the ones with leather suitcases and clean clothes, faces without suspicious scabs and sores. Peg was given the last two, bed wetters by the looks of them: the eldest was Wilhelmina, a skinny malinky longlegs, with Malcolm Aloysius, her brother, welded to her sleeve.

Peg looked at their labels suspiciously. 'Are these yins Papes? Am no having Papes in ma house.'

'I'm sorry, Mistress Nichol, but these are all that're left.' The Billeting Officer was nearly hairless with the racket and complaints.

26

'They're a mixed bunch from the Cowcaddens end of Glasgow city and that's no Kelvinside as you probably ken.

'Still, the Reverend Mackay did warn us on Sunday in his sermon: "Duty is a two-edged sword, no satisfaction without the pain of sacrifice". Is that no what he said?'

Peg sniffed, guessing that the big three of the village, Minister, Doctor and Headmaster, would have had first pickings of the teachers and their offspring, not these scruffy wee toerags. Netta had never seen so many strangers in Stratharvar, poking curious fingers into gardens and peering into windows, while pulling faces.

They loaded their reluctant cargo on to the pony and cart and headed back down the twisting lanes to the farm. It was a fine autumn afternoon, trees turning golden, wisps of white clouds in a blue sky, with the scent of woodsmoke from the stone cottages by the roadside. The evacuees stared out with glum faces.

'Where's the picture hoose and the shops, missus? It's all cows and fields,' said the girl, looking around her with dismay.

'This is real countryside,' Netta offered proudly. 'We've got burns to jump over and trees to climb, dens to make and the sea just down the road. Only the beach's all fastened up for the war, but I know a fine sandy cove to make sand castles.'

'Is that all? We've got a zoo and a swing park, a bogey park and alleys to chase, and a dose of sweetie shops. I never saw nae proper shops here . . . And ma name's Wilma, missus, what's yourn?' The girl turned to Netta with grey-flecked eyes fixed enviously on her thick coat and shiny shoes.

'Jeanette, but it's Netta at home and Nettie in the school.'

'Like yon Jeanette Macdonald and Nelson Eddy? I seed them at the Essoldo picture house. Do you like the talkies?'

Netta shook her head with disdain. 'Peg says they're the devil's flea pits, don't you?'

'Aye, you'll walk a gey long way before you'll find me in one of they time-wasters. You'll no be needing any of that stuff here, we make our own entertainment. We've a Post Office and a Jenny a' things shop, a paraffin cart and lots of delivery callers. Plenty going on on a farm tae keep you out o' mischief!'

'And in the summer the tallyman calls with his ice cream van,' added Netta, hoping to impress.

'Not any longer, he won't, hen. He'll be off to one of them camps for Eyeties and enemy aliens.'

'Whit's that stink?' The two children pegged their fingers to their noses in disgust.

'Just muck spreading . . . from the cows, you'll soon get used to the pong. It clears yer chest.'

'It smells like shite! Malky, we're goin' to have tae live in shite,' whispered Wilma.

'Any mair o'that bad language, young lady, and I'll wash yer mouth out with Oxydol!'

'Ma maw washes ma hair with Persil tae bring out the colour, so she does. She says I'll look like Jean Harlow if we keep it up. I didna want to be evaporated doon here.' Wilma hugged her parcels close to her chest. Netta looked at Peg's lips twitching into a smirk and burst out laughing herself.

'Whit are yous twos grinning at?' snapped Wilma, suddenly on the defensive.

'You've been evacuated, not evaporated . . . you're not a can of milk!' laughed Netta.

'I'm nae dumb cluck, that's whit I said. You must have tatties in yer ears.' This girl was not easily put down.

'Suit yersel, I know whit I heard,' Netta mimicked.

'Just you speak properly, Netta Nichol, I'm no having you picking up the patter frae the likes of this keelie. She's as coarse as heather!'

It was not the best of starts. As they climbed the track up to the whitewashed farm the two strangers fell silent, watching the huge fat stock cattle eyeing their progress. They clung together at the sight of Angus in his huge boots, his corduroys held up with a black leather belt. He looked like a whiskery, sandy-haired giant to them. Malky hid himself under Wilma's thin coat, cowering away from the sight of the bull calf being led out into the field.

'This'll be your job to milk him each morning,' teased Angus. Malky buried his head in his sister's thigh.

'He's just blethering, Malky, don't yous be frit. You'll soon get the hang of it.'

Netta couldn't look her father in the face. These two idiots didn't know a bull from a cow.

When they sat down to a plate of beef stew Malky poked around his plate suspiciously, picking out each lump of meat from the vegetables with his fingers. There was a stunned silence for a second.

'Use yer knife and fork, son,' whispered Peg, looking to his sister for support but she was no better. Netta was sniggering at their lack of table manners when Wilma sprang to his defence.

'Ma maw says we're to use oor fingers, it's mair hygienic. Fingers first and tongue after to lick the juice. Nae washing up after us.' She stared at Netta's gaping mouth. 'And you'd better shut yer mouth, there's a train coming.'

'Well, in this hoose, Wilma Dixey, you'll do whit we do. We eat civilised, and I'll be seeing you two eat civilised too. Just pick up they forks and knives and follow what our Netta does,' said Peg from the top of the table. The battle to tame the evacuees had begun.

Next came the palaver with the zinc bathtub and the undressing. Netta had wondered if either of the evacuees had ever seen water before, the fuss they made. Wilma was in high dudgeon, squealing for the cruelty man to rescue them from the torture of having lugs combed out and searched for nits. They were sewn into their semmits, which were lined with more brown paper against winter's chills, and afterwards Peg lifted up their clothes with a pair of tongs, dumped them in a basket and put them on the compost heap to rot down. Wilma was shown how to scrub the tatties out of Malky's ears properly. Once dried by the firelight, with flushed cheeks and shiny noses, they took on a much healthier glow. After a mug of cocoa and shortbread biscuits for supper, it was up the wooden hill for the tired pair.

Peg had made up two beds in the spare bedroom at the end of the passage, the room she hoped would one day have a cot for her own bairn, God willing. These toerags wouldn't settle down, though. Peg was up and down like a helter-skelter. 'Whit's it the now'?' she yelled from the foot of the stairs.

'Where's oor sooky Marys? I canny sleep without ma Mary. They're in ma paper bag.' Netta rooted at the bottom of their sticky sandwich bag and pulled out two grubby blue felt circles on which were sewn badges imprinted with the image of the Virgin Mary and Infant Jesus, colours faded with the dribble of years, smelling of nothing on earth.

'Father in Heaven, spare us such Popery . . . would you believe the day we've taken in idolators to this hoose? The Lord has gey strange ways, does he not?'

Angus sucked on his pipe unperturbed. 'Come on, Peg, any mother who makes sure both her weans have some comfort from their own home is a good one in my book, Pape or Proddy, green or orange. Give me their sookies. It'll nae bother my conscience to take them upstairs.'

To Netta's astonishment her father climbed the stairs and helped them settle down without another murmur.

The evacuees were now sharing the use of Stratharvar School which ran two working shifts. In the mornings Miss Armour Broun and Mr McCurdy took the local pupils, and in the afternoon Miss Lennox and Miss Murchison ruled over the visitors. Officially they mixed only when necessary but there were many informal skirmishes behind the hedges and in the dykes, and especially on the green when the Glasgow boys kicked the football and the shins of the local eleven. On the way home, however, having the advantage of the lay of the land, Netta's school friends got their revenge. There were chessie fights with conkers the size of ping-pong balls, and hit and run raids. When the locals were tied down in their classrooms the Dixeys and the Lang brothers and all the other Glasgow toerags roamed over Stratharvar district, getting into mischief, pulling down washing lines and stealing from the delivery vans.

'Wilma Dixey is so light-fingered she'd steal the salt off my porridge if I didn't watch her,' Netta moaned to her school friends. Then she noticed her pencils were disappearing, her rubber and her purple crayon too. Her satchel was no longer safe slung over the banister rail at the foot of the stairs. Her favourite tartan ribbons that finished off her two plaits disappeared next. She couldn't prove anything, but when her precious packet of ju-jubes walked out of her room, she decided to take action.

Netta found the tablet of Ex-Lax laxative, kept for emergencies, wrapped in silver paper in the medicine cabinet alongside the suppositories and Syrup of Figs. Peg kept everyone dosed in winter. Netta found some old silvery toffee paper and wrapped pieces of laxative up neatly, leaving them perched on her satchel for all to see. 'That'll teach you!' She smiled, waiting for Miss Greedy Guts to pounce. It did not take long for it all to vanish. When they were all tucking into their prunes and custard, Netta started counting her stones.

'Silk, satin, calico, lace . . . I'm lace!'

'No, yer no! It's silk, satin, cotton, rags and you's just rags,' piped up Wilma. 'I'm gonna be dressed in silk, see?'

Netta ignored her and called to Peg, 'I left some laxatives on my satchel but they seem to have vanished. Anyway I don't need them now . . . yon stuff goes through me like the Royal Scot!'

She saw Wilma going green as she bent her head. That night Netta noted with grim glee that the evacuee was up and down to the lavvy, clutching her stomach. Something to confess to the parish priest who called each Sunday to take the pair off to the little Catholic Chapel down the coast.

Gradually Wilma and Malky settled down to the routine of farm life: helping feed the pigs and clear out the byres; watching the milking. When they were naughty each was sentenced to a hundred pumps on the well handle which fed the water tank, which soon took the edge of their mischief. Everyone joined in the Hallowe'en Social, the apple dookin' and dressing up. The Battle of the Boyne was fought over again over the muted Bonfire

31

celebrations. Wilma refused even to look at the fireworks, dim though they were.

Miss Armour Broun decided in the interests of harmony that there should be some joint fundraising effort to encourage the two factions to pull together. It was decided by the Board to hold a Christmas concert in aid of Red Cross funds. All the classes were to be involved and provide sketches, songs and dances to fill the programme, but each was to keep their item a surprise.

The girls in the Qualifying and Advanced Division decided to put on an ambitious display of Physical Exercises to music. Netta and her chums put in hours of extra practice on their clubs and hoop routines. It was proving difficult to keep all their jerks in time with the music without resorting to counting out loud. As for their costumes, modesty decreed against their blackout knickers and vests in favour of pleated shorts and shirts decorated with seasonal trimmings brought from home.

Wilma was very secretive about her turn. She had a solo spot which no one was allowed to observe. One day a parcel arrived in the post from 'Maw' Dixey that sent her into cartwheels of excitement. 'It's ma costume for the show!'

Wilma seemed to be spending most of her life upside down, doing handstands and back arches: 'showing off' was what Peg called it and privately Netta tended to agree.

> 'Ma wee schule's a grand wee schule
> The best wee schule in Glesga
> The only thing that's up wi' it
> Is the baldy-headed Maister.'

Dixie was skipping and singing at the same time.

'You're not going to sing that, are you?' sniffed Netta in disgust.

Dixie kept on skipping:

> 'He gans tae the pub on Saturday night

He gans tae the kirk on Sunday
An prays tae God to gie him strength
Tae belt the weans on Monday!

'Don't be such a toffee nose, Netta! A've got something much better!'

What would Miss Armour Broun say if she heard such stuff come ringing out of Stratharvar Hall but, try as Netta might, Wilma wouldn't spill the beans about what exactly she intended.

On the night of the Christmas concert there was not a spare seat in the hall. It was a frosty night full of stars with a bomber's moon lighting the sky but so far Scotland had been spared the blitzing feared for its cities and ports. The blackouts were carefully in place nevertheless. The children were herded into the classrooms to change into their outfits and chitter in the cold.

The infants started off with a pixie dance to the tune of the 'Hi, Ho!' music from Snow White and the Seven Dwarves. The Juniors took a nautical theme and danced the Sailor's Hornpipe and sang 'Jolly Jack Tar'. There were carols for the audience to join in, recitations and Scottish dances, the homely mixture-maxture Stratharvar had come to love and expect from its pupils. Netta's group did their best but the staging was cramped and clubs kept slipping at the wrong moment, plus bits kept falling off their costumes much to their embarrassment. Everyone clapped politely but Netta thought they were more like a herd of clumsy elephants than the Women's Rural League of Health and Beauty. She stood at the back after the interval, curious to see if the 'evaporees' could produce anything better.

For all they were just from a rough city school it was not a bad showing: a boy jangling on the piano, a lad with bagpipes, and another with an accordion. A dark-haired girl with pigtails and a funny-sounding name sang 'But it's, oh, that A'm longin' for my ain folk . . .' with such sweetness that there was not a dry eye in the hall. Then Wilma exploded on to the stage in lipstick with her Persil-white hair tied up with two huge paper ribbons, looking like a doll with rouged cheeks. Her costume was a glittery two-piece bolero and shorts, the sort gypsies wore all covered with glittery sequins – a little too much on the skimpy side for Netta's liking. She sang or rather shouted 'On the Good Ship Lollipop', twirling and birling like Shirley Temple. Then she smiled and sweetly curtsied, before reciting:

> 'One, two, three alearie
> I saw Wallace Beery
> Sitting on his bumbalearie
> Kissing Shirley Temple!'

Afterwards springing into a routine of handstands and back flips, arches and split and rollovers, ending with her legs folded over her ears in front of her. They all gasped at her contortions and she had the gall to smile through it all as if it was easy-peasy! That put Netta's back up. How could she feel superior to someone who could do all that with just arms and legs?

'That bairn must be made o' India rubber,' said a wifie on the back row.

'So that's how it's done then, that's where all my rubbers have gone,' sniffed Netta. Miss Snakelegs had pulled a fast one and shown up their little routines for what they were: lumpen efforts. The audience loved this turn, cheering, clapping and shouting for an encore. But Wilma bobbed and dashed off the stage into the darkness.

Supper was served in the schoolroom and everyone basked in the success of the evening. A goodly sum had been raised and all the children had been given a Red Cross badge for their efforts. The first Christmas of wartime would not be so bad after all. They returned home in the farm van, tired but exhilarated. Netta said goodnight to Wilma with a little more respect.

'You were really good the night. Who taught you to knot yersel into a ball?'

'I went tae the circus and watched the acrobats. I sneaked in three

34

times and watched them doing warm-ups round the back. I borrowed the costume frae one of Maw's friends. She does a dancing class. Do you like Shirley Temple?'

'I like Anne Shirley better.'

'Whit picture is she in?'

'She's in a book. I'll lend it to you, if you like?' Netta paused. 'Will you teach me how to do walkovers?'

'You'll have to bend in the middle – you're skinny but you cannae bend. Loosen yer back and arch slowly, follow yer hands . . . but it's too cold now. Never do it cold or you'll rick yer back.'

'Did you enjoy our show?' asked Netta, watching Wilma undress without taking off any underlayers.

'I did so but it's no the real thing, is it? I want to go on a real stage and wear real make-up.'

'Peg says the stage's no very respectable, but she's never been tae one so take nae notice of her . . .'

'Why do you call yer maw Peg?' asked Wilma jumping into the bed.

'She's ma stepmother. I tried to call her Auntie Peggy for a while. If I had a real mother I wouldn't want to be far away from her, like you twos.'

'Aye, and one o' these afternoons ma maw will come for us to gan hame. There's nothing much to do here, is there, except read books and go to kirk?'

As if her sighs had floated away like prayers northwards, just before Hogmanay a red-faced woman, round as a barrel but with neat ankles, arrived one morning at the farm to collect her weans. Isa Dixey thanked Angus and Peg courteously for their hospitality as the children melted into her coat and she engulfed them in hugs, making Netta feel sad that no one did that to her. 'They're away hame with me the now. You think yer doin' yer best for the weans but I canna sleep for want of them. God bless yous and a Guid New Year to one and all!'

The Dixeys left a gap behind them after that first exciting Christmas of the phoney war. One by one the other city children

35

drifted back north. The farmhouse seemed silent and chill without their incessant banter and mischief. Netta and Wilma exchanged letters for a while but once the bombings started in earnest the Dixeys moved away and they lost contact for years as all of them got on with their growing up.

May 1949, Friday

Netta could feel the cramp in her thigh and thumped her leg on the loft boards. Why was Dixie's handwritten programme shoved in with the gas mask? Had Peg put it there or Father in a clearout?

Those few months with Wilma had loosened Netta's tongue and her joints. In fact, she could still do a mean cartwheel and one of these days would shock Gus on the shore with a back arch!

The Dixeys had opened her eyes to another tougher schooling where language was rich and fruity and living for the moment in blitz and bombings took nerves and courage. The colours of wartime had been so dreich with all that camouflage and blackout, gun-smoke grey and khaki everywhere. Yet Wilma with her red ribbons, Persil hair and rainbow sequins had brought sparkle to Stratharvar for a while. The evacuees who followed in their footsteps to Brigg Farm, were ground down by the Glasgow blitz and enforced separations. They never shone so brightly as that first pair.

Vida Bloom and her son Arnold came next. Vida left behind a gift so precious it had saved Netta on many an occasion. How strange that people could cross your path for the briefest of moments and yet leave their mark on you for the rest of your life. There was no forgetting those two, but was there anything tangible left her of their brief stay?

Peg clattered in the kitchen. Once woken she could not go back to sleep; an hour early in the morning was always worth two later. She liked to catch the house to herself and sit down with a pot of tea before the daily demands took a toll on her temper. The work of a farmer's wife was never finished. What time she took for herself had to be pared from all the chores of the day, gathered like shavings. They had not had a holiday since that honeymoon weekend in Edinburgh. Angus was never comfortable away from the dairy. He did not trust his men to do the jobs properly.

Sometimes she took Gus on the train to Ayr to see her own relations, but that was visiting and a duty. If she was honest Netta's arrival did give the boy days out from under her feet. She would be fifty next year and coming to that awkward time of life when she felt tired and crabbit, flushed one minute, chittering the next. She ought to see Dr Begg about the flooding each month but it would have to get worse before she submitted herself to all that poking and prying down below. She might have to have it all taken away, and who would see to things then? It was not the sort of complaint she could discuss with anyone. Peg prided herself on keeping Nichol affairs firmly behind closed doors. The less people knew about their business, the less there was to surmise. She turned to see Netta holding out a box.

'I found this in the loft: the old gas mask and a programme. Do you remember the Dixeys and the other evaporees? I thought Gus would like to see this old relic.' Peg stared at the box. 'Would I ever forget those devils! First I put up with Papes and then came yon Sheenies.'

'Vida Bloom was no trouble, nor Arnold – not like the Dixeys! I've been thinking about that time when Vida first

38

taught me to sew properly? What a wizard with her fingers and those invisible hem stitches.'

'There's no many would have all that strange palaver into their hoose like I did.' Peg was remembering the noisy arrival of the mother and son to their billet with various pots and pans and dishes to be kept strictly for their own use. They had been bombed out of their tenement in Glasgow. Mr Bloom was a tailor with the army abroad. Vida was a tiny, frail young woman with her hair falling out from jangled nerves. Her hands shook constantly, a puff of wind would have blown the poor soul away. She was also in a state about Arnold's education.

'I'm sure you'll be duly rewarded,' muttered Netta, bristling. Peg's comments were as usual icy and sharp, like water from their deepest well.

'You made enough racket at the crack of dawn. I thought we'd elephants clomping over our heads! Did you find yer mother's photographs? They'll be packed away in a box somewhere to keep them out of the light. Your schoolbooks are up there too and a load of junk. I've no touched anything.'

'If the Air Raid Warden had seen what's stuffed up there, he'd have declared you a fire hazard! Honestly, Peg, it all needs a good sort out. Gus can help me go through the cases later.'

'Plenty of time for that when we're pushing up daisies. It'll be all yours then and no doubt you'll make a bonfire of it all.'

'I just want to take my stuff back while I have transport. I'm after Mother's tortoiseshell brush and comb set, my books and photos . . . but there are so many boxes and cases, we could run a jumble sale up there.'

'You suit yersel' and let me get on with ma own work. I've nae time to be bothering with all that junk!' Peg turned to clear away her dishes. When she turned back Netta was gone.

39

It was Gus who found the dummy tucked away in a corner of the loft, covered in a lacework of spiders' webs. 'Look at this big doll.' He pulled it out to examine it further. 'Is it yours?'

Netta brushed away the dust of years and shook her head. 'It belonged to a lady who came to stay in the war with her son who was in the big boys' class. It's a real tailor's dummy. I think she borrowed it. We used to call her Mrs Sew and Sew. She could magic up the most wonderful clothes from scraps of nothing, just like Cinderella's fairy godmother! She taught me to make dresses and cut patterns from sketches. Said I had sewing fingers. Her real name was Mrs Bloom.

'Arnold was very clever. His head was always stuck in a book – not like yours. Where are all those picture books I sent you?'

Gus shrugged his shoulders. 'Mammy says there's no time for reading books in this house. Why did the blooming lady come here?'

'They had no home of their own left and Mrs Bloom needed sea air and quiet to rest her nerves. They were refugees. You know about them, don't you?'

He nodded solemnly. 'Mammy says I have to eat up all ma greens for the starving refugees.'

'Yes, and now they have to live in terrible camps or wander about. Do you know about that?' Gus shook his head.

'When you're a bit older I'll tell you all about that terrible time. That's why we went to war: to keep our country safe. All those brave soldiers who never came home . . . we must never forget them.'

'Did the lady and her son sleep in my room?'

'Yes, but they lived in the parlour like a living room and Mrs Bloom took in sewing to earn some money. Arnold's school was evacuated to Castle Douglas and she wanted to be near him for he was all she had left. I was at the big

40

Academy by then, quite grown up, and Mrs Bloom let me sit and watch her sew sometimes.'

Netta fingered the dummy, feeling the pile of the cloth body, mind drifting back to that happy, strange time when she had peered through a crack in the door, watching the firelight flickering in the parlour as the Blooms held their makeshift Sabbath meal each Friday evening. The smell of the lit candles on the tiny brass menorah, the scent of herbs in the pot, Vida Bloom with a scarf over her head speaking a foreign language and Arnold's capped head bent in prayer.

No sewing work was done until Saturday night, however many orders Vida had promised for the following week. The folds of dressmaking materials were tucked away out of temptation, the long dressing mirror stood facing the wall and baskets of threads, Arnold's clarinet case and music were piled neatly away.

When Sabbath ended work began in earnest again accompanied by music from the Third Programme on the small wireless. Peg complained much of it sounded like two cats howling in a dyke. Netta smiled to herself when she thought of the Blooms, shut away in their own private world and Peg huffing and puffing at their religious customs. Then she recalled that first wedding dress in all its glory and the faces of Stratharvar as the bride paraded to the kirk. That was when the sewing magic first began, when she and Vida were allies before all the threads of their past got knotted together in a fankle.

Dressing Miss Forsyth, June 1942

In that make do and mend world where everything was rationed, couponed or in short supply, the idea of a grand wedding in Stratharvar was a prospect to savour amongst the drab every-day routine of farm life. Of course, it was a patriotic duty not to flaunt regulations. Peg Nichol and all the other members of the Rural Women's Institute wondered just how their Chair-woman, Mrs Daphne Forsyth, would see to it that her only daughter, Aileen, went down the aisle to meet her Squadron Leader bridegroom in traditional attire without looking as if she was away off for a job interview in her best two-piece suit.

At the make do and mend demonstrations they had discussed the merits of parachute silk and nun's veiling over net curtaining and fine sheeting cotton to make the wedding gown. 'Why should she be beaten by Mr Hitler or coupons?' was the common consensus at Brigg Farm.

'A bride ought to spend her precious extra coupons on a decent woollen coat and sturdy shoes rather than a bridal dress,' declared Peg, thinking about her own modest rigout.

Mrs Bloom smiled sadly. 'A coat you can wear any day but a bride can only wear white once in her life, don't you think?'

Netta agreed, imagining herself on the arm of a Squadron Leader in airforce blue and medals, floating down the aisle like a snow prin-cess, just like the accounts of Society brides in the Galloway News.

At sixteen she still had a schoolgirl's romantic notions about marriage to a man in uniform. The only boy in her life was Arnie who tagged along the shore with her friends and lectured them about rock formations. She towered over him in height and thought of him still as a little boy tied by an invisible thread to his doting mother. One tug and he jumped like a puppet. He was not allowed to mix with the rough and tumble village boys and always stayed in to practise his music – which was perhaps as well for the local louts shouted names at him whenever he appeared by Netta's side.

Aileen Forsyth was well-upholstered, bonny but buxom. It would be easy for her to roll down the aisle looking like a couch on castors. 'Why doesn't Aileen ask Mrs Bloom to sew something for her?' Netta whispered to Peg. Vida was earning a little from doing alterations and dressmaking but Netta knew she was capable of far more than that. 'Tell Mrs Forsyth that Vida once worked in a great fashion house in London, making evening gowns from silks and tulle and handsewing sequins and beads on bodices. You did, didn't you?'

Vida blushed and bent her head. 'It feels like a lifetime ago . . . yes, I did train to do embroidery but where would I get such stuff to sew nowadays? No one wants that sort of thing here. It's far too expensive.'

'Take no notice of Netta, she's always had her head full o' dreams!' Peg ignored the information and left the two of them to their chores.

'You could make Aileen a wonderful dress, I know it,' pleaded Netta, but the little woman shook her head sadly.

'Those days are long gone, Netta. It's a sad world out there and how could I make such a garment on my own?'

'I could help you, be your assistant. It would make a change from schoolbooks and farm work. I'm sick of mucking out and feeding stock; pumping water from the well into the tank. You could teach me to do the easy bits. Go on, please? And you did say you wanted to pay for extra music lessons for Arnold. Let me ask them?'

So it was Netta who approached Stratharvar House by the grand gravelled drive and spoke to Aileen herself, suggesting she discuss her requirements with their evacuee. Two days later the Forsyths descended on Brigg Farm, demanding to see Vida Bloom and examine her work.

'A good dressmaker wears her shop on her back,' said Mrs Forsyth, peering at the little woman in her neat, well-tailored black dress.

Vida cleared the table and brought out a sketchpad. 'What exactly had you in mind?'

Ideas were thrown backwards and forwards. The difficulty of obtaining good material was only a problem until the mother offered her own lace wedding dress, packed away in mothballs somewhere, to be used as the base of the gown. It was duly sent for and examined carefully for stains and rot.

Then, in the privacy of Stratharvar House, the bride-to-be was measured from top to toe against the size of the old dress. 'I think we'll have enough if the bride promises me to take her dogs on plenty of walks,' Vida whispered to Netta. 'All brides shed pounds before the big day. I pray she'll be no exception.' Vida knew it would be a tight squeeze otherwise!

Netta watched as she separated all the precious material and spread it on the table. 'See, child, you must always shape the fabric to the body, sculpt it carefully to enhance − not conceal but glorify the wearer. We must work in cheap cotton first, make a toile and shape it round the bride before we cut all this cloth. There's no margin for error. Next we make the pattern to fit her body. Only then will I take the scissors to this cloth.'

Vida fussed and fretted over the first fitting until everyone was faint from standing still. She draped and redraped it until she was satisfied then sewed up the toile into a shape and fitted it over Aileen. Netta had pressed the old material carefully to gain as many extra inches from its generous seams as possible, working to the dressmaker's principle: 'Press after every move . . . and when in doubt, press again.

'We build like the fortress on the shore,' laughed Vida. 'First the inner layer and then the outer fabric − the cut of the gown is *its foundation. It must be as beautiful on the inside as it is on the outside. No skimping. This lace is flimsy and needs support or it will tear and pucker in the wrong places.'*

Peg watched the process, sniffing at all the palaver. 'Why couldna the lassie just wear her mother's dress?'

'Because it's Aileen's special day and she wants her own dress!' snapped Netta impatiently.

'The girl speaks the truth, Mistress Nichol. A remake of an old dress can still look fresh and original. A well-fitted traditional gown will make Miss Forsyth into a beautiful bride. And a bride must feel good on her special day, don't you think?' Vida Bloom was trying to be tactful.

The parlour now took on the clutter of a dressmaker's showroom: a cheval mirror, a sewing machine, boxes of trimmings and offcuts that Vida showed Netta how to turn into delicate rosettes for the neck trim. Every piece of the old dress was accounted for and had to be utilised to piece up the lace into a simple overskirt cut on the cross lined with an ivory parachute silk underskirt, under-layered with net to give a little more body. The bodice had a soft sweetheart neckline caught with rosettes, and padded shoulders to neaten the waistline. By the time Aileen came for her last fitting she had slimmed down enough to do justice to the outline. There were gasps of appreciation and great excitement but Vida said that there was just one thing missing – it needed a touch of added glamour to put a lustre on its plainness. 'What can we use to enhance the lace?'

The other women made suggestions but she shook her head at each one of their ideas. 'If I was in the sewing room of Molyneux now we would be adding a little row of pearls or beads to offset . . . ah, I know! Do you have beads?' Mrs Forsyth shook her head. 'Only a row of pearls for her neck, but there's an old bead purse of my grandmother's – a peggy purse for evenings. You can unpick that if it's suitable.'

Netta went to collect the purse and fingered it tenderly. It was a silk reticule, reminder of a bygone age, covered with shiny glassy beads of rose and pearl shaped into flowers.

Vida took one look and smiled. 'This is exactly what I had in mind. Beads will make the lace flowers bloom and sparkle by candlelight.'

It took hours of unthreading and sorting into sizes. Vida's face lit up with the challenge. She was in her element as she told Netta all about her days as an arpette, the lowest of pin-pickers, under the eye of a fierce dragon who breathed fire over her trainees and flung their efforts across the room if she was not satisfied. In the ateliers of a great couturier she had learned to sew gossamer stitches, make seams as smooth as liquid, to measure and cut, hem and trim, for the great maestro below.

By the firelight in the farmhouse parlour she was passing on all these skills to the willing fingers of her helper who lost herself in the intricate tasks and felt a sense of satisfaction never experienced when studying or working with farm stock. They had turned that simple wedding dress into a model gown, and putting the finishing touch of the beads raised it on to another plane.

Netta was sad when the task came to an end. She had learned so much from sitting with Mrs Bloom, watching, copying and asking questions. 'I think I'll be a dress designer,' she declared.

Vida laughed and shrugged her shoulders. 'It's the men who get the glory and the women who do the work in that business, Netta! It's a long, hard training for very little reward. I was glad to marry Izzy and leave it all behind but a decent training's never lost. It's seeing me through until he comes home.'

There was no one prouder at the church door than Vida Bloom, fussing over the photographing of her creation, with Netta bursting with pride at her own bead-sewing efforts. Aileen looked like a film star on the arm of her gallant officer. His cronies all winked in Netta's direction. How she yearned to wear a gown as perfect as that when her turn came along.

May 1949, Friday

'Are you asleep, Auntie Netta?' Gus was shaking her awake from her day-dreaming. He was standing over her, blue eyes peeping out from beneath a black helmet.

'What's that you've got on your head, young man?'

'I found it by that suitcase over there. Look, it's real! Brmm . . . brmm!'

Netta knelt up and lifted it from his head as if removing a crown, hugging it lovingly, sniffing the hard black leather, examining the ear flaps and chin straps; there was still an oily petrol smell to the inside. How did this come to be here? And what else was here?

She turned to the battered leather suitcase, pressed the rusty sneck and the hinges sprang open. She lifted the lid cautiously as if it were Pandora's Box. There was a layer of tissue paper, and folded neatly underneath a dress and jacket in lavender blue wool: her own wedding outfit. Why was this still up in the loft when it should be with her in Griseley?

How strange that she should be dreaming about the Forsyths' bridal extravaganza and forgetting her own humble outfit cobbled together in such haste. Through her tears, the colour of the dress shone like amethyst. Red hair and lilac was a bold combination but she had not been afraid of colour then. She shook out the dress and sniffed the mothballs. It looked so old-fashioned, so short and homespun, but it had been sewn in secret with such love. There were many more threads like this, tying her life together, still hidden here for the taking.

You don't choose the moment when love races like a rip tide, flooding over the shore, she thought. You don't choose your passion. It pulses like blood through your veins and roars up behind you in a leather helmet, setting the heather on fire with its heat.

All the coloured beads of her life's journey started here with this suitcase, and a lilac dress bore silent witness to her desperate time.

2

STEPPING STONES

GARNET

'Colour of blood, and earth,
Birth and violent death.
An amulet worn on life's journey,
protecting from evil and fearful
dreams.'

Rae, 1944

On first inspection, Corporal Raeburn Hunter's arrival did not impress the worthy wifies of Stratharvar. They doubted that this scruffy individual would ever suit Farmer Nichol's only daughter. The village stalwarts with spy-glass eyes who usually picked out affairs of the heart before they actually happened were surprisingly slow on the uptake about this particular courtship, being in no position to pass comment until the fortress was stormed and fair lady carried off.

Netta herself did not think much of the soldier who roared up on his Triumph Tiger 70 motorbike to the Hogmanay Social, with Dougie Mackay, the Minister's youngest son, riding pillion; two mess mates on a forty-eight hour pass from the Sixth Battalion of the Kings Own Scottish Borderers, an outfit that had been recruiting Border sons to arms since the Regiment was formed in 1689.

This particular recruit had three obvious defects. First, he was not an 'in born bairn'. The safest bet for local girls was 'to marry over the midden than over the muir'. Secondly he was sort of artist, one of they queer folk who cut off their ears if crossed. Thirdly he spoke with a pukka English accent, having been educated in a public school over the border.

To Netta he looked a tousle-haired, scruffy pup in baggy khaki trousers, roving restlessly up and down the lines of dancers as if he was looking for someone. He looked more like an Irish lurcher than a full-blooded Scottie, with his tight brown curls which even the regulation army short back and sides couldn't tame. Yet there was something intriguing about the way he kept eyeing her up as she birled across the floor doing the Dashing White Sergeant. Then, when her pals sat lined up against the wall like a set of skittles, the others nudged her and giggled. He kept staring, making her blush.

'Watch him, Nettie Nichol, he'll be getting you up for the dancing next. Look, he's giving you the eye!'

I don't want his eye, I want his arm round my waist, Netta thought to herself with surprise. Don't be so forward, she mused, let him do the running and see what he catches.

She tossed her curls and straightened her well-worn party frock of dark green tartan, its hem let down and disguised with matching green trim, trying not to feel the butterflies flitting inside her tummy.

As the evening wore on and the jollifications got rowdier and rowdier, the Corporal did not make one move in her direction but he kept on staring. Netta was so furious she began to think she had warts all over her nose. How dare he stand there eyeing her up like a farmer at a beef auction! Then she remembered they'd not even been introduced. She flounced around the edges of the dancing groups, trying to look casual, but everywhere she moved she could feel those eyes boring into her.

To her horror as she passed him by she found herself whispering, 'What you staring at?'

Quick as a flash came his reply: 'Your bones – you've got good cheeks. They should last you a lifetime if you don't run to fat!'

'Hah!' Netta stormed off, furious with herself and with him. How dare he look at her bones and not even ask her name! She hung on for the last waltz, watching even Peg and Father shuffling over the floor, feeling like a wallflower, and then left the dance early, trying not to feel slighted by the rude stranger who had spoiled her evening.

Next morning to her relief he was there in the Minister's pew, sitting meekly with the family, and she tried not to flush as she sat opposite them. Doubtless Dougie had filled him in on all the local gossip: who was fast, who was slow, and who like Netta worked *on the family farm, hardly going out, preferring her sewing, knitting stripey lace jumpers from old unravelled wool and demonstrating make do and mend to the Guides and Brownies. What a mundane wartime it was – waiting for her call up, waiting for life to begin outside the confines of Stratharvar.*

Later in the afternoon she took the farm dogs for a good stretch across the fields, down to Carrick beach to feel the sharp January breeze on her cheeks and soothe the restlessness inside her. Why did the arrival of one cocky soldier trouble her so? Then she saw him sitting alone on the shore, skimming pebbles into the water, alone with his thoughts. One of her Collie dogs bounded in his direction and he turned and waved at her as she was about to dart for safety behind a thicket of brambles. Instead her feet just walked up to him and the words shot out like bullets from a gun.

'What did you mean about my bones? What's wrong with them?'

She stood over him, furious, and he smiled a cheeky child's grin, showing white teeth and sparky brown eyes with ridiculous lashes wasted on a boy.

'They're perfect, Miss Nichol, just perfect. Dougie said you were a spitfire,' he laughed.

'What else was he saying then?' Netta rested her hands on her hips, waiting for the worst.

'He told me there was only one human subject worth painting hereabouts: a redhead with fingers as sharp as needles who lives by the shore. He wasn't wrong but I've no oils handy, just charcoal and a sketchpad. Shall I do you now?' He mimicked the ITMA catchphrase. 'Why did you leave the dance last night?'

Netta shrugged. 'You get fed up with dancing with the same faces and you didn't exactly fill up my card.' She couldn't resist a dig at him.

'I don't dance. I've never danced . . . totally useless. In fact I don't know my left foot from my right. I was afraid I'd flatten your toes. So were you sulking that I didn't dance with the prettiest girl in the room?'

53

He was teasing her and she had to smile. Why was it she could say anything she liked to this stranger? Why was it that she felt he'd been sitting on this beach all her life, like Dougie and all the other lads from Stratharvar? Yet why was it when she looked into that dark stubbly face, at those grinning eyes and that mop of hair, she couldn't breathe for the thudding in her heart? This was something strange and new, something she had never experienced before. Why did it feel like an ache inside her, it was so strong? It was easy to plonk herself down and talk about her dreams of designing dresses when this drab war was over and colour would flood back into life again.

He sketched the outline of her face as she gabbled on. Then he told her about his own life in Glasgow College of Art and the travel scholarship that he had sacrificed to do his army service. He had no family left, and the wealthy aunt who had reared him in the Borders had sent him away to England to sharpen his manners and get this artistic nonsense out of his head. It hadn't worked, of course. How could a boy who had been named after his distinguished forebear, Sir Henry Raeburn, the famous portrait painter, not fulfil his instinct to capture the world on canvas? He had built up a portfolio that got him his place at the famous College of Art but the war had intervened and now he must wait for its end to continue his studies.

'We have to set the heather on fire, Miss Nichol. Make our mark however small . . . leave something more than footprints in the sand or it's all a waste of time. I'm not one for life after death. You saw me in the kirk today but that was out of politeness to my kind hosts – and I knew somehow you'd be there. So if you want a carpet slippers sort of suitor, Miss Nichol, I'm no the man for you!' He peered at her intently and she felt a stabbing feeling deep in her stomach.

'Who says I'm wanting any suitor? I've my own plans too. I want to train up with the best dressmakers, have my own business and set my own footprints one day.'

'That sounds exciting. Don't get bogged down here in the sand . . . a body could grow gey comfortable in this lotus eater's pasture of milk and honey. London or any city's full of sharp edges to cut

54

you down to size. I bet you've never been further than Carlisle in your life!'

'I have so . . . to Edinburgh once, and Dumfries and Ayr!'

'Ah-hah! The joys of Ayr on a wet Fair weekend.' He was mocking her again and Netta rose to the bait, standing up to go.

'If you're going to make fun of me every time we meet . . . We can't all be fancy artists with cut-glass accents, Corporal Hunter. I should have thought, with all your airs, you'd be a Captain by now!'

'Ouch! I can see I'm going to have to teach you to see the jokes in my patter, Miss Nettie Thimble.'

'So Dougie told you my nickname? I prefer Netta or Jeanette.'

'And I'm just Rae. Will you write to me and let me visit you again, Jeanette? Here take this sketch . . . It must be your mother you've to thank for such cheekbones, certainly not yer pa!'

Suddenly Netta felt old maidish and silly for being so touchy with him. She didn't know what to make of this tousle-haired man with his long legs and beautiful hands, but one thing was for certain: she wanted to see him again.

He came to Brigg Farm a month later for a third-degree grilling by Peg and Angus, and was found wanting in every department. They had heard he was an unsettling influence on Dougie Mackay: an atheist by all accounts who was tempting the Minister's son into doubts. Before the war he'd had Conchie leanings and came into the regiment late. He had no immediate prospects to support a family and his pedigree was dubious. It was rumoured his aunt, who'd never married, was very mannish and lived in some reclusive mansion with a female companion. They had been found dead in suspicious circumstances.

Peg was polite enough and brought out the best china: always a bad sign in Netta's eyes. The meal was strained, punctuated by Father asking awkward questions about Rae's army career and the preparations for the Big Push which everyone hoped would not be far away. The farmer would have been happier if Rae had been one of the Galloway lads in the Fifth Battalion, now training as an Airborne Division.

How Rae managed to get the petrol for the long journey from his barracks, Netta never dared ask. Sometimes he drove through the night for a few hours of precious leave together and brought a tent to rough it down by the beach or in a barn, not wanting to overdo the hospitality now wearing thin at the Manse. Netta was furious that Peg and Father refused to encourage his visits by inviting him to stay at Brigg Farm.

They wrote to each other every day, long newsy letters as the feelings between them grew fiercer and more passionate. They walked up into the heather hills or along the shoreline for hours, putting the sad world to rights, discussing pictures and artists, sharing confidences, getting to know each other. It was getting harder to stay in control of their passionate lovemaking under the shelter of some granite crags, overlooking the bay, wrapped in his army coat and a ground sheet.

The fortunes of war were changing in favour of the Allies and the KOSBs were training intensely for the final assault on Europe. Soon the marsh orchids were springing up by the shore as rumours of a Second Front strengthened. Rae knew he would be going south soon. Time was running out for the lovers and he was desperate for a solution.

'Marry me, Jeanette? I know it's crazy but just let's go and do it before I'm sent abroad. I can't hold back any longer and I don't want to shame you. I want to give you all of me before I go, just in case . . .'

Netta put her fingers on his mouth to stop his words.

'Don't you even think the worst. How can I let you go without being a part of you? Of course I'll marry you but there's not enough time . . . How could we do it?'

'Let's go to Gretna Green, to the anvil priest – flying away like Lochinvar in this old jalopy. Why not elope by moonlight? Then no one can spoil our time together. I'll find out what we have to do if you'll promise that when I send the signal, you'll get yourself to Dumfries to meet me. Will you do it? Will you marry me? And then when the war's over we'll really set the heather ablaze! But, if you prefer, I'll run the gauntlet and ask your father.'

'Don't waste your breath, I know just what he'll be saying,' she mimicked. '"Yer too young to marry, there's a war on, wait until it's all settled. Buy her a ring if you must but no weddings yet. Don't be hasty!" Who wants to hear that, Rae, when we've only got weeks left? You do the fixing and I'll make my preparations.'

'Don't go to any trouble. Save your coupons.'

'If you think I'm going to my wedding in a threadbare Sunday suit, then you've a lot to learn about Nettie Thimble!'

How could she refuse such a romantic proposal? This was her decision and after all she was eighteen – old enough to know that loving a man like Rae would only happen once in her life. Desperate times needed desperate measures. They must take this chance of happiness before it was washed away like footprints in the sand.

It was easy to deceive everyone in Stratharvar into thinking the romance was over. Netta went about her farmwork with a face like thunder, letting it be known that Rae Hunter was just another unreliable soldier boy. Then she took to her room with her sewing machine to make a pattern and design a dress with a bolero jacket. A trip to Dumfries for the lavender wool crêpe from Barbour's store blew all her clothing coupons away in one go. Peg left her alone to her secret trousseau-making, thinking the girl was comforting herself as usual with some stitchery. When sorrow sleeps best wake it not.

Netta waited anxiously for the letter that would signal their elopement. She had sneaked her birth certificate from Father's deed box, along with her identity card and ration book; drawn out her savings in dribs and drabs from the Post office. Then, when the note came, she packed a little leather case with underwear and a nightdress sewn from parachute silk, appliqued around the edge with lacy scallops, and her bridal outfit.

She paced her room, tormented with guilt, knowing that her flight

57

would upset her parents and shame them before the district. But when love was this urgent it had to be obeyed and to hell with the consequences which would surely follow their deception.

'Oh, Mother,' she cried, 'we have to be together. You would understand, I'm sure . . . he colours my heart with fire and he's my life now.'

She passed the empty bedroom where Peg and Angus slept. The door was ajar and Netta found herself walking over to the mahogany dressing table with its kneehole and drawers to either side. In the bottom right-hand drawer was the blue box she had fingered so lovingly many times as a child. Quickly she slipped it into her coat pocket, placing a letter by the mirror.

After all, she argued to herself, I must borrow something and the necklace needs an airing: something old would be most of her bridal underwear, something new and blue was her two-piece suit. Something borrowed would bring them luck.

Rae was waiting to meet her at Gretna station. Under his black motorbike helmet his face was tired and tense. He had a ten-day pass in his pocket, enough time for the wedding and a honeymoon. They drove into the tiny village of Gretna Green and went straight to the blacksmith's whitewashed cottage, site of so many famous runaway weddings for hundreds of years. Mr Rennison, the anvil priest, in his workaday overalls, shook his head sadly at first.

'Did no one tell yous? I cannne marry you legally over the anvil, not since 1940, the churches have put a stop to a' that. You'll have to cross over to the Register Office in Gretna and give them two weeks' notice.'

'How long?' asked Netta, clutching Rae's hand.

'Fifteen days . . . to see yer papers are in order. I'm sorry.'

'But we haven't got fifteen days . . . This is embarkation leave, I've ten days at most.' Rae turned to his bride. Netta was in tears of disappointment. Cold water was being splashed all over her dreams.

'Can't you just give us a blessing, the old way, please? We can't

58

come all this way for nothing! Then, if we give notice to marry, we can come back another day and do it officially.'

Netta was thinking fast, the possibility of not being married by the blacksmith had never entered her head. Girl's romances were full of escaping heiresses crossing the border at dead of night with fathers in hot pursuit. She had heard of the blacksmith's certificate being legal tender in Scotland, irregular marriage though it was considered. A blessing would have to do for now.'

'I don't like to turn true lovers away. Sure enough I can say the words over you but what we do here is no a legal wedding, mind. It's a wedding of the heart only.' He smiled and led them through into the little room where the anvil stood, calling in his assistant as a witness.

'Can I get changed, please?' said Netta, clutching her suitcase. She was shown quickly into a little parlour where she rummaged through her case and flung on the dress and the necklace. She pinned a little piece of old lace to an artificial silk rose and stabbed it with a hatpin into her hair. Emerging, she smiled shyly at Rae and he grasped her hand. 'You look lovely.'

They stood over the anvil and the blacksmith asked them their ages and if they were here of their own free will. They clasped hands and repeated their vows.

'I, Raeburn, take thee, Jeanette . . .'

'I, Jeanette, take thee, Raeburn . . .'

He then placed his mother's engagement ring, a cluster of opals and diamond chips in a half hoop of gold, on Netta's finger. The blacksmith priest clanged the hammer down on the anvil.

'For as much as this man and this woman have consented together before God, handfasted together before witnesses, I declare in His sight only are they now man and wife. You may now kiss your bride . . . but for God's sake get yourself down to Gretna and do the job properly and don't say anything about this ceremony! I cannae gie you a certificate or register you, but we know what we know . . . Good luck to you both!'

The couple stood looking stunned in the little room with its smell of smoke and iron, dust and horse manure; a soldier in his mud-splattered uniform and Netta with most of her bridal outfit still in its case. It would have to wait for the official ceremony, for the bouquet and photographs and the brass ring they would acquire if necessary.

Outside in the spring sunshine they stood in the blacksmith's yard, reluctant to leave this sacred spot and not quite sure what to do next. It was all so simple, so tender. The world of war closing in on them was pushed back for ten precious minutes: all it had taken to join them forever.

They found the tiny Register Office down the Annan Road but it was closed. Rae slipped a note through the door, giving notice of their intention to marry in fourteen days' time. Then they roared off along the coast road and found rooms on a farm. The wife was suspicious and asked to see their marriage lines before turning them away. They found an empty byre near Powfoot on the edge of the Solway Estuary, made themselves a bridal picnic of morning rolls and cold meat, fruit and fruit bannocks. Afterwards they walked barefoot, making patterns of footprints in the mud, sketching the coastline under a cloudy sky. There was so much to talk over, fresh plans to make for the official ceremony, but more important was planning their future lives together. So much about each other's past lives they still didn't know.

Rae told her about his Aunt Freddie and her friend, Annie. 'I saw so much love between them – I never saw them as odd or different – and when Annie was told of her terrible illness they decided they just couldn't be parted. They bound themselves together with rope, face to face, and jumped into the Tweed. I wouldn't want you to do anything silly if anything happened to me . . . Promise me you will be brave and get on with your plans, with or without me? I'm sorry it's all been such a hotch-potch. I never thought to check about Gretna Green . . .'

'Stop that! I won't hear such nonsense on our honeymoon. Don't let anything spoil this time, Rae, please. No army, no wars or relatives. I wouldn't swap our anvil wedding for the poshest of *cathedral weddings with all the champagne and fancies. I just wish it could last forever.' Netta sighed, snuggling into his arms, feeling the chill of the sea breeze.*

'Nothing lasts forever, Jeanette. After Aunt Freddie died I had no one in the world who cared if I lived or died. I used to feel I was cut adrift without a rudder to guide me. Now, with you steering the ship, I know we'll set the heather on fire, search the whole world for our inspiration. The war must end once we land in Europe. I feel such hope for us.' Rae kissed her enthusiastically and they fell together to the damp grass.

Love knows no rules or regulations, no rations and blackouts, curfews and call-ups. In the cosy darkness of their straw bed they nuzzled each other tenderly enjoying this new way of loving. For these few days they owned the world. Once their notice to marry was placed with the Registrar, they crossed the border to lodgings near Carlisle and tried to order a wedding ring but there were none to be had.

As they were both Scots born, residents and over sixteen, a wedding without parental consent would be straightforward so long as Rae managed to scrounge enough time to ride over from his barracks for the second ceremony.

To Netta their real marriage had been the vows in the blacksmith's smiddy but the telegram to Brigg Farm saying: 'Corporal and Mrs Rae Hunter send greetings from Gretna Green!' must wait until later. No news of this elopement would be divulged to Stratharvar ears. Heaven only knew what lay ahead when she returned home. All that mattered now were the promises they had vowed one to the other: vows to last a lifetime. The certificate could come later. It was only a formality after all.

Summer 1944

It rained all the way home from the station, and being a Sunday there were no familiar vehicles trundling up the coast road from Kircudbright so it was shanks's pony all the way home. Netta stood under the lean-to like a drowned rat, not sure whether her return warranted ringing the front door bell. Better to press it and wait. But what if they barred the door on her? The drips from her felt hat plopped on to the end of her nose and her mac felt limp and sodden.

Peg stood back at the sight of the soaking girl. 'Look what the tide's washed in, Angus . . . So you've come back, have you, now the deed is done? I don't know what you think yer playin' at my girl. You gave us the fright of our lives, running off like that. Yer faither's fair off his head with worry. Just a note – is that all he's worth, after all he's done for you over the years? I don't know how you've got the cheek to stroll back here! What dae you think people will think when we tell them you ran away with a sojer? One that hasnae even the guts to stand and face the music at yer side! Oh, Nettie, I'm ashamed of you.'

'Rae wanted to come and explain, honest, but his leave was up. He'll come next week after . . .' Netta stopped herself. No one must know about their blunder or why he must return. 'We're going to Dumfries to get the wedding ring we ordered. It didn't come in time,' she lied. 'Am I allowed in the now or shall I walk back to the station?'

'Ach away in. Is there anything else we should be knowing?' Peg peered at her intently. 'Better to know the worst.'

'What do you mean?'

'You ken fine what I mean, lassie. Why the rush?'

Netta smiled with relief. 'Nothing like that, I promise. Rae's not like that.'

'All soldiers is like that given half the chance,' glowered her father from the doorway, eyeing her up and down. 'You've an awful lot to answer to my satisfaction, my lady. Yer own mother would turn in her grave to see the way you've treated us – running away like thieves in the night and you only knowing him five minutes. I just hope you know what you've got yersel' into. Couldn't you both have respect for each other, control yourselves and wait until this war's over like sensible human beings? Not rush to the altar like twa dogs on heat! Was it one of they Register Office jobbies then?

Netta bowed her head and said nothing, letting him continue with his assumptions.

'So off you pop to some little backstreet room. Not very elevating, to marry in some poky corner. Nae music, nae Minister and nae family: a right hole-in-the-wall affair! So where's your marriage lines then?' He held out his hand.

'Give me a minute to dry off, I'm soaked through. This is the two-piece I made and my ring belonged to Rae's mother, isn't it lovely? I told you, the wedding band is ordered.' The girl shoved her left hand in Peg's face for her to admire the moonstones and diamond chips.

'Opals is unlucky stones in my book,' sniffed Peg. 'They crack awful easy so you'd better leave it off if you want them to last.' Netta drew back her hand quickly. She was not going to be parted from her ring.

She climbed the stairs to her bedroom, to the familiar bed and tailor's dummy, the sewing machine, her farm dungarees. She smiled to herself. It had gone better than she'd expected. Lots of puff and smoke but the door was not barred and that was a relief. They had accepted her story. If she was married, however hurriedly, she was decent in everyone's eyes, and in Stratharvar appearances mattered.

She looked at herself in the dressing-table mirror: a pinched pink face with freckles dotted over her nose and cheeks, damp hair gone into a frizz. Was that a liar's face looking back at her now? she thought. No! In the eyes of God she was truly married, the blacksmith priest had said as much. The truth lay in their hearts, not on paper. She stared back at herself with a big sigh.

'Bestir thyself, Nettie Thimble, back to plain clothes and porridge, muck and shovels. Keep them sweet and keep busy.' Saturday week would soon come around, and as for her marriage lines, she had a plan to scotch that problem.

She ran to the top of the stairs and cried down, 'Oh, losh! I cannae find my lines or my birth certificate. I must have left them at the digs or on the station. They're not in my bag or my case. What shall I do?'

She started to wail with such a noise the farmhands rushed into the yard to see what the racket was about.

'Are you sure your hubby's not got them, hen?' shouted one from the kitchen door. Netta played to the gallery with her sniffles and frenzy until Father himself waved his hand. 'You can ring the Office and get another copy. Don't get yerself in such a fankle!'

'No, I'll wait and see if they're handed in. I can use my old ration book here but I wanted everyone to know I'm Mrs Hunter.'

'Tell the postie then. He's better than any notice in the Galloway News. Either way the whole district'll soon know yer business, Netta. Go to the Food Office, they'll give you advice. It's only a slip of paper and can easily be replaced.'

Netta nodded and sniffed and her heart leaped with relief.

It was to be one of the longest weeks of her life. Time dragged by so slowly when each second she kept looking at her wrist watch to check it hadn't stopped. Peg and Father were being understanding for once, not quizzing her, relieved she was back from her holiday in England: the official version of her first disappearance. Then the story changed to a surprise wedding before her husband went abroad, and a trip next week to Dumfries to see him off down south. The news was whispered from shop to farm to kirk and back. Angus drove her into town to catch the train and Netta dressed in her last pair of silk stockings and her new rigout. The necklace she had returned sheepishly to the bottom drawer, hoping it had not been missed.

The train was held up outside Dumfries by troop movements. Convoys of soldiers were piling into compartments, heading south with kitbags and cheery waves out of windows to anything in a skirt. She searched for the familiar bonnets of the Borderers, for the Lenzie tartan, patch on the sleeve, searching for one kent face among the crowds. No one could find anyone else in this crush and Rae had not promised to come to Dumfries anyway. There was just time to collect the thin gold band from the second-hand jeweller's before she took a bus to Gretna Green village.

It was a slow journey, following the convoys of trucks and armoured vehicles with soldiers hanging from the sides, waving to passers-by. Now there was plenty of time to take in her surroundings properly. The first time she had been too excited to notice a thing. She followed the outline of the Solway coast, peering into cottage windows and farms and schools on her journey south. Gretna Green was renowned the whole world over for runaway marriages. It was ideally situated between England and Scotland for lovers to take advantage of the Scottish law that allowed marriage at sixteen without parental consent. This cluster of cottages, a church and hotel and railway station, was all there was to the village, but it had been the centre of drama and intrigue for hundreds of years. She looked again at the blacksmith's shop and smiled. They must have a photograph taken outside to prove they'd done it the old way!

Netta walked to the modern end of Gretna, built around a cordite factory during the First World War. It showed a dour workaday face to the world, with plain barrack-like buildings and factory workers milling round a line of shops. There was nothing romantic about the Register Office but it served its purpose.

She was still half an hour early for their appointment, clutching a little bouquet of white heather wrapped in silver paper. Netta looked down the list of banns. They were sandwiched between a couple from

65

Annan and a merchant seaman and his girl from Edinburgh. There it was in black and white: Raeburn Francis Hunter to Jeanette Kirkpatrick Nichols.

For all it was nearly the end of May, the wind from the Solway Firth was sharp and Netta shivered in her finery. Rae was late and as the minute hand of her watch crept from ten to twenty to thirty, the time for them to be going into the Marriage Room drew nigh. The first happy couple came out laughing and friends showered dots of homemade confetti over them. The bride wore a tweed suit with a fox fur round her neck and the groom wore the uniform of a Special in the Police Force.

Netta shivered, her teeth chittering, her heart thudding, feeling tightness like a band of steel close around her chest. *He's not coming, something's happened . . . an accident on the way. Surely he wouldn't jilt me?* The Registrar peered around the door.

'Hunter party step forward.' He saw her weeping and sat her down. 'Perhaps there's a hold up, what with all the troops and lorries. They say there's a ribbon of trucks from one end of Britain to the other. Just you wait there and see if he turns up. There'll be some explanation, I'm sure.'

She sat in a side room, listening to the next bride and groom go through their ceremony. They had bagpipes to pipe them out the door and Netta could have wailed with envy. She waited until the doors were shut and the Registrar made her a cup of tea.

'I'm awful sorry. Still if he's a soldier . . . The world's on the move all right. He has to obey orders.' She could tell he was looking at her with pity, thinking, *Here's some lassie juped by the swish of tartan and a line of medals.*

'When's the next bus?' she croaked, neck stiff from looking down at her feet.

'There's one to Carlisle in a few minutes and one to Dumfries on the half-hour. You're lucky it's a Saturday, all the young fry will be off to the dancing.'

The longest week in her life turned into the longest journey home, scanning the fields and the coast, trying not to howl on the bus and the train. All dressed up and nowhere to go. How was she going to explain Rae's absence? Peg had even prepared the spare room for them, just in case. Perhaps another half-truth would do again. She was getting used to covering her tracks.

Netta ferreted in her bag, took the ring out of its box and, while none of the other passengers were looking, slipped it on her wedding finger over the engagement ring. A ring but no groom. A blessing but no marriage lines. Not a single photograph to record the event. No proof to get extra coupons to build a home for his return. But only she knew the truth of it and so it would remain. Well, this bride did have the rings and the outfit, the memories and the banns, so Mrs Rae Hunter she was going to be from now on.

Father came to meet her off the train with a worried look on his face. 'Where've you been? There was a telegram just after you left. I had to open it. See.' He showed her the slip: SORRY STOP LEAVE CANCELLED STOP WRITE YOU SOON STOP LOVE RAE.

That was the point where she broke down sobbing, much to her father's embarrassment.

'Wheesht, lassie, the laddie can't help it. Sounds as if it's all beginning, right enough. I hear they're towing some great contraption all the way from Glenluce Bay, down the west coast to Portsmouth. The war has to come first, Netta. Don't get yersel' in a state over what ye cannae change.'

Netta was in no state for consolation or company. She changed her shoes and stormed up the hill to the mound of stones behind the farmhouse looking out over the bay. Today the panorama gave her no comfort. She was ashamed of all the blame she had lammed on Rae for not turning up. Fear had turned so quickly to fury. How mean she felt to have doubted him. All their plans were scattered like confetti, for try as she might to play it down now, she knew how much that legal piece of paper had meant to her. 'Mrs Hunter' shivered in the wind at the lie she must now live to survive.

★   ★   ★

Peg could see the girl was struggling, not herself at all, anxiously scouring the broadcasts and newspapers for news of the great invasion; poring over her husband's letters as if her life depended on it. This unexpected marriage had not brought a bloom to her cheeks or increased her meagre appetite. She found no joy in the visits of old school pals who came to shower her with gifts. Angus had put a wedding notice in the Galloway News *to cheer her up but it had sent her into a fit of weeping. There was no pleasing the girl if there wasn't a letter from Rae. He was based somewhere in the south of England on manoeuvres, apparently.*

It was nothing Peg could put her finger on exactly; a shiftiness about the eyes, a reticence to give information, a reluctance to make plans for war service. No wedding photos were forthcoming which was gey strange. The two-piece came out each Sunday for church – and so it should, the amount of coupons she had wasted on such a show. But there was something not right with the girl. Perhaps she was now regretting such a harum-scarum marriage or perhaps she was just sickening for something or perhaps . . . Oh God, surely not that! Not a bairn on the way? That was not fair, not after all the years Peg had prayed for one herself.

How many times had she lain on Dr Begg's couch, being pummelled inside, only to be told: 'Sound as an ox. I could drive a coach and horses through your pelvis, dear. Not to worry, it'll come when it's ready'? As the years went on there had been a few hopes, all dashed. Now this chit of a girl was going to have a honeymoon bairn by the looks of things. It was just no fair!

All this torment Peg kept within herself for weeks, not wishing to make the tension in the house any worse. Angus kept his daughter busy on the farm, with the calves and the clipping, the haytiming. They waited for the daily bulletins on the news. D-Day plus one . . . plus five . . . plus eight. The wireless news was always encouraging but by now everyone knew that reports were shaped and vetted to keep up morale.

The morning of the twelfth of July was one of those Galloway glory days: ink blue sky above rolling hills as green as emeralds, and blossoms on the hedgerows as far as the eye could see. Netta kept peering out of the windows of the bedrooms as she went about her chores, trying not to worry that Rae's letters kept coming out of sequence. She had numbers 28 and 30 but not 29. The Borderers were rumoured to be in some big push eastwards and from the news she knew everything was still bogged down near the French port of Caen. She was following every step of the way in her heart but the dizzy spells and weakness in her stomach, the sheer exhaustion she was feeling just trying to sweep under the beds, made her head spin.

When she stood up Father was framed in the doorway, his face grey and his hand shaking as he held out an envelope. 'It's addressed to you — Miss Nichol.' Netta saw what it was immediately, collapsing on to the bed as she tore open the telegram.

10th JULY. REGRET TO INFORM YOU THAT YOUR FIANCÉ CORPL.R.F. HUNTER. K.O.S.B. KIL-LED IN ACTION STOP LETTER TO FOLLOW STOP NO INFORMATION TO BE GIVEN TO PRESS STOP.

Peg heard a scream like the howl of a tortured animal and rushed in from the yard.

'No! No! Not Rae! God help me!' Netta rushed past her on the stairs and fled down the track. The dogs chased after her hopefully.

'Come back!' yelled Peg, suddenly alarmed.

'Leave her be,' answered Angus, touching her shoulder.

It was such a warm balmy beach day, white puffs of fluffy clouds floating across the sky, the breeze soothing. But for Netta sitting on Carrick Sands it was the dead of winter. Her eyes glinted like ice, her limbs felt stiff as she looked out over a gun-metal sea. Somewhere over the water Rae lay cold, unseeing in his shroud. He would make no more footprints in the sand, set no heather afire with his landscapes and portraits, nor warm her body with his loving. She felt the crumpled telegram in her palm and flattened it open again, poring over each word in disbelief. He could still be alive? Perhaps they had the wrong name, perhaps he was a prisoner or in hiding. But, no. Deep in her gut was the certainty that he had fallen and been identified.

She tore the telegram in half, in quarters, then fed it bit by bit into the silver-grey sea. The pieces floated away like petals, like confetti . . . the confetti that would never be showered over her. All that would be poured over her head now was shame.

May 1949, Friday

'Why are you crying, Auntie Netta? Do you want my hankie?' Gus whispered, holding out a crumpled square. 'Are you like that lady on the rainbow bridge?' He watched her sniff and wipe her hand over her nose, just like he had when the old sheep dog was shot.

'I suppose so . . . It was just seeing the helmet that made me sad. It belonged to someone very precious to me. He didn't come back from the war. You can have it, if you like. I'm sure he would want you to have it.'

'What was his name? Was he a pilot?'

'Rae Hunter . . . He was a soldier and a war artist. I have his sketches on my wall in Griseley. Some of his sketches are in the War Museum. We were going to get married but . . .' Her voice went all croaky.

'Did he get deaded?'

'Yes. In the battle for the Orne river, near Caen, with hundreds of other brave men from his battalion. It was a terrible campaign. That's where Dougie Mackay, the Minister's son, lost his arm. He came back to England and brought back all my letters and Rae's belongings too. He told me what had happened and brought me a special letter that Rae had given him, just in case.'

'What did the letter in the case say?' Gus was curious. Netta shook her head.

'I can recite every word of it like a poem but it's so special and so private, Gus, no one's ever going to see it but me. Wasn't he kind to think of such a thing? It gave me the courage to go on. You would have liked him and he would have loved you . . .'

Gus looked down at his aunt. She was sitting there looking hurt like the girls in the nursery class when they played rough houses and fell down, snivelling for their mammies. He cooried into her side and said nothing.

August 1944

It took weeks for Netta to pluck up courage to read Rae's last letter properly. She had folded it and put it in a metal tin, sticking it tight into a stone dyke by the shore. On bad days, when the dagger of grief in her ribs was unbearable, she walked down to Carrick Sands to meet him by the sea, took the letter from its hidey-hole and read his words for comfort, drawing strength from his belief in her. There, sitting on the rocks, recalling that first meeting, she pored over each sentence, hearing his voice in the wind:

If you are reading this letter then you know now that you must live your life without me, but dream our dreams for me, colour the world with your creations and bear no bitterness in your heart that we are the unlucky ones. 'What's for you will no go past you,' they say. The acid of bitterness corrodes away goodness and resolve. Fight it, my darling. I am so proud to have you as my anvil wife. I fear there will be trouble ahead for you but our marriage was made under heaven and no one can deny us that.

I wish I had more than a few paintings to leave you when I carry your priceless love with me into eternity and that first vision of you on the shore with the dogs, trying to look so cross with me. Press ahead

with your plans, my darling, set the heather ablaze for
me.

    Goodbye, my own dear heart. My love for aye,
Rae

May 1949, Friday

You never love the same way twice, Netta reflected, weeping. No other love however strong could regain this first chunk of her heart. It was fortressed by a stone dyke in Rae's letter. There had been a terrible price to pay for their loving. Now she felt Gus's hand sliding into her palm.

'I think you should go downstairs now, Gus, and play outside while it's dry. I can finish off here. I'm fine now.'

'But we haven't found your photos yet and my head hurts.'

The boy shoved another box along the door and dust puffed out like smoke as sunlight from the tiny loft windows to either side of the roof shone down on the jumble. 'What's in here? Yuk!' He held up a pair of lacy bootees faded yellow with age.

'Put those down and go and get me a glass of milk if you want to make yersel' useful, young man,' ordered Netta in her no-nonsense voice.

He plonked on the helmet and saluted her cheekily. 'Righty ho, Sarge!'

She smiled reluctantly, wiping away her tears and turning back to a box that had once held knitting patterns. She knew exactly what was in here and it would break her heart.

Ten Days In March, 1945

There were rainbows and tears on Strathavar hill as Netta set off stoutly up the steep hillside, breathing breathlessly into the wind. Some things never change: the view over Wigtown Bay, the silver-blue sheen of water and grassy hummocks now torched with wedges of golden gorse edging the sandy machars of the shore. She sat on the stump of a rotten tree, searching for comfort in the familiar, and out of a leaden sky a rainbow arched down to the sea.

It was worth all the huffing and puffing just to see that arch of colour. Where was God's rainbow handle on the basket of this war-torn world? Did he care what was happening here? All the Minister's comforting words rang hollow in her ears when she pressed Rae's last letter to her heart. Her world was a hell of grey shadows and darkness without hope of his return.

This time last year there had been the colours of love in her life; crimson, gold, emerald to purple under the silken arch of Rae's protection. Today the sight of a rainbow gave no comfort for, hard as she squinted, Netta could see only a half hoop dipping into the sea and that was never a good omen. She was pushing herself to climb the hill just to share the wonder of this Galloway scenery with 'Baby Bump' who squirmed and rolled inside her body. She placed a stone on Mother's cairn which marked the summit of the hill. A girl needed her mother at such a time but Netta's was gone.

The shadows fell after Caen and Arnhem when more Galloway

sons were slaughtered. The blackness came over her in waves of anguish that Rae had died unaware there was a child on the way. How drab now were the colours of war – mourning, blackouts, khaki and camouflage – against the rainbow colours of their courtship. How could she ever set the heather ablaze without his inspiration?

She would never touch a paintbrush or a dress pattern again even though this long war was coming to an end. Netta believed that 'Bump' would get a better start here in fresh air and sea breezes. That was why she was staying put.

Everyone seemed relieved to know that she had something of Rae's to look forward to but a baby was not some souvenir to dust on a mantelpiece. It must be clothed and fed. Good wishes from friends would butter no parsnips, but at least they made up for the dour faces at Brigg Farm at her news.

Father and Peg carried on at her to sort out her widow's pension and demanded an explanation as to why stuff was arriving addressed to Miss Nichol and not Mrs Hunter. She fobbed them off as best she could in her grief, her lethargy and morning sickness.

'You're entitled to his pension at least now there'll be another mouth to feed. It should be coming to you automatically.' Father was all for writing to complain of the insensitivity of the Pensions Ministry in not giving his widowed daughter her dues.

'Rae must not have got round to informing them before they left for France . . . Don't fuss. When I feel stronger I'll make enquiries,' answered Netta warily as Father gave her one of his quizzical looks out of the corner of his eye. 'I'll take in sewing and dressmaking. No bairn of mine will go without,' she vowed.

'Now your time's up, Bump.' Netta smiled, patting the bulge. The baby was long overdue and she was hoping this strenuous outing would give it the impetus to put in an appearance.

She felt as useless as the china dogs that sat looking down from the kitchen mantelpiece. Her bulk got in the way of the Brigg dairy routines. Like a galleon in full sail in her maternity smock made from gingham curtain offcuts, she kept knocking over Peg's precious knick-knacks with the swirl of her skirts. Everyone said Mrs Hunter *was the best-dressed expectant mother in the Stewartry, war or no war. Making smocks out of blackout linings, two-piece skirts and tops from old suiting, stopped her hands from shaking. She recalled all Vida Bloom's sewing tricks as she spent long evenings listening to the Third Programme while she got on with the layette, knitting and blanket making. No wonder they called her 'Nettie Thimble' or 'Mrs Sew and Sew'. Handsmocking by firelight soothed her sad spirits.*

Staying in Stratharvar, pregnant and numb with grief, was not an ideal solution but she needed a roof over her head. Once resigned to her condition, Father made few allowances for it and showed scarcely any enthusiasm, though that was nothing new. Lately he wore the expression of a man disappointed in life; the look of a man whose women have let him down: his first wife dying unexpectedly from heart failure, having produced only one lass who had eloped and disobeyed him without so much as a backward glance; Peg no better at producing an heir for him. There would be no future for Brigg Farm once he was gone without an heir, and it had soured him.

Netta stared out to sea, hugging her knees. The March wind was chilly and her ankles were puffed up. This was no place to linger alone. It was time to return to the greystone farm in the hollows, its whitewashed byre and red-painted barns jutting out like arms encircling the house; time to check the suitcase ready for the nursing home by the coast where Nurse Plenderleith was waiting to deliver Bump.

Some things never change. She smiled at the sight far down the track of Wee Alec, the travelling draper, busy on his rounds, lumbering the mile down the bumpy track with three large cases.

He always carried them the same way: two steps forward with the first case, two steps backwards to pick up the other two, like some strange dance, forward and backwards, all the way from the station or where his old van was parked by the main road to the coast. He could not risk his suspension on the potholes to Stratharvar.

He was a cheery sight that morning: Kerr's Tailors and Drapery Store on the move to each farmhouse to mark out the seasons of the year. She could remember her own mother sifting through each of the samples in his cases in silence. 'I'm just waiting for something to jump out at me,' she would say to Wee Alec as he sipped his cup of tea, and little Netta would wait with bated breath for something to leap out of the case into her hand. It never did but Alec Kerr never went away without an order: warm shirting material, heavy stockings, interlock directoires in salmon pink or sky blue. Come hail or shine, he was always a welcome sight for there were few visitors up the long track to bring the news from Dumfries to the eager ears of the farmers' wives.

All the colours of the rainbow came in those cases: satin ribbons; winceyettes and Clydella for nightgowns; even the heathery tweed suiting brightened the long dark nights when Mother would sew up the cloth on her Singer machine. Netta's job was to catch the offcuts and make them into doll's dresses, collect the fluff into balls. The feel of fine material across her fingers was always soothing. Wee Alec brought no shoddy cloth on his rounds for farmers needed warmth and quality in their clothing to keep out the draughts and wild weather.

Netta recalled Wee Alec and his dance up the lane in those happier times when she stumbled down to meet him halfway as a child.

Now she watched furtively, ashamed to be showing her bulk so boldly. But for 'Auld lang syne' she must make an effort and drag herself down to be polite.

In the farm kitchen Wee Alec's visit was a welcome intrusion on the day's chores for Peg. The ritual never varied. First there were the formal greetings, a weather report, the state of rationing – all discussed as Alec laid out his samples on the scrubbed deal table and Peg infused the tea, buttering drop scones to accompany his forenoon cuppa.

The trek up the lane took it out of Wee Alec Kerr's stubby legs for he was now the wrong side of sixty, but he was always turned out in a dapper tweed suit, his iron-grey hair still thick with Brylcreem and sporting a trimmed moustache. Then would come the vain search for Angus in the cobbled yard to get him measured up for a new tweed jacket. His old one was not fit to be seen at the cattle market. Peg knew that getting him to open his wallet would take weeks of nagging, cajoling and downright deceit. His natural parsimony made wartime make do and mend seem like profligacy. Try as she might this district worthy shuffled about his work dressed in oilskin coats tied up with twine around the waist, patched trousers and shirts, more holey than godly, and a greasy cap which shone like leather.

Peg boiled with shame at the sight of him for they were not poor tenants. Brigg Farm was one of the finest dairies in the Stewartry, its herd of brown and white Ayrshires, the envy of many in the district. They supplied butter, cream and milk to the best creamery in the South of Scotland. Was not her front parlour stuffed with solid oak presses, adorned with silver and brassware? So why her husband needed to go round threadbare was beyond anyone's ken.

There was much about Angus she could never fathom out; that stubborn streak of Kyle stock, kindness itself to strangers but a gey strange manner of showing affection to his own kin. Sometimes it was as if he begrudged his own breath. The shock of Jean Kirkpatrick's untimely death still burned like acid within him, eroding any spark of outward warmth at times. Peg knew he would not be coming to greet Alec but went through the motions as usual then trundled upstairs for his old jacket.

'Here, can you match the colours in yon swatch with this, measure up the length of it and bring me one made up next time? If I hang it to air on the range, waft it in the byre a wee bitty, he'll no notice the difference. I've enough coupons put by and the hens are doing well. You can give me the bill this time.' Peg sat down, exasperated, and sipped her cooling tea.

'I saw young Netta on her way down the hill giving it great licks. She looks fine enough considering she's no far to find her sorrow,' said Alec, searching for his tape measure and a swatch of tweed to match up with the jacket.

80

Peg turned, shaking her head. 'Would you believe her! Stravaigin' up and down dale for all to see the size of her. It's a good job she's a willow wand or she'd never get her figure back. In my day you wore a cloak and went out at dusk. Modern women have no shame!'

Alec looked at her sideways, whispering, 'We was awful sorry about the bad news. Still, it's no the size of the dog in a fight but the fight in the dog. Netta was aye a brave wee bairn and she didna come up the Fleet on a biscuit tin, Mistress Nichols. She'll earn her own keep.'

'With her big ideas, she'll have to! You don't know the half of it, Alec Kerr. The stuff she's made for this bairn: nightgowns, barricoats, spencers, knitted bonnets, shawls. Where she got the terry towelling napkins and muslin liners from . . . I don't hold with all that spending afore a birth. It's tempting fate. She could have got the necessaries from you . . . I dare say you would have given her extra, for old times' sake?' Peg sniffed, staring at the old man with a frown.

'No, she did right to get it where she could,' he said solemnly. It's no that easy to for us to get hold of quality goods and getting worse all the time. I had tae make up a bride's costume for a young wifie in Dumfries . . . Could I get her the colour she wanted? In the end the poor soul took what I brought from the warehouse: a linen dress in rust with box pleats and appliquéd pockets. Not her colours at all but when there's a war on . . . Will Mr Nichol be long? Only I have an appointment at McQuirter's at noon.' Wee Alec was anxious to be on his way now the courtesies had all been observed, as usual.

'You'll no get much out of them the day, not now Billy's gone west. Old man McQuirter spends most of the day in the King's Head and his wife in the Catholic Chapel, so I'm told,' sniffed Peg.

'Aye, well, drinking and praying tame the strongest grief, they say. If there's anything Netta'll be needing,' Alec collected his bags, 'I'll see myself out and go and meet her.'

Once the farewells were over Peg slumped at the stone sink.

81

She could feel the tension mounting whenever Netta came into view. Why had they never taken to each other? She had tried to be understanding. They should have been companions not rivals, especially at a time like this.

Had Peg not stepped in between the arguments over Rae? And look what a disappointment she had turned out to be, running off to marry the first soldier who'd looked her way. After all Angus had done for her, insisting his girl stayed on at school. And where had it got her: not a single qualification and now not even eligible for war work. A disgrace to this house!

If Peg was honest there had been a measure of silent relief for her when Netta had waltzed off to Gretna Green with yon artist. Yet within days she was back under their roof and now the size of a bus. It wasnae fair! Try as she might Peg could never call her Jeanette, even though she was growing more and more like her mother. Roots will out, Peg mused. Trust Netta to chase after some penniless artist with only a satchel full of drawings to his name – she was after all the granddaughter of John Kirkpatrick, who'd once lived by the shore.

His derelict studio stood close to where Angus sometimes let the cattle roam and the pictures in the parlour were some of his finest. Peg wondered if they could do up the studio and put Netta and her bairn in there, out of her hair . . .

She had always been jealous of Jean. They had made such a handsome couple, she and Angus, in their hey-day; the tall farmer with his square face and sandy hair, quite a catch himself, and the fair artist's model. But their offspring would try the patience of a saint! When Netta turned up in her kitchen each morning with her belly bulging, it rubbed further salt into the wound of Peg's childless despair.

'Look what Wee Alec's given me!' *Netta breezed into the kitchen waving a dog-eared magazine in her hand:* American Harper's Bazaar. *'Maisie Kerr found it wrapped round a food parcel from her cousin in New Jersey and they thought I might like to have it.'*

Angus, after seeing the salesman's departure, was now tucking into his hot mutton broth, blowing on the spoon and slurping. He barely raised his head. 'He's got a good eye for business, soft soaping you to spend at his store.'

'Why do you always think everyone's out to diddle us? I noticed you managed to sneak in without the poor man seeing you. He was waiting to catch you,' answered Netta. The unexpected gift had lifted her spirits. It was good to have a fashion magazine to read at her leisure. She plonked down and shoved her trophy forward for Peg to admire. Angus looked up from his meal, pleased with himself.

'You two were stood there blethering ninety to the dozen like fishwives. You didna notice me. That'll teach old man Kerr to hang about! Now he'll be late for the rest of his rounds.' He stared down at Bump. 'Isn't it about time you dropped that bairn of yours or is it just wind in yer belly? If you were one of my kine, I'd be dosing you up.'

His daughter ignored the gibe and flipped through the thin pages, poring over the photographs with delight. 'Oh, look! Claire McArdell. Three pages of her designs. Isn't this wonderful?' wafting a photograph of a film star sitting casually at her mending: Miss Lauren Bacall darning her socks, relaxing in a one-piece linen lounger by Claire McArdell, New York's best young designer.

'Don't you think the line is very unusual? So sophisticated yet practical too. Look, Peg.' She peered down and sniffed. 'It looks more like a Chinese coolie outfit to me.

'Look at the belt. Oh, I do wish it was in colour and I could see the shade contrasts. That mandarin collar is so right, and the neat buttons . . . I think they'd be brass to give a military effect.'

'Stop yer running commentary. You're not on the wireless. I'm trying to have my dinner, lass.'

'Look at the sleeves, Peg, so full . . .'

'Seems a waste of good cloth to me and such plain material. I like a bold pattern, a bit of interest. They look just like plain overalls.'

'Yes, McArdell likes working materials: for leisure wear: cottons, cowboy denim, jersey. Isn't it just tickety-boo!'

'Where do you get such words? Tickety-boo indeed . . . all steamed up aboot a bit of cloth! Who's got time for leisure? This is no Hollywood. Women in trousers is for the factory floor and nowhere else. A backside isn't fit for britches, not on a woman. It's no decent,' Angus contributed, blowing the cold breeze of reality on her chatter as usual.

'Why don't you save it for when you're in bed with the bairn? It'll be something to look forward to after all the nappy pails and night feeds.' Peg was trying to be pleasant.

'I'll be breast feeding.' Netta smiled, knowing how Peg would react.

'Not in ma house you won't! That's for peasants and Papes who ken nae better, not well brought up mothers,' snapped Peg, her cheeks flushing at the very thought of such barbarism. Angus bent his head low to keep out of the crossfire. For once Netta would let this pour right over her, too thrilled by the magazine to hit back.

'You're right, I'll have to be strong and put it away. Oh, I wish the Bump would shift itself. If nothing happens the day, I'm off to see Dr Begg and Leithy to get them to do something.'

'Let nature take its course. You always did have ants in your pants. Did you turn yon shirt I gave you? Seeing as his lordship here saw fit to avoid Wee Alec and stop the moths escaping from his wallet again. Shame on you, Angus Nichol, for going round looking like a tramp.'

'I've got better things to spend my siller on than parading about like a peacock. It gives folk the wrong idea. If I look like a dandy, they'll think they can put their prices up. These shirts'll see me out.' He banged his spoon for more soup.

'Out of where, tell me?' snapped Peg, sloshing the ladle of broth in the general direction of his bowl. 'You're only fifty-five, man. You'll wear out a few more shirt collars yet, God willing.'

'I'll no have Alec Kerr thinking I'm a soft touch.'

'I'm sure he doesn't, Father. I'll turn the sleeves on your tweed jacket and put some patches on, if you like?' offered Netta.

'That won't be necessary. I've ordered the old skinflint a new one. A raggit coat arms against a robber – but I'm no going round this district with this bag of rags on my arm and that's my last word on the matter!'

At Peg's words Angus rose abruptly from the table and stormed out of the door. Netta sat in silence, head bent, suddenly overcome with tiredness, aches and pains low in her back. Peg looked up and saw the grimace.

'Don't bother about him, he'll come to by teatime. You look wabbit, my girl. Do me a bit of mending but put those puffy ankles up. I don't like you running about up the hillside. You're not a sheep. What if your waters had broken while you were out? Who would see to you then?'

'They didn't, more's the pity. I feel so restless and can't seem to settle to anything.'

'Your father would say that was a good sign. Stay close by. Save your strength for when you'll be needing it. Have you thought what you'll do when all this lot is over?'

'Don't worry, Peg, I won't burden you any longer than is necessary.' Netta bristled at the hint. In truth she could think no further than the birthing.

'I didna mean it that way . . .'

'You did. I know I'm a nuisance and I can't do much around the farm but I did want Bump born safely. Staying here seemed right at the time. I wanted to be close to . . . well, to have family around, just in case.'

'Just in case? Is there anything you're not telling me? Is there something amiss?'

'I'm fine, I just keep getting these feelings – tired one minute, excited the next. I can't explain. And then I feel fearful. It comes and goes over me like the tide. Leithy says it's all to do with losing Rae, the disappointment and all that . . .' Her voice trailed away and tears filled her eyes.

She could never talk about him without crying. Peg kept silent. The silly girl had had no marriage to speak of and now she was burdened with a bairn.

Netta was wishing her parents could have got to know him better, to appreciate he was not just any student but one who'd won prizes at the College of Art; how he'd supported himself with part-time work in a warehouse. What a brief marriage of might-have-beens. If only Netta could explain how it still hurt every time she thought of him. 'This time last year' kept ringing in her head.

'You just take it easy, my lady. If Nurse Leithy says feet up and rest, then do it.'

'Peg?'

'What now?'

'What's it going to be like?'

'Why ask me?'

'You were a nurse.'

'Just invalids and chronics, never a midwife.'

'But you must know something. The only thing I know is cows.'

'All I know about birthing can said in one sentence: castor oil, a hot bath, then use your pains . . .'

'Why castor oil?'

'It helps nature take its course and eases the passage ways, so I'm told.'

'Will it hurt? Cows don't seem to mind much.'

'Of course it'll hurt! Remember Eve's curse: "In sorrow shalt thou bring forth children". But there's joy at the end of your pains.'

'What if I die. Who will take care of Bump then?'

'Don't talk such rot. Whatever put that idea into your head? You've been reading too many of those dreadful novelettes from the circulating library. Rest is all you need, and a good dose of castor oil. There's some in the cabinet under the wash stand. If it's a bath you're after you'll have to heat up the kettle and fill the tub yourself. This isn't the Ritz, more's the pity. But mind and wait until I'm back in the house, just in case.'

86

Netta couldn't wait all afternoon for Peg to return and so dosed herself thoroughly, filled the tub and read Harper's Bazaar *in the bath. One way or another Bump would be making an appearance before the night was out.*

Bump was in no hurry to obey orders so Netta spent an uncomfortable night in and out of the bathroom, but by the morning the ache in her back had worsened into a definite pain. That was the cue to swig down more castor oil, shutting her bleary eyes with a grimace. That should do the trick.

'A ride in my old jalopy down the track should shift it nicely,' Father said as they bumped their way slowly over the switchbacks in his van along to the coast road, chugging and spluttering to the outskirts of Kirkcudbright and Braeside Nursing Home. The red sandstone villa was set back from the coast road with a shale driveway and steps up to the porch. The sun was shining on trees dripping with early pink blossom, the borders edged with crocuses. Netta could sniff the salt spray from the shore, feel the soft Gulf Stream breeze on her cheeks. This was a moment to savour: stepping proudly over the portals into an unseen world of bed pans and babies.

Nurse Sadie Plenderleith was waiting for the new arrival and ushered both of them in with their brown suitcase. 'Away you go to see Hector, Angus. A braw day for your first grandchild's coming, is it no?'

He hesitated, thinking to wait with Netta, but was hustled into the hall. 'Don't worry, Angus Nichol, we'll take good care of her. There's women's work to be done here. I need to examine her just in case she's having us all on.'

Leithy welcomed her charge through the door with a broad, beaming smile. Who could not fail to feel more confident, thought Netta, knowing the hundreds of babies she had delivered over the years, the bundles wrapped in shawls and bonnets she had handed over to proud parents? Braeside was a home for invalids and convalescents but difficult confinements were her speciality.

87

Comings and goings, births and deaths, Leithy and her brother who ran the establishment were respected in the district for cleanliness and efficiency beyond the call of duty. Woe betide any assistant who tried to cut corners or skimp rations, they were sent packing with no references. 'This is my nursing home and while I'm in charge it'll be home from home for my patients too. Cheery faces heal wounds, good food feeds the spirit. Come in and let's be seeing to you, Mrs Hunter.'

Leithy had a plump matronly air, a face framed with salt and peppery sandy hair scraped back off her freckles into a loose Victory roll at the nape of her neck. A woman in her late forties perhaps. She always wore a bottle green nursing uniform and a white starched apron which crackled, a watch pinned to her ample bosom.

Netta followed meekly as if stepping inside a warm cocoon away from all the troubles of the outside world into a special place never to be forgotten. When she left Braeside there would be a baby in her arms. Tears welled up in her eyes.

'Oh, Rae! I wish you were here, holding the case, fussing over me, trying not to look frightened,' she whispered to herself. Why did talking to Rae feel like talking to thin air sometimes?

The pains were coming tighter and harder and it was a struggle to get on to the examination couch in the front parlour. The bustle of everyday business was going on around her in other rooms; Katy Beattie from Stratharvar village was carrying trays up to the first floor, there was the distant cry of infants, the ringing of bells, a smell of Izal and polish, a whiff of steamy washing somewhere.

Leithy turned her on to her side to examine her carefully, tugging a little. 'Two fingers dilated, my girl, we're on the way.' Then the inevitable happened all over the sheet as the latest dosings took their foul effect.

'Who told you to take castor oil? What a mess, you mucky pup! You could have done quite nicely without it. Netta Nichol, how much have you swallowed?'

'A full bottle,' she confessed, pink with embarrassment.

'You must be a masochist to get all that down your throat.

88

Go and have a bath now and clean yourself up. Your innards must be red raw. Away with you while I fumigate the room. Silly chump!'

Not a good start to a long gruelling day. At each stage Netta was prodded and examined and told to relax, but every contraction brought another smelly explosion until she feared plastering the walls with her foolishness. Leithy could see the funny side of it all but the victim was mortified. If only someone had warned her! As for using the pains, that only made matters worse. At regular intervals Leithy would put her cold funnel on the bump and smile confidently. Later she brought in some instruments. 'I'm going to give the bag a wee snip to break your waters. That'll hurry it along a bit more.'

What a splashy, watery business this birthing was. There seemed to be someone else in the next room, giving it great licks, shouting the odds for her 'mammy'. Leithy patted her hand. 'You just get on with it in your own way, a good yell never did any harm. It's funny how men shout for their mammies when they're injured and lassies when they're giving birth. Don't look so anxious, it's all going splendidly.'

But Bump was proving stubborn and refused to budge much. Why did no one tell her about this pain? Netta moaned and groaned and tried to get comfortable. Never would she put herself through this torture again. Later in the evening Dr Begg popped his head round the door, his 'kent' face familiar and comforting.

'Going to give you another wee snip and put the forceps on the bairn's head, Netta. You're both getting tired now. I'll give you a jag to ease it up a bit.'

The rest was a blur of pain and pulling, of red hot pokers and strange shapes looming in and out of view. She struggled against the pain. Nothing seemed to be happening and she no longer cared but Leithy stayed close at hand. 'Come on, Netta, help us one more time – give us all you've got. I promise you, not long now . . . Use your pains!' At least Peg had got that bit right.

It was getting light when Leithy drew back the heavy drapes to show a cornflower blue sky. 'You've got a "wee scoot". Look at him! A healthy boy. He weighs eight pounds and nine ounces, no wonder you had a struggle to push him out!'

The midwife placed a warm towel-wrapped bundle in her arms and Netta peered down at the wrinkled pink face, the screwed up eyes and shock of thick dark hair. It felt like silk, an old man's face on a black satin pillow. The odours of warm towels and baby powder would always remind her of that precious time.

'Is he real?' She smiled with disbelief.

'Aye, a perfect specimen, a real bobby dazzler. Well done!'

'He's dark like his father . . . was.'

'Well, he's certainly not a Nichol. I sent a message to Angus and Peg to let them know. No visitors for you the day until you've had a good long rest. We'll just put him to the breast, shall we?'

'Am I doing right? Peg doesn't hold with the breast . . .'

The new mother struggled to raise myself and open the buttons of her nightdress. Leithy manoeuvred the bundle to the nipple. The baby struggled, sniffing blindly for the teat, latched on and began to suck away. 'Ouch! Oh, my stomach − it's collapsing! My insides hurt.'

'There's not much for him yet but what there is will keep him strong. Colostrum is full of goodness,' urged Leithy. 'Keep going. It's nature's way of closing the womb too.'

'I'm not sure nature took its own course,' Netta whispered suddenly exhausted by the effort and the tenderness of her whole body.

'With a little help from Begg. You're a slender lassie and he was a big bull calf. You were lucky we didn't have to open you. We've stitched you up nicely but bed rest for you now, my lady. We want everything ship-shape down below for the next time.'

'Next time? Never! Now I know why no one tells you anything − you wouldn't believe it if they did.' Yet a few minutes later mother and son were lying together, looking out over the Bay, safe and

well. As she looked down on that black hair there was a strange feeling of excitement surging through her body. Bump was real at last. Nothing had prepared Netta for this moment.

Oh, Rae! He's perfect. I'll never be lonely again, she thought.

On The Tenth Day, 1945

The lemon-coloured dawn radiated across the sea as Netta sat on watch from the safe haven of the bedroom window at Braeside. She had sat all night, the babe sleeping and suckling at her breast, trying to compose a letter to her sewing friend, Vida Bloom, who was living with relatives near to Leeds.

'I have to be strong for both of us now, being just the two of us, we happy breed, we orphans of the night.' *How could she sleep when there so many choices and plans dancing round her mind? Besides it was easier to think when the rest of house was silent. It must all be written down to clear the head of the ideas buzzing round like bluebottles keeping her awake.*

We may take a room and kitchen somewhere in the village. I don't want Peg fussing over my son. One look at him and they'll be slaves forever! I suppose a child needs grandparents when he's fatherless but perhaps we will stay in Dumfries and Wee Alec will find me a job at Kerr's Gowns and Drapery, but who will mind the baby all day? I suppose we could stay at Stratharvar but I'm not sure about that. Why did I not think of all this before the Bump arrived, when he was tucked up safe and warm inside me? Sometimes I wish I could put him back there or carry him around like an Eskimo all day. He won't be any bother.

I wish my own mother was here to guide me, to care for Bump. She would know what to do to keep him safe. I must stop calling him Bump. He is Raeburn Angus Hunter – I shall call him, Ray – born March 20th, 1945 when our victorious army is capturing Germany and this war is almost over. I wish Rae was coming home to help us but he can't come now. I sometimes hear his voice in my ear whispering, 'Set the heather on fire, Netta!' But how can I set heather on fire with a child to support?

How do you tell your son that he's fatherless and homeless, that his grandparents don't approve of his mother? I have to be strong for both of us, you see. I think we should stay right here in this room at Braeside where Leithy can look after us both and I'll earn my keep carrying trays to the invalids. Another pair of hands would be appreciated here. I can't sleep for thinking it all over. It's so wonderful to be a mother, to hold my own flesh tight to my breast all night in case he gets cold. Leithy says I should rest and put him down in his canvas cot by my side. But the cot is cold and damp, he might catch a chill. What does she know about babies? She has never married. My 'Ray of sunshine' is not like the other babies in the house, he is fatherless and homeless and I must be strong for both of us.

I wish you could see us here, in the pink, in a room overlooking the bay. It's like being on holiday: meals brought to my bed. There is colour everywhere, blues, golds and wonderful red curtains, shiny brocade faded to rose pink at the edges where the sunshine has burned through. I sit by the firelight imagining us in our own place. The red is so warm, it fires me with plans. I have to be strong for both of us so, you see, Mrs Bloom, how can I go back to Brigg Farm when there's so much to organise for little Ray? His bedding, a pram and canopy, a go-chair. I have no time to work. Isn't it exciting? It takes up all my time just thinking what to do next. I am drinking gallons of milk like a good girl, my breasts need to be full night and day. They are huge and sore and weep for baby so I try and sneak him into my nightie when they're not looking.

Leithy doesn't like me any more and keeps taking him away. She makes me lie in bed on my stomach to flatten the bump. I do not sleep. How can a mother sleep when she has to make plans? There are problems with my widow's pension. I can't explain: a matter of a small piece of paper, that's all. What if my precious milk dries up and he starves? I can't bear to think that I might neglect him and he might die like Mother and Rae. Please help me and tell me what to do? I am not leaving here until there is somewhere safe to go. Can I come to you? Father doesn't want us. He never wanted me, only my mother. My head is aching with all the plans hammering away in it. I cannot close my mind. I'm on sentry duty, on guard in case she comes in to harm little Ray. I have to search the room just in case, behind the curtains, under the bed. You never know where the enemy might strike.

I wish that Peg and Father could love us. They show no delight in him, no tenderness in the holding of him. I cannot bear for them to pick him up in case they soil him. Farms are dirty places, dangerous places for babies to live. Look what the place did to Mother. I do not want to go back there with him just in case. Jean, Jeanette. Racburn, Rae. See how I copy their names for comfort: the only good and certain

94

things in my life, there's magic in the very names. I am Jeanette, part of that magic. They're here beside me, watching us, waiting. Perhaps it would be better if we joined them in heaven. We'd be safe then, what do you think?

Give my regards to Arnold.

Yours cheerfully,

Jeanette and Ray Hunter

Netta's head was drooping with exhaustion but she had to stay awake and keep the letters flowing while schemes for her future danced over the clean paper waiting to be pinned down. She would send the Blooms a lock of Ray's hair and demand a gift for her son; write to the Minister, Reverend Mackay, to get him to baptize the babe quickly in case harm should come; a letter must be sent to Claire McArdell congratulating her on the designs in Harper's Bazaar *— in fact, she would write to all the London designers, to Hartnell and Molyneux and Victor Stiebel, to tell them all about herself and how she wanted to work with beautiful clothes if only as a pin-picker in their sewing department. Then they could go south and find work perhaps or emigrate to New York and join Miss McArdell's team.*

Somewhere over the rainbow *'I'll save up our fares, Ray. The Minister will help us when he calls but not Leithy.' Netta no longer trusted the nurse any more, why did she keep taking the baby away? Was there something wrong with him? Leithy kept putting him in the kitchen with the other newborns in cribs, among the smoke and the fumes to catch germs from dirty washing, and Hector in the garden. Ray must not leave their room.*

They were whispering as if she wasn't there in the room. 'I don't like to worry you both but Netta's not quite herself today. Come away into the parlour, Peg, take a pew. I'll get Katy to bring you some tea. No visitors today, dear, you're too much on edge.'

'What's up?' Angus pulled his pipe from his lips and made for his baccy pouch.

'She was fine yesterday, her milk's flowing well, but she's too chippy and excitable for my liking. I would expect the tears and doldrums by now. Mothers always have a good greet when the milk comes in, but Mrs Hunter just chatters away to herself and the baby as if he understands every word she's saying – never leaves him alone. She's spoiling him already. I tell you, Angus, I've seen this once before and I'll have to get in Dr Begg to calm her down with something. See if she can sleep it off.'

'Can we see the wee lad then?' asked Peg, who was enjoying her visits to the maternity home and the sight of the tiny creatures in their cots. 'I did notice Netta seemed awful clingy with him.'

'What's more worrying is she's no sleeping when I take him away, but sits writing letters to all hours of the night which Katy has to post – writing letters all over the country. I just don't like the look in her eye. Call it intuition if you will. She had a hard birth and recovered well. We were pleased with how she'd taken to the baby at first – not all mothers do. Now her temperature's up and her pulse is racing. Complete bed rest and sleep is what I've ordered but we find her coming downstairs hunting for the baby, naughty girl, disturbing the other patients and pacing the floor at night, don't we?' She glared in Netta's direction.

'What are you saying, Sadie, is she ill then?' Peg was alarmed at the nurse's serious expression.

'Let's put it this way: I'll keep a close eye on her but she may have to go to the hospital if she doesn't calm down. I haven't the time to spare, we're fully stretched as it is. I'll speak to Dr Begg and let you know but I'm warning you now just in case . . .'

'In case of what?' snapped Father.

'In case you and Peg have to take the bairn in for a while. If she goes into hospital, they won't take her child. It's too dangerous.'

'You wouldn't harm the wee mite? Oh, Netta, that's dreadful. Of course we'll see to him, won't we, Angus? What's brought all *this on, my girl?' Peg rounded on Netta in the bed, who turned her face into the pillow.*

'We don't know, do we . . . don't get alarmed, it may be nothing that a few knock out drops won't sort out. A big sleep and she'll be as right as rain. No need to look on the dark side. I just wondered if there was anything in the family . . . er. you know, that might be useful for doctor to know?'

'He's been around long enough to know the Nichols are sound stock. As for Jeanie's parents . . . they were artists, a bit vague but kindly. Are you suggesting . . . ?'

'I know Netta's always had her head in the clouds. Now her husband's another matter. We've heard gey strange tales of his stock. I suppose you never can tell with an artistic temperament. I hope this isn't going to be blabbed all round Stratharvar, that our Netta's going off her head?' Peg stood up to check the door was closed.

Netta hung her head, not understanding their meaning but catching the tension. She was doing something wrong but what was it?

'I did not say that, Mrs Nichol. Netta's had more than her fair share of troubles. Her mind is worn out with worry, and worry blunts the blade. All she's needing is a good rest, that'll do the trick, I'm sure. Now, no more worrying, young lady. I take it you'll have the bairn?'

'We'll do our duty, though we've nothing prepared. We thought she would be going her own road once the bairn was born but she was a bit vague about her plans, wasn't she, Angus?'

The farmer was deep in thought sucking on his empty pipe. 'What's that you're saying? You'll have to do the looking after it, Peg. I've no time, it's up to you.'

'It'll only be for a week or two until we get her rested. Once things have settled down she'll take over again, I'm sure. Go and fetch their grandson, Netta, let them have a wee peek.'

Netta went downstairs on leaden feet. Why were they taking her baby away? What was wrong with him . . . was he ill? She breezed into the kitchen and took the sleeping child, sneaked outside into the garden in her dressing gown. Soon her slippers were soaked and it was starting to rain.

Down the path she slithered and out of view of Braeside, darting across the coast road, sheltering the baby from the rain. Fire was burning in her head but the water only cooled her brow. 'I have to be strong for both of us, Bump. We must not stay where there's danger. I saw them all plotting with her. We have to get away while there's still time. They think I can't cope on my own, they want to take you from me, but we shan't let them. They can't catch me for a penny cup of tea!'

The overgrown path was prickly and squelching with mud, her slippers were sodden and the dressing gown clung to her sweating body. The wind felt exhilarating on her cheeks but whipped at her clothes and the baby was stirring. 'Walk on, Netta, walk on to the sea. Bump wants to see the beach.' There would be a rocky outcrop where they could hide to watch the tide racing in towards the fishing harbour. She loved this shore and its tangle of seaweed. So many memories to share together. She was looking for Rae. It was time he came to collect them . . .

Why was there so much clutter and so many fence posts? Why were they boarding up the beach where the purple shells and cowries lay and all the Gulf Stream flotsam treasures waited for them to explore? 'We'll play pirates and coral islands, there's so much I want you to see.' Netta smiled as she lifted the baby. Why were the rain and those sheds spoiling the view? KEEP OUT, DANGER. How dare they stop our fun! We want to play sandcastles and fish in the rock pools. I don't like this place anymore, where am I? thought Netta.

She found a gap in the defences and stepped over on to the tufts and sand dunes. 'Let's see if Mother's here, waiting for us. She'll know what to do next.' Netta's eyes searched the beach but it was deserted now. 'Oh, I remember, she's gone on before to another place. Shall we follow her then? It might be best.'

Netta edged forward to the water. It was cold and grey and at

98

her foot lay a dead bird with broken wings, its feathers stiff with oil, body twisted and barnacled, head half-detached. The sea was throwing up its dead so she knelt down to finger the salty creature. There're so many of them down there: sailors, fishermen, gunners, submariners; so many of them waiting offshore to lure landlubbers into their lonely caves. 'We won't let them trawl us in, will we, Bump?' she cried, clutching him tightly, and began to shiver, backing away from the bird of death. The tide would suck it back in anger and the mermen would throw it back again further down the coast.

Suddenly she felt cold and wet, starting awake as if from a strange dream. What was she doing on the sand dunes? There were no shadows to read the time by but it was late and Bump was crying as he snorted for the breast. Netta felt a let down rush of milk. Her bone-weary limbs ached with cold. A man was walking down the shoreline, smiling. He waved and Netta waved back. It was Rae come to collect them at long last. He had not let them down after all. She rushed towards him eagerly. Rae would know what to do.

'We found her by the beach, poor lassie, all done in.' Dr Begg sat with them all, sipping his hot tea with relish while the drugged patient drifted away from them on the bed. 'The bairn's fine, no harm done this time, but we cannae have any more of these carryings on. It's no fair on Nurse Plenderleith or her staff. When they get like this they have to be contained for their own good, made to rest in bed. She'll be off to hospital as soon as I can call an ambulance. They'll keep her under observation night and day. The next few days are critical, I'm afraid. She'll either sleep it off and be as right as rain in no time or . . . What a pity. Such a fine lass for this to happen to. You never can tell with mothers how a birth will take them.'

'What doctor is saying is, some mothers harm their babies when they get in one of these states. Do you understand?'

'You're telling me I've got a daughter off her head?' Angus

muttered. '*Running off with her bairn half-naked for all the world to see.*'

'*She wouldn't know a thing about it, couldn't help herself, a temporary lapse. There's a big name for it but little else. Just one of those things.*'

'*What happens to the bairn?*' *asked Peg, trying to grasp all that had happened.* '*You must do what is best for her, Doctor. I'm sorry we've had to bring all this on you, Sadie. I don't know what to think but I don't want it all round the district. Katy Beattie has a tongue on her the size of an ox!*'

'*She'll no say a word, I promise.*' *The nurse smiled.* '*No one need be any the wiser. Normally it would be called childbed fever but I've always prided myself on having no such infections here.*'

'*I wouldn't ask you to lie, of course.*' *Peg folded her arms and sighed.* '*Could we just say she's gone into the maternity hospital for special care? We've never had such a to do in our family before. It takes a bit of stomaching, her running off like that. I suppose we'll have to bring his lordship back with us now?*'

'*Not now, he can stay here tonight. Baby's had enough movement for one day. I'll prepare his clothing and a bassinet for you, and a timetable for his routine. After such a start in life he's going to need strict handling, four feeds and no fussing in between, plenty of fresh air and a chance to exercise his lungs out of earshot. Just see his bottom is well oiled and his head out of the sun. Drop the night feed as soon as you can, for your own sakes, you need your sleep too. I can get the district nurse to call in and advise you. Think of it as a Christian act, holding the fort until Mother comes home. A wee chance to get to know your grandchild, Angus. By the way, she's calling him Raeburn and Angus after you. You'll have to register him for her.*'

'*Come on, woman, time to be seeing to my cows. We'll send round for him in the morning. Just a temporary arrangement then?*'

The nurse patted Peg's arm. Dr Begg averted his eyes from them, looking back at his patient with concern. Poor Netta

100

Nichol was away with the fairies, not to the Maternity in Dumfries but to Park Royal, the mental hospital. Only they would know how to bring her back from the fantasies of her dreamworld.

May 1949, Friday At Noon

'I can't breathe,' Netta gasped in panic, feeling the attic walls and the clutter of years closing in on her. There were too many reminders of unspeakable times lying all around her. She could not wait for Gus to bring her the milk. She must clear her head and escape, take the farm dogs for a romp in the fields and get on with her packing.

It was time to check the radiator and tyres and ask Father to look at the oil before her long journey south: back to workaday Griseley and her business. The mission had begun with such icy courage and resolve but was quickly melting away again. How could you, after all those years of experience, behave like some tweeny of thirteen around your parents? Must she meekly beat the usual retreat once more from all her past mistakes? For all her business success far from this place Netta, the prodigal, was given the fatted calf here – but it was always dished out cold.

Peg struggled up the ladder and through the hatch, trying not to spill the milk. No whip cut so hard as the lash o' conscience and she was feeling guilty that she had let the girl struggle to find Jeanie's albums. There had been grim satisfaction at first in letting her loose to root in vain for her photographs when they were all neatly parcelled up on top of the bedroom wardrobe. Now it felt mean and callous to withhold them.

Netta's presence brought out a bad side in Peg. The young woman fair turned over her stomach, like a dose of Epsom salts. Peg's exertions went unrewarded for there was no one in the loft to greet her. She peered from the dusty gable window to watch Gus and the dogs chasing a ball and Netta trying to take a snap of them all. One more day and she would be out of their hair until Hogmanay. Twice a year: that was the unspoken agreement. Peg reckoned it had worked out for the best over the years.

She noticed the open leather case and the boxes, the clutter of years. What a sort out this place needed! One of these springs she would come up here and give the corners a fright, make a good bonfire of all this rubbish. Her eye fell on a tent-shaped object covered with an old sheet. Peg picked her way gingerly over to see what was underneath.

The black oak carved cradle rocked gently at her touch. This was an heirloom for Gus whose own children might one day be soothed by its gentle rocking. She could recall every detail of the time when it was brought down and polished up proudly for their own use: a day Peg had never believed would come. She smiled to herself. How merciful were the ways of the Lord . . .

Park Royal, Spring 1945

Peg made the trek with the leather suitcase from Stratharvar to Park Royal Hospital by train into Dumfries and then bus, leaving Angus and the one remaining Land Army girl to see that baby's bottles were made up to her instructions on the stove.

The bairn did not settle to this change of routine, fussing and screaming all night long. Peg could not believe a tiny baby could make such a din and turn the quiet regime of Brigg Farm upside down. All Leithy's instructions went by the board. She found herself pacing the linoleum in the dead of night, clasping the red-faced nuisance to her chest, patting his back in desperation. He was searching for a teat so she shoved her pinkie in his mouth. He sucked furiously and hard but the moment the baby dozed off and she tried to put him down, his blue eyes would open suspiciously and he'd start bawling all over again. Round one to baby.

Peg began to wonder if this little mite knew that his life had changed forever. Trust Angus to toss and grunt but offer no help. Next morning, however, he climbed up into the loft and fetched out a dusty rocking cradle, black with age. Peg scrubbed it clean and polished it to glass, stuffed a mattress of towels and old sheeting inside and plonked his lordship in it in the middle of the stone-flagged kitchen by the mending basket. Every so often she kicked the rockers and the exhausted infant drifted off at last. Round two to Peg.

Angus went about his farm chores, organising the yard boy and Land Army girl, saw to his beasts, but each time he returned to the kitchen he, too, would put his boot to the cradle. A man could shut out the wailing, Peg thought to herself as she peeled the tatties for the hash, but now and then she caught Angus glancing in under the carved oak hood to see the pink face and black hair, now rubbing off on to the sheets. 'This one'll be bald as a coot afore long. His eyes aren't Nichol blue, more like you see at the swimming baths. Must be the father's?'

Neither of them could bring themselves to call the child Raeburn. Perhaps he would grow into that name when he grew whiskers, thought Peg, but now it was such a mouthful for a wee mite. 'Raeburn Angus, while you're in this house we'll call you "bairn" for short. It's to the point, there's no fancy fol-de-rols in that handle – and that reminds me, you must away down the Register Office, Angus, and get this wean registered,' ordered Peg.

She had always hated hospital visiting despite her brief training. This place was better than most: set in beautiful grounds, high up overlooking the Nith Valley. It was a palatial estate of gracious buildings dominated by a huge cathedral of a kirk at its centre. Inside, however, the wide corridors of the building, decorated with panels of carved woodwork and plasterwork ceilings, were more in keeping with a baronial mansion than an asylum but it still felt like a long dark tunnel to her.

She sat on the bench waiting for the visitors' bell. Someone must have spent a bonny penny on this place, sure enough. Netta was to have the best they could afford. She was not to go in the ordinary wards but in the rate-aided department where she would be allowed to share a room and wear her own clothes.

The bell rang and there was a thud of feet down yet more corridors. No matter how many bowls of flowers were arranged to adorn the place, Peg could still detect that hospital pong.

What a carry on this was, with the mother in one town and the baby in another, she thought. It seemed all wrong to her. Yet

105

someone must do their Christian duty to bring the patient her clothes and find out just what was the matter with her. Surely once Netta heard the good news that Hitler was on the run, that the war was almost over and Stratharvar would soon be lighting a bonfire and ringing the kirk bell, she would pull herself together for the Victory celebrations. It was good to have no more blackouts and travel restrictions; the seaports round Stranraer would be cleared of landing gear, the last of the evacuees had long since been sent packing. The Nichol family had so much to look forward to when the world got back to normal again.

The ward door was locked and Peg pressed the buzzer. A young nurse in starched cap and apron asked her name and ushered her inside quickly, past a line of sleepwalking shufflers eyeing her curiously with blank stares. 'This is a secure ward, Mrs Nichol. We have to keep everything locked, I'm afraid.' The nurse smiled politely but Peg was terrified when the door clanged behind them. 'I take it you're Mrs Hunter's mother?'

'Her stepmother,' Peg replied sharply. She did not want anyone to think any of these shenanigans came from her side of the family.

'I see. Well, no matter. We must take a full history from you. It's not good news, I'm afraid. Sister will explain. You'll see a marked change in the girl. Don't be shocked, it won't last. These things have to take their course. Visiting will have to be strictly limited, just a few minutes today. In future, better to write for permission to visit just in case the patient is having treatments. I expect it's been a long journey for you from down the coast.

'Here, she's in the side room on her own for the moment. We've had to keep her separate, she's been a bit noisy . . . you'll see. I'll fetch Sister to see you.'

Peg was not prepared for the sight of Netta, sitting on the edge of her bed dressed in an old nightie. She was rocking back and forth like some strange creature. Her red hair was unkempt, standing out all over her head like Madge Wildfire, the beautiful tresses matted and dull. Her tongue was hanging out as if she was

106

panting. Netta looked up at her but the eyes did not register the visitor. Such glassy eyes, heavy with drugs.

The Sister bustled in briskly. 'Now, Jeanette, look who's come to see you all the way from Stratharvar.'

'Where's my baby?' was the only response Netta could make to her.

'He's fine.' Peg felt a lump choking in her throat.

'I want my baby!' She kept on hugging herself, rocking back and forth. Peg tried to make chit-chat. 'Look I've brought you some flowers from the garden and your summer frock. The bairn's fine,' she replied, shocked by how much the girl had deteriorated. It would break Angus's heart to see the state of her thin body with legs like spurtles.

'How long's she going to be in this state?' Peg whispered to the sister. 'I was no prepared for this.'

'She's being assessed and is under careful observation. Puerperal dementia is a very serious condition. We take no risks. Mother has to be separated from baby, of course. For everyone's benefit, you understand.'

'And it's us left holding the poor wee soul. For how long, do you think?'

'We really can't dictate how long the course of the illness lasts. It generally responds to medication and other methods if need be . . . A few weeks perhaps. I can't speculate, Mrs Nichol.'

'A few weeks! I can't keep traipsing up here every day . . .'

'And we wouldn't recommend you to either. It serves no purpose, only upsets the patient. See how she's getting agitated now. Time to go, Mrs Nichol. Better leave her alone for a few weeks. We'll keep your doctor informed if there's any change. Don't look so worried. It can happen to the very best of mothers, we don't understand it but they do usually get better . . .'

'This "purple demention" is a gey funny disease. I've not had one straight answer since it happened. How can she be right in her head one minute and mad as a hatter the next?'

'She's not insane, just mentally disturbed by all the changes

in her body after childbirth. It may be due to fever in her milk. You see we've bound her breasts with sticky tape and given her drugs to take the milk away? That will ease things, I'm sure.'

'I told her not to do the breast feeding. Look what it's gone and done!' Peg exclaimed as she made for the door, not looking back. It felt dreadful to be leaving the girl alone in here but she couldn't wait to get out of the door.

'We think it best that new babies get a natural start, Mrs Nichol. Nature knows best.'

'Not in this case it appears.' Peg had firm opinions on that score. She paused and turned to wave a false 'cheery bye'. Netta was watching with a wild look in her eye, like a tiger pacing its cage in the zoo. She jumped up and leaped forward but the nurse was quick to restrain her.

'That's enough, Jeanette! Calm down. Say goodbye to your visitor, that's a good girl.'

'She stole my necklace, my Freya's necklace! Stole all the colours of the rainbow and my jewels. She's got them!'

Peg shook her head, backing away in alarm at the sound of such ravings. She was never coming back to this madhouse with its smell of drugs and despair. Angus could do his own visiting.

The sister escorted her back to the outer door. 'Not to worry, Mrs Nichol. First visits are always a shock. It won't be long until Mrs Hunter's restored, wait and see.'

Peg was not listening to her. There was one thought only in her mind and that was how to escape from this gilded prison and get the first train home.

Netta searched and searched but couldn't find her baby anywhere. She knew there was once one inside her for there were loose folds on her stomach and pains in her leaking breasts. He must be under the bed. Bump was hiding, she thought, pacing around the tiny room. 'Nurse! Where's my baby? He was here a minute ago in the cot by the bed.' Who was that woman who had disturbed her searching?

108

Braeside had changed. The fiery curtains were gone and the seaview so she banged her head on the walls, flung herself on the floor and battered the tiles. The nurses went about their business calmly, peering in from time to time, ignoring her demands. The thick walls kept the noise insulated from the rest of the ward. Why were they hiding her baby? All night Netta paced the room, screaming and crying, terrible curses and foul oaths pouring out of her mouth like bile. That was the only ammunition she had left to hurl at these cruel women, these kidnappers who had stolen her baby. She wanted to kill them all.

After the ravings came black nights of tears when she cried for Rae to take her home. When her wildness was out of control a jacket was tied around her and she was strapped into bed but Netta couldn't understand why this was happening to her and the fear overwhelmed her. Nobody visited after that first week and she felt utterly abandoned with only Peg's accusations ringing in her ears.

'How they stomach this sort of job is beyond my ken, your nurses must be saints to put up with such carryings ons! Poor lost souls wandering up and down like ghosts in a kirkyard. You're in the best place so pull yersel together and hurry home to yer bairn . . . Oh, dearie me! We didn't deserve this shame. What would have become of the bairn? Just think if we had not come to yer aid what might have happened to the laddie, stuck in some home for waifs and strays or sent out to strangers. He's better off with his family. Ma hand tae God so he is!'

When Peg reached the haven of Brigg Farm, feeling such relief to be away from that sad place, she sat down and began to unravel some old wool, found a pair of needles from the mending basket, looked out a pattern and cast on the stitches, smiling. No more lacy bonnets for the lad, he was going to have a proper blue tammy with a bobble on the top with ear flaps tied under his chin to keep out the chill April wind. Thank goodness Netta had made such thorough preparations. She would ask around the district for the loan of a decent pram which she would put under the apple tree in the spring shade.

The telephone rang in the hall passage. The bairn stirred but it was Angus who answered the phone. He stood nodding in the doorway, holding on to the lintel, his face drawn and ashen.

'What now? Not Netta? Is it bad news?'

'Bad enough . . . I didna want to worry you but I went down to register the bairn as we agreed while you were at the hospital. I didna have the right stuff, certificates and such. I told them what I knew about the wedding and the father's name and him being killed and the mother very ill. Allan Laing accepted me as next-of-kin and said he could make enquiries for the details under these special circumstances.'

'So what's the bother?'

'They cannae find her marriages lines. There was no Hunter wedding there on that Saturday or any other day that month.'

'You've got the wrong dates then or the wrong place.' Peg could feel her heart thumping.

Angus shook his head. 'They checked. It's no registered anywhere in Scotland.'

'Oh, dear God! That can't be right, surely? She has to be married or else . . .'

'Aye, if she's not then our grandson's a bastard.'

May 1949, Saturday Morning

The holiday was over. It was time for Netta to return to Yorkshire. Time to pack up the van, to make a flask and sandwiches for the long journey, look out the AA map, pump up the tyres, check the indicators were working and say her farewells. She hated this moment above all others, seeing the look of relief on Peg's face as she shoved a package on to the passenger seat.

'I think these's what yer looking for. Safe journey.'

'Mind and stop when you get tired, Netta, and keep the radiator topped up. I've put a bottle of water in the boot,' said Father, sucking on an empty pipe. Gus was jumping up and down, waving. His fist was clenched tight around the half crown she had shoved secretly into his palm when he'd told her his throat was hurting. ''Bye, Auntie Netta!'

She headed down the bumpy track, not looking back, but in her mirror she could see him running behind her to open the gate. He waved her off enthusiastically and she turned towards Kirkcudbright and the A75 southwards to Dumfries. Crossing over the River Nith to the Carlisle road, Netta turned off right at St Michael's church and took a sentimental detour past the hospital. She parked her car and made for the open section of the beautiful

111

grounds, strolling into the parkland and the rockery, sitting on a bench to gather her thoughts.

Not many people had such affection for their lunatic asylum, this strange alma mater with its own coat of arms and mottoes. What was the maxim behind its philosophy now?

> *'Absence of occupation is not rest.*
> *A mind quite vacant is a mind distressed.'*

The treatment she'd suffered in there had served her well enough in its way. Yet her stay was like some half-remembered dream, like pieces of a jigsaw she could never quite assemble, for some of the bits were missing. She looked up at the sun-lit grandeur of the buildings. Park Royal was one of the most famous institutions in Scotland: 'A Ritz among Madhouses,' some wag had once joked to her. Within these walls rich and famous alongside poor and homeless – housed seperately, of course, in different buildings amongst the grounds – found respite from an unsympathetic world.

Here began her first exile, her trial of tears, those amber days. Why had Park Royal become such a safe haven against the terror of her illness and the harshness of those outside who didn't understand it? Netta smiled to herself, recalling all the babies she had made there.

3

AMBER

'Colour of the dancing child.
Frozen life trapped in the sun's kiss
Worn for energy
Too much orange drains the mind.'

Snapshots From The Royal, 1945

There was still a merciful mist of forgetfulness veiling those first months at Park Royal like a sea haar on a grey shoreline. Everything was bleached and threadbare like over-laundered linen, as tasteless as bland vegetables; vague memories of drugged limbs dragging themselves round the grounds, the occasional blue flash, the smell of burning rubber and taste of acid on the tongue. There must have been a progression of sorts from acute ward and restraints to a single room with an iron bed where sometimes Netta felt she was sent to bed like a naughty child for some misdemeanour. 'What am I doing in this place?' said her own voice through a mist.

Few visitors appeared: the Reverend Mackay brought news with his blessings around the beds; Father came once on her birthday in June, looking awkward in this confined space in his new heather tweed jacket smelling of bracken and open moors – the one ordered from Wee Alec behind his back. Netta could remember that incident but not her own baby's face. Angus was his usual reticent self when she begged him for news. He produced one precious picture of Ray held by Peg under the apple tree but said little. It was kept proudly by Netta's bedside locker to prove she wasn't dreaming him up and shown to everyone who entered the room.

There was no sense of time here and she was unaware of the victory celebrations, fireworks and bells ringing all over Dumfries. The seasons crawled by barely noticed: summer arrived when the

115

upper windows were opened and the brown blinds drawn against the light. The gardens were crimson and gold with bedding. There was the sound of racquets from the tennis courts where the army officers who were billeted in their own hospital quarters challenged each other to long tournaments. Autumn soon followed. Kitchen windows misted over; there was the smell of bonfires, walks among the scrunchy leaf fall, queueing for the cinema in the ballroom theatre in a fug of cigarette smoke. Then the spicy smells of a kitchen preparing for Christmas celebrations.

Her every mood swing was observed by nurses and reported to Dr Goldberg who was monitoring her progress. Over the months Netta had graduated from raving lunatic to drugged bed rest and then been allowed to shuffle along the corridor, deemed fit for occupational therapy and distraction.

She found her fingers wouldn't obey her orders. They were thick and swollen with stiff joints. She sat in the occupational therapy room watching the other patients struggling with basket work and weaving while the craft teacher guided slow fingers, chivvied restless patients into some task.

She had taken a careful inventory of all Netta's interests and skills but Netta still refused to look at a needle and cotton or knitting. It was a line of stuffed dolls that finally took her eye: dolls of all shapes and sizes, raffled and sold for funds and charities. Teddy bears and golliwogs, knitted soldiers in guards uniform, sausage dogs and draught excluders, dolls with cloth faces, puppets on strings hanging limply, and party dolls in gypsy costume. She fingered the baby dolls with matinée coats and lacy bonnets.

'Would you like to make one of these, Jeanette?' asked the therapist, gently guiding her towards the table. Netta hung back shaking her head. 'I can't, I already have a baby somewhere, you know . . .'

'Yes, I'm sure you have, dear, but why not make one to give some poor wee orphan who has nothing?'

'I can't . . . my fingers won't work.' Netta's mouth was dry

116

and her lips would barely move. Her head buzzed with the electric shock treatment. Everything was in slow motion.

'Let's just start simply then, stuffing these teddies with old rags and kapok. No needles or sewing for you yet. Let's get those hands moving again . . . See, Lizzie is showing you how.' Lizzie lived in the same house block. She grinned and nodded. This was work for hands, not minds, Netta registered but her mind seemed far away from her body.

She did notice that the teddies looked bare without a scarf or bow tie so she asked for some scraps to shape into mufflers. Her eyes never left the baby dolls. If she couldn't have her own baby she'd make herself one for company.

Her first attempt was misshapen and lumpy and she threw it on the floor in disgust. Once long ago, in a distant time, she had made a wedding dress. Why were her fingers so disobedient and her head so full of fluff now?

She looked at the creature on the floor and tears welled into a fit of weeping. You shouldn't throw babies down, they might get damaged, so Netta gathered it up into her arms and hugged it tightly, putting it in her pinafore pocket for safekeeping. It was the first-born of many babies.

Bumpy went everywhere with her after that: into the gardens for walks; to the canteen to show the other girls. He sat on her bed at night and she cuddled him in her arms, crying for the little boy in the picture who was out there somewhere, crying for herself, so obviously abandoned; crying for Rae to come and rescue her. And still nobody came.

The stuffed babies lost their appeal and the lure of materials for dolls' dressmaking was her next venture. It was like being a child all over again, choosing offcuts of shiny plain sheeting and net curtaining to make dolly brides with veils. Colours, especially bright colours, dazzled her eyes so her outfits were palest pinks and ice blues, creamy whites and beiges.

Netta could not face the adult dressmaking classes – the rows of machinery, the responsibility of not wasting precious cloth, terrified

117

her and she fled down the corridors. The door was open in the art department and the smell of paints and oils wafted up her nostrils. Here a mixed group of students, soldiers, men and women, were working quietly, bent over their boards. It was a peaceful scene until one soldier, who was scribbling furiously all over his paper with chalks, began to chunter to himself aloud.

Netta paused behind him, quietly examining the tiny cartoon-like figures squiggled all over the scene. The officer's hands were shaking: hands strangely mottled brown and white like a piebald pony. He turned round. 'What are you staring at, young lady?'

'There's a lot going on in your picture,' she commented.

'Of course there bloody is!' he screamed. 'It's an execution . . . can't you see? And that's my pal, Bigsy, getting a bullet through his brain!'

'I'm sorry . . . how awful. When was this?' She sat down beside him, staring intently at the horrifying detail with which he had drawn the event. 'Were you there?'

'Of course I bloody was! Why else does the flaming thing run through my head like a newsreel? Cowards, we were, standing to attention watching the whole damn' show!' Beads of sweat were pouring off the young man's face. His skin was mottled coffee and cream, white and suntanned in patches.

'I'm so sorry but you were prisoners too so what could you do?' It felt good to be calming him down.

'We did abso-bloody-lutely nothing but stand to attention, pardon my French!' He put his arm round his sketch like a child at a school desk hiding work from a copycat. Netta moved away.

'Would you like to join us?' asked the art teacher gently. 'There are plenty of paints and chalks. Come and join us.'

She picked up a piece of paper and charcoal and began to etch a shape, then stopped. 'I can't . . . It's been such a long time.'

'Would you like to copy something? It'll get your eye back in

118

focus. Or go outside and find some shape that interests you? Go on . . . have a try, you might enjoy yourself!'

With a chair and board Netta wandered out into the bright autumn afternoon feeling like a child again with a packet of crayons and a blank page to fill, not sure if her hands would express what she was seeing all around her.

Park Royal Hospital was no ordinary asylum, no dreaded place spoken of in hushed tones as the repository of miscreants who needed to be kept out of sight for their own good, but a baronial mansion with a fine central tower. She thought it looked more like a home for one of Sir Walter Scott's heroes with its red sandstone bricks edged with golden stone lintels. This was no fortress up a long drive lined with dark oaks; there was no studded oak door to imprison the inmates. It was an open place where patients were free to mingle and walk to take the air in all weathers. Only when she looked up could she see that some of the round galleries were criss-crossed with metal grilles.

At its great heart was a huge parish church which was filled each Sunday, a place of contemplation and solitude for those who needed to find some peace. For those in need of company and music there were recitals and a choir, but best of all were the parkland and gardens, open vistas with green hills beyond, reminding her of home.

Her mind was moving out from the cocoon of her room in Denny House, out from occupational therapy and shock treatment – dreadful though that had been to endure – out once more to the world beyond the hospital. Yet inside throbbed such a loneliness, a yearning to be with her baby, that it tore away her careful composure, reducing her to floods of stifled weeping which she was desperate to disguise. If she showed her weakness when would she ever be sent home? Would she always be stuck with a label with 'mental' written on it?

The drugs trolley still came round regularly and the patients were dosed like children. On the days when Netta was given the latest shock treatment, she soon learned there was no breakfast and waited with dread to be wheeled down the long corridors, looking up at the fine scrolled ceiling until the last moment, trying to avoid seeing the table with the straps and black box on the trolley. She was laid flat, numb with terror, as out of the corners came those dark mysterious figures holding equipment, looming over her. Then there was nothing, for days afterwards just headaches and blanks. Now the fug in her head was clearing and the taste in her mouth fading. Her course of treatment was complete.

As she sat by herself, sketching the outline of the tall church tower, her fingers clutched the charcoal tensely at first and then, as she relaxed, her hand flowed over the page filling all that her eyes could see. Not bad! she thought to herself, and to her surprise noticed that the usual black morning cloud which always floated above her head had lifted like a balloon set free. Her feet were no longer so full of lead and fresh air was stinging her cheeks. One of the young officers in the art class was leaning on the wall, dragging on his cigarette, watching her. She sensed his shadow falling over her sketch and flakes of ash wafted down on to the paper.

'Not bad,' whispered a deep voice in her ear. 'Now who was it said a church is best viewed from the outside, a public house from the inside, and a mountain from the foot? I wish I could draw like that.' Netta looked up at a shock of sandy hair, caught a whiff of tobacco breath. The voice was Scottish pan loaf, softened round the edges by years away from its native source. His uniform was smart enough but his shirt was undone and his trousers unpressed. Here was a washed out young officer eyeing her efforts like a judge at an art show. 'Not one for God-bothering myself but that's a fair attempt. Bit of a student, are we?'

'No, this is my first attempt for years. Can you get out of my light? Thank you. It's bad enough putting pen to paper without having an audience.'

'Sorry, just trying to be encouraging. Some of the stuff in there is awful. Had to get out. Fancy a stroll?'

Netta stared up again with surprise. He looked quite harmless, his face drawn and thin with sunken cheeks. His looks were certainly not the sort to grace any recruiting poster. 'Just round the block, then. I've done enough of this.'

They walked in silence, each kicking up a flurry of dried leaves, pausing now and then at fences and railings to admire the freedom of open hills across the valley.

The fresh air on Netta's cheeks felt good. Gradually she was coming back into possession of her body again. Even her monthlies had returned and she was beginning to feel normal, less weepy, wrung out and flattened. The officer stopped and lit two cigarettes, handing her one. Netta shook her head. 'I don't smoke.'

'You ought to, it's good for the old nerves and the waistline. Doctor's orders. Give it a try.' She puffed out of politeness but it made the dryness in her mouth even worse and she spat out the tip. 'No, it's choking me.'

'Suit yourself. Just trying to help. What's a girl like you doing in a joint like this?' He was trying to mimic Humphrey Bogart's accent, badly. Netta was instantly on guard.

'I could ask you the same?' She smiled sweetly and he shrugged his shoulders.

'I'm just an old soak . . . too much of the hard juice. Told me I needed a bit of a rest cure. Getting bored, if you want to know the truth. I'm as dry as a bloody prune now.'

'Are you staff?'

'Do I look like staff? You don't want to know about my escapades. I'm just another washed out soldier of fortune. Black sheep of the teetotal Stirlings, if you must know. There's always one who takes a dram too many. Andrew Stirling, at your service, ma'am.' He made a mock bow.

'This war has sorted a lot of us out, one way or another. I'm Netta Hunter, wed, widowed, babyless in just a year. Been here so long I can't even remember my own child's face.'

'That's a shame for you. Hubby in the army . . . What show was he in?'

'D-Day. He fell at Caen. I've not found out where yet.'

'They got a terrible packet there. I was involved in one of the

121

Forward Stations. I went right though with the poor sods, patched up, rested and sent back into the fire. Takes its toll, sending men to their deaths. No wonder some of us end up in the loony bin. In the end I couldn't decide if I was GB, B or going BM myself, so they decided for me and sent me to this Ritz to sort out my bad habits.'

'What's a GB?' asked Netta as she tried to keep pace with his long strides. 'Slow down, there's no bus to catch!'

'Sorry! GB means going barmy, a B means you're getting batty, and BM you've gone Bloody mental. Pardon my French.'

'Then I was a BM, first class, I suppose. I had my baby and don't remember much at all after that.' Talking to a stranger was easy enough, she found, and noticed she told him the truth about Rae and the whole sorry tale, as if it had all happened to someone else.'

'You poor sod! Nature can pull some cruel tricks on a woman. Sounds like post-partum dementia. Very rare. What rotten luck. Have they treated you well in here? I'm sure it gets better – eventually.'

'How would you know? I have had the doubtful pleasure of experiencing the miracles of modern medicine: potions and pills and regular electrocution, bed rest and occupational therapy. At last something's shifting. I have never stayed in one place long enough to draw a picture until now, and I can tell you this without bawling. No one has really bothered to explain it to me. I thought, at first I had done something dreadfully wrong.'

Netta stopped in her tracks. He was her own height and abruptly pierced her gaze with his clear-eyed stare. 'Believe me, you did nothing wrong. No one can explain it yet. Hormonal change after childbirth is as near as they'd probably get. You're definitely OTM!'

'What's that?'

'On the mend.'

'Thank you, Doctor, and what is your fee?' They had walked full circle back to the church. What a strange man, talking as if he knew something about her terrible experience. Netta decided it was better to humour him.

'Call me Drew, and can we meet again? Do you go to the dance hall? I hear it's pretty swish inside. Didn't expect such a bevy of pretty patients and nurses around the place. You're better than a G and T. Meet me tomorrow, promise? That'll be my fee.'

'Tomorrow it is but I'll meet you inside.'

Netta paused to admire the pond and the late-autumn flowers in the rocky banks. An evening with Drew Stirling should be quite an experience; not quite the art therapy she had intended but it would pass the time, give her a chance to dress up and put a face on. She had not felt like doing that for months. Something was shifting inside her and she felt a leap of excitement. A bit of singing and dancing would do no harm.

Drew raised his arm instinctively to salute her then put it down and bowed. 'Tomorrow at seven. I say, a date in the loony bin – how bizarre!'

Netta washed her hair and curled it under in a pageboy style. She wore a gathered skirt with panels of alternate navy blue and white, a white shirt with navy blue cuffs and collar, and her only pair of decent court shoes. She dabbed on perfume behind her ears and made her way to the ballroom to listen to the band striking up with all the Forces favourites. She tried not to think about Rae, taking comfort from the fact that he'd hated two-steps and waltzes and the jitterbugging craze. Dr Stirling looked the sort of guy who would push her round the floor like a sweeping brush but beggars can't be choosers and one day she would laugh about his antics. There, it was happening again, she thought, I can think funny things, see the funny side of this strange exile. Oh, Ray, Mummy'll soon be coming home to you.

The ballroom had a sprung floor that bounced in the middle. There was a stage at one end and a gallery at the other. It was the most splendid dancing space she had ever seen. The tea dances were popular with patients and staff alike and everyone mingled in the crush to hear the latest tunes from the hit parade. Park Royal was like being in one big ark: a shelter from the storms outside for a while, a haven for wounded souls. For seven months this had been her home and the thought that she might leave this place of safety soon terrified her. Here was order and dignity; out there would be coldness and chaos.

There had been no word from Stratharvar for months. Netta had written for news about Ray but short formal notes had been the only reply. His photograph was worn and cracked with fingering now.

Drew pounced on her as soon as she wandered to the edge of the dance-floor, introducing her to a bunch of other officers but waltzing her straight out of their reach. As Netta had feared his idea of ballroom dancing was an exuberant exhibition of twirls and turns which made her head spin. Like a demon possessed, he flung her this way and that until she staggered off the floor in a tizzy.

'Isn't she just lovely, you guys? So fresh and wholesome, like a buttered scone – and me such a poor haggis. If I'd had someone like you to come home to, perhaps I'd not have returned such a wreck. Come for a stroll in the moonlight, Netta, I've something to show you.'

Drew was wild-eyed and earnest as he elbowed her towards the door. Netta hesitated. 'I promise to behave. Please, I want to show you my special tree.' His eyes were brilliant, burnished like amber, sparkling mischievously like a child's. Netta threw caution to the wind. Why ever not?

The moon wasn't full but the autumn sky was lit with stars. Frost was already in the air and she was glad of her jacket as they tore down the path towards the trees.

'What's so special about a tree in the dark?' shouted Netta as he guided her into the darkness towards a gnarled old specimen with a broken stump.

'Trust me, this is purely in the line of science. I want to share the secret of my success with you,' Drew yelled back

124

as he leapt on to the broken branch like John Wayne astride a saddle.

'What on earth are you doing?' Netta peered among its branches as he climbed further.

'Just fishing . . .' His voice faded with the effort to root inside the hollows of an old oak's trunk. She could see dimly that he was embracing it with a hug and wondered if it was safe to be out with this madman. 'There, got it! Come and see my liquid gold.'

He sat swinging his legs on the branch, waving a whisky bottle that glistened in the moonlight and shimmered temptingly. 'Water of life, I dream of thee, slaver at the thought of your warm kisses. How I miss thee!'

'I thought you were supposed to be off the juice?' Netta crossed her arms, disappointed, shaking her head.

'Oh, I'm dryer than a nun's arse, pardon my French, but the sight of this sort of tops up the old resolve. My test piece, stashed away to prove I can live without my little comforter. See, it's still sealed, untouched by human hand, I promise. I just thought you'd like to see what a good boy I've become. A black sheep needs something to ease the pain, believe me, to hide uncertainties behind a show of strength. Soldiers want false hope and bravado, not dour Scots honesty, when they go over the top into battle. It's expected of officers but when we crack up, boy, do we know how to paint the town! It took three Redcaps to tear me off that jerk who said our Tommies were lily-livered. On my way to a discreet discharge until some kind soul recognised that we all have limits to our endurance. So here I am, the Wreck of the Hesperus, proving I can kick the urge once and for all.'

'Your family must be relieved.'

'My family know nothing of this little escapade nor must they. They're missionaries in South Africa running a clinic, dear pious souls. They think I'm on some training course and there's no one waiting at the station to clasp me to their bosom. After all that battle grub and mud, I've earned a few weeks in this gilded slammer, all mod cons and first-class cuisine, don't you think?'

'I can't wait to be out of here, to see my little boy and pick up the threads of normal life again. I can't believe it's been over six months now.'

'Something to aim for . . . That's what this getting better is all about. Something to replace the joys of juice. To think that all my training and do gooding is reduced to a craving for liquid gold slurping down my throat.'

'You must be on the mend if they let you out on the town with the others now?'

'They watch out for me and keep me out of the bars but there's been a lapse or two. One snifter and it's anchors aweigh again, I'm afraid.'

'At least you seem to understand what's going on.'

'It doesn't make it any easier, believe me, knowing the theory. Sobriety and comfort – the two don't mix easily for me. One day at a time is just about bearable, but never to be able to drown my sorrows in alcoholic oblivion again . . . Perish the thought! Can you understand any of this?' He slid the bottle down into the hollow with a sigh and patted the tree, afterwards jumping down beside Netta.

'When Rae was killed, I couldn't imagine another day of life without the promise of his return. I didn't believe it was true for months afterwards. I kept on going down to the shore or up into the hills just to talk to him and feel his presence again. He wasn't there and I wanted to die but there was this tiny creature inside me who wanted to live, who needed me, and that kept me living. But now I've not even the pleasure of my baby to comfort me. If I thought I'd never be with him again, I think it would be the end for me too . . .'

'You'll go home to your bairn, sure as death. There has to be some justice in this rotten world. Not that I've seen much of it so far but we must live in hope.'

'Hope is what we must pray for in 1946, Drew. That you'll find your purpose again and I'll be with my baby. That's not too much to ask, is it?'

126

'I suppose not. You're a tonic, Netta. Let me kiss you for good luck! I didn't expect to find such common sense in the loony bin. A lass who delights both ear and eye, I'm going to keep tabs on you.' He drew her gently into a hug and kissed her on the forehead. 'You are lovely! Who needs a dram when you are in the room?'

Netta tossed her head back and laughed. 'And you are an awful tease! It's time you walked me back to the dancing, I'm freezing out here!'

After such an enjoyable evening they met regularly at the kiosk, the cinema, the ceilidhs, and Netta saw Drew's cheeks begin to fill out. She had not expected to make a friend in the asylum but Park Royal was no ordinary hospital.

Drew Stirling found his days brightened by the company of the flame-haired beauty but could not bring himself to tell her of his real shame. Few knew his rank or the real reason for his enforced rest cure. He himself didn't want to think about any of it now the war was over. He would give the coming Remembrance Service a miss. It wasn't going to bring any of his comrades back, the shrouded bits he had buried, the broken minds and severed limbs that disturbed his dreams each night.

All that carnage and waste . . . the burden of his unbelievable knowledge took its toll. No wonder he drank to anaesthetise himself from memories of carcasses, burning flesh and the stink of death.

How can anyone stay calm in the face of continual slaughter, seeing a handful of fine riflemen return from a sortie, all that was left of a company? Shivering wrecks of humanity that he was expected to patch up and send backwards, forwards or sideways into burial pits. At best he could secure them a few days' respite at an exhaustion centre further back down the line. As they shoved forward from street to street, avoiding mines and snipers, ambushes and bombardment, performing miracles of minor surgery, stemming the blood and guts, mud and gunge, the strain took its toll on all his staff.

In his arrogance Drew had thought doctors were invincible to the suffering around them behind masks of dispassionate professionalism. He could observe the madness of sadistic officers, logistical cock-ups, the stupidity of some orders, but the cover up of the tent massacre was the final act of needless carnage that yanked him adrift from his moorings.

A tent full of sleeping soldiers was mown down by a drunken driver out on a spree, a futile accident. He had to peel men off the tent walls. Just another needless waste of life that no one would talk about. A single slug from the whisky ration was no longer enough to quench his thirst or calm his anxieties after that. He was a doctor and could control his anaesthetic, or so he thought, but no white coat could switch off his feelings or his fears.

Only long hard bouts of boozing could keep him operational. Other ranks could go to the exhaustion centres to see the trick cyclist but Drew had been raised with a puritanical outlook, a tendency to regard mental illness as mere evasion of duty and a sign of moral weakness. He was now beginning to think otherwise.

How he tried to be strong for his men! And if that meant two bottles of juice a day, so be it. But then he was caught paralytic in the First Aid Post and sent down the line in disgrace. No one wanted to know about his nightmares or his panics. He was a label with 'Nervous Exhaustion' written large on it. The fact that he was a medic only added to his shame.

What followed was a blur of cold turkey, lectures and enforced drying out. Only his military record saved him from immediate discharge. He was put in some square-bashing barracks in the Borders and told to sort out the A1s from the C grades.

Drew puffed smoke into a ring, thinking of that final bar-room brawl that had landed him in Park Royal. This time he was for it. As he stared at the church and the green lawns and gracious buildings, he felt only despair.

He did not want to be around when the bugles blew the Last Post. He was sick of brass and uniforms and orders. He was ashamed that he had not seen out the last few weeks of war with his men. Someone had shoved a book of Wilfred Owen's poems in his hand and he had found them oddly comforting. They were honest and stark, straight from the heart. No one cared a toss what was in Drew's heart, it seemed. The doctors and nurses here were kindly enough but reserved with a fellow medic who would not take their orders. He hated being beholden to anyone.

There was really no point in hanging around in here any longer. Time to leg it over the wall and take a hike south. Pity! He would miss Netta's turquoise eyes but she too was on her way out soon. Better not start what you can't finish, Andrew. Quit while you're ahead.

Netta was looking out for her friend at that first solemn Remembrance Day parade amongst the marching officers and the poppies, the dignitaries processing to the church. She sat in her pew, trying to find his shock of sandy hair and sloping shoulders. She asked around among the crowds who poured out of the service in silence. No one would give her a straight answer. They had arranged to take a stroll but Drew stood her up and she was puzzled.

In the grey mist of that November afternoon she found herself making her way down to the stumpy oak and the secret hollow. Perhaps he was waiting for her there. She darted into the undergrowth and shinned up to the hollow, fishing with her hand for the bottle. She smiled with relief to feel it there. When she pulled it up into the light, she saw that it was open and empty. Drew must have drained every drop. So much for hope, she sighed as she made her way back up the slope towards Denny House. You're on you own again, Netta. It's up to you now!

Ray's photograph kept Netta moving forward, away from that black fog of despair by the rivers of tears. The cocktail of drugs in the egg cup changed its taste and smell from sweet to metallic to a more normal flavour on her tongue.

In the dayroom she watched the snow falling with excitement, and when it was exercise time the group threw snowballs at each other and danced around in the snow. Dr Goldberg promised a Christmas revue and asked for volunteers. Netta offered to help with costumes, some of the staff put on a show and they invited in a dancing troupe to cheer the patients up.

She was given a trunk of old costumes to sort out. The trunk was musty and some of the costumes moth-eaten, reeking of camphor candles. 'These must have been here since the Ark!' Netta laughed, prancing around waving a flimsy gauze evening dress. She fingered the materials lovingly.

'These aren't costumes, they're real! Look at the beadwork on this bodice – and the lining of this waistcoat is pure silk.' They were handling ancient dresses of a bygone era, handstitched, full of exquisite embroidery; gold filigree needlework on crumpled uniforms. This lot should be in the Stewartry Museum not a dressing up box in a madhouse, thought Netta as she salvaged the best of the costumes before showing them to the Revue Committee. She felt the texture of them, rubbing the materials against her cheek; the green velvet pile with the gold braid, the orange damask brocade with ivory lace edging. The greys and duns of the dreary past months disappeared in this visual feast. Colours were coming into focus again: she noticed the whiteness of the snow dusting the red bricks, turning Park Royal once more into a fairytale palace, not a mental hospital. The cloud of depression and weariness no longer pressed down on her forehead.

With such rich colours close at hand Netta could forget all her sadness and knew release could not be far away. The last promotion was to go before the panel for a final assessment. How many times in those last weeks did she imagine holding Ray in her arms, cradling him to sleep, hugging away baby tears while singing her favourite lullaby?

Dr Goldberg assured her that the shock treatment was working. It had, however, taken much longer than anyone had expected to get her back on an even keel. There were great gaps in her memory, holes which the past had slipped through somehow, but she trusted him when he said that she was now fit to go before the Panel Board for assessment.

130

He shoved a newspaper in her hand and told Netta to read up about what was happening in the world outside. She was sent on day trips into Dumfries to find out the prices of post-war rationing, get used to traffic and the crowds milling around her. It had been a worry to be so out of touch with the real world. She looked for Drew but he had vanished. The thought of a winter journey back to Stratharvar made her feel faint with anticipation. How would it feel to see the pram and baby in it? How would it all work out?

She sat nervously before a line of worthies; some with kindly faces, others who never looked up from their paperwork.

'What's your name?'

'Jeanette Hunter.'

'Your mother's maiden name?'

'Jean Kirkpatrick.'

'What is today's date?'

'December fifteenth, 1945. I was nineteen on the tenth of June last,' she added for good measure.

'The reports before me state that this woman is said to be fit to leave subject to the usual regulations. She must see her doctor on release.'

'I just want to go home and see my baby.' Netta smiled at the assembly.

'All in good time, Mrs Hunter. We don't want to rush things. You will be under strict supervision. The little mite's managed fine without you so far, don't want to upset his routine. Take it slowly, let yourself into it gently. Your family doctor . . . er . . . Dr Begg will want to see you first. Don't go making a fuss. Remember, you've been away for eight months and the war's over now.'

'I just want to see my baby!' Netta could feel her throat tightening with fear. Were they going to send her away from Stratharvar?' She bowed her head and shifted the rising panic.

131

'That's better. Mother mustn't fuss so. We don't want any relapses, do we?' His words did not register with Netta. Once she arrived on the doorstep of the farm all would be well, she knew.

May 1949, Saturday Morning

A plane flew overhead, jolting Netta from her half dream. Was she hurtling backwards or forwards to Griseley? She must stir herself off this bench and get on her way if she wanted to arrive back before dark. She took one last lingering look at Park Royal. You served me well, dear green place, but you couldn't prepare me for what was to come.

Hogmanay, 1945

Home for Hogmanay! Every Scot's dream is to let in the New Year with his 'ain folk' across the border. Netta couldn't stop grinning as she watched those snow-tipped Galloway hills flash past the carriage window. What a surprise they would get when she arrived home early with a suitcase stuffed to bursting with all the sewing she'd done for baby: smocked rompers and stuffed toys, embroidered hankies as gifts, and tammies and mufflers knitted from the unravelled wool of old jumpers. Nettie Thimble knew 'Mrs Sew and Sew' was on the mend when she picked up needles once more, trying to teach Lizzie down the corridor how to cast on.

The morning of departure Netta woke as usual at about four o'clock but this time there was no sickening panic fluttering in her guts, only a surge of joy that at last she would be seeing her son for the first time in eight months. Netta dressed quickly and sat by the bed, packing and repacking a battered leather case, not quite believing this day had come. How she was raring for release from this gilded prison but felt so sorry for those who must spend the festive season here, wishing them all well, hugging her neighbours, making promises to visit and last-minute farewells. She thanked each of the nurses and Dr Goldberg, who had kept his promise and brought her back to normal. It was warm and bright in Denny House with decorations and cards everywhere. The first Christmas after war was over and everyone was in festive mood. Here she felt safe and sheltered but her spirit was eager for release into that chilly outside world.

Soon the smells, voices, shapes and colours of Park Royal would be only shadows and echoes, silhouettes on the wall by lamplight. She trusted she would never have to stay in there again.

Telephoning Stratharvar took all her reserves of courage but try as they might there was no reply from the telephone in the hall and Miss Dennison at the Exchange promised to send a message through to inform them of her imminent arrival. It suited Netta to make a simple homecoming with no fuss, just a few moments alone with Ray to sniff his head and feel the warmth of his body close to her chest. Would he be sitting up and smiling? Would his hair be red and stick up straight like hers did as a baby? How she had pored over his photograph until it was crinkled and cracked, faded from exposure and fingering. Film was scarce but the first thing she would do was have a portrait taken: mother and son together. Start as you meant to go on, Netta, into 1946, into a New Year of peace and a new beginning for us both. She smiled, fists clenched with determination.

There was no one waiting at the station halt, just the old porter who smiled and doffed his cap. 'Home for Hogmanay, a Guid New Year to ye!' She was just another weary traveller returned from abroad. His cheery wave gave her the confidence to feel normal. There was no prisoner's circle of shame on her coat, no label 'Mental Patient Out on Parole'. Yet shame was stained deep inside her wounded heart: shame that she had ever had to be sent to Park Royal in the first place. How would Netta ever brave company with that lead overcoat weighing her down?

The rain turned to sleet, lashing down in gusts; the wind tearing at her coat buttons. She stopped to pull out a muffler and beret, pulling the hat down over her ears against the squall. The inside of the hospital was always so warm. Now she felt the full blast of the westerly on her cheeks, the sting of sleet in her eyes, the icy welcome of a solitary homecoming.

She wondered now if she should have written to them and

waited, but no! Netta had been determined to leave at the first opportunity. She legged it down the hill along the country road, hoping against hope that Father was just late and racing to meet her along the twisting lanes. Eventually it was the postie van on its collection round that stopped for her and the familiar schooldays face of Donnie Gillespie who told her to hop in the front seat and rest the suitcase in her lap. He quizzed her gently and Netta fenced her answers carefully. Donnie eventually dropped off his grateful passenger at the foot of the farm track.

As she lifted the case out, thoughts of Wee Alec the draper and his bag-dance up the track to the farm buoyed up Netta's courage as she trundled onwards and upwards: each step bringing her nearer and nearer to Ray. It was no afternoon for a pram to be outside in the yard but she searched for it just the same.

Dusk was falling when she walked through the kitchen door, the lamplight burning. The heat of the range wafted on to Netta's face as she scanned the room. Ray was sitting strapped into an old high chair, his mouth coated with egg yolk, his chubby fingers gripping a wedge of toast. She stood for a second, transfixed by the sight of his dark curly hair. He looked up at the stranger with his piercing blue eyes and quickly turned to the woman by the sink who spun round,

'Netta! What in the name of goodness are you doing here?' Peg wiped her hands on her apron as Ray lifted up his hands to her, looking at the figure in the doorway with suspicion.

'Can I hold him?' Netta moved forward, eager to clasp him, but he turned from her, burying his face in Peg's floury pinafore. Netta tried to wrench him out of Peg's arms but the baby writhed and howled. She was a stranger and he was frightened. He smelled of kitchen and stale nappy. Peg grabbed him back. 'You've startled him! He's not used to strangers . . . There, wee Gus. Here's a lady come to see you, smile for the lady . . .'

'For God's sake, I'm his mother!' Netta whispered, trying not to scare him further. The lovely reunion of her imagination was being spoiled.

'He disnae know who you are, Netta. This is the only place he knows. Why didn't you let us know you were coming? Have they let you out for good?'

'I asked Miss Dennison at the Exchange to let you know. She couldn't get through.'

'I expect the line was down with the gale. You should have waited for your father to collect you. We're no prepared for visitors. What with wee Gus having a cold and the Ne'rday crowd, your room's not even aired. Dr Begg said nothing about you coming home. Surely he knows you're back?' Netta shook her head.

'You make it sound as if I'm just out of jail, Peg. There was a bit of a rush to send as many as possible home for Hogmanay. I haven't gone AWOL, I promise you. I've been so keen to see Ray. Isn't he dark? He's so like his father, all those Shirley Temple curls. Spoilt on a big laddie like you, aren't they, Raeburn?'

'We've called him Gus . . . he answers to that. We didnae know how long you'd be away so we just got on with it our way, the best we could under the circumstances . . .'

'I know, Peg. You've held the fort and I'm ever so grateful. It can't be easy trying to run the farm, and the war . . .'

'I'm not grumbling, am I? Wee Gus just had to fit into the routine of things, didn't you?' Peg put him back into the high chair, strapping him into the makeshift harness. 'We were awful scared he'd rock himself out of yon contraption on to the flag floor and crack his skull so your father's tied it to the table just in case. There now, you show the nice lady how you can hold a spoon . . .'

Gus looked up suspiciously, not sure if Netta was going to take his toast soldiers, banging his horn spoon on the tray and bursting into a broad grin at the noise he was creating.

Netta knelt down, slowly this time, to his level with tears in her eyes. Being so close to him and yet not to be able to hold him pierced her like a dagger. There was so much she didn't know about him and he knew neither her smell nor her voice. To him she was just a pretty lady with a caseful of gifts. He was Gus, not Ray

137

and suddenly fear twisted her stomach. Was he Peg's baby not hers now? No, never!

Lots of parents were separated from their offspring by the war, she argued to herself. In refugee camps and prisons, children sent abroad to Canada and Australia and now returning on ships to England had been separated a lot longer than Gus and her. It would take them time to adjust, of course. I must go gently and not force myself on him, she decided. Peg would let her help with his care and get to know his routine. Netta would jiggle him on her lap and sing lullabies by his cot. It was not too late, please God, to be reunited with her own baby.

Netta's knees were locked with cramp and she sat back on the floor to stretch them. Gus leaned over the side of his chair and saw her struggling to straighten her legs. He gurgled with curiosity at the funny lady's yelping. For one second their eyes locked and she smiled at him through her tears. 'What a silly mummy!'

'Let's have none of that,' snapped Peg, whisking him out of the chair. 'There's only one mammy in this house – the one that's fed and done for him night and day, who walked away his colic and sat up with him when he was sick. It's no right to confuse the bairn. Away and unpack your suitcase if you're staying . . . You can come and finish off the tatties for our tea while I see to his lordship.'

How could Netta answer back, for Peg was right on every score? Netta was the failure who'd had to be sent to an asylum while Peg alone coped with the nursing. Surely I have a right to come and take him away, though? She cried to herself. Yet I've frightened my baby and put Peg's back up. Good start, Netta, ten out of ten, go to the top of the class!

Her knees buckled as she climbed those familiar stairs. All the thrill of the homeward journey, the walk in the wind, the disappointment of being unexpected and unwelcome, was exhausting. The Ray she had yearned for was a figment of her imagination. In the kitchen sat a very real Gus who knew her not. She sat on the carved oak landing chair like an old woman as Peg bustled around with nappies in the newly tiled bathroom.

'You look done in, my girl. I'll go and infuse the tea. You're still peaky and your arms are like matchsticks. You need to put some weight on, pull yourself together before you think about the future. We can manage. We've managed so far just fine. I have baby to a strict routine. He knows who's the gaffer and what's what. So don't go upsetting the applecart over Ne'rday.

'My cousins, the Hustons, Sandy and Eileen and Morag – she's about the same age as Gus – are coming for the night. It'll be a chance to have a good blether and knees up at the Church Social. You can help me with the cooking.'

Alone in the spartan bedroom of her childhood with a hot water bottle airing the bed, joylessly, unpacking parcels, hanging her coat and one decent dress in a wardrobe smelling of mothballs, only then did a wave of sickness and dread engulf Netta's spirit. Later at the tea table there was not one word of welcome home. Father was quiet, his head down, eyes flitting from Peg to his daughter, backwards and forwards. The silences were awkward and full of menace. Something hung unspoken in the air.

It was a relief to creep into the boxroom where Gus's cot almost filled the room. He lay fast asleep, arms splayed out by his head, cheeks pink. He was wrapped in a woollen blanket coat, the flaps turned over into an envelope to keep his legs and feet cosy. The dressing gown was blue and looked new, not second-hand. It would have taken many coupons to purchase such a garment. The baby had kicked off his blankets so Netta leaned over to tuck him in; the first time she had seen her beautiful child alone.

Peg appeared from nowhere like a silent shadow. 'Don't touch him! He's fast asleep!'

'I was only tucking him in,' Netta whispered.

'That's my job, I'm his mother now.'

She lay awake all night, hearing those words repeated in her head. Had she forfeited the right to her baby because she'd been ill? Netta cried into her pillow. Surely not? He was her flesh

139

and blood, not Peg's. He grew under her heart, not Peg's. She was not even his real grandmother. How dare she claim him? And yet . . .

Nothing was going to turn Peg's preparations for Hogmanay from their traditional course. The black bun, like a pastry brick filled with spiced fruits, stood in the pantry; a rich Dundee cake glazed with hoarded nuts sat majestically in the round tin. Angus had killed a fat cockerel for the pot. The attic bedroom was cleared and aired for the Hustons' visit, with a cot borrowed for Morag. Netta's unexpected arrival had kept Peg awake all night. What a time to impose herself on them! Peg kept her busy in the kitchen like Cinderella, allowing her a dispensation to give the baby his midday slops, change him by the hearth and wheel him down the path to sleep in his bucket pram. Netta made herself useful doing his hand washing and steeping the nappies, feeding the livestock and poultry, content to hang around his lordship all day if Peg didn't chivvy her away.

Peg hovered over her like a hawk ready to pounce on any infringement of her own routine, gritting her teeth to choke back the frustration. Resentment at Netta's return hung in the air like a bad smell. It made the girl clumsy and flummoxed. 'It's a good job you weren't carrying the bairn with your butter fingers,' Peg sneered when Netta almost dropped a batch of scones.

With two pairs of hands they could polish the furniture in the parlour to a sheen; the log fire was lit to air the room and decorations strung across the ceiling, the faded pre-war paper bells which reminded them both of happier times.

Christmas was never the main celebration here but a side show in which they all trooped off the kirk and then politely exchanged a few small gifts. Angus had made the bairn a fine wooden cart full of bricks to push around when he was walking; hours of work he had put into the toy. All Netta produced for him were hand-made clothes which Peg dismissed as 'coming in handy and very serviceable when he grew into them'.

New Year was to be the main event, the climax of this year's

140

end when lucky relatives with petrol coupons drove for miles to first foot. The darkest-haired would cross the threshold after midnight bringing a lump of coal for good luck; then the singing of 'Auld Lang Syne' and the wee dram of whisky and slice of black bun to toast in 1946. Peg was dreading Netta's making some scene in front of company. You never could tell with mental patients what they would come up with next. It was not often that her relatives came to visit so she kept the myriad questions she had for that young lady until after their departure.

If Netta thought she could just waltz off with wee Gus into the sunset then she was in for a big surprise! He was beginning to get used to Peg's handling him and singing to him. She loved the way he cocked his head like a sheepdog to listen to her voice while he dribbled out the last spoonful of Sister Laura's gruel. He was beginning to roll over and crawl to the edge of his playpen where he howled to be let out.

The first battle came over Netta's wanting to lift him out. Peg told her it would spoil him. It was dangerous for a crawling baby on a farmhouse kitchen floor. Netta complained when he was sat on his potty for hours until he performed, his bottom encircled with a red rim. 'He has to learn obedience and good habits. It's never too soon to begin,' Peg argued. Did the girl not see that babies were wilful and needed to be tamed and trained by a strict regime? Peg knew that when she left the room Netta would rush to pick him up and cuddle him to stop his crying. He would struggle against her, his eyes on the door searching for Peg's return, and it choked her heart with relief to be first and best in his world. No one needed her like Gus had needed her all those months. Nothing had prepared her for such a welter of emotions.

On New Year's Eve the Hustons poured out of their little Austin Seven which was piled up at the back with a metal rack on which was strapped a collapsible go-chair. Peg had never seen such a contraption before and decided that Gus would be getting about in one of those. It could be shoved in the back of the farm *van for trips into town. Eileen struggled out of the back seat with Morag on her knee from where they were sitting next to a crate of bottles ready for the celebrations.*

Morag was dressed like a little princess in a pink woollen coat edged with swan'sdown, leggings and a matching peekaboo bonnet but she had been sick down the front of her coat and stank to high heaven. Nobody had ever warned Netta how foul a soiled nappy could be, especially one that belonged to somebody else's child. Morag had a podgy face and piggy eyes, not the most appealing of little girls, and Peg was proud that Gus was so handsome with features that were defined and strong.

Eileen was surprised to see Netta. She had been told she was away on war work.

'It's a long time, Netta, since we had a chin wag. You home for Hogmanay? Here, Sandy, take the wean, my arms are stiff. Where's that gorgeous nephew of mine? Isn't he a doll? Peg's so proud of him. After such a long time they must have given up hope . . .' Her words exploded like an incendiary bomb.

'But he's . . .'

Netta tried to catch her attention but thankfully Morag's foot was trapped in Sandy's jacket and she was making a din. Peg rushed into the breach.

'Eileen! Here at last, are the roads bad? I've put you in the loft, you see we've got a visitor in the spare bedroom. Netta's come to stay a while . . .' Eileen turned again to the daughter of the house.

'I was so sorry to hear your bad news. Not much of a marriage, was it? Robbed of your man so soon. Still the boys are coming home so I'm sure some other young man will take your eye . . . What a slender willow wand you are, you must take after your mother. Nothing like a baby to fill you out, is there, Peg?' She smiled, patting her stomach.

'But . . .' Netta lurched forward and Peg held her breath. This time it was Angus who came to the rescue, grabbing her arm and holding her back.

142

'Whisht! Not now, Netta, now's not the time.'

'What do you mean, not now? Do they think that Peg had my baby?' As Peg hustled her visitors quickly through the door, Angus took Netta to one side.

'They don't know about your troubles, it's not the sort of thing you speak about in company. They think we adopted Gus . . . during the war. Don't make a fuss and spoil the visit. Wait until they've gone and we'll have it out then. Let Peg have her day. She's been a good mother, you know.'

'I'm sure she has but I'm home now and he's my responsibility. Pretending he's yours isn't going to help anybody in the long run.' Netta was so angry she could hardly get the words out of her mouth. Peg watched anxiously from the hallway as he tried to calm her down.

'Not now, Netta,' he pleaded and for the first time she saw real torment in his grey eyes, fear that his daughter would take the baby away from them. Speechless, Netta plonked herself down by the fireside to listen to the prattle of baby talk, the comparisons of who had how many teeth, what injections they had endured, who was sleeping through the night. All that sacred mother knowledge she knew nothing about, all the babyhood she had missed.

They ignored her silent presence until she rose up and left the room, to hide in the kitchen, away from the lies and the boasting.

Peg sat on the edge of her seat . . . uncomfortable in case Netta made an exhibition of herself, screaming and cursing, and they might have to send for Dr Begg and an ambulance to take her back to Park Royal. To her own horror Peg was feeling a certain grim satisfaction in that scenario, but then all sorts of skeletons would have to come out of the cupboard and she did not want the Hustons to know there was weakness in the family.

Say nothing, keep calm, go along with the pretence, it's only for a few days . . . But Netta's obvious sulking soured the celebrations. She refused to attend the Social in the Memorial Hall. Said she was under the weather and did not want to be a damp squib

143

but offered to babysit. Peg was suspicious at first but went to get dressed and made light of the threats hanging in the air. Alone in the kitchen with the wall clock chiming in midnight hour, sipping a burning dram of whisky and eating some cake, with two babies asleep upstairs blissfully unaware of the dramas below, Netta would come to her senses once she realised they held all the trump cards.

'How dare you pass off my bairn as your own!' she yelled as they sat supping porridge, stony-faced and hung over. The Hustons had departed early for there was talk of snow on the hills, the sky was leaden grey. But Netta was in no mood to be fobbed off any longer.

'We did what we thought best, Netta. We did it to protect you from talk.'

'Ach, away! How can ye kid yerselves that Ray is your adopted son?'

'But he is . . . leastways we've got the care of him. I saw the doctor, he said we were his guardians. He's better off with us. What have you to offer him?'

'Ma hand tae God, I'm his mother!'

'Don't blaspheme, Netta, not in this house,' said Father sternly. 'You're in no position to argue the toss. We've put a roof over your head and his, and many a father would have turned you out the door for all those lies.'

'What do you mean?'

'Do I have to spell it out, Mrs Hunter – or rather Miss Nichol? It's about time you told us the truth. Are you married or not?'

'Yes, I was married.'

'That's not what the Register Office would have us believe. There was no marriage there to their knowledge.'

Netta froze like a rat holed in a corner. 'We were married over the anvil and then we had the banns read.'

'By a Minister of God or some anvil priest?' shouted Peg.

'Does it matter?' Netta screamed back. 'It was a wedding of

144

the heart. Fate intervened to prevent us . . .' Tears were rolling down her face.

'You have shamed us before the Stewartry! They marriages are worth nothing in the eyes of the law, and you know it. They stopped them years ago . . . stopped young hussies making fools o' themselves. Well, Mrs Hunter you've made yourself so Mrs Hunter you'll remain, but in the eyes of the Almighty you're nothing but a common-law wifie. What's done cannae be undone, can it, Angus?'

Angus Nichol sucked on his pipe and stared hard at his daughter.

'What fools you've made of us. I even went to the army to demand your pension. How do think I felt when I was told Corporal Hunter had never registered a wife? But no grandson of mine is going to be a bastard. He's been registered in my name and be done with it. We have the care of him. You're not fit to be his mother!'

'Oh, but I am. All I've worked for in hospital is to get home to look after him. I can stay here and get a job to support us both. I won't ask another penny from you but Raeburn is mine, not yours!'

'That's not what's best. How can yous look after him after all that carry on in the hospital? I saw you dribbling like an imbecile, your tongue hanging out, not knowing if you were Donald or Agnes . . . There must be a weakness somewhere, there must be, and we don't want wee Gus exposed to any of that carry on again.' Peg was enjoying her moment of triumph for she had indeed seen Netta at her weakest and Netta had known nothing about it.

'Dr Begg'll tell you, it was a one in a thousand chance. I was unlucky,' Netta pleaded.

'Unlucky or no, it happened and I'm not letting wee Gus go oot of this house until I've a certificate in my hand to prove you'll no go doolally again!' Peg's mouth was a mean thin line. She banged her fist on the table, dark brows knitted together.

145

'I don't need a certificate to make me his mother, I have the scars to prove it. The birth certificate is all I need.'

'Well, you're no getting it frae us . . . It was your father who had to register him as you were away with the fairies!' Netta turned to Angus, bent over his bowl saying nothing. Surely he could see her pain?

'I'm sorry for all the trouble. Don't do this to me, please . . . I love Ray, he's all I've got left of his father.'

'We never did think much of yon soldier. It makes no odds now, he's gone and can't provide for you both. Get yourself a proper job, prove to us you are a fit mother by doing something with your life and we'll think again on the matter. Until then he stays with us, here by this hearth, the only place he knows.'

'Where his future will be all mapped out for him. He's not just from farming stock. How do you know he'll want to be tied to Stratharvar?'

'Because he is of Nichol stock as well as Kirkpatrick. We've been here as long as the oaks. He'll grow up knowing no different, I'll see to that. He's the son I need to keep this farm on the map. Don't deny him his chance or you're no a daughter of mine.'

Netta was sobbing now, great gulps coming out with each words.

'Please, don't make me leave him behind . . . I've lost so much of his babyhood already.' She turned to the playpen and the baby looked up, beaming a smile. 'See, he's beginning to know his own mother now. How could you be so heartless as to separate us?'

'Netta, you must understand that it's the best for Gus and his future. Don't make it harder on yourself. If only you'd told us the truth from the start . . .'

She was no longer listening. She leaped from the table, slammed the door and strode down the braeside track to the Strathavar. She must tell Dr Begg what they were doing to her.

'Be strong,' said a voice in the wind. 'This is a test of your strength, hold fast, child,' whispered Rae's voice in her inner ear. 'You are his mother, you will always have a claim on him. Watch

146

over him at all times, keep close to him whatever it costs you . . .
one day . . . one day.' 'One day what?' Netta cried out. 'How
can I exist if he's not by my side?'

Netta ran all the way to Dr Begg's house at Stratharvar, once
the gracious grey-stone Rectory of the old Episcopalian Church,
with high gabled roof and Georgian windows. The coach house
was converted into a waiting room and surgery. She rang the bell
at the side entrance where an elderly maid in starched apron and
cap opened the door.

'Oh, it's you, Netta. Home from the wars at last, are we?
They said you were away doing war work, and you with a bairn.
Still Peg's doing a grand job for you. He'll make a fine farmer's
son for Angus. You'll be wanting the doctor, I suppose? Go and
wait across the yard. He'll be in shortly.'

Dismissed to the waiting room and its collection of ancient
magazines with curling pages that Netta could swear had been
there since her childhood, she thumbed through a few dog-eared
Picture Posts, *seeing the smiling faces of tired soldiers embarking*
on battleships, film stars supporting the war effort and Victory
parades. She flipped over the pages anxiously. Nothing had
changed but Mima Garvie's opinions rankled. How dare the
maid assume she'd dumped the baby on her parents? It appeared
no one locally knew the truth about her absence: both a blessing
and a worry. By now her heart was thumping with fear as it
always did around a white coat or a ward.

'Well now, who's this coming to cheer my day?' Dr James
Begg breezed in as if she was a regular at his door. He took
her hand in his as he ushered her into his consulting room full of
cluttered instruments, files and a huge desk which he sat behind.
This was the man who had put her in that place. She was in
no mood for his jovial banter.

'Well then, Jeanette, good to see you abroad at last. I was
giving you a few days to settle in but you've beaten me to it.
Haven't they done a grand job?' His beady grey eyes peered at

147

her over half-moon spectacles. 'Let's have a look at you – thin as a lath but that's to be expected. Peg and Angus will soon put some flesh on your bones – then you can look to the future. Nice to have you back in the land of the living. Park Royal may be a palace but it's a bit of a barn. The best in south Scotland for your sort of thing, though. Did the trick. Got you sorted as I knew it would. How's your memory, still a bit fuddled I expect. Early days . . . early days.'

'Why? Dr Begg, why did you let them take my baby? Why has this happened to me?' His dismissive small talk was pushed aside by her pleas.

'If I knew that, my dear, I'd be a rich man. Just one of those things, a one in a thousand chance and you were the unlucky one. Not your fault, my girl. Have to put it behind you now. No more worries, no crying over spilt milk, Jeanette.'

No worries indeed! she was sick to the stomach with all the developments going on behind her back. Surely he would understand that?'

'They won't let me have my baby! Dr Begg, please help me. I find my baby is called Gus not Ray, and I'm not allowed to go near him without Peg watching over me in case I drop him. Father accuses and doesn't look me in the eye. What's going on?' she pleaded.

'Steady the Buffs, old girl, don't get all het up. It's early days, your release was unexpected. I suppose they wanted to clear the decks for Hogmanay. I've had a letter to say you've passed muster but you must go slowly. Surely you didn't expect to walk in and take over as if none of this had happened? Your father paid for the best care and under the circumstances I think he's been a Trojan. I'm sure he'll support you for as long as is necessary but the bairn doesn't know you from Adam, does he? Peg stepped into the breach like a real trooper, beyond the call of duty if you ask my opinion, especially as she can't have a bairn of her own. They are the "kent" faces baby Nichol turns to and they love him like their own. Why should they let you

148

walk away with him, with no home, no income, no place to call your own?'

'That's no my fault, you've just said so!'

'Aye, but a real mother wants what's best for her bairn and won't just upsticks and dump him in a day nursery while she earns her living, will she?'

'Thousands of women had to do that in the war,' Netta argued.

'But the war's over, Jeanette, and you weren't there to see them flocking back to their hearth and home to be housewives and mothers again. Think about it. A good mother never sacrifices her child's welfare and chance of education. She wants the best for her child. Do you catch my drift, young lady?'

'Are you saying I should leave him at Stratharvar, walk away from my baby as if he'd never been born?'

The Doctor leaned back on his chair, fingers pressed together, and said nothing.

'Are you telling me to give him over to his grandparents?'

'You did that once already, Jeanette, when you were ill. They stood by you then and saw you got the best treatment. You've already made the sacrifice. They'll make good parents and give him a fine education, a secure home in beautiful surroundings. Many girls in your situation would gladly yield up their babies to a home such as theirs.' Netta was shaking at his meaning, trembling with indignation. He was not listening to her pleas at all.

'But it doesn't have to be like that, Doctor. I can get a job nearby, rent a cottage. If I'm careful we'll get by. We can all share him. He can spend as much time as he wants to on the farm,' she argued. Dr Begg shook his head. 'No, dear, you misunderstand. He'll only be confused. It's either one or the other. With you a life of uncertainty, with them an assured future. It's not going to be so easy for you to get a job now with all the soldiers returning home. They want their jobs back, of course. And you'll have to keep quiet about where you spent the last eight months. People have closed minds about mental institutions, palaces or not. References *might be asked of me about your suitability . . . I can't guarantee there'll be no lapses in the future. If you were married, perhaps, but you've told lies, Jeanette. Your mother would be very disappointed in your behaviour.*

'Think carefully. A single woman with a child and no one to back her up will give a son no father to model himself on. At Stratharvar wee Gus'll have the best of fathers who'll set him fair for the future. Doesn't it make sense?'

'But my father can still take on this role.' All the sense was leaking out of her head. It was difficult to form her arguments logically. He was battering down her opposition. 'I didn't come here to be told I must give up my baby, I can't do it, surely you can see that?'

'Then just bide a while, leave him settled and sort yourself out. Get some work, get to know him, visit when you can, leave him here until you can make a proper home, prove you are a stable person, find a nice young laddie to help bring him up . . . over time perhaps it'll all pan out. Just wait and see.'

'I want my baby now!'

'We cannae always have what we want in this life, Jeanette, we get what we need. Look at your father when he lost his wife, left with a lassie to bring up on his own. He married for your sake and it's no been a bad union. They've supported you when many another would have thrown you out. Don't ask for the moon. You're not in a fit state to rear a kiddie yet with nothing behind you.' His voice was cold and his manner haughty now and Netta felt like a small child in front of the headmaster: foolish and frightened. Yet she was not going to give in easily to his arguments.

'Thousands of war widows like me are doing just that on a meagre pension. No one is telling them they've not got the right to bring up their children, are they?'

'That's not the point. I see I shall have to spell it out to you. You never married and so forfeited the right to compassion. We just can't have that sort of behaviour in our midst, shoved in our

faces. It's no example to the children of this parish, is it? Bairns out of wedlock! I think you're still in a fragile state of mind, easily upset, volatile, and I should check your sedation. We don't want to have to readmit you, do we?'

Netta's mind was racing. She could hear the veiled threat in his patrician pan-loaf accent. Shut up, let him think you're being obedient, be a good little girl, she told herself. The warning had been given. Nothing must make her return to Park Royal. She must take no chances. Dr Begg was wrong, all her instincts were screaming, he's wrong! Her baby should be at her side now, not at Peg's . . . But Netta bowed her head in submission, swallowing her thoughts. It was time to stay silent.

A Secret Outing

Netta wrapped the baby tightly against the chill wind, packed the base of the bucket pram with his best outfit and a bottle of juice to pacify him and told Peg that they were going for a walk. 'Don't go far,' she yelled as usual. 'No, not far,' Netta replied, racing down the track for the coast road, hoping for a lift. She had telephoned ahead for an appointment and waited by the bus halt for the morning coach, leaving the pram at the bottom of the ditch, hood up and canopy hidden from view.

In the bus she sat with Ray on her lap looking outwards, pointing to the rugged cattle in the fields, jiggling him until Kirkcudbright harbour came into view with its castle ruins and fishing fleet. They alighted near the square and made for the photographer's studio off the High Street. He was set up and ready for they were late.

Ushered into the back, she changed Ray into his smocked romper and put on the jacket of her two-piece wedding suit in lavender crêpe with its embossed lapels and collar. It had been waiting in the wardrobe all those months she'd been away, perfumed with mothballs but almost as new as the day it was first put on. It hung on her shrunken frame and when she fixed her hair into a smart Victory roll Netta felt suddenly older and greyer, drained of colour. Once dressed she placed over Ray's neck Mother's rainbow necklace which she had found at the back of Peg's knicker drawer, still in its battered blue cardboard box from Laing's of Glasgow.

There had been a frantic search for Ray's birth certificate but it must be locked in Father's deed box. The necklace hung like a charm over his chest and he played with the stones, chewing on the chain.

Archie Lambert fussed over their poses, placing them this way and that on his brocade settee. He had a black umbrella and waved at Ray from behind the camera. The baby was mesmerised by the lights, blue eyes sparkling like sapphires.

'Mother, hold the baby . . . just a little more to the left.' How Netta relished being called 'Mother', smoothing and preening Ray's dark hair with his baby brush, trying to make a quiff. He soon began to wriggle and squirm so out of a basket came the squeaking toy and Ray burst into giggles of delight. Flash! The explosion of light startled him. Netta could afford only two poses, one of mother and child and one of baby alone. Ray was plonked on on a rug and Netta lay down in her finery to catch his eye, dangling toys. The stones of the necklace glinted in the lights. Flash! The photographer snapped them both in this intimate precious moment. Just another young mum having her picture taken to send out to hubby somewhere in the Forces, for an anniversary perhaps. It was the first time she had been truly alone with her son.

'Do you want it hand tinted, Mrs Hunter?' Archie had not recognised her as Netta Nichols. She nodded. 'And don't forget to tint the rainbow colours of the necklace.'

'Boys don't usually wear jewellery,' he commented.

'I know, but it was my mother's and I wanted something of her in the portrait.' Netta smiled sweetly and he accepted this strange request. It was time to change out of their finery and as she sat in the Paul Jones Tearoom to give Ray juice and herself a cup of tea, she awarded herself a brownie badge for all the times she had shut her lips, bent her head and swallowed Peg's lecturing. It was another hour before the bus took them back to Stratharvar. It was raining and getting dark but Netta stayed under shelter in the shops until the last moment. The portrait proofs were to be ready in two weeks.

By the time she got off the bus at the bottom of the track the rain was lashing and to her horror the pram was no longer tucked under the hedge. She cooried Ray into her thick coat and struggled up the track to the farm. There was a row of strange cars waiting in the yard. She recognised Dr Begg's Wolseley and Sergeant Kerr's black Austin Saloon. Something must have happened. Netta dashed into the kitchen to see them sitting at the table supping tea with worried expressions. Every eye turned on her.

'Where in goodness's name, have you been? We've sent out a search party! How dare you take the bairn out in this weather . . .' shrieked Peg, grabbing the child and examining him carefully.

Netta stood stunned by the accusation and the look on Dr Begg's face. 'What have I done wrong?' she answered. 'I was just taking him out.'

'You creep out of the house without so much as a word and steal our baby, what do you expect us to think in your state of mind?' Peg was in high dudgeon, shouting at the top of her voice. 'We found an empty pram by the bus halt. What were we supposed to think – that you had run away to Carlisle on the train? Netta Nichol, you've gone too far this time. I want you out of this house! Dr Begg, you see what we're dealing with . . .'

'Hold your horses! Peg, I just took him on the bus to Kirkcudbright. I left the pram under the hedge for the walk back, that's all. Just a wee trip, the two of us. When it disappeared I thought the tinkers had been up the lane again. Get him out of those damp things before he gets chilled.' Netta took off her coat and hung it on the banister knob. Her father saw the dress. 'What are you all dolled up for?' he asked.

'This is my wedding outfit and in this bag is the romper I made for Ray in Park Royal, as if you didn't know. I wanted us to have our portrait taken at Archie Lambert's . . . Just the two of us together.'

'What's that thing doing round your neck? You've been fishing in my dressing table. Look! She's even stolen my necklace, Angus.'

154

Netta yanked the chain over her head. 'Here's your bloody necklace. It was my mother's and you never wear it so I put it over Ray so there was something of a Kirkpatrick in the photo.'

'She's barmy! Boys don't wear necklaces. You see what we have to put up with? That's why we cannae have her cluttering up the kitchen. Two women in one kitchen never works. It can't go on,' Peg pleaded with Dr Begg who turned to Netta.

'Why didn't you tell them where you were going, Jeanette?'

'A mother and her son shouldn't have to tell the world their business. This was a private outing. I knew there would be trouble if I asked. I'm not an invalid. I can arrange an outing and come back safely.'

'We thought you'd run away and were worried about wee Gus.' Her father's voice sounded weary.

'Then I'm sorry to have worried you but it's not easy to be alone with him here, is it, Father? Peg doesn't trust me.'

'That's no true.'

'It is so.'

'She has a point, Peg, the girl needs time with the bairn,' said Dr Begg, for once on her side. 'You'll have to learn to share if she stays here.'

'I'm no having her round my feet forever. She'll have to find a job out of my hair. You know what I think.'

The Sergeant stood up to go. He was embarrassed by all the argy-bargy. 'I'll be away the now, no harm done. Nice to see you back home, Nettie. We were all sorry to hear about your husband. Did you know our Tommy didna make it back either, crossing the Rhine? 'Bye the now.'

Once the policeman had left there was silence around the table. No one wanted to open up the issue again but Dr Begg wanted his say.

'So, what in name of thunder are you all going to do?'

'She'll have to go. I can't be doing with this carry on.'

'Angus?'

'It's up to Netta, I suppose, she knows what I think.'

155

'Jeanette?' Everyone focused their eyes on her. All the resolve and strength were draining away from her. Netta bowed her head wearily.

'I'll go at the end of the week . . . sort out a job and then I'll be coming back for Ray. I shall see a lawyer about this too. He's my son but this atmosphere will make me ill if I stay when I'm not welcome. It doesn't do my baby any good either. He's the most important thing in my life from now on. His needs must come first, but I shall be back every moment I can. Don't think for a minute I'm going to disappear out of his life ever again.'

Saturday, Midday on Shap Fell 1949

Netta drew the steaming van to a halt by Shap summit. The long drag from Carlisle was taking its toll on the engine. As usual she could boil a kettle on the radiator. It was time for a breath of air, time for a a stretch of cramped legs, strolling along the track among the lorry drivers sipping tea from the makeshift kiosk on top of the moors. The bottle of water in the boot would top up the cooling system until she got to Kendal where the engine would have a chance to go cool again. Peg's package of photographs sat on the passenger seat but this was not the time or place to examine them closely.

The majestic Cumberland fells rose like bosoms in every direction: ochre, purple, grey and green. To the south-west, in the far distance, a shimmer of coastal water glinted on the horizon pointing the familiar route back to Yorkshire: back to the solace of work and friends.

A curlew's lament echoed her own sadness on leaving the Borderlands. Netta strolled to the fence, away from the car fumes, to clear her head in the stiff breeze, but the pounding drumbeat of guilt thundered in her ears.

How many times had she come south with her heart in her boots? But never as badly as that first time with demons driving her on into the unknown. How many times had she tortured herself with regret that she had not snatched her baby the day when they went for their portrait together? Why had she not taken her chance then? Netta shook her head knowing exactly why.

Because you were always your father's daughter and duty is your middle name. But how could you just have walked away from your baby? Did you think you were leaving for him or for yourself because you hadn't the courage to stand up to Peg's bullying? Were you trying to repay Father for the expense of your treatment? Oh, you coward! You hadn't the guts to stay there and take the flak, to claim your rights. Was it because you loved Ray so much that you wanted only the best for your baby? Peg and Angus had the best that was going then. And you walked away down that track like an automaton on a musical box, going through the motions, numb, too fearful to look back. And now you've done it again.

If only . . . but turning back the clock is never an option. Wretched and exhausted from your illness, you just caught the first train south from Dumfries, not bothering where it ended up in that bleak winter of 1946. Nobody cared if you lived or died. They let you walk out of Brigg Farm with a wad of banknotes, in your best coat and hat with a suitcase full of nothing but flimsy promises and a heart as black as coal.

Netta Nichol was doing her duty, leaving her little mistake behind and being the obedient daughter of the house. Little did they know how close she came to finding the perfect solution to the whole sorry mess.

4

JET

'Colour of grief and penitence
Treasure of darkness and shadows,
Absorbing all other hues
In its intensity.'

February 1946

The waiting room was crowded: a poky parlour in one of a row of tired terraced houses with a doctor somewhere in the back, living over the shop in a makeshift flat no doubt. This surgery was about as far away from Dr Begg's gracious premises as it was possible to imagine but it would do, thought Netta. She sat huddled in her camel coat in the corner chair, listening to the thick Yorkshire accents, the hacking coughs and rusty voices of old men in caps and women in curlers and carpet slippers. Now and again someone would glance at her with interest as if to strike up a conversation but she buried herself in the dog-eared magazines, trying to be invisible. She had registered herself as an emergency, a visitor, showed her identity card and was told a Dr Anwar would see her at the end of his list.

How had she managed to land herself in this foreign mill town amongst a forest of black chimneys, cobbled streets and terraces of some West Riding town? It was just like a Lowry painting come to life as she stepped out of the station and made her way up the parade of shops, sheltering from the drizzle under the gracious wrought-iron canopies which kept the shoppers dry enough to browse along the row.

Somewhere behind the main street she sampled the greasy mysteries of a fish and chip bar but couldn't stomach the food and asked directions towards a decent bed and breakfast establishment.

She was pointed towards the Skipton Road where the houses were bigger but still blackened with soot.

Netta knocked on several doors before a landlady eyed the cut of her best camel coat and sensible brogues and decided she was indeed a respectable young war widow looking for work in the district. The room was basic, drab and worn. It would suit her purposes. Netta said she was feeling unwell after a long journey and needed to see a doctor.

'Up the road, turn right down the side street. Doctor'll see you, I'm sure, but don't go falling sick on me in the night. My man's on day shift. He needs his sleep. Staying long, are we?' said the landlady in her flowered overall and turban headscarf.

'Not long, just passing through for the night,' she replied, feeling utterly exhausted by the slow journey from Dumfries. The train had stopped at every station, from sad memories of Gretna and Carlisle to hill halts on windswept Cumberland moors to country stations amongst rivers and wooded valleys. At each screech of the brakes she just wanted to rush off the train and go back home but her limbs were strangely disobedient to her will. All the energy had drained from her. In her eyes was a picture of baby waving her off with his pudgy hand. Rage burned inside her head. If anyone else had told her that it was all for the best that she should go south and find herself work, she would have hit them.

Dr Begg had arranged for her to stay at some temporary hostel near Leeds. She even had Vida Bloom's old letter in her hand with her last address, the one 'kent' face she could find in a foreign land. There was a regular train service northwards and it was promised she could come back anytime to measure baby's progress. Peg was full of smiles and Father was generosity itself, putting enough money in her Post Office account to tide her over until she found work.

As the train rattled over the bleak Yorkshire moors and the sky grew grey and dark, so her spirits sank deeper into hopeless despair. What was the point? After sea and shore, hills and streams, this dark industrial landscape of exile sapped the last of her confidence.

There was only one thing left to do and once the thought pushed its way into her head, her feet sprang into action and she jumped out of the train at the first busy station.

'Mrs Hunter, Doctor will see you now.' *A loud voice interrupted her thoughts. Netta shuffled down the hall passage, sniffing the surgical spirits and hospital smells of Park Royal again. She entered a small room on the right that was dimly lit by a lamp. It was difficult to focus on the man sitting at the desk in his crumpled tweed jacket. All she could see were the dark pools of his eyes watching her. She shoved her trembling hands into her coat pockets and sat down, averting her own eyes.*

'How can I help you?' *His voice much to her surprise was foreign, cultured but with a curious Scottish lilt. She looked up but the light dazzled her eyes.*

'I can't sleep, Doctor, I need something to help me to sleep.'

'I see. You're not one of my regulars, are you? What part of Scotland are you from? I trained in Glasgow, it's a beautiful country.' *She bent her head and muttered.*

'From the south, Galloway . . . but I've come visiting and don't want to disturb my hosts. If you could just give me something to tide me over . . .'

'You're on holiday, then?' *He was quizzing for answers, peering at her closely, and she stiffened.* 'I'm very tired. I need to rest.'

'You live alone?'

'At the moment. I'm a war widow. Just give me something to sleep, please. Then I can get on with things . . .'

'Mrs . . . er . . . Hunter, I'm not in the habit of dishing out sleeping tablets to people I've never met before. Why should you be the exception?' *Netta was trembling with embarrassment. Trust her to find the one over-concientious doctor in the district who wanted a history from his patient before he prescribed anything.*

'Because, Dr Anwar, I've just come out of Park Royal near Dumfries. No doubt you've heard of that establishment? After eight months in there I need to make a fresh start and I've used*

163

up my medication. I'm tired and don't want to be a burden on anyone.'

'So what took you in to Park Royal? If I'm to help you, I'll need to know all your details.' He sat back in the shadows, patiently awaiting her reply.

Netta began slowly with just the barest details: the baby, the fever, Peg and Angus. Then out it all poured, the whole sorry tale: Rae, her disgrace, this banishment. What did it matter if he knew the truth. Who was there to tell but strangers? 'Now you see why I need to rest.' Tears rolled down her nose and she fumbled for a handkerchief and buried her face from his gaze.

'I'll give you something just for tonight but I want you to call in again in the morning . . . just to make sure. Where are you staying?'

Netta mumbled the address. He stood up but she did not look at him, too ashamed. 'Thank you.' She turned to the door.

'Hang on! Don't forget this chitty to take to the dispensary down in the back room. They'll need to see your identity. And please, Mrs Hunter, make another appointment for tomorrow. You can talk to me again then.' Netta sensed him searching her pallid face with the dark circles under the eyes. She took the prescription, blindly nodding her thanks, went to the dispensary then fled out of the back door.

She wandered the streets aimlessly, feeling the box in her pocket for comfort. She bought a cheap bottle of medicinal brandy, splashed out all her sweetie coupons on a big bar of Fry's Five Boys chocolate. Why shouldn't her last hour on earth be comforted by childhood favourites?

The bedsitting room would have done Dickens proud. It was threadbare and stale smoke from the previous occupier fouled the air but it was clean enough and the bed had enough blankets to coorie under. There was a gas fire with a meter. She had everything she needed for her purposes.

Inside the pill box there were only two tablets: not enough to send a mouse to kingdom come, but with a gas fire turned on

164

and a towel stuffed by the locked door, she would know nothing about it.

She would leave no note so nobody could be blamed or little Ray shamed. Just a tragic accident. Perhaps she had better not block up the door, though . . . It was the only solution. Netta could not go on living with this constant pain in her heart. She was tired of struggling, of failing, of making mistakes. Why not clear the decks and leave them all to it? Time to sleep for eternity. If she were lucky Rae would be waiting for her.

Netta swallowed the tablets with the brandy and sucked away the bitter taste with chunks of chocolate. She closed the curtains and turned on the fire, sank into the pillow and all her sorrows rose over her head. How easy it was to go to sleep when you are tired of living, was her last thought.

Somewhere far away there was a banging and a crashing. Voices and rough arms were pulling her this way and that, dragging her out into cold air, walking her away from the warm bright tunnel of light. She was gasping for air, gulping down draughts, vomiting, choking, and the urge to keep breathing grew stronger, but still she cursed them wildly. 'What are you doing?'

'Mrs Hunter . . . Mrs Hunter, can you hear me? Come on, young lady, wake up. For the love of Allah, wake up! Take some deep breaths, damn you! Wake up!' Netta opened her eyes, a strange and yet familiar voice echoing in her ears. 'Let me go back to sleep,' she muttered, going limp.

'Just keep her walking, let me check her pulse . . . The ambulance will be here soon. Poor woman.' Somewhere there was a screech of wheels and the ring of a bell, a stretcher and the slamming of doors and then darkness once more.

Netta woke up in a hospital ward, contained tightly by stiff sheets, feeling sick, her head thumping. This was not heaven and the nurses who clomped past her bed tutted as they passed her by. 'Whatever possessed you? You should be ashamed of yourself, taking up a busy bed. It's a sin against God to commit such a

165

crime. Think of all those poor dead soldiers who gave their lives for us, and you try to waste yours!'

Netta's mind was racing with the fear they might shut her away in an asylum again. 'I'm sorry,' she kept whispering. 'It seemed the only way to ease the pain.'

In her heart she felt such a failure. She could not even take her own life. Yet there was a strange relief that someone had rescued her in time. If someone had bothered to save her, perhaps she was not meant to die yet.

When the lights were dimmed and she was half asleep Netta could see shadows flickering at the end of her bed. She could make out Sister's triangular headdress and a man in an overcoat standing loking at her.

'How are you?'

'I don't know, Doctor.'

'I was just on my rounds, thought I'd pop in to see how it was going. You nearly made it! We had to break down the door. There was just something in your eyes, making alarm bells ring. I couldn't settle after our consultation. An instinct warned me about you and I had to check. You owe your life to giving me the right address, telling the truth. Don't waste your second chance.'

'What'll happen to me now?' Netta felt small and vulnerable, looking up at Sister who was checking her pulse and tutting.

'I'll be giving your a good talking to before we send you out of here,' she said darkly.

'I'm sorry.'

'Don't be too hard on the lassie, there's quite a story behind all this. She's not a soul in the world to turn to. I think she was just at the end of her tether. Mrs Hunter will come and see me again and we'll talk it all through. Promise?

'I promise, and thank you.' They left her bedside and went into a huddle out of earshot. Netta strained to hear them. Dr Anwar had understood her pain. He had saved a stranger, followed her to drag her back to life. At least there was someone who believed in her enough to think her worth saving.

166

In the morning she stood on the balcony of the day room, looking out at a misty blue sky and hills in all directions. They were not the gentle green hills of home but dark high Brontë moorland with black stone dykes running in all directions, sooty sheep dotted like boulders amongst the last of the purple heather now burnt into a burnished coppery hue. Where the heather burnt were rainbows and Rae. 'Set the heather on fire, my darling.'

His last words scorched her heart with shame. How could she have forgotten his precious orders, abandoned her bairn and given in to such temptation? How could she think so little of her life when he had had to give up his?

I'm sorry, dear heart, she cried silently. I'll never do it again, I promise. I'll try to set the heather on fire for you and make our baby proud of me. I don't know how I'll do it but if Netta Nichol could find a way to end her life so determinedly and fail, there must be a way Mrs Hunter can find it again and succeed!

Nothing To Write Home About, March 1946

The other women left her to it each lunchtime. Netta pored over her sewing machine, finishing off the tailored coat and leggings she was rushing to finish for baby's first birthday. The shoulders were padded expertly and she was attaching a velvet collar just like the little coat she had fingered so carefully at Matthias Robinson's store in Leeds; the coat she would have bought if only she could have afforded their prices. This replica was made from factory floor offcuts and lined with satin from the market stall. It had to be done in her own time, secretly, and parcelled off before his birthday.

She was trusting it was the right size, preferably on the big side for him to grow into. The fact that her neck ached and her back was stiff after a long shift with no break must not spoil her workmanship. Nothing was too much trouble for her son. How she wished she could be there on the day but it was too soon and she had no money to spare for fares. It was a comfort to know he wouldn't know much about his special day either.

This temporary job at Saloman's garment factory was nothing much to write home about. It was a glorified sweatshop making skimpy coats with thin linings like tissue paper for the cheaper end of the rag trade. She lived now in the heart of the Yorkshire textile industry with mills on every street and factories up every back alley, churning out demob suits and coats by the thousand. Somewhere in the midst of the shoddy there must be quality clothing factories but she was grateful for any job in this grim climate.

Most of the girls came to work in iron curlers and headscarves, with overalls to keep the oose of their own clothes. It got up your nose and in your hair. They kept their distance from Netta since the job had been found for her as a favour from the boss to a relative and they considered she'd stolen someone else's job. She was an offcomer, not one of them, and therefore probably a spy. Netta kept her head down, working fast and efficiently, gave no bother or lip and was politely ignored.

So much had changed since her long talk with the Egyptian doctor. Taking her courage in both hands she had caught a bus to Leeds and found Rosamund Street where Vida Bloom was still living. The door was opened to her with surprise but the stranger from Scotland ushered in warmly. Number five was one of a line of back-to-back terraced houses on four storeys: cellar kitchen, living room, bedroom and washroom, attic with a roof light in the ceiling. The houses rose up in a sprawl from the city towards the University with its grand steps and clock tower, up to Woodhouse Moor and another warren of terraces: these like sooty lichen clinging to black walls, stretching ever outward to the river valleys and green fells lying just out of sight over the horizon. The names of these posher districts were listed on bus destinations: Headingley, Lawnswood, Adel, Cookridge, Bramhope, Otley, Ilkley and the Dales beyond.

Vida had aged since she was widowed suddenly at the end of the war, her dark eyes heavy and ringed with shadows. Arnold, judging by the line of proud photographs of him in uniform, had shot up several inches, filled out and was fast becoming a mother's boy, destined to replace Isadore Bloom as Mummy's favourite companion. He had left the Army Pay Corps and was now articled to a firm of Chartered Accountants in Leeds. How Vida's face lit up with delight as he pushed his bike through the door. 'Arnie, you'll never guess who's turned up on our doorstep?'

He looked at Netta with disbelief, taking in her shabby coat

169

and ankle socks, her battered hat. He nodded shyly, a look of resignation on his face. Netta recognised the mark of the beast, another offspring who shared duty as their middle name. He shook her hand weakly. 'Pleased to see you, Nettie. What brings you to our grand city?' His Scots lilt had been overtaken, flattened by northern vowels.

'It's a long story.' She gave them a sanitised version of events, skipping over the usual difficult areas. Being an unmarried mother, having a breakdown, sent packing from her homeland to find her fortune. 'Fancied a wee bit of a change. I'm looking for work. I always said I wanted to be a dress designer, didn't I, Mrs Bloom?'

'You won't find any openings for that here, love, just factory work. But what about your baby? You wrote me such a long letter when he was born, so full of plans. How can you leave him behind?'

'I have to start somewhere. He's staying at home until I can find suitable accommodation. Do you know of anything?'

'Leave it with me. We may not be the richest end of the family but Blooms, Frankls and Levys have connections in the trade from buttons to handbags, carpets to threads. Where are you staying?'

'A hostel in Hunslet, an old army barracks. Not exactly the Ritz but a roof over my head. It'll do for now.'

'You could stay here but you see how it is . . . What with the sewing, the bike and our rules, it would be difficult. But you must come whenever you like. We go to concerts, perhaps we can all go together?'

'I'd like that. And if you hear of anything, I would be grateful.'

The city of Leeds went about its business briskly despite bombsites and rebuilding, gaping terraces with wallpaper hanging off the bedroom walls, crowds of shoppers packing the market hall each Saturday when Netta took herself out of the grim coke-fumed Nissen huts and lines of damp washing steaming over the stove, to lose herself among the fabric stalls. For a time the novelty of

170

theatres and cinemas, music halls and concerts, distracted her from the sadness of being without Ray. The return to barracks each night, to the loud wireless music and the smoke and the coarse chatter of strangers, brought back the grim reality of her situation, pierced the bubble of all the colour and sounds of theatre fairyland.

It was sewing that kept her sane. Each weekend she browsed among the fent stalls for cheap offcuts from the textile mills to sew into rompers and smocked shirts for her son. She lost herself in the smells and sights of rolls of printed cottons and shirtings, woollen tweeds and suitings, fancy brocades and satins, velveteens and corduroys, fingering the textures, sniffing colours graduated like crayons in a Lakeland pencil set. Who could be sad at such extravagant sights: bold patterns, stripes and polka dots, checks and ginghams, florals and chintz?

There were boxes of offcuts for cushion covers and curtains too. How she longed for a place of her own to furnish with cushion covers and curtains, bedspreads and table napkins. She always saved the best until last to fortify herself for the bus ride back to the dingy hostel, wandering in a trance around the bridal fabrics and dress velvets, stroking the pile, silky smooth like the ears of a dog; comforting like the top of a baby's head. Sheer organza and silk netting, all the colours of the rainbow at her fingertips.

Close by were the trimmings stalls, Aladdin's caves, cluttered with cards of ribbons and braidings, hat trimmings, artificial flowers and cherries, neat drawers of buttons, zips, embroidery silks and displays of cottons. There were dress trimmings with glittering sequins in wondrous shades like jewelled brooches, instant glamour for a few pence to garnish the plainest of garments. Netta's fingers were itching to play with all these treasures so she bought packets of sequins to satisfy the urge, a treat better than a teacake in Fuller's for it was still there when she got back to Hunslet.

Sometimes she felt as if she had been whisked up and plonked in an alien planet among foreigners and wept for the hills of home and the sea breeze. This was exile indeed. Vida Bloom, true to her word, had quickly fixed her up with work at Saloman's but

171

she and Arnie were no substitute for Galloway folk. The Blooms had their own community, faith and friends. Netta would always be an outsider there.

She kept her promise to Dr Anwar, giving him regular progress reports, returning to the little back street surgery and the warmth of his interest. He listened to her sadness with a kindly nod of the head, his strange accent oddly comforting. He liked to talk of his time in Scotland. He had seen far more of it than she had ever done and assumed she knew Skye and the Cairngorms, the Trossachs and the Western Isles intimately.

'When I first went to your country, it was so wet and damp, I could not get warm. I did not think I could live in such a climate but there were a few fellow countrymen scattered in the University, as lonely, cold and miserable as I was. Enough to make a friend or two, enough to make it bearable. We talked of home and kept our festivals. It is true that you must find your own amongst strangers. Follow what you love and it will lead you where you need to go. It's the only way for you to survive here, young lady. You must find a bit of your own country here, in music or books, I ken not, but you'll recognise it. Keep yourself busy with your sewing. Be hopeful and on the look out for that bit of sugar to sweeten the bitter pill.' He smiled at his little phrase. 'Enough is a feast, as you say?'

Netta looked gratefully at the man who had saved her life. He spoke of hope like the soldier in Park Royal before he fled over the wall in search of liquid gold. How strange she should think of him now. The two men had talked sense in such different ways. 'Thank you, Dr Anwar, you give me hope. How can I ever repay you?'

'By putting one foot in front of the other, slowly, until a path opens up before you. One day this strange journey will make sense to you but not now. It is too soon. Remember, a mountain is climbed from the foothills. Find some of your own people, they will help you.'

172

Homeward Bound, July 1946

Netta was so relieved when she boarded the Thames Clyde Express at last. The factory was shut for the annual Wakes week and she had saved hard for her first holiday back home. She had treated herself to a new hair cut. Off went the Victory roll in favour of a soft bob framing her freckled face. She'd made up a linen two-piece suit in beige, two cotton skirts with bibs and braces and a pair of slacks copied from a Claire McArdell original in the Vogue magazine that she shared with Vida, poring over it like a Bible.

Staggering from the hostel under the weight of cases full of sewing to the bus stop, she paused for breath. Every spare penny from her wages was spent on making clothes for Ray. She was going to arrive home looking chipper, not a down-at-heel factory girl. She pressed her nose to the window as the train drew into Kirkcudbright station to see if anyone was waiting to greet her. There, to her amazement, stood Peg on the platform with the baby who was toddling on his own, bow-legged around his thick nappy. He clung to Peg, eyeing Netta with suspicion again, a reminder of that first visit home from Park Royal.

The coat she had sent for his birthday was discarded in favour of a summer coat that looked shop-bought not home-made.

Netta tried to enthuse about her new life in Leeds but it sounded hollow. The only truthful bit she could add was how she was going to help make another wedding outfit with Vida Bloom for one of the

173

girls in Saloman's office. She gave them all the gen about Arnie, and the Blooms' house, but no one seemed very interested.

Peg sifted through all Ray's new outfits with a sniff. 'Dinna waste yer money on all this fancy stuff. He cannae muck about the place in these frilly shirts. He's a laddie not a lass. He disna want printed cottons at his age. Dungarees and overalls, something more serviceable if you want to make him anything – and make them the right size. Yon last lot you sent him for his birthday were awful skimpy. I passed them on. We can take care of his clothing, you know.' It was never going to be an easy visit after that.

The worst moment was when Father dangled the baby before the mirror and whispered, 'Gus.' The toddler watched his lips intently and spat out, 'Gust!' All hopes of ever giving him his original name were quashed now but Netta swallowed her fury and disappointment. Nobody must see how this rejection of her choice was hurting her.

She wanted to spend every precious moment with her child: going on walks to the shore, paddling by the sea, getting to know all his funny ways. It would be a long route march to New Year and her next official visit. On the way to it she must pass through all the 'this time last years'. The anniversary of Ray's death had left her weak and Remembrance Sunday would be painful to observe again. She still had no picture in her head of where Rae was buried but Father gave her a certificate of condolence from the King which had arrived for her at Brigg Farm.

As Netta pushed the go-chair back to the farm along familiar lanes, pointing out landmarks and flowers to her baby; she wondered if she dare ask to have Ray to stay with her for a while, but in her heart felt it was hopeless even to venture such a suggestion. The hostel was no place for a bairn. She must work all hours if she was to find herself a proper home for him. And who would care for her baby all day? Besides, Peg scarcely let him out of her sight when she was around. The days rushed by and soon it was time to hand him back and kiss him a tearful farewell.

That second journey south went quickly and this time she got off at Leeds Station determined to find proper lodgings with open spaces to wheel a pram, somewhere closer to fields and trees where the sprawling suburbs thinned out into the country. Within two weeks she had found a room and kitchen close to Kirkstall Abbey and the River Aire where she could walk among parkland and over the hilly streets to Rosamund Street and the Blooms.

She cheered up the room's shabbiness with a flurry of curtain making and cleaning, covering the dull moquette of the sofa with covers and cushions made from offcuts. It kept her hands from shaking with the yearning to hold Gus, as she must now call him. The name choked in her throat but she must thole it. Her room overlooked open spaces, the nearest she would ever get now to countryside. Only Dr Anwar's words kept her from crumbling. Step by step she would shift herself further out from these black sooty streets towards green hills. One day she would have her own place with a garden where her son could play and roam safely, a place where she would be proud to entertain her relatives, set high above the twinkling lights of the town. One day she would make them all proud of her.

It was Arnie's birthday and Vida had a streaming chesty cold. She was anxious he didn't catch it and suggested he took Netta to the pictures instead as a friendly gesture for helping with Edna Gresty's wedding dress.

'You do understand, Netta, I'm trusting you with my boy. He's not for you, I hope you realise there can be no matchmaking? He's spoken for. He must marry into his faith with a suitable girl, someone who can share his interests. He's still got a lot of exams, there must be no distractions.'

Netta smiled to herself at this broad hint. Arnie had raised his thick black eyebrows in her direction once or twice but she had soon cooled his interest with little sisterly put downs and teasings. He was not on her hit list of possible suitors. Interest in him could never exist in her scheme of things for there was only one man in her life and he was two hundred miles away in his cot!

'He seems so tired with it all. No time for his music now and he was so good at his clarinet,' Netta ventured.

'Just a hobby, Netta, music's his hobby. Business is where the money lies: qualifications, articles and charters. He'll make his mother so proud! When your boy grows to be a man, you'll understand. You want only what's best for them and mother knows best! I hope you don't mind being disappointed? I wondered when you came at first if it was to see my son again, you were awful pally in the war?'

'We were children, babes then. Now it's different. I know my place.'

'Now you're offended. Like I say, it's all for the best. But we're friends and we work well together, yes?'

Netta shrugged her shoulders. 'Aye, Mistress Bloom, there have to be rules.'

Arnie chose to let his hair down for a change, rejecting a piano recital in favour of the latest revue at the City Variety Theatre in Leeds. It was a famous little theatre, a compact smoky atmosphere where the punters yelled and cheered if they liked an act and bawled if they didn't. It was the usual mixed bill: comic turns, animal acts, dancers and singers and acrobats. One of the speciality acts was Karenza the Snake Woman, a contortionist who slithered on to the stage in a snakeskin body suit while an exotic-looking man in oriental costume played some pipes. What a figure the artist had and could she twist her body and put her legs where legs were never meant to go! It made Netta's bones creak just watching her.

At the end of her act Karenza stood up and took a well-deserved bow before the audience, whipping off her mask and skullcap. Out popped a cascade of bleached blonde hair in bunches and Netta recognised instantly who it was: Wilma Dixey. It must be.

'That's Dixie!' Netta screamed, jumping out of her seat to wave at her. Arnie held her back whispering, 'Shush! She's a furriner.' He thought Netta was going bananas and tried to pull her down but she was determined to see if it really was her old

176

sparring partner. At the interval she made him troop round to the stage door to ask if they could speak to Miss Karenza herself. The doorman wouldn't let them cross his threshold but did allow Netta to scribble a note to the artist instead. 'Hi there! Greetings to the Evaporee from Stratharvar! How's Malky?' *Her hand was trembling with excitement. Arnie did not know where to put himself for shame at her antics.*

'What will Mother say?' *he mumbled.*

Within minutes a woman shot out of the door in a glamorous dressing gown lined with swan'sdown, 'Ach, away ye go, hen. Is it really yous?'

'She's foreign, right enough,' *whispered Arnie.*

'That's not foreign, it's broad Glaswegian! Have you forgotten yer Scottish education already?' *Netta laughed and gave Wilma a bear hug, introducing the astonished Arnie who seemed dazzled by her false eyelashes, make-up and glamorous air. Wilma looked like a Hollywood star now but underneath Netta sensed that she was still the same rough and ready Dixie.*

At the end of the show she took them both for a late-night meal in a cellar where there was a jazz band and dancing. The music was sizzling and Arnie's feet never slopped tapping. It was the best birthday night out ever, thanks to Dixie's nous. She knew city hot spots better than any locals. The night began for her only when the curtain dropped. They missed the last bus home and Arnie walked Netta all the way to Kirkstall. 'To think we grew up in the same city,' *he said,'* and dinnae ken each other.'

'I don't think yer mothers washed in the same Steamie, Arnie. Peg never got over having Papes and Jews as refugees, and her such a good Presbyterian. What a coincidence we should all meet up again, even if she's just passing through.'

'She's off to the Grand in Bolton, next week. Wasn't she wonderful . . . those costumes, and such a smart act? To think we've so much in common. I'll take Mother to see her tomorrow.'

'I don't think so, it's Friday,' *whispered Netta tactfully. Poor old Arnie was smitten by the sight of Karenza in the footlights*

177

and the lure of her greasepaint. Vida was not going to be happy about this at all.

'I do think you were thoughtless to let him roam the streets with yon keelie, Netta. I'm disappointed in you. You know he has work to go to in the morning.' They were finishing off the last fitting for Edna's wedding dress in the sewing room at Rosamund Street. Netta sucked on her pins, trying not to swallow them.

'We all had work to go to. And Arnie had a wonderful time at the jazz club, I've never seen him so relaxed. It was his birthday, surely you don't begrudge him a good time?'

'He's been back there again, you know, three times.'

'Good for him!'

'But his studies . . . what about his exams? I don't know what's got into him.'

'Flexing his wings a little. He's over twenty-one, old enough to do as he pleases.'

'Well, I don't like it,' snapped Vida Bloom, spitting pins.

I don't suppose you do, thought Netta, burying her head in the hem, out of the crossfire.

Netta watched the solemn procession: the silver band, clergy, civic dignitaries carrying poppy wreaths, scouts and cubs carrying their flags and the local territorials and British Legion walking stiffly behind. There was a steady stream of ordinary people following carrying little wooden crosses with names on them. Women with small children, older couples and widows, all in sombre clothing, walking together on that solemn morning when the city streets were silent and still and the bell from the parish church tolled in remembrance of fallen heroes.

Netta took her place with her own small cross of poppies: another sad face in the crowd as they reached the Cenotaph on which were inscribed the newly engraved names of the dead. It had to be done. A public display was the least survivors could offer to Rae and his friends for their sacrifice, but how Netta wished she was holding

178

her own child in her arms for comfort as a token of their love. One day, she vowed, Gus would go with her to find his father's grave. She would teach him then about sacrifice and duty. It was the least she could do.

She was going to give Christmas a miss this year. What was there to celebrate after all? Netta swallowed her sadness. For two long days the whole world would fall silent and the curtains in Aireview Street would be drawn tight against the darkness. There was a carol service at the parish church if she was desperate, music on the wireless for company, plenty of outwork from Vida to be getting on with. She promised herself a long walk along the river in the afternoon of Boxing Day, with a basket of alterations on the go to keep her mind from yearning for Stratharvar. She wondered if Ray would like his parcel of soft toys sent through the post? The dungarees and leggings, and the siren play suit, would wait for final fitting when she saw him once more. She was not going to make the same mistake again. This time she had made sure her sewing gifts would be acceptable.

Her mind was full of sewing plans when Dixie turned up unexpectedly at Netta's digs one Sunday lunchtime en route to a mysterious assignation. Miss Karenza was requesting a new sequinned costume for her pantomime appearance and Netta was to have the order.

'I've never done anything like this before.' She shook her head, looking at the sketch in surprise, but Dixie just winked and shrugged her shoulders. 'I'm sure you'll do me fine, hen. How's that handsome fella of yours?' She smiled at the photograph of mother and son on the mantelpiece. 'You're a dark horse and no mistake! I couldn't believe it when you told me about yer wean. A shotgun wedding, was it, up the aisle with an elastic waist? I bet Peg was charming about that?'

'Not exactly.' Time for Netta to spill some of the beans but her audience just roared in response, 'You divil! Running off to Gretna Green like that. How romantic – and an anvil wedding, what a hoot!' Dixie was not the type to be shocked by a mismatch of dates and certificates. 'But how can you bear to leave the wean with that dragon?'

'I can't keep him here.'

'There must be good nurseries for working women. Better than living apart, surely. And if you got piecework at home . . .'

'I haven't space here to swing a cat. Children aren't allowed. I'll move to somewhere bigger as soon as I can.' How easy it was for Dixie to shrug off her shame as some minor indiscretion. And Netta longed to confide in her how much it really cost her to live two hundred miles from her own baby, but the moment passed. Dixie waltzed off in her fine fur coat to meet Arnie somewhere for tea, leaving behind the other joker she had thrown into the pack of cards when she challenged Netta about a proper sewing career.

'You're wasted on a factory floor. If you sew everything to this standard you ought to be making dresses for a living, not killin' yerself after midnight for bawbees!'

'Making what, though?' Netta mumbled.

'You know fine what I mean: costumes like these, fancy stuff, theatricals, ballgowns, bridal dresses to order. You can do the lot. You've got an eye for colour and detail with that special bitty flair and sparkle. Yer own clothes have real style and you cannae buy that in shops these days.'

'Style won't pay my digs and board, Dixie, or buy messages at the store. I need regular work but yer right enough – I do so much moonlighting, I can hardly raise my neck it's that sore. Sometimes I wake up in the night and I'm dreaming fabrics: fents and cotton reels and buttons dancing round my head even in the dark! I count bobbins, not sheep.'

'Think about it, hen. You only come round the once. Why waste yer talents? I should talk to Arnie's mum, see if she can help. No flies on that one when it comes to making a bob or two, I'd say, if he's anything to go by.'

'Are you seeing him?' asked Netta. Dixie flashed her big eyes like

180

a Kewpie Doll, putting one scarlet-fingered nail on her lips. 'Mum's the word!' They both giggled.

Dixie's suggestions were unsettling with Christmas so close and no one to discuss it all with but the festivities were only two days in the year after all. It would not be long before Netta would be back home to hold her boy again. Then they would take the road down to Carrick beach and she would tell him all about these scary possibilities. One step at a time, Dr Anwar had said. Was a golden path of opportunity opening up for Netta at last?

Saturday Afternoon In Kendal 1949

Netta descended down the A6 to Kendal and parked the car by the river. She climbed up towards the town, pausing to browse in the shop windows and the indoor market. She drifted from one street to another looking for a café to slake her thirst. The town was full of holiday makers jostling their raffia shopping bags and ice creams, kiddies in sun bonnets whining for toys and treats on hot pavements. Youths lounged outside milk bars and old men in flat caps and open shirts chivvied their wives to be quick about their purchases.

It was late afternoon, close and sticky. She must find somewhere for afternoon tea to clear her dusty throat and throbbing head. There were still hours of driving ahead. Netta was swept along the street through the swing doors into Woolworth's store which were jammed open to let in some air.

It was the usual layout: sweet stalls and tables spread with buckets and spades, toys, colouring books, leftover paper flags and souvenirs, haberdashery, fancy goods. Netta was pushed to the back of the store where the hardware was stacked high and began to feel queasy and faint, light-headed and short of breath. She turned to get out of the door but the thronging shoppers were bearing down on her and she clung to one of the counters to steady her rising panic. She couldn't find the way out and her chest began to tighten, her throat constricting so she couldn't breathe. I'm dying, she thought. I'm going to die on this dirty floor if I don't escape. The room was spinning around her head.

She woke up on the floor with someone waving a paper over her face. They carried her to a chair by the door and her head was shoved unceremoniously between her knees. A glass of water appeared and she was fanned like an oriental princess by one of the young assistants. Netta felt like a freak show with everyone staring at her. 'I'm sorry, it must be the heat. This has never happened to me before,' she lied. In fact it was becoming an all too frequent occurrence in crowded places when she was tired or upset.

She drank in the fumes and smell of horse dung on the busy road as the traffic crawled through the town. It felt safer now, in the fresher air and the shaded part of the street. She thanked everyone and made for Finkle Street to a corner café up a flight of stairs that was her usual stop for tea and scones. She lit a cigarette to steady her nerves, ordered an iced lime soda, slurping the fizzy pop through a straw and scooping out the creamy ice with a long spoon. It cooled her thirst and reminded her of childhood treats at Angelini's. She relished the blast of cold on the back of her throat and wished Gus was there beside her to share the sensation.

Netta fingered the package of photographs that she had stuck in her large straw handbag. There were enough here to start another album after all: a special tartan one with tassels. Here was her mother and herself, tiny specks on the shoreline taken when she was five, more school snapshots, some of her letters packaged up and a printed card of her very first sewing venture in its infancy. She fingered the gold lettering lovingly. Where would she be now without her dressmaking?

5

CITRINE

'Sacred colour of midday,
Worn for purpose of mind and spirit
For wisdom and courage on the journey.'

In The Winter Of 1947

All Netta's resolutions froze solid on her return to Yorkshire. No one was prepared for the winter of 1947 when snow blanketed Britain for week upon week. It could only be endured. Pavements were piled high with icy mounds and Netta struggled by foot to Saloman's through tunnels of ice. Everything ground to a halt, pipes froze up and the power failed. Coal supplies were difficult and factories began to seize up, laying off their workforce. Business was slack at Saloman's and the girls who did make the effort to get themselves to work were often turned away again when there was no power.

Netta had never known such cold. Her bedsit was like a block of ice with no heating when the power failed and ferns of frost crusted the insides of the window pane. The rooflight was thick with ice. She piled on layers of clothing, struggling to keep out the chill, but her gumboots were at the farm and her bootees thin, giving her chilblains on her heels. In desperation she ran out into the Abbey grounds to dance away their itching, barefoot in the snow.

The daily tramp to Saloman's was agony. The wind whistled from the steppes of Russia, chilled to iciness by the North Sea and the bleak moors, biting into her face until the ends of her nose and lips were raw.

The only comfort in all of this freezing mayhem was the beauty of the scenery, the wonderful snowscapes and drifting sculptures that hung from the Abbey ruins by the river skating rink. Netta loved to watch the children tobogganing down the slopes and hoped that Father would make Gus his own snowman in the farmyard. Even Aireview Street looked like the castle of a snow princess, dripping with icicles, crusted with rose-tinted snow in the sunlight, all its grim shabby reality disguised by the dazzling whiteness. Her fingers were too raw to sew fine work, no one was in the mood for making clothes and Netta was bored, lost without something in her hand. She walked up the slippery street to see if Vida Bloom needed a hand with anything.

When she arrived there, shivering on the doorstep, Vida ushered her in before a warm coal fire, gave her a glass of strange spirits. 'That'll warm you up better than any hot water bottle!'

It burned Netta's throat but fired her brain with Dixie's challenge. She leaned back and told Vida how Dixie had suggested she set up her own dressmaking business.

Vida shook her head vehenently. 'She's right, it's time for you to move on from the factory floor but not to this, girl, sewing up dresses for millgirls. It suits me for the moment, I've seen the big time and it's not all it's cracked up to be. But you need experience of the better end of the market first, where the real money is to be made – the carriage trade in Harrogate or Ilkley. Get yourself some experience there in retail fashion, get to know your customers and what they want.

'Arnie and I were only thinking the other day that when the coupons go there'll be such a rush for decent clothes and new ideas. Everyone's so fed up with threadbare suits and coats. The garment factories will be spinning for years, just wait and see.'

'But I don't want to make utility clothes. I want to make the stuff of dreams and glamour and hope for the future . . . beautiful gowns, couture concoctions with yards of material, all flounces and furbelows, silks and satins, buttons and bows . . .' Netta had slumped over the table for the brandy had gone to her speech as well as her knees. 'I want to make Cinderellas into princesses not pumpkins. How can I do that with ration books under my nose?'

'I know warehouse garments are like gold dust, expensive to buy and scarce to order with all the restrictions on purchase and export, but where money dwells there's always a way round restrictions, believe me. You'll just have to be patient, one step at a time. Learn your trade in a quality retail establishment, that's a start. Look in the Post, smarten yourself up and go for interviews. See what comes up.'

'But if I made a simple collection of unusual gowns and hired them out together: Scarlett O'Hara ballgowns and Bette Davis cocktail and party frocks?' Netta was carried away with her ideas, already in the realms of fantasy. It was Vida who splashed cold water on her dream.

'Not so fast, love, keep it simple and safe. Think big ideas, yes . . . just start slowly, focus on finding the right clientèle. Who would want such stuff round here? Where would you get the capital outlay for materials, workshop equipment and saleroom hire as well as advertising? I'm sure I could get you wholesale on materials and I could give you a hand with the sewing sometimes. It's a grand idea making dresses for Yorkshire princesses but hold yer sweat and start off at the bottom with the top people. That's my advice for what it's worth.' Mrs Bloom paused. 'Have you seen Arnie lately? He's behaving very oddly. I don't like the look of him.'

'Perhaps he's sickening for something,' muttered Netta, stifling a smile. Vida Bloom looked wearily at her over her glasses.

'What are you grinning at? It's not funny. I don't get a straight answer out of him these days. He's taken up his clarinet again. Not for Mozart but that dreadful wailing stuff they play on the Light Programme.'

'The Blues. It's Jazz, Mrs Bloom. He's taken to Jazz that's all.' Netta sighed with relief that this change of subject had shifted them away from the real cause of Arnie's distracted air.

'It all sounds like two cats in a dyke to me.' Netta smiled, thinking those were the very words Peg had used about Vida's Third Programme. There was no accounting for musical taste.

*   *   *

189

The proprietress of Maison Dorelle surveyed Netta with disdain, sniffing over her homespun suit like a bloodhound, searching in vain for a loose thread, uneven hem, any visible flaws in her sewing skills. 'I wouldn't be interviewing a factory gel if I wasn't desperate. Why I should be taking you on, I don't know. This reference from a Mrs Bloom, a back street dressmaker, no doubt, is hardly worth the paper it's written on, Mrs Hunter. I don't take marrieds but as you're a widow I suppose I can make an exception.

'My ladies like familiar faces when they disrobe, clean fingernails and sweet breath. Do you smoke?' Netta shook her head. 'I want no stale smells on our garments. This is all highly irregular but that harpy just upped and left us without a moment's notice and with the summer season to prepare for . . . You'll have to do, I suppose. You're the least offensive of the bunch and your accent is at least tolerable. My ladies can manage a bit of Scotch as long as it's not broad and common.

'Pity about your hair. Not a fashionable colour at all, too brash to the eye. We'll have to cover it up. You'll be on a month's trial. If you fit into our ways, then we'll see. This is a very respectable establishment founded by our father, Mr Percival, God rest his soul, departed these two years. Everyone here knows their place and I won't have slackers. Do you understand me?'

Netta almost bobbed like a servant girl. 'Yes, ma'am.'

'And it's Miss . . . Miss Venables to you. I shall expect you at eight sharp, tomorrow morning. We shall take it from there. You will answer to Jeanette when called upon to render assistance to our vendeuse, Maybelle.'

Netta gulped as she studied the bus timetable to see what unearthly hour she must rise to get back to Griseley in time. Beggars can't be choosers, she sighed. Of all the jobs in all the papers she had written to and asked after, this was the only one to come up trumps. Mrs Danvers from the film Rebecca, that was who Miss Venables looked like, and she came to a sticky end. If this was the grilling for a humble alterations seamstress, heaven knows what a sales assistant must go through to be acceptable. Still *it was a job in fashion retailing, the next step forward. As Netta stared from the top of the bus the sights around her looked pleasing enough. Griseley was almost countrified with moorland stretching into the distance as far as the eye could see and it was on the road to Ilkley with fine houses with huge frontages and gardens, an elegant parade of shops, broad streets and an air of prosperity about the shoppers even in these shabby times.*

The last of the terrible snow lay melting in piles on the sides of the pavements but the hills were clearing fast. There was no white in the hollows, a sure indication that the snow would not return. Spring was late but it had come at last and her spirits soared with excitement at this new opportunity. Vida had been right when she'd said Netta should find the right clientèle. There would be so much to learn about Maison Dorelle even though it was old-fashioned. Who nowadays had 'Gowns, Furs and Overmantles' printed in faded gold lettering above the window? There were no prices in the window displays and that meant expensive, exclusive and quality. If she was going to be a dress designer then this was where she must start.

In the days that followed her arrival across Maison Dorelle's hallowed portals, Netta found herself on her hands and knees to the great and good of the county. Miss Venables was a stickler for pecking orders, procedures and propriety. 'You stay in your corner, Jeanette, until called. Speak to no one unless spoken to. Maybelle makes the sale and you obey her orders at all times. She will nod. Do not hover and above all make no suggestions. I will not have pin-pickers altering my garments without my say so. No contact, no comments and no connection with our customers. Is that understood?'

Netta was banished to the cubby hole at the back of the shop; a tiny workroom with a bench and machine, just a few shelves and a sink. She was expected to make tea for customers as they browsed through the latest collection of summer wear. She was also expected to prepare dresses for the part-time mannequin, well past the full flush of youth, to parade before the customers who could

191

not be expected to disrobe themselves for fear of catching a chill. Their measurements were kept discreetly in a cardboard box and occasionally they submitted themselves to the tape measure for a renewal of the sad statistics.

'We specialise in portly fittings,' said Miss Venables as she sifted through the files, chucking the unfortunates who had not made it through the harsh winter into the bin. 'Yorkshire ladies all like their puddings and it shows.'

When the bell rang, Netta made her discreet entrance through the plush curtain in a dove grey overall, an exact match to the carpet, pins on her chest lined up like medals, tape around her neck like a stethoscope, to grovel silently at the feet of the client while Maybelle talked them through possible alterations and Netta adjusted seams, tucks and length swiftly, trying not to put cold fingers on their delicate flesh.

How bare and vulnerable these bodies all looked in the harsh mirror and some smelled as if they had not had a wash for weeks. Some of the richest women did not care how they were dressed but flung on several dresses and then flung them off again on the floor for their poodles to trample on. These were not the women she wanted to make dresses for, they were old and tired and corseted into unnatural shapes. She longed for young flesh and bright colours, stylish modern cuts in glamorous fabrics. How dowdy were the rails of colours, maroons and dark blues, black and every shade of mud: dull as dishwater colours on plain women, all reflecting the taste of Miss Venables and 'Our father who has gone before'.

Then there were the tweed brigades who lived in draughty barns out in the country. They wanted serviceable and sensible and more sludgy country colours. Some were young enough to smarten up and Netta hoped their evening wear would be brighter and more alluring, but even Maison Dorelle could not get everything they ordered from the tired-looking trade reps who called hopefully each season. A quota of Utility designs seemed be the best value but their bridal wear turned out to be skimpy and plain beer. No wonder customers went elsewhere for their evening wear.

Hadn't they heard of the 'New Look' in the fashion magazines? Christian Dior was the talk of the trade. Netta had scoured the fashion magazines when she first began to hear of this bombshell exploding in Paris. Christian Dior's look was rocking fashion houses all over the world. He was doing the unthinkable, lowering skirts, shaping women into tiny waists and full bosoms, using yards and yards of tulle and taffeta to plump out skirts into bells.

'I think his designs are disgusting, emphasising curves in such a suggestive manner . . . a waste of materials, such decadent ideas,' condemned Miss Venables. 'Our father would turn in his grave to see such a betrayal of wartime spirit. It won't catch on. Our ladies have more sense!' Netta said nothing about seeing the latest newsreel pictures and how his ideas were taking fashion by storm in London. She wanted to be the first girl on the High Street to sport such advanced fashion and stayed up all weekend to run up a printed cotton dress with a tight bodice and full skirt which hovered just above her ankles. If only she was a real designer she could grab these ideas and translate them into the most wonderful ball gowns and wedding dresses too. Make everyday women glamorous and feminine again. She wrote to Brigg Farm to tell them all about her new position and turned up for work on the brightest of mornings, knowing that her visit home was only two weeks away.

'Take that off at once, Jeanette Hunter. You look ridiculous. Don't make such a spectacle of yourself. Whatever next!' Her new outfit was banished to the workroom and it was on with the uniform once more. But she was going to wear it for Gus when she stepped off the train.

Neither Peg nor Angus could see the point of her dressmaking idea. 'It's all a bit of an airy-fairy scheme. Why don't you stay in this dress shop and be done with it?' argued Peg.

'But anyone can run a dress shop. I want to make clothes out of my head. The world has gone wild with the New Look and Royal wedding fever, or hasn't it reached these parts yet?'

Peg shrugged her shoulders. 'It's all one tae me, lassie. You should ken, there's mair to marriage than dressing up, Princess or no!'

'Oh, Peg, don't be a wet blanket!'

'Better a wet blanket than living with ma head stuffed in the clouds. It'll take more than a bit of confetti and ribbon to make yer fortune. It changes nothing.'

'Nothing . . . what?' asked Netta, not catching her meaning.

'Gus stays here with us where he's settled. You're in no position to take on a kiddie with all they daft schemes of yours.'

All her pride and excitement in her progress suddenly evaporated with these cool words. Was she always to be punished for her mistakes? Would her own needs and desires ever be respected by them? It seemed not, but Netta would keep on trying whatever it took. One day she would be a success despite them and then nothing would stop her from being a mother to Gus.

The Texas Rangers, Autumn 1947

Each night Netta stood wearily at the bus stop, sheltering from the downpour in a shop doorway. One evening she saw the poster announcing: 'Come Scottish Dancing'. Memories of jigging it down the Memorial Hall at Stratharvar flooded her with nostalgia and homesickness. 'Find your own' the doctor had suggested. If she stayed on after work and caught a later bus back to her rooms she might enjoy the music and the company. It was a warm thought on a cold night and cheered her all the way home.

The windows of St Andrew's church hall were steaming, the parquet floor groaning under the thunder of the dancers who swirled around the room until the gramophone jerked its needle, throwing everyone into confusion. They were mostly young women and a few older men who were shared out fairly to learn their steps. Netta was welcomed with open arms because it was obvious she didn't have two left feet. St Andrew's Night was fast approaching and the troupe were hoping to lead the Yorkshire Scotia at the annual bash in the Royal Hotel.

All those years pounding the Memorial Hall dragging reluctant pupils came in useful and she sent for her black leather lace-up pumps from Brigg Farm. They were a friendly bunch of nurses and teachers, butchers and housewives, and her own partner was the matron of some Cottage Homes close by. It was good to hear familiar accents en masse, not just a stray Scots voice on a bus.

195

The Scotia Club members who were turning up to polish their steps were a different breed, mostly second-hand by marriage with a sentimental attraction to tartan and pipe bands.

The late influx of official members was dominated by a loud horsy set of snappy dressers who roared up to the church hall in flash MGs: the sort Netta surmised who had wealthy parents or husbands who shelled out petrol coupons, fodder bills and clothing allowances. Here were her future customers: youngish, many still single, an untapped source of wedding dress potential perhaps. She was going to stick close to them and observe.

The leader of the gang was Ginnie Mackeever. Jean, the matron, whispered that the girl was the daughter of the biggest builder's merchant in the district. He had started out his career as a humble Glasgow brickie but now lived in some grey stone villa on the outskirts of Ilkley with his own stable of hunters.

'Watch out! Here come the Texas Rangers,' Jean warned. 'You watch, they'll push their way in and ruin all our rehearsals. I wish they could dance as well as they can ride! We do all the serious stuff, charity displays and dancing classes. They get all the glory turning up in a posse of fur coats and a cloud of blue smoke.'

But Netta couldn't take her eyes off Ginnie Mackeever. She looked like a mannequin, tall and curvy with a stylish perm. As she twirled, the diamonds on her engagement finger flashed in the gaslight. How confident she looked and how wildly glamorous. She was wearing a New Look full skirt cinched by a waspie waist band in the very latest style. Even her boat-neck sweater was straight out of Vogue: such casual careless elegance, cutting her own workaday homespun clothes down to size.

Jean was watching her partner, eyeing her enviously. 'Forget it, they Texas Rangers take no prisoners. Many are called but few are chosen. We're no in their league. To be one of them you have to ride like the devil, own your own horse and drink like a fish. Oh, and have some poor soul up yer sleeve to fund all they fun and games, hen.'

You could be useful to them, Netta thought to herself, sew

them up outfits as up to date as any they are wearing. But if you want some of their clothing allowance you'll have to run yourself up something stunning for the Ball, something they will notice and want to know where you bought it. Yes, St Andrew's Night must be the next stepping stone on her path to success.

The buffet supper was demolished. An afterglow of speeches and toasts lay like a smoky haze over the assembly. The hotel ballroom glittered with silver buckles and tartans in the lamplight, from deepest scarlet to midnight blue: Macgregor, Macduff, Macleod, Black Watch, Scott, Ogilvie, all the colours of the rainbow set against black velvet and white satin.

Tonight Netta felt the colours around her so keenly that she could almost taste them. Carmines smelled of burnt rose petals; yellows brought a tinge of mustard and gorse flowers; greens were the newly cropped fields of grass, and blue and purple brought whiffs of smoke and heather honey to her nostrils. She sat back to admire the guests, glad to have joined the dancing group.

The troupe had led the floor in a short display of reels and Netta's white dress, boned and scooped out at the neck, with layers of rustling underskirts made from net curtain lace and offcuts, had been much admired. White was the purest, harshest of hues on a redhead so she had softened the fabric with a soaking in tea. Working with pale shades was soothing. Was it because it was a safe and female colour? Did it make up for so much that was murky grey in her own life? Why was she pondering such gloomy thoughts when she was safe among her fellow exiles, listening to the chink of raised glasses?

For the first time in many months she could relax, away from the strains of the dress shop and her shabby rooms. One day she would be one of the Scotia club when she was Jeanette Hunter, dress designer, with her own little business on the High Street. How she envied the Texas Rangers the comfortable security of solid homes and local connections, all that noisy exuberance. They belonged because of who they were. Ginnie didn't have to budget

197

and scrimp, stay up all night to finish her dress or worry about a secret child so far away. They must be about the same age but Netta felt so old and staid in comparison. The sparkle had gone out of her life. She sometimes felt almost invisible amongst them and it hurt to be ignored.

There're other exiles here besides you, though, thought Netta. The soldiers in their dress kilts, the butchers, builders, teachers, policemen, wives and nurses, doctors, shopkeepers and landowners. Exiles who found nostalgic comfort every now and then in recalling the homeland with its bagpipes and folk songs, mountains, lochs, tenements, tram cars and pawky humour. What was it that really made a Scot? What a mixed bunch the members were with only their birthplace in common. Yet this St Andrew's Night was going to be an evening to savour when she was back hemming miles of tulle under Miss Venables's hawkish eye.

Then Ginnie Mackeever swept across the floor in her white lace dress amd tartan sash, flouncing across the ballroom with her fiancé on her arm. 'Come and meet the natives, darling. This is our own Moira Shearer . . . such red hair it makes me go out of step just looking at it. Is it really that colour,' she whispered,' or are we looking at some quality henna? Love the dress . . . Who's your dressmaker? A little bird told me you're the star stitching up Dorelle's. Poor girl, however do you suffer Maudie Venables?' Ginnie's accent sounded as if it had never crossed the border in its life.

Netta averted her eyes, feeling Ginnie's sharp eyes roaming over her dress with reluctant admiration. 'Quite the little Schiaparelli! Not bad, is it, my sweet? Meet Dr Andrew Stirling, my fiancé . . . Darling, meet the crowd.'

He nodded casually, putting his hand on the table to steady himself for he was a bit the worse for whisky. The hand lay spreadeagled in front of Netta's nose, a hairy freckled pigment on the wrist. She looked up out of politeness, waiting to shake hands, but her arm froze at the sight of the man. She would have recognised that mottled face, those waves of sandy hair anywhere.

198

A flash of recognition crossed his face and his mouth twitched into a small smile.

Netta glanced away, her neck flushing with the effort to stay calm. 'Pleased to meet you.' She bent her head down with relief but couldn't help noticing he was still staring at her. She stared back at him, warning him with a brief shake of her head. Would he blab it out to Ginnie? It would be all over the club in minutes. Suddenly a feeling of dread flooded over her and she couldn't breathe. Netta rose to find the ladies' room, to steady her nerves and calm this awful shaking.

Drew leaned on the table to catch his breath. Good grief! What a shock to see that mane of flaming hair and those sea-green eyes wide as saucers at the sight of him. What on earth was she doing in Yorkshire? He lit a fag to steady his nerves while Ginnie flitted from table to table like a noisy starling. Smiling to himself, he thought of the poster which had been stuck on the Sunday School wall as a child. BE SURE YOUR SINS WILL FIND YOU OUT. This meeting could call his bluff with this crowd, but somehow he knew Netta was a safe bet.

Nevertheless he had been thunderstruck by her slenderness and elegance and the warmth of her smile. He had forgotten how luminous those eyes were.

She had been discharged by the time he found his weary way back to Park Royal. After weeks sleeping rough and sorting his head around his raging thirst, the crabs crawling through his mind, Drew had returned to complete his treatment in the hospital like a penitent child, kow-towing to the regime like a model patient.

On his discharge he had been determined to put formal medicine behind him. Not for him the surgical ward or the surgery for he had seen enough drama and blood. He settled for a safe option behind a desk as a public servant. A few locum jobs were all it took to convince him he was hopeless with the ailments of hypochondriacs. In the end he took a post with the West Riding of Yorkshire

School Welfare Association, providing screenings and medicals to local schools.

The contact with children was refreshing although depressing at times. There were so many city children who were malnourished and downtrodden by wartime disruption, but kids in general were honest and uncomplaining. They allowed Drew to drift on the surface and avoid extreme reactions.

Then came the fateful outing to the Yorkshire Show when he saw Ginnie Mackeever take a bad throw in the show jumping ring and rushed to give her first aid. Her father was distraught, worried that his only child should be seriously injured, but she must have had the devil's luck and a spine of steel to walk away so easily from what could have been a wheelchair outcome.

Ginnie's crowd was, at first, just the tonic Drew needed to complete his social life. Horsy but generous, with no bourgeois hangups about spending lolly by the bucketful: the eat, drink and be merry brigade who welcomed him into their charmed circle. Ginnie bubbled like pink champagne, dazzling his senses with her glamour and horsemanship.

He had ridden as a child of the Manse in Perthshire but needed many lessons even to begin to keep up with this crowd. How he'd got himself in to Fattorini's the jeweller's in Leeds to choose an engagement ring was all a bit of a blur. After some boozy party, no doubt. But Billie Mackeever had welcomed him as a fellow Scot and a tame quack in the family. Ginnie thought the whole romance a hoot. Why shouldn't he enjoy himself after all those wasted years in the Forces? His parents sent a letter of congratulations from their clinic in the African bush, hoping Ginnie and Drew would make up the loving team needed to steer through the stormy waters of modern marriage. Ginnie had roared with laughter at their old-fashioned ideas.

As the time to make wedding plans drew nearer he felt anxious about the commitment he was taking on but relieved at least that young Ginnie was in no rush to canter down the aisle. Long might it continue.

When Netta walked past the bar, Drew was propped up there, close enough to touch her arm. 'We meet again.' He saw her mouth tremble. 'Never expected to see you again. Don't worry, your secret's safe with me.' He was grinning with amusement.

'It's not funny! You stood me up, as I recall, on Remembrance Day. I wondered what happened to you.' She muttered the words like a ventriloquist's dummy.

'The usual, I expect. One too many, over the wall and far away. I came back but you were gone by then. Don't look so po-faced.'

'You're drunk!'

'I'm as sober as a judge but this sort of shindig always gets me reaching for the bottle. All this tartan glory makes my eyes water. Sorry, but it's not my thing.'

'Well, it was mine until you turned up.'

'What brought you to Yorkshire?'

'It's a long story.'

'There was a baby, I recall?'

'That's the long story, but I live in hope. And you, did you find yourself some hope too or is the Texas Ranger your last chance saloon?' He roared with laughter at her phrasing, drawing everyone's attention to their conversation and Ginnie quickly to his side.

'I can't leave him alone for two seconds before he's chatting up some skirt. You never told me you knew each other?'

'We don't. Just passing the time, aren't we, Mrs Hunter? Nice to meet you.' Drew put his arm around his fiancée and smiled sweetly. Netta watched as they swayed back to the dance floor. Ginnie gripped his arm, giving Netta a long hard look that signalled: Do not muscle in on my property. Keep to your place in the pecking order.

Netta watched Drew staggering, Ginnie draped all over him like a stole. To look good in Highland dress a man needed firm full calves to show off the skean dhu in his stocking, broad shoulders and a neat waist to give the jacket and kilt definition. There was nothing distinguished about Drew Stirling. He was too lanky and spindle-legged with a slight stoop to his shoulders as if he was afraid to uncurl himself to his full height. Yet it was that very stoop that caught Netta's eye as she could see him sobering up fast, trying to concentrate among the chatter, glancing furtively in her direction. What strange misalliance of stars had brought those two lovebirds together? she wondered.

She no longer felt safe, knowing Drew Stirling was living at such close range. What he knew about her private life could bring down her fragile house of straw with one puff: all the little half-truths of its façade scattered by his first drunken gaffe. So he was a doctor? That was why he had been quick to make a diagnosis of her illness. Was he still practising medicine or had he been dishonourably discharged from the army? She was curious but would never risk a function at the Scotia again just in case.

Ships that pass in the night was all they had meant to each other in Park Royal but he had recognised and remembered as much of her as she did of his sad story. Billie Mackeever, the builder, was quite the elder of the kirk now, indulgent with his daughter perhaps but not enough to want her to marry a drunk, whatever his nationality.

Netta's knees had stopped shaking. There was no reason for them ever to meet again socially. It need not stop her dancing on Thursday evenings. As for the Texas Rangers, it was a fantasy to think any of them would ever use her services when there were big stores locally and London only hours away.

Netta caught sight of the silver-mounted cairngorm buttons on his black dress jacket, flashing in the light like the fear in his eyes. There was an odd solace in knowing somebody else was just as discomfited as she. Their strange encounter in Park Royal was a secret shared only by them, she was sure. Now they must collude in a mutual silence, an alliance of deceit. Each had power over the other in this affair; a disturbing thought. It was time for this

Cinderella to change back into her rags and put all this behind her. Nothing was going to stop her progress, not even the joys of Maison Dorelle awaiting her in the morning.

Spring 1948

There was cherry blossom dusting the pavements of Griseley High Street like pink confetti and wedding fever was in the air. The Royal wedding back in November had set its stamp of romance on the nation and Yorkshire brides were rushing to the altar in modest replicas of the ivory satin Hartnell creation which had staggered the world with its glorious embroidery and appliqué work. Vida was snowed under with cotton and net, farming out as much work to Netta as her weary eyes could manage. Dorelle's were struggling to supply its quota of mother of the bride two-piece outfits and accessories. Netta crawled through the winter on her knees making alterations.

Even Maudie Venables had bowed to the inevitable and at last bought in some fashion stock. With every stitch of overtime and bridal piecework, Netta was counting more pound notes. At last she was on the move from Aireview Street to upper Griseley, renting a stone end-terraced cottage, two up, two down, on a ledge of houses halfway up towards the moors.

Her own place at last! No more early morning bus rides in the dark, no more grim streets and sooty smuts on her sewing for this was above the chimney line and away from the prevailing winds. Her thimble had been red hot with the effort to reach this milestone. Now she would have the right place to bring up her son, with schools close by and a nursery in the town. This was what she had been working towards all these years. So what if it had damp patches on the walls and a funny iron range with a will of its own, rickety steps up the middle of the house and an outside toilet in the backyard? For joy of joys, it also had its own front garden, just a fenced off little patch with a latched gate and a privet hedge with a view right up into the fields and the sky. Nothing had prepared her for the pleasure of such a momentous move.

When Netta was not sewing bridal wear, she was sewing cushion covers and loose covers and decorating the little box room for Gus. Vida Bloom had pointed her to auction sales and house clearances where she picked up beds and a table, an oak linen chest and sideboard, a corner cupboard and a set of shelves for her son's room. She distempered this in duck egg blue with gingham check curtains made from an old tablecloth, stuck transfers on the painted wood and fresh linoleum on the floor. Then she bought a pegged rug from her neighbour to cover the stone flags in the kitchen. The walls were three feet thick and she had to bend under the beams here and there, but outside she could breathe fresh air and step out of her gate along the terrace and up on to the moors to stretch her aching back.

Netta set up her treadle machine and ironing board in the front parlour with a sheet on the floor to protect all her sewing. There was no electricity connected but the range heated the water and she lived off griddle scones and oven stews. At the end of each weary day she could close her own front door and sew again by storm lamp, listening to records on the wind-up gramophone that Arnie had kindly donated to the cause.

It was through him that she heard where Dixie was performing and how he visited her on station platforms each Sunday while she crossed the country with her theatrical trunk to the next Variety revue. Sometimes he brought his music and gave Netta a rendition of his latest Jazz piece. He sometimes stood in for someone at the Cellar but his mother didn't like him taking time off work the morning after so he pretended to be on some audit out of town and kipped down in Gus's room. Everything was ready and prepared. All Netta wanted now was her own child under her roof.

It usually happened somewhere between Carlisle and Dumfries as the train rattled northwards along the Solway coast line. Then all Netta's Griseley layers of confidence and purpose slipped away, along with her assurance that her plans were set fair for the future. Somewhere on that journey homewards her neatly pressed suit was exchanged for the cotton overalls of a subservient farmer's daughter. But this time it was all going to be different for all her self-imposed targets had been met.

She had taken the precaution of registering Gus's name at a little private nursery near by where he would be picked up after work each day. It had taken months to organise everything so that his homecoming would be as perfect as possible. At long last she was fired up to reclaim her son once and for all. This time she would take no refusals from Peg. They had had their fair share of him. Now it was his mother's turn.

What a shock Arnie and Vida would have when she introduced her son to them. Netta had taken the precaution of getting a statement of her financial affairs from the Penny Bank to prove to her father that her account was at long last in credit.

She had even made a confidential visit to Arthur Worthington, a local lawyer, to check what rights she had concerning her son. He had assured her that according to English law there should be no problem since Netta had never signed him over for adoption in the first place. She was entitled to ask for him back. As far as his investigations could discover, Gus was not listed as a ward of any court in Scotland. This knowledge armed her even further with the righteousness of her claim.

This time she made no song and dance about her return to Stratharvar, arriving unannounced and making her own way from the station by bus. She settled into the holiday routine as if nothing was changed but her heart was thumping for the right moment when she would spring her plans into action and take them by surprise.

Peg for once was relaxed in the glorious sunshine, chatty, even ready to admire the photographs Netta had brought of her cottage and some of her brides in spectacular creations lined up for approval. She showed Father her accounts to prove how well she was progressing, drew in a gulp of breath and dropped her bombshell at the tea table on the second night of her visit.

'It's time Gus came home with me. I have kept ma word and done everything you've asked of me. Stayed away when my fingers itched to hold him. Made no fuss with the lawyers and such like. Now I've got a lovely wee room for him to call his own and set everything in place for him to return with me at the end of the week. I never signed any papers so I know he's mine by rights. He's always been my son, hasn't he? I was just too feared to make a fuss.'

She watched the two of them shooting glances at each other, faces flushed with surprise at this outburst. Her thunderous news was bursting over their heads and for once they were silenced.

'We didna think it would be so soon . . .' Her father pushed his dinner to one side.

'Three years I've been waiting for this moment. He's all I've lived and worked for — to be successful enough to prove I can keep him myself. That was the promise. You knew it would come to this one day. It was what was agreed.'

'Dinna be hasty, Netta, bide a while more. The bairn'll have to get used to the move too. He's hardly seen much of you, has he?'

'And whose fault is that? I've come when I'm bidden and welcome. I've bit ma tongue not to just turn up.'

'Aye, you've done well enough but there's a sour tip on yer tongue the now. You cannae just spring this on us. I'll have to speak to ma lawyer. We have oor rights too!'

'What grazing right is this? Keep a bairn on yer pasture for three years and automatically he's yours to keep? He's no a cow!' she heard herself shouting.

'Ach, not that at all. In his eyes we're his mam and paw and

207

you're his Auntie Netta. Tell me how we just let him upsticks with you and flit to another country with no preparation? He's only three and at a difficult stage,' pleaded Peg.

'It seems tae me every stage is difficult. First he was a bairn and needed routine, then he was a toddler and now he's three. He can use a potty and talk. He's not at school yet. Do I have to wait until he's left the Academy before he's ready to live with me?'

'I think we should all sleep on this. Gus can be an awkward little cuss when he's having a tantrum. He's awful strong-willed the now. You've no experience. You just see him high days and holidays in short bursts. You come bearing gifts and sweeties, far too many in ma book, and he's all over you. I know . . . that's what visitors do. I suppose you need to do that to compensate for not being around, but you've no the full picture of things here.' Peg twirled her cup round and round on its saucer, hardly able to hold back the tears. Netta was not going to be swayed.

'At the end of the week he comes away home with me. We shall have a holiday on our own to settle him in his new surroundings. You don't know how long I've been preparing for this day. Don't try and stop me or I shall just walk out with my baby and you'll never see him again. It's not that I'm not grateful for what you've done here. I suppose I had to go and prove myself, set the heather ablaze after such a bad start. Now there's nothing left to prove.

'Griseley's a fine town. He'll have the best of both worlds there. You can come and visit him any time. I won't put restrictions on you. It's not as if I'm taking him to the other end of the world, now is it?'

'You might as well, for all the chance we'll get to leave the farm and visit. He's a country boy not a townie, used to roaming fields in safety, not traffic. How safe will he be in mills and muck?'

'There's enough country on our doorstep, rivers and riding schools, good schools and cities to visit. He'll have the best of both worlds. He'll soon make friends of his own age there. I shall see to that, don't worry.'

'And when you go to work all day? Where will he go then?

Cooped up in some nursery, I suppose, like a caged animal. Is that what you want for a farmer's boy?'

'He's not just from farm stock. Gus must have a broad enough education to choose his own path. Rae would have wanted that for him. This farm can still be part of his life, in the holidays.'

'Think what yer doing, Netta. Why such a rush? Why not come back here and get to know him better before you whisk him away?' Her father's eyes were frightened and suddenly he looked old and weary.

'I have my living to make. I cannae just leave it when it's just taking off. I like ma work too, you know! Giving girls what I didna have myself, I suppose. For three years I've had time to think about this day and I won't be fobbed off.'

Gus sat at his high chair, sensing the tension in the air. He climbed on to Peg's knee, sucking his thumb. For once she did not check him.

He began to say no to everything Netta suggested, hanging back, clinging on to Peg's apron and looking up at Netta with suspicion.

'Shall we go to Carrick beach today?'

'Nope!' Gus turned and ran out into the yard.

'Come in and let me wash your hands. We're going for a walk.'

'No! Go away.'

Gus ran round in circles like an aeroplane and refused to listen to her cajoling. She had to pick him up, kicking and screaming and wriggling from her grasp.

'Look, Gus . . . we're going to go on a big train soon. Shall we choose some toys to take for your room?' He looked at her as if she was speaking some strange language and laughed.

'How long's he been like this?' she asked Peg, puzzled by this fierce little boy who was always defying her.

'For months now. I told you, he's at that awkward stage. Tears and tantrums, paddiwacks and cuddles: that's all we get. He's needing a nap and his Yumpy bear.' But Yumpy was nowhere

to be found and Gus lay on the floor and howled like a puppy in agony until Angus couldn't stand the din any longer, whisking him over his shoulder. He took him up the stairs for a rest, settling him down with firm words.

For the first time Netta felt at a loss to understand his behaviour. This was not the little boy she knew and loved but a stranger who could bring the whole household to a standstill with his screams. Was he sickening for something? Was he normal?

She sneaked glances how Peg dealt with his tirades, by ignoring him mostly and then humouring him out of his screams. It was Father who really had the measure of him and took only so much cheek before he spanked the child's legs sharply and took him out of the room to cool down.

'I hope you'll be able to handle this when he tramples all over your bridal fabrics and shames you before your customers!'

'Oh, it won't come to that,' said Netta with a half-hearted smile. But as the rain poured down that week and she was cooped up in the farmhouse watching the rivers of water streaming down the windows like tears, she felt her confidence slipping away. What if she took him home and he screamed? How would she cope? What if he didn't settle at the nursery and they sent for her to take him away? How would she complete her orders? What if he was so upset he became ill and wouldn't be consoled? How would she console him?

Peg and Father withdrew into polite silence. They just left her to deal with Gus and whenever he played up he was passed to her to manage. Netta was exhausted and gave in to his whims to humour him. Gus was now confused as to who was running the show so went from one to the other of them in search of attention. Netta tried to appear confident but dogs and children can sniff a phoney at fifty paces and Gus was no exception.

To her horror she found herself afraid of the power of her child to humiliate her and frustrate her orders. He was sapping all her confidence. Parenthood was not some ready-to-wear garment you could slip on and off when it suited. It was like a shift, a hair

210

shirt at times. You wore it all the time and it could scratch and pinch next to the skin. She was feeling shirtless and exposed. But surely a parent and child could just settle down together if given privacy and time together?

Netta kept up her spirits by sorting through Gus's bedroom, dividing stuff to pack and stuff to keep at Brigg Farm.

The other word that Gus kept on screaming at her was: 'Why?'

'You're going to come with me.' She smiled excitedly but he looked at her with Rae's blue eyes and said, 'Why?'

'Because you belong to me now and we're going to live in our own little house . . .'

'Why?' he asked, not interested in her packing, pulling out his toys as she pushed them in the trunk.

'Because I'm your mummy now and we must live where I work.'

'Why?'

'Because it's the right thing to do. We're going to have a holiday, just you and me. Won't that be fine?'

'Holly . . . day?' He looked at her, not understanding. 'Why?'

Netta felt a flush of irritation at his questions. This was not how it was supposed to be. The stupid child didn't understand about holidays, but why on earth should he? Gus had never been on a proper holiday in all his three years. He didn't need to when there was sea and sand, lochs and forests, and such beauty all around him. Then it struck her that Gus had hardly left this farm at all, just the usual weekly visits to town and the clinic perhaps. This was his world and she was going to yank him out of it at the end of the week and transplant him into a strange Yorkshire town.

She could see Gus didn't understand why she was packing up his toys. Holiday was just a word to mimic. How could she explain to this little boy that he must leave everything he had ever known? Then, to her horror, with one sickening, gut-wrenching jolt of understanding, Netta suddenly realised that she was expecting young Gus to do what had been doled out to her three years

211

earlier only she had been an adult then: to be packed on a train, in exile from loved ones. Would he feel as abandoned and rejected and confused as she had then? Netta was nineteen and it had nearly killed her. How would she explain to a three year old that his little Shetland pony, Bruce, or his heifer calf couldn't fit into their luggage? That Peg and Angus must be left behind on the station platform?

Netta gazed through the window up to the brow of Stratharvar hill and prayed for help from her mother, but there was no guiding voice in her ear. Instead in her mind's eye there was a snapshot of Gus standing woebegone at the nursery school door, in his blazer and cap, with his pump bag wrapped across his shoulder, looking bewildered and lost: just a baby abandoned to strangers while she was busy at work. Who would wipe his nose and cuddle away his fears or find Yumpy when he wandered? Who would explain all this to him in Griseley?

Netta slid down the wall to the floor, crouching into a ball, weeping at her foolish fantasies. Gus was far too young to be separated from everything at Brigg Farm. Perhaps in two or three years? Perhaps when he was ready for school? How could she have been so selfish and blind not to see that this was all about her need of him, not his need of her.

You're taking him back like some trophy to show off, she told herself. Look what I've got everybody, like a rabbit out of a hat. Your precious secret, indeed! How could you be so ignorant and so selfish? You don't even know how parenthood works. You're going to have to learn a lot more about Gus before you try this exercise again.

Netta wept for all her false dreams and the shattering of precious hope then dried her eyes and went downstairs.

No one spoke at the tea table. The atmosphere was chilly before she broke the silence. 'I've been thinking over what you said, Father. It is too early to take Gus back with me. It would upset him, I see that now. It doesn't mean I'm not going to come back for him, only I shall wait until he can understand who I really am and why I

212

want him to live with me. So you can eat your tea in peace now, Peg. He's all yours for the moment.' Netta speared a spud with her fork, waiting for their grateful reaction.

'You've put us through hell this week, my lady. Don't you ever do that to us again! In his eyes we'll always be his parents and you know it! That's the way it'll stay for the next few years, until he's old enough to make up his own mind. You can come and visit, of course, far be it from us to deny you your rights! Being a parent isnae as easy as it looks, ma girl! You've a gey lot to learn.' And Peg tucked into her stew and dumplings with relish.

Saturday Teatime In Kendal 1949

The Kendal waitress was anxious to sweep up the café floor and close up. Netta's tea had gone cold while she fingered each of her precious photographs: staring sadly at the one of her stone cottage and thinking about that first lonely return there from Stratharvar. The nursery bedroom, smelling of paint and newness, looked accusing. The satin eiderdown quilt plumped up for its new occupant a haunting reminder. It quickly reverted to being Netta's summer sewing room.

She smiled wistfully at a snap of Gus taken on his first day in the nursery class in Stratharvar. How silly she'd been to think she could whisk him away with no thought for his feelings and needs. He was not some plaything to toss about to distract her from her loneliness, even now when they'd grown to understand each other better. How that one miserable experience had sapped all her resolve. Somehow it'd never been the right time to ask for him again. Until now. The years had just rolled by. Mother and son in two different worlds, always running in parallel lines like ladders, with her making visits like rungs across the divide, to keep in touch with his growing up.

Why can't you stand firm and rock solid when the panic waves come crashing over your head? Why do you waver like flotsam blown this way and that by the tidal forces around you? Why didn't you stand up to Peg just one more time? How will you face yourself if you run away now from the young friends you've created for yourself, your adopted family in Griseley? When it comes to those children you can be as tough as leather in their defence, but did you find them or did they find you?

6

JADE

'Colour of growth and cleansing,
The great harmoniser,
A resting point balancing
Past and future.'

Dancing On The Green, Summer 1948

What was the point of carrying on? Netta flung her sewing across the bedroom in frustration. Since her return from Stratharvar all the purpose of her work had evaporated in the summer heatwave. If she couldn't have her son by her side why bother building up all her connections, why stay here? Why not move back to Dumfries and start all over again, closer to home and not so easily ignored? There was nothing to keep her here but a dreary, back-aching job.

Suddenly her cottage felt dark and ice cold in the sunshine. She slumped into a lazy routine, shoving her appliqué work into the basket until Vida Bloom called in person to demand where all her trimmings for the bridal dresses were, catching Netta in her dressing gown.

'If you're going to let me down every time you have a setback then I shall have to find someone else to do my embroidery. I'm surprised at you! You never struck me as the type of girl to give in to despair. So you can't have the boy back yet? So you failed at the last hurdle? That's no reason to give up now. It's not the size of the dog in a fight, it's the fight in the dog, Izzy used to say. Think of that song Arnie plays about picking you up, dusting yourself off and starting all over . . . Where's that Dunkirk spirit gone?

'Come on, Netta, don't let me down now. I want you to get that business going. I'm looking forward to visiting your little bridal

shop, knowing I gave you a start. There, that's the truth told and the devil shamed.'

'You sound just like Peg on her high horse. I'm sorry, I've just let things slide. It's been an effort to drag myself out of bed each morning to face Miss Venables without biting her head off. I don't think I can stand much more of her.'

'What about your dancing class? Have you been to any summer gala displays or shows?'

'No, I can't be bothered,' Netta confessed.

'Can't be bothered? What sort of mother can't be bothered to make the best of herself, get out and face the world? What example is that to your son? Where would Arnie be if I didn't chivvy him to do his studies? No one hands success to you on a plate. You have to work every step of the way, every stitch of the way in your case, if you want to make your mark. Work hard and play hard. So if dancing's your hobby, then do it and stop whining about yer lot. There's many far worse off than you: all those poor souls in the concentration camps who lost their children, and refugee families. Your boy lives and breathes, never forget that. He is safe and secure with those who love him. One day he will be yours, God willing, but slouching about in a sulk won't get him back . . . getting on with your life will. There I go again!'

'I know you're right but I feel so wimpish to have come back empty-handed again. What must I do?'

'Give it time, Netta. Just time.'

Vida's words touched her heart for they were true and honest. Netta reached for her thimble and went back to her Thursday class. Jean Brownleys was especially pleased to see her.

'I know you're busy but I have a big favour to ask of you. The Scotia always dance at the Cottage Homes annual garden party and I want some of the younger girls to put on a wee bit display themselves for our patrons. They need costumes, something simple that our older girls can run up, but as usual it's all last-minute. Could you help them sort something out – a straight up and down shift with a bit

220

of decoration? I know it's a cheek, I was hoping to see you earlier. Have you been ill? We've missed you.'

'I've been very tied up, back home to Scotland, just family stuff,' Netta fudged.

'Nothing serious, I hope?' asked Jean, with her nursing voice and warm eyes. Netta smiled and shook her head.

'Can you come next week to meet my girls? A nice bunch, eager but a bit hamfisted at times.'

'Of course, I'll do my best.' Netta wondered what she was letting herself in for. The Oldroyds Home was only a name on a collecting box to her so Netta needed instructions on how to find the orphanage. The dancing troupe always performed at the open day. Netta imagined that it was one of those gala occasions when the tartans swirled before the great and the good of the district on an expanse of green lawn, lit by the summer sun glinting through broad-leafed trees.

The house itself was half-hidden up a country lane leading high on to the moor: a gracious Victorian millowner's mansion bequeathed to the town for the benefit of homeless orphans. There were bay windows like turrets at each corner of the main house and two blackened brick extensions to the building that made it look like a private boarding school. In the grounds were staff cottages and the stables were converted into a nursery for the infants.

Netta prepared a simple pattern for a short shift dress, like a ballet dancer's rehearsal tunic with slits to either side. She found some end-of-roll bridesmaid taffeta in four shades to donate for the costumes. The girls would have to make a simple side dart and sew up the side seams of each outfit then they could decorate them how they pleased. A wreath of crêpe paper flowers for a headdress would finish the costume off perfectly. True to her word, she walked through the country lanes to make her first visit to Matron Jean.

She welcomed her visitor warmly and proceeded to give Netta the full tour of the Home. She was a brisk, buxom ex-Army nursing sister who ran Oldroyds like a main line train station, keeping to a strict timetable of activities. Netta was immediately

221

reminded of Peg's maxim: 'An idle brain is the divil's smiddy'. She soon saw how Matron Brownleys liked to see everyone fully occupied in some useful task. When Netta saw the dormitories and the row of iron bedsteads crammed into each room she wondered when the children ever got any privacy to daydream and play alone. Perhaps it didn't matter. Since that her last encounter with Gus, she realised what she knew about young children wouldn't cover a button.

The boys and girls slept in the purpose-built wings and shared the large communal rooms that made up the original house. The old drawing rooms and gracious high-ceilinged reception rooms may have seen more gracious days but now they rang with the laughter and noise of children. There were scuffed skirting boards and smears up the wallpaper, a clutter of gumboots and gaberdines in the hallway. The managers had done their best to furnish it like a real home but the regulation green paint and treacle-coloured woodwork, with a canteen smell of boiled vegetables hanging over all, gave it an institutional air.

In the stable block the infants were playing on tubular seesaws, with nurses in starched uniform waiting for the older children to return from their day schools around the district. As they piled out of a school bus Netta was relieved to see that they were all in gymslips and cardigans, in the local school uniform, not set apart in the orphanage grey garb of the Cottage Home children who had come to Stratharvar School during the war.

Four girls of about fifteen were summoned to meet her, to be instructed how to cut out the pattern and make up the costumes. Four very different girls sat silently, taking in Netta's own pretty dirndl skirt and neat blouse with its Peter Pan collar, examining her strap sandals. There was Vera who wore thick-lensed glasses and Pat whose face was one blotch of erupting pimples. Beryl was the smartest of the bunch in a neat cardigan and bottle green gymslip with white ankle socks. She had braided her hair in a criss-cross of plaits over her head. Then there was Polly Liddell: a hawk's face on a sparrow's body. Her wide sad brown eyes reminded Netta of that

222

cornered look on Dixie's face at their first encounter at Brigg Farm: sharp, defiant and nervous.

Netta sat them down away from the rumpus of school children letting off steam along the corridor. She showed them her choice of material, a sketch of the simple outfit and the pattern block she had made for them to use. She brought out two already made up pieces and showed them where to place the darts and where to join the seams. Netta had checked with the matron that all the girls could tack up, hem and use a sewing machine. She suggested they each ran up five slips in one of the colours. They discussed how they might decorate the costumes with paper leaves or appliqué and told them she would return in two weeks to see how they were progressing.

Beryl asked about Maison Dorelle and if they could have a look at her workshop sometime as she was very interested in clothes. Pat and Vera nodded their heads but Polly said nothing. 'I would have to ask Miss Venables if you could look round once the shop is closed,' Netta told them.

'My little sister wants to be a ballerina, miss. She'll be a long time waiting for lessons,' Polly piped up in a squeaky voice. 'I think dancing's silly!'

'Why?' answered Netta.

'It's stupid prancing about,' she argued.

'Take no notice of her, Miss. She's a right Scrooge.'

'I'm not! My gran said . . .'

'Well, your gran's not here, is she, or you wouldn't be in here, would you? Or Lil or Jack?' This seemed to silence Polly's outburst and she folded her arms and said nothing more.

Netta was surprised when Polly turned up with the other girls after school in gaberdine macs and berets at the shop door. Netta tried to persuade Miss Venables to give them a tour but she looked down her nose and turned them away.

'We don't want riff-raff in here. Kindly refrain from making an exhibition of my premises without my permission in future.'

Netta asked them to wait outside and then took them all back home to show them some of the private sewing she was doing –

223

a bridal dress and bridesmaid's outfit – trying to make this tour interesting, showing them all the fabrics and the swatches of material, the half-made gowns. She demonstrated how the pattern block was turned into a cotton toile which was pinned on to the bride to form her own body shape. She showed them how the pattern was cut then on to the proper silk fabric, and fitted and refitted until it was perfect. They examined some of the pattern pictures in the sample books for customers to choose from, oohing and aahing over the drawings like love-sick brides.

Beryl and Polly called in by themselves the following week for a chat as Beryl wanted to ask if they needed a tea girl on Saturday afternoons in Dorelle's. Netta gently told her it would not be a good idea to ask there. Polly hung back, saying nothing, but she fingered the last of the bridal gowns slowly.

The day of the annual garden party drew closer and it was time to inspect the girls' costumes just in case they needed redoing. Netta hoped against hope that they had pressed everything at every stage as she had insisted. There was still time to repair puckered seams and dippy hems.

Lily Liddell and the other small dancers paraded in pink, lilac, blue and green costumes. Each of these efforts was good enough to use, Netta saw with relief, but one set of costumes jumped out at her for their quality and flair. These were not covered in paper leaves or felt appliqué but hand embroidered in satin stitch, quilted and padded into lustrous trailing ivy leaves with green toy beads threaded here and there to add texture to the decoration. There were hours of work in each of these dresses: work that would not have shamed an apprentice dressmaker.

'Who made these?' asked Netta, lifting up the costumes, intrigued by the sheer exuberance of this handiwork. No one spoke then Beryl pointed to the corner.

'Her, miss. Polly's a divil with embroidery. All day and all night, never leaves it alone. Allus stitching summat.'

Polly had gone scarlet and darted out of the room with the little girls.

'Where's she gone? I only wanted to congratulate her. You've all done very well.'

'Polly's gone with her sister to take her little brother a walk, he's still in the baby house. Not quite there is Jack Liddell but Polly's dead good with him.'

It was Matron Jean who told Netta the full story of how the Liddell family came to Oldroyds Home two years ago when their mother had been killed by a hit and run driver in a peasouper of a smog. She had been carrying the boy in her arms and as she was struck his head hit the kerb and he was left unconscious for several days. When he woke up he couldn't speak or walk. Polly had nursed him fiercely ever since. They were all brought into Oldroyds so as not to be separated but Polly was due to leave her school at the end of term and find work. Lily Liddell was nine and Jack four.

'She wants to be able to support them on her own, a tall order for a lass of her age,' Matron sighed.

Netta nodded: one look at those costumes had convinced her that Polly was a sewing natural, an apprentice worth training up. If ever she rose to the dizzy heights of having her own premises, then Polly was the helper for her.

The garden party was a great success and the scorching heatwave brought everyone searching for shade as they watched the little ones go through their paces in the home-made costumes. Netta was resting from the exertions of the Scottish dancing display, walking in the shade of the old woodland path, when a familiar voice called her name and she spun round. It was Drew Stirling.

'Netta Hunter . . . Thought it was you jigging in the sunlight. Must be mad, dancing in all this heat. So we meet again in the undergrowth!'

'Not you again! What are you doing here? And where's Miss Mackeever?' Netta shaded her eyes to see him standing under a branch in a pre-war crumpled linen suit and open shirt worn with a Panama hat cocked at a rakish angle and a cravat skewered with a gold pin.

225

'Lord knows. Buying up Harrogate, no doubt. This isn't her sort of occasion, and it's strictly business for me. I'm on the Management Committee for the Local Authority, a sort of MO. Come to lend moral support and all that.'

'You're still a doctor then?'

'Heavens above! why not? Doctors're a valuable commodity these days with this new National Health Service about to appear any day. "From cradle to grave" – where would you be without us? You don't just get chucked out for liking a dram or three. There'd be no quacks left if that was the case.

'No, I'm one of the new breed of public servant, school doctor if you must know, nothing too taxing. I just line them up, stick a needle in their arm or a stick down their throat, poke in ears, up noses, examine their skin like a vet. Try to catch anything before it hurts. And, boy, is there plenty to catch in Leeds with all the slums and shortages!'

He pulled out a hip flask from his pocket and offered it to her. 'Fancy a swig? All this jollification makes me thirsty. I never know where you're going to pop up. You make me nervous. Ginnie usually does enough talking for both of us. Come and have a stroll in the shade, just like old times in Park Royal.'

Netta brushed aside his offer of a drink but walked along the dusty path with him, trying not to catch the undergrowth on her best dancing dress. It was cool under the dappled shade with the music of a silver band echoing across the long garden.

'Jean Brownleys asked me to help the older girls do the costumes. I've enjoyed it. It's made me think how lucky we are to have families, however distant and troublesome.'

'Matron Jean is a good egg, just right for the place, efficient but motherly. The walls of this house should weep for some of the kids in here, orphaned by bombs and blitz. The worst cases are those who've been dumped here by their own parents, the children of some brief wartime fling. There's been an influx since demob of unwanted babies turfed out by returning soldiers who won't have some stranger's kiddy in their house as a reminder. There's a few brothers and sisters

226

who can't be separated, some backward ones nobody wants . . . a rag-taggle of sadness, I suppose. Anything you can do to support this outfit will be welcomed with open arms. Better than throwing a few pennies in a collecting box. I can see the wings sprouting out of yer back already!'

'And I can see your horns! Why do you always put things down?' Netta's heart was saddened by the thought of bairns with no home of their own. At least Gus wanted for nothing, especially love. It made her ashamed of all her past sulking. Vida was right, there are always others less fortunate than yourself. It was time to change the subject.

'How did you and Miss Mackeever meet?' she asked, more out of politeness than interest.

'At some horsy bash last summer. She fell at a hurdle and I was Sir Galahad to the rescue. Big Billie Mackeever made a fuss over me and the next thing I knew we were choosing rings. The poor girl ought to be marrying a horse, not me. I can't keep up with her in the saddle, she's like a streak of lightning and fearless over the jumps. We're a pair, the two of us, both stubborn as mules. That's another reason for keeping out of general practice – I can't see Ginnie sipping tea with the Vicar's wife in twinset and pearls or being the angel of mercy on the phone at two o'clock in the morning. She's not exactly the soul of discretion but a real sweetie. I sense you don't like her much?'

'We've not much in common coming from such different circumstances. I don't know the colour of her heart yet.'

'What a funny expression, Netta! I must call you that. I've only known you as Netta and it's not exactly Mrs Hunter as I recall.'

'How kind of you to remind me, Dr Stirling. The colour of a heart, my mother used to say, is lightened or darkened by shades of kindness and thoughtfulness, putting others at their ease, warmth and generosity. It's not the splash of brightness on the outside, all the clothes and possessions, but what's inside of us that matters. When you live by yourself you soon see who is friendly and who is not. Matron Jean has a heart of

227

gold, welcoming me to the Scotia Club. Ginnie's crowd made me feel an outsider, small and insignificant. I'm sorry but you asked me.'

'Aye, she's young and had it easy.' Drew came to his fiancée's defence. 'I'm sure she's a diamond at heart.'

'I hope not, for your sake. Diamonds are brilliant but very hard. I'm sure that's not what you meant. Here we go again, putting the world to right and making judgements.'

'You'll see some pretty black despair and blue hearts in Oldroyds. Life can be cruel and unfair to children through no fault of their own. To be honest, it's a grim job but Ginnie is a great distraction. She's the only girl I know who can dance all night and down her bubbly faster than me, but she seems to stay sober and be up with the lark each morning. Funny, isn't it?'

'Sewing does that for me. Times flies so fast when I'm lost in it.' Netta told him about her hopes to open her own bridal shop, fill a gap in the retail trade. 'All very modest, just in the planning stage, but one day I'll make it happen.'

'Good for you! I wish you luck. You'll need it with all the restrictions.'

'Apart from Gus, sewing's the only thing I ever wanted to do. Rationing can't last forever.'

They came to the parting of the ways back to the crowds and the tea tables. 'Hope to see you about this place, Netta, your help is much needed here.' Drew raised his Panama hat and smiled. She nodded and walked back to the Scottish dancers. It was time for their second display.

Drew watched the dancers swirling around the lawn and one in particular always caught his eye. It was funny how he could say anything to that girl and she listened as if she was interested. He would like to have told Netta how he had been approached by the Legion to talk to a group of ex-prisoners of war about aftercare and rehabilitation. There was some concern about the Jap POWs who were still not fully recovered from their ordeal. Some of the stuff they came out with to each other was a revelation to Drew. His

228

own European experiences had been harrowing enough but theirs were something else.

They usually sat in a pub on a no name, no shame basis, awkward and suspicious at first. When they saw he could down the pints as quickly as they he felt he was halfway to gaining their trust. It was going to be a hard slog to open them up and he was not sure what good it would do to reopen past horrors. There was some evidence from the Military Rehab Units that talking in groups was useful but he had yet to be convinced.

From now on Oldroyds was no longer just a name but a place where Netta was always welcome to visit. At weekends she sometimes took some of Lily Liddell's friends for a picnic, high among the heather on the moors, and wondered if the Scotia Club dancers might band together to plan an outing for the children to Bridlington by coach. How she wished that she could share her own beautiful Carrick seaside with those less fortunate than herself.

Only two weeks later, when she called into see her adopted sewing group, she was met at the door by Drew. He was wearing a white coat, his face like thunder. He held up his hand firmly and shooed her out of the door.

'Out, Netta. I'm afraid the place is in quarantine. No visitors. We've got fever in the place. It's in the district . . . all this hot weather's a breeding ground. Dreadful business. Infantile paralysis in some cases, kids going down like flies. I've just rushed three off to the isolation hospital for tests. One's in a bad way, I fear. Respiratory failure.'

'My sewing girls – Polly, Beryl, Lily?'

'Just tummy bugs but poor little Jacky Liddell's very sick. I don't hold out much hope. Don't come any further, call back in a few weeks. I'm sorry to bear such sad news.'

'What about Jean?'

'Rushed off her feet but fine. Don't worry.'

'Are you OK? You looked washed out.' She noticed he was grey about the gills and his cheeks were sunken again.

229

'Fine. Oh, what the hell? Fancy a brew? Come in the office.'
Over a cup of Camp coffee and sterilised milk, Drew Stirling began
to relax.

'It makes me fume to think of the unfairness of all this, you
know. These kids deserve the best, and what do we do? we herd
them all together in dormitories so that any Tom, Dick or Harry
sort of infection goes on the rampage amongst them like wildfire, far
faster than if they'd been in their own homes. It's always the weakest
who suffer in this world. I hope this new National Health Service will
iron out such social differences but it's only early days and I have my
doubts. I'm just impatient, which makes matters worse.

'A bad start in life is a bad start, the constitution is weakened
and impaired and easily defeated. Poor housing and food, damp
conditions, it doesn't help to fight illness.'

'Is that the cry of conscience I'm hearing? So much for the
dispassionate distance of a school doctor. Yer mask is slipping, Dr
Stirling. Shame on you!' Netta teased. He shot her glance and she
blushed pink.

'How do you manage it? Each time we meet you keep me on
the straight and narrow. Just when I was about to pull the golden
liquid from the filing cabinet, up you pop like Tinkerbell to call,
"Time, gentlemen, please." I think I'm going to need you as my
friend. Who else knows me like you do? You've cheered up a dark
morning. Call again any time.' Drew smiled and Netta suddenly
felt the heat of his gaze.

'I really came to see Jean but I'll call back later. Give my love
to all the patients. Tell them I'll see them when I can. I must go.
Thanks for the coffee but I'll leave it, if you don't mind.'

'Me too, it's awful stuff.' Drew rushed to open the office door
for her in a flurry of mock courtesy which made Netta smile.

'See you around, Drew.'

'My pleasure, Netta. Away to your needles.'

In the weeks that followed such tragic events when the town was
full of the dreaded polio epidemic, Netta found herself drawn to

Oldroyds, to Jean but especially to Polly and her sister Lily. Their brother Jack had not survived his illness. She caught glimpses of Drew Stirling in the distance. He waved and would have made his way to her side but she chose to keep her distance. His friendship was a marker of sorts around some of the greatest milestones of her life: her breakdown, her newfound sense of purpose here in Griseley. It was a strange friendship of conspiracy based on mutual secrecy, as sort of affinity which each of them felt.

Outwardly, she supposed, they made an odd pairing: he a doctor and manager and she only a seamstress and volunteer. He was almost a married man and she would never be any part of their circle so it was best to keep to the surface of things, not delve too deeply into feelings and fears. She was here to support the Liddells after all.

Netta dreaded that first meeting with Polly after the outbreak. She did not know what she was going to say to her. The girl came up the stairs in the cottage looking like crumpled linen, in an over-large smock with pins already lined up on her chest like medals. She'd brought her dolly bag containing a clean handkerchief and a silver thimble. Her eyes were tired and red-rimmed, hair scraped back in a dancer's ponytail making her face look pale and pinched and her ears stick out. Netta ushered her into the workroom amongst the other silent girls, trying to put them at ease. *Just watch what I do and ask whenever you see me doing something you don't understand.*

'Yes, miss.'

'Mrs Hunter will do, Polly. Tell me where you learned to do such lovely embroidery?'

'My granny, Miss . . . er, Mrs Hunter. She taught me to do tatting, crochet work and lace. She was a ladies' maid and did alterations, but then her fingers swelled up into sausages and she couldn't hold a needle so she taught me. She died . . .'

'And your mother, could she sew?'

'No, miss, she just stayed in the back kitchen baking. Lily liked baking.'

'And your father? What did he do?

'Dunno, miss, can't remember much about him.' Polly bent her head, embarrassed by this grilling in front of the others.

'I was so sorry to hear about Jack . . .'

'It's OK.'

'How's Lily?'

'She's OK now.' And that was the sum of conversation that Netta could raise from Polly Liddell, but her concentration and interest were like blotting paper, soaking up all the sights and tasks. Netta recognised another who was losing her sorrows in her work.

She showed them some fashion magazines where the New Look was at last hitting bridal fashions and customers were clamouring for full or ballerina-length bell-shaped skirts, with tight-fitting waists in the Christan Dior padded style. Pathé News was a great inspiration too, showing the latest Paris collections. Shawl collars and off-the-shoulder dresses with boned bodices were much in demand, with beading and lace trimmings. Beryl wanted to make a straight skirt with a kick pleat at the back.

Netta started them off by making fancy bows, showing them how to line and stiffen the bow, to shape and design it for different lengths and effects. Polly was a stickler for detail and more interested in fancy embellishments than overall design. They were going to make a good team if Polly could relax into her sewing, but now was not the moment to pursue the matter.

Showdown

Netta paused twenty yards from Dorelle's to gather herself for the day's onslaught. As she saw the discreet sign on the three-storey soot-blackened building her heart sank. The shop was along a smart parade of similar properties with overhanging glass canopies that sheltered shoppers from the squalls of rain off the moors. There was a solid, no-nonsense quality about this row of buildings: the very stuff of smart Griseley. Dorelle's was the exception. One day Netta would have her own premises down this row and they would be the smartest.

Miss Venables was waiting for admiration of her latest attempt at window dressing. 'Where have you been? You're late again.' She pointed Netta towards the back room.

Netta engrossed herself in the usual stream of drab outfits to be altered, bending her head to the daily tasks. It was Maybelle's day off and there were just the two of them in the showroom. It was quiet first thing. Madam Maudie would demand that the mirrors be polished and it was Netta's job to vacuum the velvet pile of the dove grey carpet, dust the copper beech leaves arranged in a cracked lustre vase and check the cubicles for any stale smells while Miss Venables just checked the post and tidied along the hangers, picking over the stock as if it had fleas.

Dorelle's customers were not window shoppers. A price tag was of no consequence to many of them so none was evident. From the

233

moment they walked through the door they would be at the mercy of Madam Maudie.

It was the future Mrs Herbert Batley of Batley's Mill who opened the batting on that miserable wet morning, coming in to make the final choice for her bridal two-piece outfit.

'I'm going to try on that pink job again – the one you ordered for me, Miss Venables, just to be sure.'

Netta brought down the sample dress and jacket. Elsie Cumberbatch peeled off her clothes and tried it on. 'What do you think?' She had squeezed herself into 'Aurora' but it was a tight fit. Elsie was to be the second wife of one of the wealthier mill owners; a war widow whisked from her loom in Cinderella fashion. Poor lassie would never have dared cross these snooty portals once upon a time but her husband's wallet, being as full as any in Griseley, meant his intended would have only the best of wedding outfits.

'What's the problem?' sniffed the proprietress. 'Mrs Cumberbatch, aren't we satisfied?' Netta could clearly see the bulges round the waist and the unsuitable colour.

'Not really, I just felt like another look before I make up my mind. I do love the idea of a two-piece but it's a bit like candy floss on me hips and it sticks out a bit . . .' This was only a sample model but the client was already hesitating at the sight of herself in the mirror. 'Herbie will want me to stick out but not this much. It's both us big day after all. What do you think, Jeanette?'

Netta took in a deep breath. The drab beetroot shade drained all the colour from Elsie's plump baby-faced prettiness and the platinum blonde fluff of her expensive perm. She had also expanded since the last session and the length was unforgiving.

It was written in tablets of stone that no alterations minion should venture an opinion. This being the case many customers were allowed out of the door in the wrong length of sleeve or hemline or the wrong design for their shape, whatever the price of their dress, grateful to have anything new to wear. Every defect was put down to 'shortages in the trade' and the 'best goes for export', which Netta knew was blatantly untrue. 'We never lose a sale. If needs be, we sell our ladies short;' was Maudie's secret maxim. Quality and class meant dishonesty and disrespect in this establishment.

Elsie was going to look like a puce beer barrel in that suit. Maybelle was not here to run the show and Miss Venables was called away by telephone so Netta whispered, 'It's not the best colour for you, it drains your lovely suntan, and where will the honeymoon be?' She paused, seeing Miss Venables approaching fast to clinch the sale.

'To Madeira like the cake – quiet but rocky, my Herbie says. Just his sort of place. Still, at our age . . . The gardens are supposed to be nice. Not the same second time around, I reckon.'

'Well, you'll look lovely on your day, I'm sure, but maybe not in that pink, and I'm not sure about the waistline. The "Aurora" is quite a tight-fitting suit, it would need re-shaping completely. Is that style really what you had in mind? Another shade perhaps, a larger size. Did we try on the "Margaret Rose"? It's a bit simpler . . .'

'It looked a bit plain on the hanger, didn't it, Miss Venables? But if you think . . . is me bum getting in the way of things or me tum this time? Eeh, what it is to be young and have a figure like you! At least Madam Maudie keeps me company.' Elsie was clearly wavering.

Miss Venables flushed with fury and pointed a dagger-like finger to the stockroom. 'The seamstress will get it for you. Sometimes dresses that look limp on a hanger are stunning on the figure.'

Netta scurried to find their largest sample of 'Margaret Rose'. Maudie whisked away the 'Aurora' and guided Elsie into the new dress and jacket, emphasising all its good points. 'It's a generous cut, with three-quarter sleeves and a plain neckline. Ideal with jewellery, don't you think?' She stood back to admire the effect. 'We can start with this and add any details you require.'

The art of selling was simple; a dress was bought not sold. But this one was even worse than the first. Netta noted with disappointment that it was even less flattering on Elsie's sturdy hips and there were plenty of Batley pearls and clasps to emphasise her bulging bosom. Elsie was smiling as she twirled before the carefully chosen flattering mirror ordered especially for the cubicles to lengthen the figure.

'You know, Jeanette, you're right as usual, this drains me too. I could get some wear out of it for parties if it were a better shade, happen, but I'm not sure . . . It always cheers me up, coming in here, to have your honest opinion. I'll call back when yer new stock comes in and try again, happen. Cheery bye.'

Silence thundered in the cubicle as Netta gathered up the outfit.

'How dare you lose us that sale, Jeanette? She would have taken the first one but for your big mouth!' hissed Miss Venables after Elsie's departure.

'But it didn't suit her and she's a nice lady. It's her big day, surely she has the right to look her best?'

'My clients are grateful to know that our label is in the back of their dresses. That's sufficient in itself. These days people are grateful for what's on offer. Giving them too much choice only confuses them. You have been very disobedient. I've a good mind to give you your notice . . .' Miss Venables paused, arms folded, waiting for her menial to grovel in repentance.

'And I've got a good mind to snap your mean hand off and take it! How can you face your conscience, knowing that Dorelle's is famous in Griseley for its three Ds: designs as dull as dishwater fit only for the three Bs-batty, boring old biddies!'

'Get your coat on this minute, you impudent hussy, and never darken my door again.'

'It'll be a pleasure. And regards to "our father". He still seems to be running the show from the other side.'

Netta flounced into the autumn rain with a flourish. How sweet the air was after the staleness inside. Then she stood stock still, sweating. What had she gone and done? But nothing would induce her to step back inside and as she hurried along the pavement, not looking, she bumped straight into Elsie Cumberbatch, coming out of the bakery clutching a bag to her bosom. They collided.

'In for your elevenses? Don't look what I've bought but I was that fed up with being fair, fat and forty I bought mesel' a vanilla slice to cheer myself up. You look like you lost a bob and found a tanner. Was Madam Maudie mad I never bought that dress? You were right, I looked like a jelly mould — all of a wobble.'

'I've had ma cards, if you must know.' Netta smiled weakly.

'For speaking up about them suits . . . I've a good mind to give the old skinflint a piece of my mind! Poor love, what'll you do?'

'What I should have done months ago. Set up on my own and give Maison Dorelle a run for its money.'

'You do right, love. And let me be yer first customer. It's not too late to run me something up, is it?' Elsie rummaged in her bag for a pencil. 'Here's my address. Come and see me, bring some patterns. If I'm going to spend an arm and a leg, I'd rather be suited by you, eh?' She smiled at her little joke, shoving a note into Netta's hand and the paper bag. 'If you're going to run a tape measure round me, I'd better give this cake to you as a downpayment. Next week, then?'

Netta walked up the hill from Griseley in the pouring rain, her mind racing with all the possibilities. How would she manage, working from home on her own? A new stitch overlocking machine would be necessary to see to the hemming but everything else would have to do. Then she remembered there was no electricity to power any machine. She would need to rent a small workshop somewhere plus a little showroom for her samples and stock. There would have to be a bank loan and an order book, working capital to set up the venture . . . so much to think about.

On the mat was letter from Dixie asking if she would run up a cocktail dress for Christmas, something spectacular, a surprise for Arnie. She was sending the fabric through the post for Netta to look at and would come for a fitting as soon as she could. Another order! What she needed was printed cards and an advertisement in the local Echo. What should she call herself?

Fear stalked Netta through the night; fear of failure, fear of not paying the rent, fear of not being up to the job, running out of ideas, making a hash of precious cloth. Fear drove her to the sketch pad to sketch out a shape that would suit Elsie's figure.

In the small hours she banked up the stove and made a bowl of comforting porridge to soothe the gnawing pangs in her churning

237

stomach. *Fear made her write down every penny she would need to survive for three months ahead. Her savings would have to last. Perhaps Father would chip in too. She would have to have extra help with basic work. Perhaps Vida Bloom might help and introduce her family in the wholesale trade. Now was the time to ask if Polly would like to be her apprentice. So much to think about . . .*

She dozed and woke suddenly with a poster before her eyes: LET NETTA NICHOL DESIGN FOR YOU. Why not use her real name? It was sharp and neat. Jeanette Hunter was only the pin-picker at Dorelle's. Netta Nichol was her own boss. A new name for a fresh start.

Follow what you love and it will lead you where you need to go . . . who was it had said that? Out of the window she saw the turquoise dawn rising from the east, streaked with pink and orange. It would set the shepherd tapping his barometer but after such a dark night it was just the sign Netta needed. Today was her new beginning.

Christmas, 1948

'Not another present for wee Gus! Netta, you spoil that wean! I ken they Pelham Puppets is all the rage in the toy shop windows but are you sure that's what he wants? Surely those farm animals are more up his street?' said Dixie, grabbing her friend's arm away from the tempting display.

'Oh, but puppets are more fun. He can make his own theatre and plays. I can't decide between the Wizard, the Cowboy or the Soldier.'

'Come on, hen, I'm starving. You can come back later. This wind is going right through me,' moaned Dixie, wrapping her fur coat round her chest. It was a chill north-easterly blowing down on to Briggate in Leeds and the first flakes of snow landed on her sleeve. Dixie was appearing here in the pantomime Aladdin as the top speciality act. This outing was a chance to hand over her party dress and for Netta to find presents for Brigg Farm. Gus was not going to get another stuffed toy this year whatever the cost.

They found seats in a smoky café off the Headrow and collapsed with all their shopping bags to sink their teeth into toasted teacakes dripping with margarine which tasted like farm oil.

'Hand it over then, how much do I owe you?' Dixie peeped in the box. 'Arnie didn't see it, did he?'

'No, why should he . . . but it's all crumpled in that little box, why couldn't you let me bring it to the theatre later? What's the

239

rush?' The red slipper satin sheath with the sari silk overskirt streaked with gold threads was going to look stunning by candlelight. True to her word Dixie had turned up for a fitting, strangely silent for once, examining the dramatic effect without her usual banter.

She puffed a loop of blue smoke into a ring. 'I want it to be a surprise for him, that's all. How's it going? I'm so glad you got off yer bahoochie and left yon dragon's lair of a dress shop. Is it working out?'

'Early days but my orders for spring are looking better than I expected. Elsie Batley has passed my name on to her friends. I found a small room, not exactly the Parade but near enough for clients to call in for fittings. Polly will start after Christmas when she's fifteen. I wish I'd done it sooner. I shall go to Stratharvar, of course. I can't wait to see Gus's face . . .'

'Promise me you'll send for the bairn now? Snatch him if you have to but stop shilly-shallying. Waiting to see if things get better never works, believe me.'

'Is anything wrong with you and Arnie?' asked Netta seeing the furrow of concern flash over Dixie's smooth brow.

'Just the usual. His mammy sticking her nose into everything, making him feel guilty. Nags, nags nags at him all the hours when his heart's not in the jobbie. Can she see it? There's none as blind as them as dinna want to see . . . She'll learn the hard way. Poor lad's torn in twa pieces. Still, ye can shape a bairn's coat but not the way he wears it.'

'Dixie, what's that supposed to mean?'

'Wait and see, hen, wait and see, And thanks for the tip. Show us yer presents then.'

Netta pulled out a paper bag full of little naked dolls with brassy gold hair in ruffles. 'Not exactly Rosebuds but imitations for the girls at Oldroyds. I'm going to dress them up as wedding dolls for Lily Liddell and her gang . . . a job lot from the market hall. I got some face powder and lipstick for Beryl and Polly. I do hope it's all still on for Oldroyds Home to come backstage after the panto? Thanks for letting them have those seats at the front. The managers are giving them a special tea at the Albany Hotel and then on to your theatre. What a great outing on Christmas Eve!'

'An' we can promise you a good show this year. The Principal Boy's not exactly David Whitfield but Danny Larado can croon the pants off you, I promise. Not a dry eye in the hoose!'

'I just hope it doesn't snow and block us all in like last year. My first proper Yorkshire Christmas and I thought I'd come to the Arctic wastes!'

'When are you going north?'

'For New Year's Eve. I can't wait to see Gus's face when I produce two puppets. We can make our own show.'

'Netta, will you call and see Vida sometime over Christmas? I'm not exactly welcome in the hoose. Now I'll have to love you and leave you, hen. Time for rehearsals. See you sometime and here's what I owe you.' Dixie plonked down the pound notes, gathered her parcels, gave Netta a theatrical kiss on the cheek. She fled out into the darkening street, leaving more questions than answers hanging in the air.

There was so much to finish off before the Christmas holiday: two last-minute alterations, dressing the Rosebud dolls, sending off the Christmas parcel. The Stratharvar parcel arrived early and Netta shoved it under her little artificial tree. She was going to be spending Christmas alone again. It was her choice but that didn't mean there weren't decorations to be put up, paper chains and lanterns, bringing in holly and ivy from the garden to trim up her fireplace. She was so busy there was no time to brood. The girls from Oldroyds would bring Christmas to her hearth. Each would have one of the sequinned quilted stars she had made for her tree.

On Christmas Eve it was snowy enough to look like a Christmas card. The road was still clear down into Griseley town centre and the mill chimneys sparkled with hoar frost as the charabanc edged its way cautiously from Oldroyds, packed with excited children, steaming up the windows and writing love hearts and messages for passers by to see. Netta didn't know who was the more *thrilled to be going to the theatre on Christmas Eve: she or they.*

Tea was a bunfight, a noisy affair with paper hats and crackers. Father Christmas, who looked suspiciously like their Medical Officer, handed round sweets and balloons. Then they trooped the party across the slushy streets to the theatre where they chattered like flocks of starlings until the house lights went down.

As the orchestra struck up the Intro, the children's faces lit by the footlights were a picture of anticipation. Matron and her assistants sat scattered among the boys, with Drew and Maggie, Netta and Mary Finlayson, sitting alongside the girls. How they all jeered at wicked Uncle Ebenezer, cheered on the handsome Principal Boy crooner and Princess Sulima, and shouted at Widow Twankey to watch out for the ghosts hiding behind the screen. Then Karenza the Snake Woman came on as the Genie's mate in a turban, doing a fire-eating turn. Lily Liddell cooried into Netta's lap as poor Aladdin was trapped in the treasure cave, believing every word of the drama. Netta saw Drew down the row, fast asleep, and wondered how many noggins Father Christmas had knocked back in the Albany. He was so unpredictable.

At the end of the show the children trooped backstage to meet the stars, tongue-tied and shy with Danny Laredo, gobsmacked by all the glamour of scenery, costumes and bustle. Dixie showed them her sequinned snake suits and headdresses, her box of make-up sticks, the dressing rooms and the scenery stacked up behind the stage. The stage was cleared enough for the children to have a bottle of fizzy pop, a bar of chocolate wrapped in amethyst paper and a packet of crisps each while they collected autographs from their favourite stars.

'Isn't it grand? And Father Christmas is on his way too,' yelled Lily over the back of the coach seat later. 'Matron says we're last on his rounds so we've not to wake early and put the light on or he'll think he's been and we'll get passed o'er! Is he coming to your house, miss?'

Netta nodded. 'He's already been and left some parcels under my tree because grown-ups can be trusted not to open them until Christmas Day.'

'Will you come and see what he's brought us?'

'Of course, in the morning. I'm coming for dinner.'

They all sang carols as the coach chugged up the hill but Polly was looking out of the window, not joining in. Netta touched her arm. 'Are you thinking about Jack?'

'Mrs Hunter, do you think he's with Mam in Heaven?'

'Wherever he is, I'm sure he knows you're thinking about him with love, and yer mammy too. I lost my own mother when I was about Lily's age. Each Christmas I hang up a star on the tree, one for her and one for Rae who died in the war. It doesn't seem right, does it, to be enjoying ourselves without them?'

'No. Lily can forget, she's still nobbut a babby, but I can't. It's not fair. Why him? He'd not done owt wrong.'

'I don't think it works like that, Polly. Some diseases are too strong for us, but one day soon someone will find a way to cure them.'

'Jack would have loved that show, all them lights and noises and colours. I'd love to make dresses and costumes like them. The way they shimmered in the light . . . Theatre costumes have to be different from everyday ones, don't they? They have to stand out and sparkle so you can see them right up in the Gods . . . sparkling like lights in the dark. Fireworks. It cheers you up to see all them colours. I suppose wedding dresses are a bit like that, an' all?' Polly smiled and her tired face relaxed for once.

'I've never thought of it like that before but you're right. For one day in her life a girl puts away her everyday clothes to be lit up like a holy candle, shining before the altar so everyone can see her.'

'A bit of magic, like a rainbow painting the sky. There isn't much magic about in Leeds, is there? But we're magicians, making costumes for magic to happen. Was your wedding magic?'

Netta felt her answering voice tremble. 'It was wartime, not that long ago but things were different. Many of us were calico brides, not shiny satin ones like nowadays, but we felt like shining stars inside just the same. Yes, love, it was a sort of magic.'

No use telling this girl that magic never lasts. Polly knew that already.

Matron took the helpers back to her office for a snifter and they helped her wrap up the last of the children's presents. Afterwards Drew offered to run everyone home. He was in no hurry to drive up to Ilkley, making sure he did a complicated detour which dropped Netta off last of all.

'Happy Christmas!' He paused and shut off the engine. 'Can I come in and see your decorations?' He'd been feeling decidedly queasy all evening, the after effect of all the kids' shouting and the whisky.

'Shouldn't you be going back? Ginnie will be waiting for you . . .'

'Like hell she will! The party's been going on for hours already. I'll turn up when most of them have gone. To be honest I can't stand some of the hunting crowd — such bores. Horses, horses, horses is all they talk about. It's cold standing out here but the view looks good to me.' He wasn't looking at the stars.

'You're half cut again. Oh, Drew, I thought you'd turned your back on the bottle,' Netta sighed, green eyes wide with disapproval.

'It's Christmas! I shall have to tank myself up to get through Christmas with the Mackeevers.'

'What about your own family?'

'Far away overseas still.' He paused in the doorway to the little room. 'This is cosy and beautifully furnished. All handmade, I expect?'

'Of course.'

'What's under the tree? Parcels — goody. Go on, open them. It's almost midnight.'

'Not quite. I'll make some spiced tea, hot and strong and then you can help me open Gus's parcel. The rest can wait, all the bedsocks and hot water bottles, hankies and soap.' Netta was dying to read the Christmas letter from the farm and to think of Gus tucked up

*in his room with that stocking waiting at the foot of his bed. It was
nearly Christmas Day after all.*

*She brought out some tree candles that gave a soft rosy glow to
the room and stoked up the fire to put the kettle on the hob. Drew
had had enough booze for one night. Tearing open the brown paper
and sealing wax, she plunged into the parcel for the Christmas card:
a snow scene with glittery frosting on the front and a letter neatly
attached in Father's square hand. She smiled as she read out:*

Dear Netta,

Peg and Gus join me in wishing you all the best
for the season. We hope you have a lovely day with
your friends in Griseley and our gifts make up for the
disappointment of not being together this Hogmanay.
We hope you don't mind but we'll be away this Ne'rday,
visiting Peg's cousin, Eileen Huston.

She's in the family way and can't travel to us this
year so we decided on a wee change so Gus could play
with Morag. It'll make a break for Peg. I've got John
Paterson's son, Alan, to do the milking. Hope you're not
too disappointed but I'm sure there'll be plenty going on
for young fry in Yorkshire. Have a Guid New Year.

Aye yours,

Father, Peg and Gus

*Drew watched Netta fling the letter across the room and burst into
tears. 'How could they just spring this on me? So that's why their
parcel arrived earlier than normal this year and I just pushed it under
the tree as a treat to savour. I did what I always do, saving it for
Christmas Day. It's not fair, Drew, they know how much a visit
means to me! I've been so busy trying to build up the business,
but not to see Gus or be able to give him his present . . . If only
I'd known in time . . . to make arrangements, go on the train for
Christmas. How stupid! They think I don't care. Perhaps it's not
too late to catch a train on Boxing Day. Oh, Drew, it's not fair!'*

'I'm sorry, poor you. Not much of Christmas then but we can have our own party here. I've a bottle of wine or two in the car and some chocs. Light the candles, put on the gramophone and find some glasses. We can cheer each other up.'

They sat by the firelight, glasses drained, listening to the Winter movement of Vivaldi's Four Seasons, huddled on cushions on the floor. Drew watched the flames flickering in her emerald eyes. He was in no hurry to shift himself to the grander party up the road. Their silence was oddly comforting, their friendship a strange hidden sort of affair, unknown to others.

He wished he didn't drink so hard and fast and wondered what drove him to seek solace in a bottle. Now was not the time to ask such a deep question, when Netta was so grateful for company, so down at heart about her letter. They were leaning against each other, swaying with the rhythm of the music, letting the sound soothe away all the tension. So much so that they slid slowly down on to the flag stones and the peg rug and lay back, laughing.

'This the true spirit of Christmas, Netta: a warm welcome on a cold night, the laughter of children, the heat of good wine in the belly, and above all to be side by side with a good friend – one who understands and doesn't judge. Better than a load of stuffy wallahs in dinner jackets blethering about nothing.'

'Thanks, Drew, you've made this evening bearable. At least someone wants me.'

He raised himself on to his elbow to admire the view again. 'Netta you're lovely, how many times have I told you that?'

'Words, Drew, only words. That's all I've ever had for years. I'm still young but I feel a hundred sometimes.'

'Let me show you how lovely you are with those sea-green eyes and foxy hair.' He reached over and ruffled her hair playfully. 'And I like the way your nose tilts up like a ski jump.' He fingered her cheek and put his lips to hers in a long and lingering kiss.

The power of his touch shot through Netta's body, waking her from this half-dream. 'No, Drew . . . don't. It's not fair. I can't. There's Ginnie . . .'

246

'If I know my wife to be, she'll be hard at it with someone under the mistletoe. No one knows . . . We could be good together, you and me.'

'Call me old-fashioned but two wrongs don't make a right. Please, get up. My arm's gone to sleep. Don't spoil what we have.'

'What've we got that's so different from anyone else? I think you're special. I want to kiss you now. Where's the harm?'

'If you think me some silly damsel you can disarm like a knight of old when you're sozzled and I'm squiffy then you don't think of me as that special. You can go right now, Drew Stirling! I pity your poor bride if you take every drunken opportunity that falls your way.'

'I'm not drunk, just merry. Don't be such a spoilsport.'

Netta sat bolt upright and looked down at him with a scowl.

'Take a long, hard look at yourself. Call yourself a doctor? I pity any patient who comes to you for a stitch when you're half seas over. What is it drives the demon in you? How can you be so unreliable, so slap-happy and unaware? How many times have you been dried out?'

'I didn't know you were a card carrying Temperance Worker.' Drew sat up, hair standing out like a hedgehog, puzzled by her change of tone.

'I know when to stop. You can't. That's the difference between us. I can't face Christmas without seeing my child and you can't face anything without a drink. What a pair of misfits we are! I don't like Ginnie very much, but I won't lie here with you whispering sweet nothings in my ear either. Go and sort yourself out. Don't make matters worse than they already are for me.'

Netta rose pulling down her skirt with embarrassment. Drew staggered to his feet, looking woebegone.

'I was only trying to help . . .'

'I know, but you've just gone and spoiled it all, so hop it.'

'Shall I pop in to see you again?'

'What do you think? I'm not your patient.'

'Perhaps not then. I'll find my coat.' He shuffled to the door and

247

cracked his head on the beam. 'Damnation! Must you live in such a tiny room.'

'It suits me fine. Mind how you go.'

Drew paused at the gate. 'Happy Christmas to you, Netta.'

She picked up a lump of frozen snow and threw it at his back. It cracked him on the neck. Drew turned round in surprise but the door was already shut.

Window Shopping In Kendal, May 1949

The shops were shutting for the day as Netta dawdled down Strickland Gate, browsing in the shop windows with tired eyes. She was putting off the moment of decision, wasting the best of the afternoon driving light, reluctant to return to the van and take the long winding road south. She looked at young couples pushing go-chairs with babies in sun bonnets, their mouths plugged with rubber dummies. There were still busy shoppers trundling along the street together, peering in the windows or waiting at bus stops; older couples hand in hand enjoying an afternoon stroll, unworried by the sun setting behind the buildings. She thought of Drew and Ginnie planning their wedding as they cantered over the moors together. All the world was paired up and she felt utterly alone. Then she saw the dress.

It was turquoise, shimmering like a peacock's feathers, a shantung silky fabric that caught the light. It had a simple line, a bold shawl collar with no sleeves. It was perfect, safe and unobtainable for the shop was now in darkness. She stood transfixed by the colour, drinking in its effect. She thought of kingfishers by the river flashing in the sunlight and the sea shimmering on a summer's day, rippled with silver. Turning her back, she hurried down to the parking space by the river bank.

7

TURQUOISE

'Colour of inspiration,
Sadness and yearning
Coolness of heart to
Keep plodding forwards.'

Into 1949

In that saggy hummock between Christmas and New Year when everyone was back at work and the children at Oldroyds received visits from whatever relatives they could muster, Netta stayed indoors with just her sewing for company, mulling over her amorous tussle with Drew on Christmas Eve and wondering how young Gus was going to enjoy his visit to Ayr. How would he sleep in a strange bed? Would there be squabbles with Morag Huston over toys? Had he missed the fact that Auntie Netta was absent? Did any of them care that they had let her down badly?

Tossing and turning in the dark she wondered if she ought to go to Stratharvar and await their return but the pressure of being her own boss did not allow it. If Polly were to join her workshop then orders must be prepared and the workroom kitted out properly. Only new orders would finance her outlay. Nevertheless Dixie's challenge was still ringing in her ears: 'Go back to Scotland and grab him, stop shilly-shallying.' Now was not the time but it would be her New Year's Resolution, she vowed. This is the year she would make it all happen and bring Gus home. This time she would succeed.

Then the postman shoved some letters through the door and she shuffled sleepily over to see who was late with their greetings cards. The postcard on the mat had a familiar picture on it and its contents sent Netta rushing for her clothes and boots, scurrying down the hill to catch the bus to Leeds. She must go and see Vida Bloom at once.

The curtains were closed but there was a strange wailing sound coming from inside. A nosy neighbour shook her head from an upstairs window. 'There's been a bereavement in the family, love. She's sitting shivah or something, poor soul, and her a widow and such a hard worker. If you're not one of them, I wouldn't go in. Best let them get on with it. The whole tribe of Israel's been knocking at her door, weeping and wailing. I wouldn't bother, if I were you.'

Netta was not so easily put off so she banged harder. A strange face came to the door. 'Yes?'

'I've come to see Mrs Bloom. Please, I must see her.'

'She's seeing no one, there's been a sudden bereavement . . .'

'What has happened? I got a postcard from Arnie only this morning. I have to know. Please let me in to give my condolences. That's what you do, isn't it, visit the mourners?' The woman in the sheitel wig hesitated and opened the door. 'Just one minute, she's very tired. To lose a son, an only son . . .'

'But when? Where? Are they killed . . . Arnie and Dixie?'

'Don't mention that shiksa's name in this house. Is that you, Netta? You have robbed me of my only joy.'

Vida Bloom was sitting on a chair surrounded by women. From upstairs came the sound of men at prayer. She had aged overnight, her eyes red with crying, and the lapels of her jacket were torn, hanging down from her suit. 'This is what it comes to when I trust my son to you . . . you traitor!'

'Tell me what I've done? I just had a postcard from Gretna Green from Mr and Mrs Arnie Bloom. Did something happen to them?'

Vida rose with an effort. 'He has married out . . . to that slum keelie of yours – yon dancer from the show. I will not say her name, coarse, Catholic and common as it is.'

'Don't say that, Mrs Bloom, they must love each other. At least he's happy,' Netta pleaded, looking at a photograph torn to shreds in the hearth. 'Was that their wedding photo? Is that why you're so upset?'

'Aye, lass, and all your doing. Look at the dress. See, the one *you made up for the scarlet woman and brought for me to finish off. To think, I made the wedding dress in my own home! You gave them the notion of Gretna when you told the yenta about your own runaway marriage, did you not?'*

Netta blushed, bowing her head.

'I'm so sorry, it was only a passing mention. I didn't know they would run off themselves, but what were they to do if you wouldn't speak to them about their feelings?'

'You don't know the half of it. He's left his job . . . my son, the accountant is now just a jobbing jazz musician, following her all over. Well, he's dead to me now. How can you live with that?' screamed Vida.

'Calm, Davida, remember what the doctor said? Tears won't bring him back,' said the friend, pointing Netta to the door.

'He's not dead – he lives and breathes. Remember what you said to me? "Be grateful he lives when others have perished. Blame keeps wounds open, only forgiveness closes them." You said that to me once but Arnie's better off without a mother who wants happiness only for herself and not for her child. Don't worry, I'm leaving. I won't trouble you again. They'll always be welcome in my home. I envy them their happiness and pity you.'

'Don't think I shall put any more work your way. You walk yer own path from now on.'

'I always have, Mrs Bloom. Believe me, it's a lonely road and you won't be far behind.'

February was a bleak month for any bridal trader. No one wanted to shed layers and parade down the aisle in the muck and mire of a Griseley winter. Then came Lent when no one married and the order book looked so thin that Netta wondered if she ought to lay Polly off. They beavered away on the few orders coming in for Easter. Sometimes sales reps in smart suits came to show off their latest fabric ranges and bridal accessories but mostly it was quiet and Netta busied herself making hire samples to lift the heaviness in her heart. Then the bell on the showroom door ding-donged, announcing a customer. Netta whipped off her overall and found herself face to face with Ginnie Mackeever who was clutching a magazine.

'Don't get excited, Jeanette, I'm just browsing round. Dr Stirling seems to think you'd be able to sew me something rather spectacular for the nuptials so I promised to show you what I want. I can't seem to make the Leeds stores deliver to my standards: all these shortages. Isn't it boring?'

'Congratulations! I hope you'll both be very happy.' Netta smiled through gritted teeth. 'How do you think I can help?'

Ginnie plonked a calfskin leather glove on the table and fingered for the page in her magazine. 'There, that's what I want, an exact copy of that. If I could fly the real thing across I would. A design from Priscilla of Boston, all the rage in the States. This is from American Vogue.'

Netta was looking at a vast gown of ballroom dancing proportions with a bodice that cascaded and flounced down the back in an elaborate peplum. It would take acres of material. 'I'll have a go – but the cloth . . . I have only a small quota.' Her wholesale supply had mysteriously dried up since Arnie's marriage and there had been no reconciliation with Vida Bloom.

'Don't worry, Daddy has ways and means, leave it to me. I want pink lace guipure. With silk underlining, of course. I shall wear a picture hat like Margaret Lockwood in Wicked Lady. That should knock 'em dead in the aisles! I want it for June but I shall be away in May so we'd better put our skates on.

'You can come to the house, of course, this is far too poky for a decent fitting. I'll catch my death stripping off in here. Do you think you're up to it? Speak now, for God's sake, or forever hold thy peace. Andrew seems to think you are, always singing your praises: you're quite the favourite aunt at some Home or other.'

'How is Dr Stirling?' Netta had been relieved to have seen nothing of him since Christmas.

'Like a bear with a sore head, poor darling. Always off to some damn' meeting or another. He can be quite a spoilsport with all his boring shoptalk. He gets so involved with it all. I don't know what

256

he sees in a bunch of whingeing ex-soldiers, sitting over their pints moaning on about the war. Thank God it's all over, I say. Let's forget about it and get on with the good times. Don't you?'

'It's not so easy for some, I expect. Bad injuries to live with . . .' She was glad Drew was branching out with his work.

'Rubbish! Life is for living now, not harping on about what you can't change. It's making him quite a misery guts but a few whiskies and he lightens up, thank God!'

Netta did not want to make this dress or copy someone else's creation, however far away, but she needed the order and the prestige of the Mackeever name. It was what she had always planned but now it was happening there was no excitement, only apprehension. The thought of Drew being yoked to this hard heart was not a satisfying one but that was his business. This order would keep them afloat.

Netta smiled sweetly and brought out the diary. It was full of embarrassing gaps that the sharp-eyed Ginnie was quick to notice. 'Oh, dear, we're very new at this, aren't we? You'll be opening a bottle of champers after my visit, won't you?'

Netta forced her face into a semblance of a smile.

'I should really be going to London to have it made up but Daddy has this quaint notion of supporting local tradespeople. Very noble of him, don't you think? Herbert Batley told him you're the best in the district and did his little Elsie proud.' She sniffed at the rail of half-finished garments. 'Judging by these, I'm sure you'll come up trumps. Even if it is a bit out of your usual league.'

'All my bride's dresses are special.'

'The wedding's in Leeds parish church, of course. So many guests to cram in. Lots of publicity for you if you hit the mark.'

'It all sounds very grand. We'll have plenty of time to sort you out, won't we?' Netta refused to be patronised.

Ginnie shrugged her shoulders. 'Must dash, masses to organise. See you next week.'

Love's got one eye and is awful deaf, thought Netta as the bride swept out of the shop.

'Dr Stirling's got a right one there,' smirked Polly from the shadows.

'I couldn't have said it better myself,' Netta replied with satisfaction. Just the thought to cheer a body up on a cold winter's afternoon: the sight of a floating blancmange rustling down the aisle to her Prince Charming. But it would be the most beautiful blancmange ever seen on this planet, if that was what she wants.

She banged the iron down to shake herself out of this strange mood. Netta Nichol Designs must embark upon a strawberry sea of silk and lace.

'Shall I make us a brew?' said Polly from her machine.

'Yes, and put a slug of gin in mine. I think I'm going to need it. Sometimes, Polly, I think this business's like the weather . . . there's no pattern to it.'

Forks In The Path, March 1949

The iron grip of winter loosened its hold on Griseley. Snowy white patches gave way to the greeny-yellow of early spring and still Netta had not returned north to see the boy. There were too many demands on her time: training Polly; pattern making into the small hours until her eyes ached with weariness. She must get ahead with the spring bridal wear and snatch some time with Gus in May before the final onslaught of the Mackeever extravaganza.

There was little pleasure in copying someone else's creation, however loosely she interpreted the design. How she wished for Vida's advice but there was no word from that quarter, only postcards from Dixie and Arnie who were blissfully unaware of the estrangement, on tour around the country.

Netta stifled the guilty feeling that she had stayed away too long from Brigg Farm. She parcelled up a lavish present for Gus's fourth birthday, one she could ill afford. Her New Year resolution to bring him back to Yorkshire had faded under a flurry of orders. Somehow the success of Netta Nichol Designs, beating the odds and staying solvent, was taking over her life. There was always some other pressing priority, leaving little time even for the Home visiting and relaxation with her young friends there.

Polly had her own crowd and went to the local pictures and the Town Hall dances, dressed in offcuts. There was talk of her applying for a bursary to do a college course at night school.

She was staying at the Home until she was sixteen. Polly's gang made Netta feel ancient and washed out with all their crazes and pashes. She felt lonely, cast adrift on a tide of busyness; a silent observer peering through the curtains into other people's happiness. She watched the cherry blossom in full bloom on the Parade, eager for its petals to be shed and to hurry on Maytime when she would be returning home to make her stand over Gus's future.

Drew Stirling was in the bath when the telephone rang. Ginnie was on her second Martini, stamping her high heels impatiently in his flat in West Park on the outskirts of Leeds. 'For God's sake, get your skates on! We'll be late for the theatre again. Five mins and I'm off without you . . .'

She lifted the telephone receiver. 'Dr Stirling's residence.'

'Is that you?' said a man's voice.

'Do I sound like him? He's off duty now. Can I give him a message?'

'Tell him it's Arthur Bates. Sorry to trouble him but he said I could call this number anytime.'

'Not now you can't! Dr Drew is just going out and he's late. Give me the number and he'll call you back later.'

'Who is it?' shouted Drew from the bathroom.

'Just some Arthur chappie, sounds a bit squiffy. Really, Drew, you shouldn't encourage them . . .'

Drew shot out of the bath dripping his way towards the phone. 'Give me that.' The line was dead.

'Was it Arthur Bates? Did you get his number?'

'No, why should I? I told him to call back. I'm not your secretary!' Ginnie pouted, her hands on her hips.

Drew shook his head, 'Oh, Ginnie, you should have let me speak to the man. He needs help.'

'And make us even later than ever? Darling, it's after six. Even a school doctor has a private life. What's so important about one drunk?'

260

'Nothing you would understand, my silly darling. What would you know about torture and imprisonment, failure and agony?'

Drew poured himself a whisky and stormed back into the bathroom, troubled by the phone call. Things must have been desperate for Arthur to make it. He was one of the members of the voluntary group that met regularly at the Red Lion, a quiet unassuming man who had hung back from the general discussions about prisoner of war experiences. Things were not going right for him at work or home and he'd found he couldn't hold down a job. He had confided to Drew in the Gents that he had nightmares and sweats and couldn't settle to anything. He had lost two jobs after he'd clocked in drunk. Drew had suggested they met up on their own to talk about his symptoms and perhaps refer him to someone in Leeds who specialised in rehabilitation.

At the theatre Drew sat through the performance, wondering if Arthur would ring him back. He was the quietest of the bunch, always sitting in the corner supping slowly, listening, nodding, but saying bugger all. He'd been in some camp on the Burma Railway, starved and worked almost to death like most of them, but he'd had a pal, a bit of a singer and concert party star. The pal was executed in front of him. Drew guessed that Arthur was hard up and didn't want to miss his round so he only came once or twice.

Drew was finding all this talking about their past feelings disturbing. He wasn't trained for this sort of palaver himself. Needles and pills, yes, anything physical. But he couldn't get a handle on this invisible pain. The stuff that goes on in somebody else's head was properly speaking a job for a trick cyclist. It was a relief at least to know they had arranged to meet later that week.

But back at the flat an overwhelming urge to find Arthur took over him. This sense of urgency got him ringing round discreetly to find out Arthur's home address, but nobody knew it.

Two days later Drew arrived early and sat at their table in the Red Lion, waiting for Arthur to turn up. He didn't show. With a sinking feeling he sat there for hours before he got in the car and drove to Rawdon. He found Arthur's address by asking around the

261

pubs, saying he was an army pal. Drew knocked on his front door, feeling apprehensive. A tired woman in black opened it. One look at her face and he knew that Arthur was dead.

'I'm Dr Stirling. I was concerned about Arthur.'

'Come in,' she whispered. 'He's not here, I'm sorry. He's gone. He went missing two nights ago . . .'

Drew bent his head, thinking, It's all my fault. I could have helped him but I was in the bloody bath.

'What's happened? How did he die?'

'He took a tow rope and hung himself in the local park two nights ago. Some children found him swinging from a tree. He had a note in his pocket saying he didn't want to stick around in this rotten world anymore. He was very low. Didn't think that what he fought for was worth a toss to people now and so he was better off with his pals. He was never the same when he come home. Not my Arthur, more like a stranger. I never thought he'd shame us like this, though. He wouldn't want to scare kiddies like that. It must have been the booze. He were teetotal before the war.'

Drew listened in silence with a sinking heart. He made the right noises and left in a turmoil. He did not want to be alone.

He took the high winding road northwards on to the moors away from the cold comfort of his flat in West Park, parking his car to face the twinkling lights flickering through the mist from the city below. It was lashing with rain. He opened the door to feel the water splashing on to his face, stinging his cheeks, then closed it quickly. On the windscreen the raindrops bubbled down, full of faces trapped like ships in bottles: faces of long-dead comrades and dying soldiers, children. Bobbing in front of him the pudgy, pale face of Arthur Bates glistened: such a quiet, sad man. All the torrent of rage and sadness tearing his soul apart had been hidden by his unassuming exterior.

Drew banged his fist on the glass. How could he have misread such misery? His own sense of failure thundered like a punch in the gut, taking his breath away. What sort of doctor are you, Stirling? he asked himself. He felt under his seat for his usual comfort but *there was not enough left to anaesthetise a flea. He revved up the engine and headed for the nearest off licence.*

How he found his way to Netta's door was a mystery of automatic driving. Drew stepped out of the shadows in the pouring rain, looking like a drowned rat holding a bottle of whisky. Netta couldn't make out at first if tears or rain were dripping down his cheeks. Then she saw it was both. 'Drew, for goodness' sake, away inside. You look like death warmed up. What's happened?'

'I've been standing soaking in the rain, staring at this damn' bottle, looking inside for an answer until I'm numb. Liquid gold, my little comforter. Tonight for once it's let me down. I can still feel the pain and there's no answer inside any bottle, is there? So I thought, Do I buy another or do I come and see my friend one more time? That's what I thought to myself: the bottle or Netta. And for once you won.'

'And I'm supposed to be flattered? I haven't the faintest clue what this is all about. Has Ginnie left you?' Visions of that pink marshmallow wedding dress and the fat cheque floating away over the horizon flashed before her eyes.

'No such luck! Ginnie sticks to me like a plaster. Dear beautiful Ginnie, not a flicker of conscience in her diamond heart to trouble her. She can't help me on this one but you might . . .'

'I see,' sniffed Netta as she put the kettle on the hob. He was going to need sobering up before she got any sense out of him. 'Have you eaten?' Drew shook his hair like a puppy, scattering drops in all directions. 'Take off your wet things, dry your socks on the fender rail. Warm up and tell Auntie Netta what on earth's been going on? Bacon and egg, I think. One rasher's all that's left of my ration but there's plenty of fried bread. Go on, I'm all ears.'

Drew told her the bare bones of his story, his hands shaking. 'I could do with a fag. It's all my fault. I might as well have handed him the rope when I didn't answer his call. If only . . .'

'You were unlucky. He called you so he must have thought

*something of you. It was unfortunate. You must have faced sui-
cide before?'*

'Yes, but they were just names to me, people I didn't know or
much care about. Arthur was a good chap. He deserved better. There
must be thousands of war veterans, suffering silently, surviving with
guilt, pushing down their panic and memories, trying to live normal
lives. I should know. Even I saw enough on my fighting patch to turn
the stomach. Battle is torture. Arthur's right, it's a rotten world if you
are weak and vulnerable. Only the tough and uncaring survive.'

'That's not true and you know it.'

'How can I face the other men and tell them about Arthur? Did
all our talking stir it all up and make it worse for him? Talking about
stuff is dangerous. You never know where it'll end. Look at you and
me: I talk to you. Ginnie and I don't talk — we just pass the time
of day, swap anecdotes, crack jokes. You and I, we bare our souls.
We're best pals. What shall I do, Netta?'

'Don't ask me. At least you chose to tell me about it, not drown
your sorrows again. Surely that proves something? It's a start. Go
and tell the group the truth and see if there are any others who
are as desperate as Arthur was. Use what has happened to help
someone else and then his death won't have been in vain. That's
all you can do.

'As for you and me, yes, we're friends but you ought to
try and find that palship with Ginnie in your marriage. You
can't run the two of us, side by side like tram lines: Ginnie
for sunshine and fun, poor old Netta for showers and sorrow.
You can't keep bobbing up out of the blue when you feel like
it to lumber me with all your troubles, leaving me anxious and
sad while you swan off back down the road to the High House,
free to dance to Ginnie's beat. It's not fair on either of us.
I'm really sorry for what happened tonight. I know what it's
like to have nowhere to turn and feel life's not worth living.
You once said to me, "Cling on to hope and honesty", remember?'

'Aye, I know, but where is all this leading me?'

'I don't know. It's your life. One step at a time, Drew. Follow your heart, don't go against your instincts. Look what happens when you do.'

'Where do you find all these gems of insight . . . from a Patience Strong calendar?' He was grinning.

'Don't mock. That particular one came from a far better doctor than you'll ever be if you don't use your compassion. A man who saved my life by following his instincts.'

Netta shoved a mug of cocoa in his face. The story of her own suicide attempt could wait for another time. Drew's burden of guilt was hard enough for the moment. They sipped in silence and she saw weariness fill his face. He fell asleep in the chair and she saw no point in disturbing him. Covering him with a quilt, she blew out the lamp and went upstairs.

High House was another Oldroyds but untouched by the local council, a private residence set up a long winding drive into Rombalds Moor, overlooking the whole of Wharfedale. This solid mansion bearing witness to Victorian grandeur had stables to the side in a cobbled courtyard. Netta had long ago decided that the tradesmen's entrance was her proper port of call.

She parked the hired van on the gravel and carried her precious cargo in a coffin-like cardboard box. The housekeeper helped her up the stairs to a large dressing room where the cupboards were attached to the wall in the contemporary fashion with mirrors for doors. There was a sink of turquoise enamel and a shower by its side. A separate door led into Ginnie's own suite of rooms overlooking the valley below — quite the most luxurious apartments she had ever seen. Netta smiled, thinking of her own hurried ablutions in the zinc tub in front of the kitchen range.

Ginnie was late for her fitting. She bounded up the stairs in her jodhpurs, her cheeks flushed with exercise. 'Won't be a sec! Just a quick shower.' And she flung off her clothes, going through the door. On the four-poster bed were laid out a fine French corselet and silk underslip in coffee silk trimmed with blue lace. Netta unpacked the

265

pieces of the wedding dress carefully. This was the first trial fit of the bodice.

She had to admit the colour suited Ginnie's fairness, a rich fizzy pink with tinges of oyster, apricot and a hint of cream. Ginnie called it, 'My pink gin and champagne.' The guipure lace was heavy, sculpted into florets, every piece handstitched and appliquéed into one flowing whole. No seams were to be visible to the naked eye. Polly was spending hours preparing the lace and now the three layers of bodice were ready.

'Only got half an hour to spare. I hope it fits this time. You know I'm off to France with the girls for my trousseau in May? Going to have my hen party in Paris. Meeting Dr Stirling now, off to dinner with the Macmurrays. You won't know them, Irish not Scotch. Ouch!'

Netta pulled out the offending pin with satisfaction. The bodice was perfect but the line of the panels at the back needed attention. She gave Ginnie a stiffened petticoat to wear underneath to see the effect. She twirled excitedly in the mirror. 'Hmm . . . Andrew was right. You can sew! I wish he'd take a bit more interest in the wedding . . . left to muggins as usual. Just hasn't had the time, poor darling, all this National Health nonsense. I've told him when he moves in here, Daddy will find him plenty of customers for a private clinic.'

'But . . .' Netta bit her tongue. She was not supposed to know that he had rejected that offer already. 'You'll both be staying here then?'

'Of course. Daddy would rattle round this place like a pea in a jar on his own. And I'm not leaving my horses. Masses of room for all of us. I don't intend to live in some street down there.' She dismissed the whole of Ilkley with one flick of her elegant wrist.

It's none of your business what your customers do after their wedding, thought Netta, but her heart lurched with pity for Drew. Dr Begg's grand surgery came to mind. She could not see Drew in the same mould, not after what had happened last week. Ginnie was not the right girl for him. She needed all her corners knocking off: this spoiled daddy's girl who would not give up any

266

comfort for her man. Surely one-sided giving came to nothing in the end?

Netta fled from High House in confusion. This was the most exacting commission she had ever had. The hardest dress she would ever make. She realised with an ache in the pit of her stomach that every stitch would be agony, for it would be made in sorrow not joy. When it was finished she would lose Drew Stirling forever.

Late Afternoon In Kendal, May 1949

The sun was setting behind the slate-grey houses of the Lakeland town as Netta made for the van parked by the river. Business, business . . . the past few months had fled by in a flurry of tulle and satin, fittings and alterations. Polly would be anxious for her to return to Griseley to finish off Ginny Mackeever's gown. It was not going well.

So what had happened to that New Year's resolution again? Did it get swamped by all the sewing orders or was that just an excuse? She watched the River Kent rushing over the boulders in full spate, under the bridge she must drive across to carry on southwards.

Netta turned back towards the van with a heavy heart. She'd had a week to complete her mission. How could she have driven all this way, more than halfway home, knowing she'd funked her task? She sat down in the driving seat, placing the straw bag like a passenger to one side of her. You've done it again, she brooded, broken your promise, let yourself down.

She switched on the ignition and yanked the choke out but nothing happened. In frustration she pulled again and the engine spluttered as it cut out. Her fist hit the steering wheel. A man stuck his head in the open window.

'Have you flooded the engine, love? Don't be hasty. Put

the choke back in and leave it a while. Mind on, don't rush, give it the gentle touch.'

He winked and walked off, smiling to his wife.

'Thanks.' She winced at her own ignorance, slumping back into the seat with frustration. Even the wretched car didn't know what to do with itself. She was stuck! Forwards or backwards, which was it to be? Neither option looked promising from where Netta was sitting: forwards to work and the 'Royal wedding' or a long drive backwards to battle for her son. Why was life so complicated now? It was all Drew Stirling's fault. Why couldn't he stay away? He was to blame for her confusion, damn him!

Netta turned on the ignition tentatively, hardly daring to believe that it might start up. 'Turn again, Whittington,' she prayed and the engine fired perfectly. She reached the river crossing and paused, knowing it was now or never. What should she do? Cross the Kent or turn back north into the hills of home. Trust in what you love and it will lead you . . . Dr Anwar had better be right but why, oh, why, was her own loving never straightforward?

8

LAPIS LAZULI

'Mysterious colour of midnight oceans and sky,
Torching a path from the darkness of fear
To the indigo brightness of intuition.'

The Same Saturday Afternoon At Brigg Farm

Once Netta had left for England Peg sighed with relief that the visit had gone without a hitch even though Gus sulked and moaned as usual about his head hurting and didn't want to do his farm chores. His girny gripes just got on her nerves as she stripped the visitor's bed and tidied up the room. It was going to be a fine day for a stint in the front garden, a chance to prune the rose border that brightened up the side of the pathway to the front door.

When she came in at teatime Gus was nowhere to be seen and she called out to the yardboy to go and find him. When he returned empty-handed she began to get anxious and searched the byres herself. It was just on the off chance that she popped her head round the bedroom door and smiled. Gus had tucked himself up on his bed and gone to sleep with Yumpy.

She felt his forehead. He was hot but temperatures were often highest in the early evening so she closed the curtains to let him sleep off his sulks and over-excitement. If he woke up later he could have supper downstairs. She told Angus that Netta had worn out the poor child with all their stravaigin' about the coast. Measles, chickenpox, mumps . . . Peg reeled off all the childhood illnesses one by one. He had been vaccinated for smallpox and diphtheria. He must have

273

picked something up playing with Jamie Paterson. He was just overtired.

The boy seemed better in the morning and had some porridge but his cheeks were still flushed and his eyes glassy. He waved Angus off to the church service in Stratharvar and then was promptly sick, which took the stuffing out of him. His head was hurting and he had a sore back so he curled up in the leather armchair with Yumpy in the heart of the kitchen, a bucket at the ready. By late morning he had taken himself off to bed again and Peg felt relieved that he was out of her hair, sleeping it all off. It was just some 'summer tummy' going round the district, no need to worry. Peg was never one for overfussing but some instinct kept making her check on the boy. Tomorrow he would probably be as right as rain and twice as noisy. Rest and plenty of fluids would do the trick. Nature would take its course in such a healthy young bairn.

Gus lay back, docile and limp. It worried Peg far more than if he was complaining. He pushed aside picture books and models. It hurt his neck to bend and all he wanted was Yumpy to suck. He asked if Auntie Netta would tell him a Viking story. Seemed to think she was still here, rambling on. His temperature was up again and he was sweating, his pulse racing. Peg brought a bowl and face cloth and began to sponge his forehead, trying not to panic. Perhaps this was not a normal fever after all. She peered out of the window to the winding track, willing some cheery body to reassure her. She prided herself on not bothering the doctor for trifles, especially on the Sabbath. Where was Angus where she needed him?

For all her nursing experience, Peg was nonplussed by Gus's symptoms. He seemed to have gone very weak and floppy and it was as much as she could do to force liquid down his throat. Suddenly she was feeling very unsure and very alone. A strange feeling was burning into her, as if something terrible was about to happen, as if something was going to change their life forever. If only Angus hadn't gone to church! But Gus had seemed fine when he had left. How everything seemed to change in just a few hours!

Alone with time on her hands, she began to frighten herself with lists of complications, the worst of which was meningitis. But there was no rash or spots, no obvious localised stomach pain. Peg racked her basic medical knowledge for some simple explanation. It must be gastric flu, some virulent form of infection. All that stravaigin' with Netta . . . perhaps she too was suffering the symptoms.

For the first time in years she searched through the address book for the telephone number of the Bloom woman in Leeds and put in a trunk call to reassure herself. A woman answered. 'Mrs Bloom, how can I help you?'

'I'm sorry to trouble you but could you get a message to Netta, Mrs Hunter, please?'

'I'm sorry, I don't know her whereabouts . . . Who's speaking?'

'Peg Nichol from Stratharvar. You once stayed with us in the war. She left us yesterday and she was heading straight home, or so she said.'

'I'm sorry, Mrs Nichol. I've not seen Jeanette for months. Is anything wrong? She has her own business now, try ringing there.'

'I'm not sure of the number. I'd like tae check something out with her. Sorry to have troubled you.'

'Not at all. So glad to be speaking to you, Mrs Nichol, after all these years. Don't worry, I expect her motor's broken down or something.'

'It's no her I'm afeared for!'

They were cut off at this point and Peg slammed down the phone in frustration. Trust Netta to disappear just when she was wanted. Such an unreliable girl! If she'd given wee Gus this infection there'd be hell to pay!

Peg lifted the phone again and called Meg Paterson at

Fordhall Farm to check on Jamie. It was such a relief to hear that he was being sick and was confined to the house. It was just something the bairns had picked up playing together, no doubt. On the strength of this good news, Peg made herself a cup of strong tea and got on with her housework, brushing the stairs down, finding clean linen for Netta's bed and dusting the banister rail. She was panicking for nothing.

When she heard the engine stop in the yard she flew to open the door, thinking it was Angus home early. It was only the old van she had waved off yesterday. Netta was stretching her long legs out of it while the silly sheepdog was racing round in circles yapping.

'Oh, it's you! Where've you been? I've been ringing all morning and not a sign of you. What have you been up to?'

'I came back. I had to. There's a lot of stuff we need to talk about, stuff to be sorted out once and for all.'

'Not now, Netta. Were you unwell? You'd better come upstairs and see for yourself. It's Gus – he's awful poorly, since you left yesterday. He's been so feverish, sick and achey. Jamie Paterson's in his bed too. Are you feeling fine?'

'Not a twinge, just tired. I got as far as Kendal in the Lake District and then I turned back to Penrith. I stayed overnight in digs. I rang my assistant to tell her not to expect me for a few more days. I meant to ring you but I just wanted to come back here. I drove and drove, felt uneasy . . . Let me see him.'

Netta was racing ahead up the stairs even as she was speaking. She paused at the bedroom door and tiptoed inside, Peg following behind.

'He looks so wee in his bed, all curled up. Surely he's shrunk? How long's he been like this? Where's Father? You've sent for the doctor?'

'Well, no . . . I didna want tae bother the man, but Gus's no picking up, is he? I'm awful worried. I've never seen him like this before. Gus, wake up, son. Here's your Auntie Netta to read you a story. He was asking for you . . .'

He opened his eyes but his focus was blurry. 'I can see rainbows, Auntie Netta. Can we play rainbows again?'

'For God's sake, Peg! Phone Dr Begg. The boy's delirious and burning hot.'

She tried to lift him but the child moaned and grimaced.

'Cannae lift ma neck. It hurts. Mammy . . . I want my mammy.' Gus cooried into Peg's stomach as she sat beside him, trying to sponge him down.

Netta said, 'I'll go and ring for Dr Begg. You should have done it sooner.'

'Ma head hurts so!' he was crying.

The two women lifted him higher on to the bolster but he flopped down and moaned like a whimpering animal.

The two women sat by his bedside for a while.

'Where on earth is Dr Begg? You rang ages ago. Minutes are like hours, I suppose.'

'He'll come when he can. If there're others like Gus to see to . . . it's going to be a long morning ahead, full of anxious mothers. Come on, Peg, you looked wabbit. Come down and I'll put the kettle on. It's the only cure. Thank God I came home! I nearly didn't but this little voice kept saying, "Go back, Netta, go back!"'

'I'm glad you did, hen. I wouldna like to be here on ma ain fearing the worst. All sorts of silly things go through your head . . . I'm fair shaking with the look of him.'

'I know, Peg, but when the doctor comes he'll tell us what to do. Come away down the stairs and let Gus rest. Sleep is the best cure for him.'

It was after lunch when they heard the scrunch of tyre wheels. Ian Begg came through the door with his Gladstone bag, looking pushed for time. 'Another one with the squitters, is it? Where's young Master Gus, in the kitchen?'

'No, Doctor, he took himself to bed yesterday and he cannae move. He's running a temperature, his neck is stiff and his head is burning. He's only been sick the once and no runs so far.'

Ian Begg went to the bedroom and the women hovered by the door silently, not wanting to interrupt his examination. As thorough as his father before him, he took temperature and pulse, throat, glands: all the usual stuff. But then he drew back the covers and took his little hammer to Gus's raised knees, they would not stay up. 'Can you feel that?' He smiled, tickling Gus's toes.

'A bitty,' said a weak little voice.

'And this?' The doctor pricked his foot.

'A bitty,' came the reply.

'Any tingles, young chappie?'

'Ma legs jingle-jangle all of the time.'

The doctor tried to move his lower body but there was no life in his limbs.

'How long has he had no movement down here?'

Peg shrugged her shoulders, puce with embarrassment. The doctor's face had tightened from his usual jovial banter into a mask, stern and carefully composed, giving nothing away. He was taking his time and choosing his words. Peg knew he had no good news.

'What is it, Dr Begg?'

'Where's your phone?' he answered crisply. 'I need to make some calls.'

She pointed down to the hall table where the black phone lay on a white lace doily. He went to the bathroom and washed his hands then slipped downstairs.

'I dinna like the look on his face, do you?' Peg was trembling and wringing her hands. Netta was moved to touch her arm.

'He'll tell us in a minute. Hold on, not in front of Gus, He mustn't see we're afraid.'

There was a tremor in her voice too. She hovered at the top of the stairs, hearing snippets.

'Ambulance straight away ... isolation ward ... precautions ... contact authorities ... second case this week.'

Netta darted back as he came into the room.

'Now, young man, I'm going to take you on a ride to the hospital in Dumfries to see a nice doctor who knows all about this sickness of yours. He can run a few tests and sort out what we're going to do with you. Don't look so worried. The nurses'll have you on your feet in no time and you'll be kicking nine bells out of Jamie Paterson before very long.'

Gus smiled weakly.

'Just you lie back and rest a while longer. Don't worry, you'll get lots of fuss and ice cream and jelly when you're feeling better, I promise. I just need a wee word with your mother.' He paused, seeing the look of anguish in the other woman's eye. 'And Auntie Netta, of course.'

They sat stiffly in the parlour, still cool in the afternoon rays. 'I can't be sure at this stage exactly what Gus has contracted but it is serious. He must go into hospital. To the Infectious Ward, I'm afraid. We need to do more tests in Dumfries. His limbs are flaccid. He has feeling but no muscle action. I don't know how much else of his body might be affected.'

'It's infantile paralysis, isn't it?' Netta's voice was cold and calm.

Peg looked up in surprise. What did she know about that? 'That's a dirty disease ... from the swimming baths. You didn't take him to the public baths, did you?' she accused.

'Poliomyelitis can be caught from many sources, not just bathing, Mrs Nichol, but Mrs Hunter might be right. Have you come across this recently?'

'Only last year, at an orphange near Leeds. There was an outbreak and two children died,' Netta answered calmly.

'Oh, dear God! Have you brought this with you?'

'Calm down, Mistress Nichol. Last year saw many epidemics in the heatwave. I'm sorry but I have to take precautions. It may not be that at all but Gus must be in the safest place.'

'What about Jamie? Is he stricken too.'

'A milder form, just a fever and tummy upset. It can go either way, but don't look so worried. It's not in his throat or chest, so far as I can tell. Bed rest and lots of peace and quiet, and we'll get someone to look at those legs. Chances are he'll make a full recovery in time. The ambulance will be here shortly. I would gather a few things for him to take. It's better if he goes alone. I shall write a few notes and details. You can follow later for visiting time between six and seven.'

'Thank you, Doctor. I'm glad we weren't wasting your time.'

Ian Begg put on his cheery mask again and raised his hat. 'You should have rung me earlier. Gus is very sick. It's good Netta called me when she did. The sooner we can find out what exactly the young chap's caught, the sooner treatment can begin. Get Peg a stiff whisky, Nettie, she's taken a bad shock.' He left them standing stunned in the hallway.

Peg collapsed on the bottom stair. 'Not polio? Oh, what will Angus say? Will Gus end up in an iron lung, no able to breathe for himself?'

'We have to be strong for him now. It may not be the worst form of paralysis after all. We'll pull him through . . . Do you mind if I make a few phone calls? I need to clear the decks.'

'Are you away the now, back down to Yorkshire?' Peg suddenly felt exhausted and confused. If Netta left now, how could she cope on her own?

'No, of course not. My son is poorly. He needs me. He needs us all and here is where I'll be staying until he's on the mend. Polly'll have to manage without me somehow even if it means closing the workshop.' Nothing was going to shift Netta from her son's side.

Staying On, June 1949

The ambulance was gone. The farm felt suddenly empty. The two women sat by the hearth, stunned by Gus's tearful departure. Netta had offered to follow behind in the van but Dr Begg insisted she should stay on to disinfect Gus's room and wait for Angus's return.

'You'll have to clear out all his stuff, I'm afraid, burn what you can't boil. Keep Mistress Nichol as busy as you can. Visiting will be restricted, of course, in the interests of hygiene.'

On such a beautiful day, to be stripping beds, yanking down mattresses into the sunlight, making a bonfire of Gus's toys and books as if he was already departed from them for good. When it came to Yumpy, Netta was adamant. 'We can't burn his sucky.'

'Why not? It's been stuck close to him. It must be full of germs. I'd rather burn it than cremate ma wee bairn! Give it to me.' Netta could not bear to watch and went inside to phone Jean Brownleys with the awful news.

'Leave the shop to Polly. She'll cope. I'll go through the order book with her and cancel early fittings. Polly can do the rest. We can send up some of your sewing if needs be. Forget about Griseley, concentrate on what's important. It's only dresses, after all . . .'

281

'But I don't want to let my customers down!' Netta cried.

'You won't be. Gus needs you and so do your parents. They must come first. Here's Stirling, he's in my office doing medicals again. He wants a word with you.'

'Oh, Drew! What shall I do if anything happens to him? They think it's polio.'

Drew's voice was steady, calming her panic. 'Look, don't worry. Everything they're doing is routine so far. They'll run tests. It could be either meningitis or poliomyelitis. There's a non-paralytic variety or, if we're unlucky, acute asymmetric flaccid limb paralysis . . .'

'Drew, slow down! I can't take it all in. Which one's infantile paralysis then?' Netta as straining to catch his words.

'Netta, are you still there? Remember, even if it's the worst sort, over half recover with no permanent damage. Hold on to that hope. "*Courage, mon brave*". If he's unlucky there's still plenty that can be done.'

'Tell me the truth – will he die? Don't give me false hope. Drew, he looks so ill. Will he be in an iron lung?'

'Only his doctors can tell you that. Be patient. We'll face what has to be faced, when or if it comes to it. He needs you to be strong and cheerful. The little chap's going to need all the courage he can find. I'll ring you for a bulletin later this evening. I wish I could just drop everything but I can't abandon things here, forgive me. What a good job you turned back. This is your chance to show them your true mettle. I'll be thinking of you and I'll come when I can. Chin up.'

It took nerves of steel to walk down that long hospital corridor with its oh-so-familiar smells, not knowing what would be waiting for them in the Isolation Ward. Netta strode out briskly with a falsely confident air, trying to chivvy on Peg who shuffled to catch up, clutching parcels and gifts. All

282

their old rivalries had vanished in the heat of such a tragic turn of events.

The world quickly shrank into one hospital bed where Gus hovered between life and death, barely conscious, while his body was examined, injected, poked and invaded. There had been no respiratory collapse and that was the best news that was on offer. Netta soon learned that information was spoon-fed in measured doses to anxious relatives. They watched from behind a screen, helpless and useless, and Peg fled from the first sight of him in tears.

'That's no ma bairn in there, that poor waif, all on his own. A mammy should be in with her wean at such a time, no forced to sit behind glass once a week while strangers see to him!'

'I know, Peg, but rules is rules and it's all for his own good. We have to trust they know what they're doing . . . It's their job to nurse and they say that too much visiting disturbs the children. We mustn't let Gus see we're upset. Wave to him and hold up all the presents we've brought.'

'All these toys'll have to be destroyed in here when he leaves. What a waste! Why can't I go in and help?'

'The day he leaves this hospital, I'll gladly burn everything he's been given myself. Think about it: that happy day when he leaves to come home. Getting him through's all that matters now! We must do as they say, Peg. Don't make it harder on yersel.'

When Angus and Peg went in the following week they were reeling from the news that Gus was suffering from the dreaded asymmetric flaccid paralysis and the outlook was not good for his legs. The fever was destroying nerves in his body. They crawled back to Brigg Farm drained and aged with worry, pacing the floor all night, while Netta stood out in the farmyard looking up at the bright stars in the violet sky, also pacing up and down. It was balmy summer night, the smell of blossom on the soft wind. How could the weather

283

be so fine when they were so stricken? She was in no mood to be lulled by starlight.

'You will live, Gus Nichol! You will live and get back on your feet. Just keep breathing for us. I won't let you die. I will die before you. That must be the order of things. Come on, all you guardian angels. Where are you all? Mother . . . Rae . . . loving spirits. See that you pull a miracle out of the hat. Do something for your child. He mustn't die . . . He won't. I won't let him.'

Netta shook her fist into the night. No one was going to take Gus from Stratharvar, from Peg and Angus, tear him from her heart. She was not even going to consider the possibility.

Do you hear me up there? If he has to stay here at Brigg Farm forever, if I have to keep on visiting him, year in and year out, I don't care now. If that's what it takes to keep him alive, then so be it. I surrender my claim to him as long as he lives. Do you hear me? Gus has to live. I can bear the rest.

Their pain was made bearable only by the kindness of others. The Strathavar folk rallied to make a rota for milking which gave Angus the chance to visit the hospital each precious hour on Saturday and Sunday. Steak pies and sponge cakes appeared out of the air on the kitchen table to sustain their broken hearts. Gus's little pals sent cards and letters and gifts for him. Peg wept each morning when the school bus passed at the bottom of the track, knowing that Gus was lying so far away from all that was normal. Netta no longer cared what was happening in Yorkshire. If the business was ruined so be it, but Polly kept her informed and loyally kept up her sewing.

A flow of kindness from her Griseley customers came through the post. The Oldroyd girls send a parcel of magazines addressed to Gus. Elsie Batley sent a huge bouquet to the farm and a box of fancy chocolates to boost Netta's morale. There were even greetings from the Scotia crowd and prayers of encouragement from the church folk. Peg and Angus were humbled that so many strangers were concerned for the plight of their child.

Drew came up by train to meet up with them outside the hospital and Netta introduced him shyly to Peg and Angus as they made the trek down to the ward. Her parents were impressed by the way he could ask the sort of questions in medical language that got pertinent answers, not evasions. He explained every procedure to them in simple terms. Netta took him in briefly to see Gus who was now out of immediate danger but very weak. 'This is Dr Stirling who's as keen on Leeds United as you are on Queen of the South.'

In the quiet of the Station Hotel he was able to explain what might happen next in Gus's treatments. 'He's being transferred to orthopaedics now, being rested on a firm bed with lots of massage and therapy on his limbs. Perhaps he'll need calipers for a while to strengthen them. He's over the worst but there's still a long way to go. He's a spirited wee lad. He'll do fine, I promise.'

Netta wished she could believe him as they walked along the platform. It felt strangely comfortable to have him to herself in the very place where she and Rae had met so many years ago. Another man and another farewell.

They sat on the bench. Drew was quieter, more reserved, and there was something different about him. He stared along the track with vacant eyes, opening his mouth as if to say something but shutting it again like a goldfish.

'I think you should consider coming back to Griseley. It's going to be months before he comes out, you know.'

'I'm not leaving until Gus is on the mend. I'm sorry, I know this scuppers Ginnie's dress. It's half-finished but Polly isn't up to the rest. I've written to Vida Bloom to see if she can come to the rescue. I don't want to let anyone down but you see . . .'

'Don't worry about that now.'

'Oh, Drew. What a mess. He will be all right? We hardly see him and he's very quiet.'

'You're welded to that hospital bed, aren't you? And here's me, rabbiting on. He's going to be fine.'

'He's going to be crippled.'

'Have some faith in the medical profession even if not in my puny efforts.'

'I'm sorry, Drew. I can't joke at a time like this.'

'I'll take myself back now but don't forget there's a wee something Polly sent in that parcel – to keep yer hands busy, Netta, in the long weary hours. Something to keep you going forward. Practise what you preach. One step of the way, remember?'

Two weeks later on Sunday afternoon who should pop into the ward but a glamorous blonde in a pretty pink duster coat. Dixie and Arnie Bloom had made a special detour from Glasgow to visit Gus and Netta. Larger than life and twice as loud, but a lovely sight all the same.

'How are you both? What a surprise! Did Vida tell you to come?' said Netta, hoping they had had a reconciliation.

Arnie shook his head sadly. 'I knew what would happen if I married Dixie. It's mother's loss but we're sad she took it out on you too.'

Dixie gave her a hug. 'I was bursting to tell yer all about ma dress being a wedding dress but we thought what you didn't know wouldn't harm ye. Still, that's families for ye. It takes twa to make a fight.'

They shook hands with Peg and Angus who stepped aside to let them in. Dixie blew a big kiss to the boy. 'So this is the famous Gus! Do you know, when I was your age I used tae live on yer farm, did I no? And this man here used to take us up the stairs to ma bed and telt me stories.

'Netta and me fought like cat and dogs. She never used to pick me for the games. Do you remember? "Silk, satin, cotton, rags . . . you are oot!" And this yin here used to stick up her toffee nose and say, "I'm no cotton or rags . . . I'm lace." Well, she's certainly had plenty of lace in her life. We called in at your new place and Polly telt us all about it.'

Netta blushed. 'She's such a bletherer, Gus, take no notice of her.'

Dixie had brought a box of games for Gus to play with on his bedside table. He was sitting up unaided now and that was giving the nurses hope for his recovery.

Sometimes, in the privacy of her own room, Netta wept at the thought of him crippled, in a wheelchair. How would Peg and Angus cope at Brigg when they grew older? What if he never got the strength back into his muscles? She had seen how his limbs were like sticks. He could not bump a chair down to the shore. How weary they were all getting from their weekly trips to see him. How she ached to stay by his side and play games with him, read him stories and see to his comfort. He preferred to have Peg and Angus by his side.

Why didn't she get the infection? Why Gus? Why couldn't he recover in a few days like Jamie Paterson, with nothing more than a sore back? As long as she lived Netta would never understand a happening that shot out of the sky like a bolt of lightning from the blue.

Netta caught Father buried in the milking parlour, pretending to clear up. But she could sense he was skulking out of sight, bleary-eyed from lack of sleep. 'I've worked like a navvy to build up this place. Gus was our future hope. How can a cripple manage to run Brigg? Netta . . . I'm that choked I could smash all these damned new machines! It's no fair, why us!'

'Don't talk about him as if he's dead and gone. He's alive and he'll recover. I know it now. Why should the Nichol family be preserved from troubles? Don't tell me life's ever fair . . . Didn't we learn that when my mother died and Rae was killed and all that followed? You have to believe what Drew

287

tells us. He *must* walk again. Drew says half of polio victims suffer no long-term effects, and another quarter have only minor problems. It could be much worse. Gus has everything on his side. He's so young and he's fighting to get well.'

'He's a good yin, that Dr Stirling. I take ma hat off to you, you've made some good friends. He's no much of a looker but I like a man who looks ye straight in the eye. You could do far worse.'

'Away ye go, we're just good pals the now. I'll have to go back soon to finish off his girl's wedding dress. We all have to pull together to get Gus back on his feet. Now the worst of his fever is over, the hard work really starts: all that physiotherapy. Don't they have long words for everything? His muscles are wasted. He has to build them up to take his weight again and we'll just have to let the nurses get on with it. His legs may have to be braced in calipers for a while.'

'No bairn of mine's going to be put in leg irons!'

'If it gets him back on his feet quicker, then surely it's for the best? Drew says it'll straighten his legs and help him take the weight.'

'He doesn't have to put them on now, does he?'

'Oh, Paw! If only I could wear them for him, I would. We're going to have to grit our faces and watch and worry. Do what is best for Gus and help him bear it.'

Angus moved forward out of the shadows and faced his daughter.

'I'm proud of you, hen. I know it's been a long time coming but I've watched you keep us all afloat, paddling the canoe like fury, baling out the water, buoying up Peg's sinking spirits. I don't know how we'd have coped without you. You've got so much of Jeanie in you . . . not just yer looks but that steely-eyed look she had when she was determined to go her own gait: stubborn but with a golden heart. You have that same golden heart. "That's what matters most . . . the colour of yer heart," she used to say. Now away afore I start greetin' like a bairn. Away inside and see if there's any food on the table. I'm starving!'

Netta pressed her hand into his. 'Thanks.'

The praise of her own father rang strangely in her ears, once yearned for, now welcome for it marked her transition in his eyes from troublesome child to valued grown-up. How Gus's illness was changing everything at Brigg Farm!

Gus opened the parcel with dull glassy eyes. The banner fell over the bed like a tablecloth. 'Polly made this for you and I added some bits. Lift it up, see, here's a rainbow made out of ribbons. There's you in the hospital bed at one end and here's the farm and Brucie waiting for you at the other. That's Jamie and there's Maisie. Peg is standing by the door with Father. She made it out of materials like a picture. I sewed on the sea and the golden sands with sequins as shells. One day we'll all go back to Carrick and play there again. Would you like that?'

Gus turned his face away from the rainbow and sucked his thumb. He had forgotten the beach and his room. This bed was his home now, with the stripey nurses who tugged at him and hurt him. No one came when he cried and he didn't like the smells.

'We won't go away, Gus, I promise. It's all still there, waiting for you under the rainbow. We're counting the days . . .'

'I don't want it . . . put it away!'

'I'm sorry, we thought a picture on the wall would cheer you up. I have to go back to Griseley soon to get on with my sewing but I'll come back every weekend to visit you.'

'Go away! I don't like you. I want the nurse. Go away!'

His words tore at her heart on that second journey southwards in the van. Perhaps it was time to sell up or close down and come back for good. Sewing was no longer her first priority though it had always served her well to date.

Mustn't rush into anything. There was too much still to sort out. She could never be without a thimble on her finger. Perhaps the business was part of that too. She had to go back to sort things out. Poor Polly must be floundering or wondering if she was going to have to find other work!

In her heart Netta knew Gus was on the mend when he started to complain. He was weary of hospital and all the fiddling about and adjustments to his leg braces. He fought them at first then accepted that they had to stay on, but he was too young to understand why he was hurting.

No one had bothered to explain to him why he should be massaged. Netta asked if she could attend some sessions to learn how to help the boy but was shooed away. No one from Brigg Farm was there to praise his first steps.

Peg and Angus busied themselves in a flurry of cleaning and decorating. Gus's room was transformed ready for his homecoming. Netta stuffed a brand new Yumpy complete with a fresh suit of clothes. She would tell him that old Yumpy had been retired to a home for old suckies and his nephew, Yumpy Junior, had come in his place. He would not smell or taste the same but, given a few weeks to settle in, he soon would.

Netta smiled, thinking of Peg's words, 'You spoil the bairn.' She had replied, 'Listen to the kettle calling the pot black. Who bought a new candlewick bedspread and linoleum for the floor? What laddie would notice any of that?' Then Peg said she was worried how he'd get up the stairs but Netta had asked if they were practising that in the hospital therapy room. She'd been informed that they were and the Nichol boy had a very stubborn streak.

'I'm not surprised!' Peg smiled. 'We've had enough of you to know where that came from!' Peg was actually smiling! At long last she had acknowledged the special bond between Gus and his mother.

Netta sniffed away the tears. It was still Peg he cried for

when they worked his legs. On her last visit he had looked at her so angrily. 'I want my mammy – not you, my mammy!' The rebuke was breaking her heart.

9

AMETHYST

'Colour of the moon in soberness.
From this rainbow's end
Earth and Heaven reveal themselves.
Time to cross over into the unknown.
To begin again?'

Back To Griseley, June 1949

Netta flung open the windows and doors of her cottage to let the breezes air the rooms and shift the fusty unlived in smell of the place. The garden patch was knee-high in rogue grasses and corn poppies, dandelions and buttercups, as she waded to the stone wall and sniffed soot not salt in her nostrils. Coming back gave her no relief from her concern for Gus. There would be so much to catch up on if she was to get back to Dumfries again at the weekend.

She had deposited the van at the garage and called in to see if her workshop was still standing. Polly had done her best to keep the work going but no sixteen year old could be expected to run someone else's business. The unmade pieces of outstanding orders were packed away neatly and Ginny Mackeever's gown hung on the rail waiting for its final fitting at High House for the wedding in two weeks' time. Its full lace underskirts swamped the room. Everything would need adjusting. Netta fingered the fabric. She would be glad when this wretched thing was out of her sight.

She wanted to thank Polly for her banner and the thoughtfulness behind the design. She must have been lonely here each day. It was no place for a young girl without company. In fact she had thought over Polly's future very carefully on the long journey back. Training and experience at college would be far more beneficial for her natural talent than being shut up in a back street workshop. Polly hankered after theatrical costumes and designs, embroidery and textile fashions. It was only fair to offer her the chance to take up that place at college in September should it be offered.

She must let Polly go, she pondered, but where did that leave Netta? Where would she be in September when Polly left and Drew was married? What if Gus was still in hospital? How would she manage then? Griseley or Galloway: where would her heart settle? When home is one place and your roots are elsewhere, something has to shift.

Life had been so hectic in Stratharvar in these past few weeks, seeing to farm chores, helping Peg, visiting and catching up with handsewing. Suddenly this little cottage felt poky, dark and silent and Netta was utterly alone.

Drew sat in the darkened cinema transfixed by the action on the screen. Not his usual sort of film but a gripping colourful fairytale about a ballerina trapped by her red dancing shoes, torn between her lover and the lure of ballet stardom. Ginnie was asleep beside him after her exhausting shopping trip to Paris with her cronies. They had partied their way all over the city and brought back enough contraband to sink her sports car and the ferry.

He couldn't take his eyes off the heroine, Moira Shearer, as she flitted across the screen with her flame hair and beautiful sea-green eyes. He was stunned by her resemblance to Netta; the same innocence and wide-eyed expressive smile. As the story unfolded he became more engrossed in her dilemma and found himself choked at the end as she was carried dying from the railway track. It was all so sad. Would Netta spend her life torn between her son and her talent, never finding satisfaction in her life?

He shook Ginnie awake for the National Anthem and they made their way out of the Ilkley cinema into a fine June evening, strolling uphill back to High House. Once inside, Ginnie on her second wind offered him some whisky.

'No, thanks,' he said smugly. Since that business with Arthur Bates he no longer found satisfaction in a bottle of spirits. He was wary of his drinking habits and realised that when he was busy and interested in something he never drank. Boredom and frustration, not thirst, sent him looking for a glass. Now was such a moment.

'You're getting to be such a sobersides, Andrew. Come on, a glass of malt will relax you,' Ginnie ordered, shoving it under his nose.

'No! I'm fine the now, don't fuss . . .'

'I'm not fussing. It's just you keep going quiet on me lately. The girls have noticed it too. When I hug you, I'm not sure you're in there anymore. What's got into you?'

'I'm tired.' He swallowed back 'and bored'.

'I know . . . but when we're married and all your stuff is moved in here, there'll be no more trekking up and down to Leeds. There's Cook and the staff to pander to your every whim. The decorators have started on our rooms. Isn't it exciting?'

'Look, we've been through this before. I don't think it's a good idea for us to start off married life with your father. I prefer to stay nearer my work. You'll enjoy making a new life together.' Ginnie never listened to a word he said if it didn't suit her plans.

'Don't be silly, darling. It's all been agreed. Daddy has tons of space and what about the horses?'

'What about the bloody horses? You have two grooms. Daddy Mackeever can fend for himself.'

'You really are a bore, Andrew. This is my house and I don't see why we should move into some semi in Headingley. Daddy says you can convert the stables and run a private practice from there.'

'Are you deaf? I believe in this new National Health

297

Service. I happen to like working with kids. In fact, I'm seriously thinking of retraining. There's lots of opportunities for a medic to specialise . . .'

'This is too much! What future is there in that? How can we go hunting midweek?'

'When have I ever hunted with you in the middle of the week?'

'But I thought we could go off on holidays, trekking. We might as well stay as we are then. I don't intend to leave High House to answer your phone calls.'

'I wouldn't dream of risking you at that after the last one you misdirected!'

'You're not going on about that again? Ever since that man topped himself you've been like a bear with a sore head. Snapping at me every time I mention the wedding. Anyone'd think you'd got cold feet!'

'If we can't agree on my job, where we live, how I spend my time, what's left to get married for . . . well, the rest we've done already.' Drew smiled.

'Don't be coarse!' Ginnie lit a cigarette and opened the veranda windows. 'Now you tell me, two weeks before the day. So gloves off, is it? Well, let me tell you, you're no great shakes in *that* department either and since you've taken the pledge you're about as much fun as flat champagne! Boring on about your army group and dressmaker's sons with polio . . . what do I care about any of them? You're a bore, Andrew Stirling, and I'm not marrying a bloody bore!' Ginnie pulled off her engagement ring and flung it into the shrubbery. 'There! That's better!' He could see the tears in her eyes.

'Yes, it's a wee bit of a relief. Tell the truth and shame the devil! The only thing you and I had in common was the booze. Since I got my act together we're not the cosy little couple we once were: Andrew, Ginnie and a bottle. I'm advising you, it wouldn't do you any harm to cut back your own tippling. I'm no ready to put on a collar and lead.

Some tame lap dog running to heel at your or your father's beck and call. I have ma own life to lead and if you don't want to share any of it, I just don't see the point, do you?

Drew stood in the doorway, watching her bend over the handsewing with total concentration, oblivious of everything but her task. 'You're back.' She looked up and smiled at him then realised it was the wedding dress in her hands. 'Shut your eyes, don't look, it's bad luck!' Netta fumbled to clear away the dress.

'Dinna fash yerself, hen,' he mimicked. 'The wedding's off, I'm afraid.'

'Oh, Drew, I'm sorry,' she lied until she remembered all those unpaid hours of work on the gown. As if reading her thoughts and her panic, he raised his hand. 'Don't worry, all bills will be honoured. You won't be out of pocket.' He lifted up the dress. 'Is this it?' She nodded. 'It's terrible . . . I feel sick just looking at the colour. I hate pink.'

'So do I,' confessed Netta with a wry glimmer of a smile. 'What happened?'

'Fancy a stroll and some fresh air?'

They walked on top of the ridge overlooking the Wharfe valley. It was clear and Netta could see for miles. A skylark babbled above them. Lapwings dived and twisted in the fields where the fat lambs nestled with the ewes. Drew had told her about the quarrel and its aftermath. 'It's all your fault, you know.'

'What have I done now?'

'Got me back on the wagon. After Arthur died I was shaken up. I knew I couldn't spend the rest of my life hiding in a bottle. If alcohol is your weakness it will always be your weakness so I wanted to see if I could cut down. I even had a session with a trick cyclist friend of mine and he put me straight on how to go about it. Now I like waking up in the morning with a clear head and not a doormat for a tongue. I like that rinsed out, fresher feeling. I sound like a toothpaste advert but it's the little things you notice. Ginnie and I moved in boozy circles and once I stepped away from them, I could see more clearly that we had nothing in common any more. She's mad as hell with me but she'll survive.'

'What'll you do?'

'Stay where I am for a while, but I want to do some more study. I'm interested in new research stuff coming out about the effects of separation on children. I think it's going to be important work. I'm reading up my psychology theory again and there are lectures in London I can attend. Just a hunch but working with the POWs opened my mind. There's so much going on under the surface of people's lives we don't understand yet. It intrigues me. That's a start, I suppose. One step at a time. Who was this precious doctor who gave you all these sayings?'

Netta took a deep breath, plonked herself down on the grass and told him the full story, holding nothing back this time. Her fingers wound a necklace of daisies as she talked. She told him about Polly's plans and her own quandary.

'I ought to stay here and build up my business.' She sighed wistfully.

'Don't be so conventional! You can be in two places at once if that's what you want. Sewing fingers travel anywhere so go where your heart dictates. Finish off your work here and take yourself back to Galloway. It's not impossible. What's stopping you?'

'I shall miss you and the Oldroyds gang.'

'I hadn't intended to be so easily disposed of, Miss Nichol. I shall be here, there and everywhere for a while but petrol rationing won't last forever. There are trains and buses even in Galloway, telephones and postage stamps. I hope we'll make our own bridge, if you think there could be a future?' He edged closer.

'I'd like that very much. Old friends should stick together.'

'Not so much of the old, please. And I'd hoped we would be more than that, Netta.' They linked arms and huddled together, staring at each other with fresh eyes.

'I hope so too but there'll always be Gus in my life.'

'What's yours will be mine, I hope.' Drew smiled.

'Am I dreaming all this? Just a few weeks ago the world was so black. Now it sparkles with possibilities.'

'And it will be grey and dreich again, Netta. But just for today you can touch rainbows if you reach out for the light and follow your heart. There, that's worthy of Dr Anwar's motto collection!'

Netta punched him in the arm, tussling on the grass with him while the sheep watched their antics in alarm.

On Carrick Sands, September 1949

The celebration picnic preparations in the kitchen were nearly complete: the sandwiches cut and wrapped, the cakes in their tin, the flask warmed. The two women sat in silence, each waiting for the other to speak. It had come at last, this day of reckoning.

'So what are yer plans, Netta, now your assistant's away to college?'

There was a silence and Netta drew in her breath to speak slowly. 'I shall stay on in Griseley to finish my orders. Now that Gus is home from hospital . . . it's time to think again.'

'You're welcome to stay here as often as you like. What we would have done if you hadn't made me ring Ian Begg . . . you saved his life. I expect that's what you'd want, to be back here with him?'

'I don't know what I want. I prayed so hard for him to live and my prayers were answered. If he recovered, I vowed, I'd make no further claim on him. I sometimes feel he's never really been mine. When I saw you together in the hospital it was always you he wanted not me. This is his home, not mine. He belongs here with you and always will. I'm not going to take him away.'

'He's no been the same wee boy since he came out of that place. I think he believes we wanted him put away. He wets the bed every night. We could do with you close by to give a hand. Come back to Kirkcudbright. There's room for a dressmaker there. I cannae drive you away again, lass.'

'You're not driving me away. I'll think it over carefully but only on one condition, Peg: that we stop the lies and tell the bairn the truth or as much of it as he can understand. Drip it into him, like yon contraption in the hospital. He can get used to it slowly. Nothing'll change. I shall always be Auntie Netta to him but that doesn't stop me being the best auntie in the world, does it?'

'I can guess what it must have meant to you, leaving him here?'

'I don't think you can, Peg, or I would never have been sent away. But what's done is done. I made a vow and I'm keeping to my bargain even if it breaks my heart. Gus must stay here to recover. I may set up a workshop locally.'

'There's your grandfather's old studio going to rack and ruin . . . you could use that?'

'Perhaps.'

Gus sat on his chair like a king among courtiers surveying his domain, trying to capture the moment in his drawing, fingering his crayons for the right colours. It was autumn. The sky was still powder blue with cotton white clouds and the sea shone like silver. When he looked closely the sand was in the mucky water of his painting jar, the travelling rug beneath his feet was scarlet and the grass was speckled with purple flowers. A brown fluffy spot darted across the scene as Brucie scampered towards Ardwall Island, splattering over the ripples of mud. Auntie Netta was frantically trying to catch the silly dog before it dashed to chase the sea. Mother was knitting furiously by his side, looking at her wristwatch to see when Father would arrive in the van with their picnic basket.

Gus had dreamed of this place in hospital when no visitors came through the ward and he'd tried to be a big boy and not cry while they were hurting him, tugging his legs to get them working again. Now it felt strange to have everyone there together. This was something new but since he came home from hospital everything was different. There were visitors popping in all the time. Even his bedroom was all done up for his return, tidy and smelling of paint. He was not sure about the Yumpy Junior in his bed but his ears were tasty.

He wished his legs would get a move on and he hated the caliper on his left leg, it felt like a cage, but Dr Begg said he was a brave boy and gave him a whole half crown to spend.

Now they had the beach to themselves for all his pals had started school. He would be starting one of these days when his leg got better. What a long summer it had been. He turned to see the van bumping its way cautiously over the hummocky sand track and Father hooted his horn. He had never come to a picnic before so this must be a special occasion. Perhaps they were taking him back to hospital again.

Out of the back came the laundry basket covered with a tablecloth that was spread over the grassy bank. This was not the usual chittering bite of bread and jam pieces and lemonade but a full meal with cups and plates. That was because it was a special party. He knew they had a surprise for Auntie Netta hidden in the basket. Out came a flask of mutton broth and chunks of bread, then there were bridies and Scotch eggs, enough sandwiches to feed Stratharvar School and Gus's favourite fruitcake with nuts on the top. There were gingerbread squares and millionaire shortbread, celery and cheese, and the last of the rasps from the garden. What a bunfeast!

Gus wished he could chase around with Brucie like he used to do but he was learning a new word called patience. He'd thought it was a granny's card game but now he knew it meant slow down, give yourself time to lift one leg in front of the other. But it was tiring. He noticed everyone was sitting around quietly, waiting for a signal for someone to speak, looking sideways at each other and at him, munching their mouths like cows. Gus wanted the picnic to follow the usual pattern with a story digestive, the bit where you had to let your food settle or it would hurt. After the food Auntie Netta must tell him a story.

'What's it going to be today? Not another soppy one?'

'No, Gus, today I'm going to tell you a true story. I want you to listen very carefully and tell me what you think? Everyone's going to chip in and tell bits of it as well. Are you sitting comfortably?'

He squirmed. 'Not another Listen with Mother! I'm sick of listening to they stories on the wireless.'

'No, but fair dos, all good stories start with once upon a time . . . There was a little girl who played on this beach who was sometimes good and sometimes awful like the girl in the nursery rhyme with the curl on her forehead. She went to Stratharvar School like you and when she grew up she met a handsome soldier called Rae, on this very beach. They loved each other so much that they ran away on his motor bike to get married but when they found a place to marry the shop was closed. There was no time to wait for it to open so she went back home and he went to war. He was killed in a terrible battle in France. Then a little boy was born but the mother was so ill she had to stay in hospital, just like you, but for many more months, and her parents, who were cross with her, had to look after the bairn until she came home again.'

'What was the baby's name?' There was a cough and then Auntie Netta whispered, 'Gus . . .'

'But that's my name!'

'Yes, and it was me who had to go into the hospital . . . I just couldnae look after you.' Auntie Netta bent her head.

'I hate hospital. If I'm naughty, do I have to go back?' Peg dropped her knitting, shook her head and continued the tale.

'So we brought down the old crib from the loft and you lived with us. I wasn't able to have a bairn of ma own so you were very special . . . After a while everyone thought of you as our wee son, not Netta's bairn. And that's how it's stayed.' Then Father leaned forward to add his piece.

'We didna ken if Netta would be fit to look after you herself but she came back as soon as she was well to take you away. We couldn't let her take you away so she had to go and find somewhere to live all by herself.'

Now it was Mother speaking again. 'Auntie Netta went to live in Yorkshire and worked hard at her sewing to prove that she could look after you just as well as we could. It made her very sad not to have you by her side so she came up as often as she could to see you. She's always wanted you to know that she's your real mother, not your auntie or your sister, but we wanted you to go on thinking of us as your parents too. Can you understand all this, son?'

Gus stared at them unblinking. 'I've got two mammies then?' No one spoke and then Father added some more in a hurry.

'That's right, two mammies to fuss over you and spoil you, and me who's trying to show you how to be a farmer. One day Stratharvar will be all yours. I wanted a son to follow on the line o' things so I made you mine.'

'What about Auntie Netta, can't girls be farmers?' There was silence again and Auntie Netta spoke softly.

'Farming's no for me, you ken the sorts of stuff I make, but what I do mind is you not knowing who I really am. I didna want some laddie blurting it out to you in the playground. They might say that you were not Father's son but mine and you wouldn't understand and get teased. I got used to being called Auntie Netta years ago. You're a special wee boy to have two mammies who care for you.'

Gus looked puzzled. 'Now I've got two mammies, do I get two paws as well?'

They were all looking at each other, spluttering crumbs, and Father added his sixpence.

'Your brave daddy, Rae Hunter, died in the war. He's no here to look after you so I'm doing it for him.' Auntie Netta was smiling with damp eyes and a soppy look on her face. It was time to ask a better question. 'Did you buy me at the hospital then? Jamie Paterson said they bought his wee sister at the Cresswell or was the shop closed?' There was silence again. That had shut them up. Auntie Netta was blushing and Father was scratching his head, flummoxed.

'You don't buy bairns in hospitals, son. You helped me pull out Maisie when she was born . . .'

'But she's a cow, just an animal,' he argued.

'And we're just animals when it comes to birthing. Babies grow big in their mother's tummies in a safe watery nest, just like Maisie!'

'Yuk!' Gus looked around again. They were all looking queasy and red in the face. Grown-ups could tell such silly stories. 'Shall I show you my picture? See . . . that's you and you . . . and I've put a rainbow bridge in the sky like my banner but there isn't one here at the moment. I shall paint it when I get home to remember. Is there any more cake? I'm starving. Do I have to go back to hospital?'

His parents were ferreting in the bottom of the basket for a box that was hidden under Father's serviette. He coughed like the Minister before the Sermon. 'It's handy us all being together on the occasion of wee Gus's coming home. We wanted to thank you, Netta, for all you've done these past weeks. I hope we can all find a way to make things work for the young chap but we wanted you to have something, just a wee tochar to help you along.' He was handing her an old blue box and she opened it and started snivelling. Inside was a necklace, the one in the story with stones on a gold chain.

'That's the rainbow necklace,' Gus said promptly. 'You like rainbows.'

'Aye, it belonged to Granny Jean and Peg but I . . . we want you to have it now.' Pa looked awful embarrassed as if he was afraid she'd hug him. Auntie Netta looked pleased and dangled it in the sunlight.

'Thank you, you know how much this means to me.'

What was the matter with grown-ups? Why did they bite their lips and sniff when they really wanted to blubber and greet? What a strange picnic this was turning out to be and no one was answering his question, thought Gus, as he turned to finish off his drawing. He was tired and not sure if he wanted two mammies to fuss over him. But he didn't want the nurse hurting him in hospital again.

The sun blazed down on the party, the flies buzzed over the crumbs. They retreated into a companionable silence. Father was lazing on the rocks with a pair of binoculars, pointing out the sea birds to Gus. Peg snoozed over her knitting and Netta just stared out to Ardwall in a daydream. Something momentous had shifted that afternoon. Their honest exchanges, however hesitant, had been made. Gus knew the score now. It wouldn't change anything much. She would always be just his Auntie Netta.

There would be tensions galore and the rivers of frustration, jealousy and rivalry to ford if she came back north. So much uncertainty. Best to ford rivers at the burn or the source, deal with what came along sooner rather than later. That was surely something all of them knew now. Netta would always be rooted to this spot because of Gus but Griseley had its charms too. Where would her heart settle? Could she keep on shifting it from one place to the other? And there was Drew.

With Peg and Father no longer against her, surely there was nothing they couldn't work out, given time and space, to make Gus's future a happy and secure one? He would take many more months to recover his mobility. Her instincts told her that Gus needed to be in familiar surroundings with

308

friends and pets, not flung into a strange town or school. He was going to be a difficult patient. She had to do what was best for her child. There would be Drew's visits and outings together and who knew where those might lead?

Netta thought about the vow she had made on that dark, dark night when Gus's future looked so bleak. She had let go her claim to him then and he had lived. Now even Peg and Angus were learning to loosen the tight cords of control. Here on Carrick shore they were all beginning a journey of hope and trust. It must succeed for it had cost them dear.

Netta fingered the necklace of coloured stones sparkling in the sunshine; garnet, amber, citrine, jade, turquoise, lapis lazuli and amethyst, shielding her tears from view. There was no rainbow in the sky to seal their promises today but who needed rainbows when such a crock of gold was sitting beside her on this pebbly beach?

In the beginning there was colour everywhere from orange-red to purple: birth to death. But now there was a rainbow of colour in her heart, no longer dulled with the jet of despair but tinged with a hint of gold, the colour of love. That was enough for now.